# MEH
## A STORY O
### MARS
#### B
## SABINE BARING-GOULD

CHAPTER I.
THE RAY.

Between the mouths of the Blackwater and the Colne, on the east coast of Essex, lies an extensive marshy tract veined and freckled in every part with water. It is a wide waste of debatable ground contested by sea and land, subject to incessant incursions from the former, but stubbornly maintained by the latter. At high tide the appearance is that of a vast surface of moss or Sargasso weed floating on the sea, with rents and patches of shining water traversing and dappling it in all directions. The creeks, some of considerable length and breadth, extend many miles inland, and are arteries whence branches out a fibrous tissue of smaller channels, flushed with water twice in the twenty-four hours. At noon-tides, and especially at the equinoxes, the sea asserts its royalty over this vast region, and overflows the whole, leaving standing out of the flood only the long island of Mersea, and the lesser islet, called the Ray. This latter is a hill of gravel rising from the heart of the Marshes, crowned with ancient thorntrees, and possessing, what is denied the mainland, an unfailing spring of purest water. At ebb, the Ray can only be reached from the old Roman causeway, called the Strood, over which runs the road from Colchester to Mersea Isle, connecting formerly the city of the Trinobantes with the station of the count of the Saxon shore. But even at ebb, the Ray is not approachable by land unless the sun or east wind has parched the ooze into brick; and then the way is long, tedious and tortuous, among bitter pools and over shining creeks. It was perhaps because this ridge of high ground was so inaccessible, so well protected by nature, that the ancient inhabitants had erected on it a rath, or fortified camp of wooden logs, which left its name to the place long after the timber defences had rotted away.

A more desolate region can scarce be conceived, and yet it is not without beauty. In summer, the thrift mantles the marshes with shot satin, passing through all gradations of tint from maiden's blush to lily white. Thereafter a purple glow steals over the waste, as the sea lavender bursts into flower, and simultaneously every creek and pool is royally fringed with sea aster. A little later the glass-wort, that shot up green and transparent as emerald glass in the early spring, turns to every tinge of carmine.

When all vegetation ceases to live, and goes to sleep, the marshes are alive and wakeful with countless wild fowl. At all times they are haunted with sea mews and roysten crows, in winter they teem with wild duck and grey geese. The stately heron loves to wade in the pools, occasionally the whooper swan sounds his loud trumpet, and flashes a white reflection in the still blue waters of the fleets. The plaintive pipe of the curlew is familiar to those who frequent these marshes, and the barking of the brent geese as they return from their northern breeding places is heard in November.

At the close of last century there stood on the Ray a small farmhouse built of tarred wreckage timber, and roofed with red pan-tiles. The twisted thorntrees about it afforded some, but slight, shelter. Under the little cliff of gravel was a good beach, termed a 'hard.'

On an evening towards the close of September, a man stood in this farmhouse by the hearth, on which burnt a piece of wreckwood, opposite an old woman, who crouched shivering with ague in a chair on the other side. He was a strongly built man of about thirty-five, wearing fisherman's boots, a brown coat and a red plush waistcoat. His hair was black, raked over his brow. His cheekbones were high; his eyes dark, eager, intelligent, but fierce in expression. His nose was aquiline, and would have given a certain nobility to his countenance, had not his huge jaws and heavy chin contributed an animal cast to his face.

He leaned on his duck-gun, and glared from under his pent-house brows and thatch of black hair over the head of the old woman at a girl who stood behind, leaning on the back of her mother's chair, and who returned his stare with a look of defiance from her brown eyes.

The girl might have been taken for a sailor boy, as she leaned over the chairback, but for the profusion of her black hair. She wore a blue knitted guernsey covering body and arms, and across the breast, woven in red wool, was the name of the vessel, 'Gloriana.' The guernsey had been knitted for one of the crew of a ship of this name, but had come into the girl's possession. On her head she wore the scarlet woven cap of a boatman.

The one-pane window at the side of the fireplace faced the west, and the evening sun lit her brown gipsy face, burnt in her large eyes, and made coppery lights in her dark hair.

The old woman was shivering with the ague, and shook the chair on which her daughter leaned; a cold sweat ran off her brow, and every now and then she raised a white faltering hand to wipe the drops away that hung on her eyebrows like rain on thatching.

'I did not catch the chill here,' she said. 'I ketched it more than thirty years ago when I was on Mersea Isle, and it has stuck in my marrow ever since. But there is no ague on the Ray. This is the healthiest place in the world, Mehalah has never caught the ague on it. I do not wish ever to leave it, and to lay my bones elsewhere.'

'Then you will have to pay your rent punctually,' said the man in a dry tone, not looking at her, but at her daughter.

'Please the Lord so we shall, as we ever have done,' answered the woman; 'but when the chill comes on me———'

'Oh, curse the chill,' interrupted the man; 'who cares for that except perhaps Glory yonder, who has to work for both of you. Is it so, Glory?'

The girl thus addressed did not answer, but folded her arms on the chairback, and leaned her chin upon them. She seemed at that moment like a wary cat watching a threatening dog, and ready at a moment to show her claws and show desperate battle, not out of malice, but in self-defence.

'Why, but for you sitting there, sweating and jabbering, Glory would not be bound to this lone islet, but would go out and see the world, and taste life. She grows here like a mushroom, she does not live. Is it not so, Glory?'

The girl's face was no longer lit by the declining sun, which had glided further north-west, but the flames of the driftwood flickered in her large eyes that met those of the man, and the cap was still illumined by the evening glow, a scarlet blaze against the indigo gloom.

'Have you lost your tongue, Glory?' asked the man, impatiently striking the bricks with the butt end of his gun.

'Why do you not speak, Mehalah?' said the mother, turning her wan wet face aside, to catch a glimpse of her daughter.

'I've answered him fifty times,' said the girl.

'No,' protested the old woman feebly, 'you have not spoken a word to Master Rebow.'

'By God, she is right,' broke in the man. 'The little devil has a tongue in each eye, and she has been telling me with each a thousand times that she hates me. Eh, Glory?'

The girl rose erect, set her teeth, and turned her face aside, and looked out at the little window on the decaying light.

Rebow laughed aloud.

'She hated me before, and now she hates me worse, because I have become her landlord. I have bought the Ray for eight hundred pounds. The Ray is mine, I tell you.

Mistress Sharland, you will henceforth have to pay me the rent, to me and to none other. I am your landlord, and Michaelmas is next week.'

'The rent shall be paid, Elijah!' said the widow.

'The Ray is mine,' pursued Rebow, swelling with pride. 'I have bought it with my own money—eight hundred pounds. I could stubb up the trees if I would. I could cart muck into the well and choke it if I would. I could pull down the stables and break them up for firewood if I chose. All here is mine, the Ray, the marshes, and the saltings,[1] the creeks, the fleets, the farm. That is mine,' said he, striking the wall with his gun, 'and that is mine,' dashing the butt end against the hearth; 'and you are mine, and Glory is mine.'

[1] A salting is land occasionally flooded, otherwise serving as pasturage. A marsh is a reclaimed salting, enclosed within a sea-wall.

'That never,' said the girl stepping forward, and confronting him with dauntless eye and firm lips and folded arms.

'Eh! Gloriana! have I roused you?' exclaimed Elijah Rebow, with a flash of exultation in his fierce eyes. 'I said that the house and the marshes, and the saltings are mine, I have bought them. And your mother and you are mine.'

'Never,' repeated the girl.

'But I say yes.'

'We are your tenants, Elijah,' observed the widow nervously interposing. 'Do not let Mehalah anger you. She has been reared here in solitude, and she does not know the ways of men. She means nothing by her manner.'

'I do,' said the girl, 'and he knows it.'

'She is a headlong child,' pursued the old woman, 'and when she fares to say or do a thing, there is no staying tongue or hand. Do not mind her, master.'

The man paid no heed to the woman's words, but fixed his attention on the girl. Neither spoke. It was as though a war of wills was proclaimed and begun. He sought to beat down her defences with the force of his resolve flung at her from his dark eyes, and she parried it dauntlessly with her pride.

'By God!' he said at last, 'I have never seen anywhere else a girl of your sort. There is none elsewhere. I like you.'

'I knew it,' said the mother with feeble triumph in her palsied voice. 'She is a right good girl at heart, true as steel, and as tough in fibre.'

'I have bought the house and the pasture, and the marshes and the saltings,' said Elijah sulkily, 'and all that thereon is. You are mine, Glory! You cannot escape me. Give me your hand.'

She remained motionless, with folded arms. He laid his heavy palm on her shoulder.

'Give me your hand, and mine is light; I will help you. Let me lay it on you and it will crush you. Escape it you cannot. This way or that. My hand will clasp or crush.'

She did not stir.

'The wild fowl that fly here are mine, the fish that swim in the fleets are mine,' he went on; 'I can shoot and net them.'

'So can I, and so can anyone,' said the girl haughtily.

'Let them try it on,' said Elijah; 'I am not one to be trifled with, as the world well knows. I will bear no poaching here. I have bought the Ray, and the fish are mine, and the fowl are mine, and you are mine also. Let him touch who dares.'

'The wild fowl are free for any man to shoot, the fish are free for any man to net,' said the girl scornfully.

'That is not my doctrine,' answered Elijah. 'What is on my soil and in my waters is mine, I may do with them what I will, and so also all that lives on my estate is mine.'

Returning with doggedness to his point, 'As you live in my house and on my land, you are mine.'

'Mother,' said the girl, 'give him notice, and quit the Ray.'

'I could not do it, Mehalah, I could not do it,' answered the woman. 'I've lived all my life on the marshes, and I cannot quit them. But this is a healthy spot, and not like the marshes of Dairy House where once we were, and where I ketched the chill.'

'You cannot go till you have paid me the rent,' said Rebow.

'That,' answered Mehalah, 'we will do assuredly.'

'So you promise, Glory!' said Rebow. 'But should you fail to do it, I could take every stick here:—That chair in which your mother shivers, those dishes yonder, the bed you sleep in, the sprucehutch[2] in which you keep your clothes. I could pluck the clock, the heart of the house, out of it. I could tear that defiant red cap off your head. I could drive you both out without a cover into the whistling east wind and biting frost.'

[2] Cypress-chest.

'I tell you, we can and we will pay.'

'But should you not be able at any time, I warn you what to expect. I've a fancy for that jersey you wear with "Gloriana" right across the breast. I'll pull it off and draw it on myself.' He ground his teeth. 'I will have it, if only to wrap me in, in my grave. I will cross my arms over it, as you do now, and set my teeth, and not a devil in hell shall tear it off me.'

'I tell you we will pay.'

'Let me alone, let me talk. This is better than money. I will rip the tiling off the roof and fling it down between the rafters, if you refuse to stir; I will cast it at your mother and you, Glory. The red cap will not protect your skull from a tile, will it? And yet you say, I am not your master. You do not belong to me, as do the marshes and the saltings, and the wild duck.'

'I tell you we will pay,' repeated the girl passionately, as she wrenched her shoulder from his iron grip.

'You don't belong to me!' jeered Elijah. Then slapping the arm of the widow's chair, and pointing over his shoulder at Mehalah, he said scornfully: 'She says she does not belong to me, as though she believed it. But she does, and you do, and so does that chair, and the log that smoulders on the hearth, and the very hearth itself, with its heat, the hungry ever-devouring belly of the house. I've bought the Ray and all that is on it for eight hundred pounds. I saw it on the paper, it stands in writing and may not be broke through. Lawyers' scripture binds and looses as Bible scripture. I will stick to my rights, to every thread and breath of them. She is mine.'

'But, Elijah, be reasonable,' said the widow, lifting her hand appealingly. The fit of ague was passing away. 'We are in a Christian land. We are not slaves to be bought and sold like cattle.'

'If you cannot pay the rent, I can take everything from you. I can throw you out of this chair down on those bricks. I can take the crock and all the meat in it. I can take the bed on which you sleep. I can take the clothes off your back.' Turning suddenly round on the girl he glared, 'I will rip the jersey off her, and wear it till I rot. I will pull the red cap off her head and lay it on my heart to keep it warm. None shall say me nay. Tell me, mistress, what are you, what is she, without house and bed and clothing? I will take her gun, I will swamp her boat. I will trample down your garden. I will drive you both down with my dogs upon the saltings at the spring tide, at the full of moon. You shall not shelter here, on my island, if you will not pay. I tell you, I have bought the Ray. I gave for it eight hundred pounds.'

'But Elijah,' protested the old woman, 'do not be so angry. We are sure to pay.'

'We will pay him, mother, and then he cannot open his mouth against us.' At that moment the door flew open, and two men entered, one young, the other old.

'There is the money,' said the girl, as the latter laid a canvas bag on the table.

'We've sold the sheep—at least Abraham has,' said the young man joyously, as he held out his hand. 'Sold them well, too, Glory!'

The girl's entire face was transformed. The cloud that had hung over it cleared, the hard eyes softened, and a kindly light beamed from them. The set lips became flexible and smiled. Elijah saw and noted the change, and his brow grew darker, his eye more threatening.

Mehalah strode forward, and held out her hand to clasp that offered her. Elijah swung his musket suddenly about, and unless she had hastily recoiled, the barrel would have struck, perhaps broken, her wrist.

'You refused my hand,' he said, 'although you are mine. I bought the Ray for eight hundred pounds.' Then turning to the young man with sullenness, he asked, 'George De Witt, what brings you here?'

'Why, cousin, I've a right to be here as well as you.'

'No, you have not. I have bought the Ray, and no man sets foot on this island against my will.'

The young man laughed good-humouredly.

'You won't keep me off your property then, Elijah, so long as Glory is here?'

Elijah made a motion as though he would speak angrily, but restrained himself with an effort. He said nothing, but his eyes followed every movement of Mehalah Sharland. She turned to him with an exultant splendour in her face, and pointing to the canvas bag on the table, said, 'There is the money. Will you take the rent at once, or wait till it is due?'

'It is not due till next Thursday.'

'We do not pay for a few weeks. Three weeks' grace we have been hitherto allowed.'

'I give no grace.'

'Then take your money at once.'

'I will not touch it till it is due. I will take it next Thursday. You will bring it me then to Red Hall.'

'Is the boat all right where I left her?' asked the young man.

'Yes, George!' answered the girl, 'she is on the hard where you anchored her this morning. What have you been getting in Colchester to-day?'

'I have bought some groceries for mother,' he said, 'and there is a present with me for you. But that I will not give up till by-and-bye. You will help me to thrust the boat off, will you not, Glory?'

'She is afloat now. However, I will come presently, I must give Abraham first his supper.'

'Thank ye,' said the old man. 'George de Witt and me stopped at the Rose and had a bite. I must go at once after the cows. You'll excuse me.' He went out.

'Will you stay and sup with us, George?' asked the widow. 'There is something in the pot will be ready directly.'

'Thank you all the same,' he replied, 'I want to be back as soon as I can, the night will be dark; besides, you and Glory have company.' Then turning to Rebow he added:

'So you have bought the Ray.'

'I have.'

'Then Glory and her mother are your tenants.'

'They are mine.'

'I hope they will find you an easy landlord.'

'I reckon they will not,' said Elijah shortly.

'Come along, Glory!' he called, abandoning the topic and the uncongenial speaker, and turning to the girl. 'Help me with my boat.'

'Don't be gone for long, Mehalah!' said her mother.

'I shall be back directly.'

Elijah Rebow kept his mouth closed. His face was as though cast in iron, but a living fire smouldered within and broke out through the eye-sockets, as lava will lie hard and cold, a rocky crust with a fiery fluid core within that at intervals glares out at fissures. He did not utter a word, but he watched Glory go out with De Witt, and then a grim smile curdled his rugged cheeks. He seated himself opposite the widow, and spread his great hands over the fire. He was pondering. The shadow of his strongly featured face and expanded hands was cast on the opposite wall; as the flame flickered, the shadow hands seemed to open and shut, to stretch and grasp.

The gold had died out of the sky and only a pearly twilight crept in at the window, the evening heaven seen through the pane was soft and cool in tone as the tints of the Glaucus gull. The old woman remained silent. She was afraid of the new landlord. She had long known him, longer known of him, she had never liked him, and she liked less to have him now in a place of power over her.

Presently Rebow rose, slowly, from his seat, and laying aside his gun said, 'I too have brought a present, but not for Glory. She must know nothing of this, it is for you. I put the keg outside the door under the whitethorn. I knew a drop of spirits was good for the ague. We get spirits cheap, or I would not give you any.' He was unable to do a gracious act without marring its merit by an ungracious word. 'I will fetch it in. May it comfort you in the chills.'

He went out of the house and returned with a little keg under his arm. 'Where is it to go?' he asked.

'Oh, Master Rebow! this is good of you, and I am thankful. My ague does pull me down sorely.'

'Damn your ague, who cares about it!' he said surlily. 'Where is the keg to go?'

'Let me roll it in,' said the old woman, jumping up. 'There are better cellars and storeplaces here than anywhere between this and Tiptree Heath.'

'Saving mine at Red Hall, and those at Salcot Rising Sun,' interjected the man.

'You see, Rebow, in times gone by, a great many smuggled goods were stowed away here; but much does not come this way now,' with a sigh.

'It goes to Red Hall instead,' said Rebow. 'Ah! if you were there, your life would be a merry one. There! take the keg. I have had trouble enough bringing it here. You stow it away where you like, yourself; and draw me a glass, I am dry.'

He flung himself in the chair again, and let the old woman take up and hug the keg, and carry it off to some secure hiding-place where in days gone by many much larger barrels of brandy and wine had been stored away. She soon returned.

'I have not tapped this,' she said. 'The liquor will be muddy. I have drawn a little from the other that you gave me.'

Elijah took the glass from her hand and tossed it off. He was chuckling to himself.

'You will say a word for me to Glory.'

'Rely on me, Elijah. None has been so good to me as you. None has given me anything for my chill but you. But Mehalah will find it out, I reckon; she suspects already.'

He paid no heed to her words.

'So she is not mine, nor the house, nor the marshes, nor the saltings, nor the fish and fowl!' he muttered derisively to himself.

'I paid eight hundred pounds for the Ray and all that therein is,' he continued, 'let alone what I paid the lawyer.' He rubbed his hands. Then he rose again, and took his gun.

'I'm off,' he said, and strode to the door.

At the same moment Mehalah appeared at it, her face clear and smiling. She looked handsomer than ever.

'Well!' snarled Rebow, arresting her, 'what did he give you?'

'That is no concern of yours,' answered the girl, and she tried to pass. He put his fowling piece across the door and barred the way.

'What did he give you?' he asked in his dogged manner.

'I might refuse to answer,' she said carelessly, 'but I do not mind your knowing; the whole Ray and Mersea, and the world outside may know. This!' She produced an Indian red silk kerchief, which she flung over her shoulders and knotted under her chin. With her rich complexion, hazel eyes, dark hair and scarlet cap, lit by the red fire flames, she looked a gipsy, and splendid in her beauty. Rebow dropped his gun, thrust her aside with a sort of mad fury, and flung himself out of the door.

'He is gone at last!' said the girl with a gay laugh.

Rebow put his head in again. His lips were drawn back and his white teeth glistened.

'You will pay the rent next Thursday. I give no grace.'

Then he shut the door and was gone.

CHAPTER II.
THE RHYN.

'Mother,' said Mehalah, 'are you better now?'

'Yes, the fit is off me, but I am left terribly weak.'

'Mother, will you give me the medal?'

'What? Your grandmother's charm? You cannot want it!'

'It brings luck, and saves from sudden death. I wish to give it to George.'

'No, Mehalah! This will not do. You must keep it yourself.'

'It is mine, is it not?'

'No, child; it is promised you, but it is not yours yet. You shall have it some future day.'

'I want it at once, that I may give it to George. He has made me a present of this red kerchief for my neck, and he has given me many another remembrance, but I have made him no return. I have nothing that I can give him save that medal. Let me have it.'

'It must not go out of the family, Mehalah.'

'It will not. You know what is between George and me.'

The old woman hesitated and excused herself, but was so much in the habit of yielding to her daughter, that she was unable in this matter to maintain her opposition. She submitted reluctantly, and crept out of the room to fetch the article demanded of her.

When she returned, she found Mehalah standing before the fire with her back to the embers, and her hands knitted behind her, looking at the floor, lost in thought.

'There it is,' grumbled the old woman. 'But I don't like to part with it; and it must not go out of the family. Keep it yourself, Mehalah, and give it away to none.'

The girl took the coin. It was a large silver token, the size of a crown, bearing on the face a figure of Mars in armour, with shield and brandished sword, between the zodiacal signs of the Ram and the Scorpion.

The reverse was gilt, and represented a square divided into five-and-twenty smaller squares, each containing a number, so that the sum in each row, taken either vertically or horizontally, was sixty-five. The medal was undoubtedly foreign. Theophrastus Paracelsus, in his 'Archidoxa,' published in the year 1572, describes some such talisman, gives instructions for its casting, and says: 'This seal or token gives him who carries it about him strength and security and victory in all battles, protection in all perils. It enables him to overcome his enemies and counteract their plots.'

The medal held by the girl belonged to the sixteenth century. Neither she nor her mother had ever heard of Paracelsus, and knew nothing of his 'Archidoxa.' The figures on the face passed their comprehension. The mystery of the square on the reverse had never been discovered by them. They knew only that the token was a charm, and that family tradition held it to secure the wearer against sudden death by violence.

A hole was drilled through the piece, and a strong silver ring inserted. A broad silk riband of faded blue passed through the ring, so that the medal might be worn about the neck. For a few moments Mehalah studied the mysterious figures by the fire-light, then flung the riband round her neck, and hid the coin and its perplexing symbols in her bosom.

'I must light a candle,' she said; then she stopped by the table on her way across the room, and took up the glass upon it.

'Mother,' she said sharply; 'who has been drinking here?'

The old woman pretended not to hear the question, and began to poke the fire.

'Mother, has Elijah Rebow been drinking spirits out of this glass?'

'To be sure, Mehalah, he did just take a drop.'

'Whence did he get it?'

'Don't you think it probable that such a man as he, out much on the marshes, should carry a bottle about with him? Most men go provided against the chill who can afford to do so.'

'Mother,' said the girl impatiently, 'you are deceiving me. I know he got the spirits here, and that you have had them here for some time. I insist on being told how you came by them.'

The old woman made feeble and futile attempts to evade answering her daughter directly; but was at last forced to confess that on two occasions, of which this evening was one, Elijah Rebow had brought her a small keg of rum.

'You do not grudge it me, Mehalah, do you? It does me good when I am low after my fits.'

'I do not grudge it you,' answered the girl; 'but I do not choose you should receive favours from that man. He has to-day been threatening us, and yet secretly he is making you presents. Why does he come here?' She looked full in her mother's face. 'Why does he give you these spirits? He, a man who never did a good action but asked a return in fourfold measure. I promise you, mother, if he brings here any more, that I will stave in the cask and let the liquor you so value waste away.'

The widow made piteous protest, but her daughter remained firm.

'Now,' said the girl, 'this point is settled between us. Be sure I will not go back from my word. I will in nothing be behoven to the man I abhor. Now let me count the money.' She caught up the bag, then put it down again. She lit a candle at the hearth, drew her chair to the table, seated herself at it, untied the string knotted about the neck of the pouch, and poured the contents upon the board.

She sprang to her feet with a cry; she stood as though petrified, with one hand to her head, the other holding the bag. Her eyes, wide open with dismay, were fixed on the little heap she had emptied on the table—a heap of shot, great and small, some penny-pieces, and a few bullets.

'What is the matter with you, Mehalah? What has happened?'

The girl was speechless. The old woman moved to the table and looked.

'What is this, Mehalah?'

'Look here! Lead, not gold.'

'There has been a mistake,' said the widow, nervously, 'call Abraham; he has given you the wrong sack.'

'There has been no mistake. This is the right bag. He had no other. We have been robbed.'

The old woman was about to put her hand on the heap, but Mehalah arrested it.

'Do not touch anything here,' she said, 'let all remain as it is till I bring Abraham. I must ascertain who has robbed us.'

She leaned her elbows on the table; she platted her fingers over her brow, and sat thinking. What could have become of the money? Where could it have been withdrawn? Who could have been the thief?

Abraham Dowsing, the shepherd, was a simple surly old man, honest but not intelligent, selfish but trustworthy. He was a fair specimen of the East Saxon peasant, a man of small reasoning power, moving like a machine, very slow, muddy in mind, only slightly advanced in the scale of beings above the dumb beasts; with instinct just awaking into intelligence, but not sufficiently awake to know its powers; more unhappy and helpless than the brute, for instinct is exhausted in the transformation process; not happy as a man, for he is encumbered with the new gift, not illumined and assisted by it. He is distrustful of its power, inapt to appreciate it, detesting the exercise of it.

On the fidelity of Abraham Dowsing, Mehalah felt assured she might rely. He was guiltless of the abstraction. She relied on him to sell the sheep to the best advantage, for, like everyone of low mental organisation, he was grasping and keen to drive a bargain. But when he had the money she knew that less confidence could be reposed on him. He could think of but one thing at a time, and if he fell into company, his mind would be occupied by his jug of beer, his bread and cheese, or his companion. He would not have attention at command for anything beside.

The rustic brain has neither agility nor flexibility. It cannot shift its focus nor change its point of sight. The educated mind will peer through a needlehole in a sheet of paper, and see through it the entire horizon and all the sky. The uncultured mind perceives nothing but a hole, a hole everywhere without bottom, to be recoiled from, not sounded. When the oyster spat falls on mud in a tidal estuary, it gets buried in mud deeper with every tide, two films each twenty-four hours, and becomes a fossil if it becomes anything. Mind in the rustic is like oyster spat, unformed, the protoplasm of mind but not mind itself, daily, annually deeper buried in the mud of coarse routine. It never thinks, it scarce lives, and dies in unconsciousness that it ever possessed life.

Mehalah sat considering, her mother by her, with anxious eyes fastened on her daughter's face.

The money must have been abstracted either in Colchester or on the way home. The old man had said that he stopped and tarried at the Rose inn on the way. Had the theft been there committed? Who had been his associates in that tavern?

'Mother,' said Mehalah suddenly, 'has the canvas bag been on the table untouched since Abraham brought it here?'

'To be sure it has.'

'You have been in the room, in your seat all the while?'

'Of course I have. There was no one here but Rebow. You do not suspect him, do you?'

Mehalah shook her head.

'No, I have no reason to do so. You were here all the while?'

'Yes.'

Mehalah dropped her brow again on her hands. What was to be done? It was in vain to question Abraham. His thick and addled brain would baffle enquiry. Like a savage, the peasant when questioned will equivocate, and rather than speak the truth invent a lie from a dim fear lest the truth should hurt him. The lie is to him what his shell is to the snail, his place of natural refuge; he retreats to it not only from danger, but from observation.

He does not desire to mislead the querist, but to baffle observation. He accumulates deception, equivocation, falsehood about him just as he allows dirt to clot his person, for his own warmth and comfort, not to offend others.

The girl stood up.

'Mother, I must go after George De Witt at once. He was with Abraham on the road home, and he will tell us the truth. It is of no use questioning the old man, he will grow suspicious, and think we are accusing him. The tide is at flood, I shall be able to catch George on the Mersea hard.'

'Take the lanthorn with you.'

'I will. The evening is becoming dark, and there will be ebb as I come back. I must land in the saltings.'

Mehalah unhung a lanthorn from the ceiling and kindled a candle end in it, at the light upon the table. She opened the drawer of the table and took out a pistol. She looked at the priming, and then thrust it through a leather belt she wore under her guernsey.

On that coast, haunted by smugglers and other lawless characters, a girl might well go armed. By the roadside to Colchester where cross ways met, was growing an oak that had been planted as an acorn in the mouth of a pirate of Rowhedge, not many years before, who had there been hung in chains for men murdered and maids carried off. Nearly every man carried a gun in hopes of bringing home wild fowl, and when Mehalah was in her boat, she usually took her gun with her for the same purpose. But men bore firearms not only for the sake of bringing home game; self-protection demanded it.

At this period, the mouth of the Blackwater was a great centre of the smuggling trade; the number and intricacy of the channels made it a safe harbour for those who lived on contraband traffic. It was easy for those who knew the creeks to elude the revenue boats, and every farm and tavern was ready to give cellarage to run goods and harbour to smugglers.

Between Mersea and the Blackwater were several flat holms or islands, some under water at high-tides, others only just standing above it, and between these the winding waterways formed a labyrinth in which it was easy to evade pursuit and entangle the pursuers. The traffic was therefore here carried on with an audacity and openness scarce paralleled elsewhere. Although there was a coastguard station at the mouth of the estuary, on Mersea 'Hard,' yet goods were run even in open day under the very eyes of the revenue men. Each public-house on the island and on the mainland near a creek obtained its entire supply of wine and spirits from contraband vessels. Whether the coastguard were bought to shut their eyes or were baffled by the adroitness of the smugglers, cannot be said, but certain it was, that the taverns found no difficulty in obtaining their supplies as often and as abundant as they desired.

The villages of Virley and Salcot were the chief landing-places, and there horses and donkeys were kept in large numbers for the conveyance of the spirits, wine, tobacco and silk to Tiptree Heath, the scene of Boadicaea's great battle with the legions of Suetonius, which was the emporium of the trade. There a constant fair or auction of contraband articles went on, and thence they were distributed to Maldon, Colchester, Chelmsford, and even London. Tiptree Heath was a permanent camping ground of gipsies, and squatters ran up there rude hovels; these were all engaged in the distribution of the goods brought from the sea.

But though the taverns were able to supply themselves with illicit spirits, unchecked, the coastguard were ready to arrest and detain run goods not destined for their cellars. Deeds of violence were not rare, and many a revenue officer fell a victim to his zeal. On Sunken Island off Mersea, the story went, that a whole boat's crew were found with their throats cut; they were transported thence to the churchyard, there buried, and their boat turned keel upwards over them.

The gipsies were thought to pursue over-conscientious and successful officers on the mainland, and remove them with a bullet should they escape the smugglers on the water.

The whole population of this region was more or less mixed up with, and interested in, this illicit traffic, and with defiance of the officers of the law, from the parson who allowed his nag and cart to be taken from his stable at night, left unbolted for the purpose, and received a keg now and then as repayment, to the vagabonds who dealt at the door far inland in silks and tobacco obtained free of duty on the coast.

What was rare elsewhere was by no means uncommon here, gipsies intermarried with the people, and settled on the coast. The life of adventure, danger, and impermanence was sufficiently attractive to them to induce them to abandon for it their roving habits; perhaps the difference of life was not so marked as to make the change distasteful. Thus a strain of wild, restless, law-defying gipsy blood entered the veins of the Essex marshland populations, and galvanised into new life the sluggish and slimy liquid that trickled through the East Saxon arteries. Adventurers from the Low Countries, from France, even from Italy and Spain—originally smugglers, settled on the coast, generally as publicans, in league with the owners of the contraband vessels, married and left issue. There were neither landed gentry nor resident incumbents in this district, to civilise and restrain. The land was held by yeomen farmers, and by squatters who had seized on and enclosed waste land, no man saying them nay. At the revocation of the Edict of Nantes a large number of Huguenot French families had settled in the 'Hundreds' and the marshes, and for full a century in several of the churches divine service was performed alternately in French and English. To the energy of these colonists perhaps are due the long-extended sea-walls enclosing vast tracts of pasture from the tide.

Those Huguenots not only infused their Gallic blood into the veins of the people, but also their Puritanic bitterness and Calvinistic partiality for Old Testament names. Thus the most frequent Christian names met with are those of patriarchs, prophets and Judaic kings, and the sire-names are foreign, often greatly corrupted.

Yet, in spite of this infusion of strange ichor from all sides, the agricultural peasant on the land remains unaltered, stamped out of the old unleavened dough of Saxon stolidity, forming a class apart from that of the farmers and that of the seamen, in intelligence, temperament, and gravitation. All he has derived from the French element which has washed about him has been a nasal twang in his pronunciation of English. Yet his dogged adherence to one letter, which was jeopardised by the Gallic invasion, has reacted, and imposed on the invaders, and the v is universally replaced on the Essex coast by a w.

In the plaster and oak cottages away from the sea, by stagnant pools, the hatching places of clouds of mosquitos, whence rises with the night the haunting spirit of tertian ague, the hag that rides on, and takes the life out of the sturdiest men and women, and shakes and wastes the vital nerves of the children, live the old East Saxon slow moving, never thinking, day labourers. In the tarred wreck-timber cabins by the sea just above the reach of the tide, beside the shingle beach, swarms a yeasty, turbulent, race of mixed-breeds, engaged in the fishery and in the contraband trade.

Mehalah went to the boat. It was floating. She placed the lanthorn in the bows, cast loose, and began to row. She would need the light on her return, perhaps, as with the falling tide she would be unable to reach the landing-place under the farmhouse, and be forced to anchor at the end of the island, and walk home across the saltings. To cross these without a light on a dark night is not safe even to one knowing the lie of the land.

A little light still lingered in the sky. There was a yellow grey glow in the west over the Bradwell shore. Its fringe of trees, and old barn chapel standing across the walls of the buried city Othona, stood sombre against the light, as though dabbed in pitch on a faded golden ground. The water was still, as no wind was blowing, and it reflected the sky and the stars that stole out, with such distinctness that the boat seemed to be swimming in the sky, among black tatters of clouds, these being the streaks of land that broke the horizon and the reflection.

Gulls were screaming, and curlew uttered their mournful cry. Mehalah rowed swiftly down the Rhyn, as the channel was called that divided the Ray from the mainland, and that led to the 'hard' by the Rose inn, and formed the highway by which it drew its supplies, and from which every farm in the parish of Peldon carried its casks of strong liquor. To the west extended a vast marsh from which the tide was excluded by a dyke many miles in length. Against the northern horizon rose the hill of Wigborough crowned by a church and a great tumulus, and some trees that served as landmarks to the vessels entering the Blackwater. In ancient days the hill had been a beacon station, and it was reconverted to this purpose in time of war. A man was placed by order of Government in the tower, to light a crescet on the summit, in answer to a similar beacon at Mersea, in the event of a hostile fleet being seen in the offing.

Now and then the boat—it was a flat-bottomed punt—hissed among the asters, as Mehalah shot over tracts usually dry, but now submerged; she skirted next a bed of bulrushes. These reeds are only patient of occasional flushes with salt water, and where they grow it is at the opening of a land drain, or mark a fresh spring. Suddenly as she was cutting the flood, the punt was jarred and arrested. She looked round. A boat was across her bows. It had shot out of the rushes and stopped her.

'Whither are you going, Glory?'

The voice was that of Elijah Rebow, the last man Mehalah wished to meet at night, when alone on the water.

'That is my affair, not yours,' she answered. 'I am in haste, let me pass.'

'I will not. I will not be treated like this, Glory. I have shot you a couple of curlew, and here they are.'

He flung the birds into her boat. Mehalah threw them back again.

'Let it be an understood thing between us, Elijah, that we will accept none of your presents. You have brought my mother a keg of rum, and I have sworn to beat in the head of the next you give her. She will take nothing from you.'

'There you are mistaken, Glory; she will take as much as I will give her. You mean that you will not. I understand your pride, Glory! and I love you for it.'

'I care nothing for your love or your hate. We are naught to each other.'

'Yes we are, I am your landlord. We shall see how that sentiment of yours will stand next Thursday.'

'What do you mean?' asked Mehalah hastily.

12

'What do I mean? Why, I suppose I am intelligible enough in what I say for you to understand me without explanation. When you come to pay the rent to me next Thursday, you will not be able to say we are naught to each other. Why! you will have to pay me for every privilege of life you enjoy, for the house you occupy, for the marshes that feed your cow and swell its udder with milk, for the saltings on which your sheep fatten and grow their wool.'

The brave girl's heart failed for a moment. She had not the money. What would Elijah say and do when he discovered that she and her mother were defaulters? However, she put a bold face on the matter now, and thrusting off the boat with her oar, she said impatiently, 'You are causing me to waste precious time. I must be back before the water is out of the fleets.'

'Whither are you going?' again asked Rebow, and again he drove his boat athwart her bows. 'It is not safe for a young girl like you to be about on the water after nightfall with ruffians of all sorts poaching on my saltings and up and down my creeks.'

'I am going to Mersea City,' said Mehalah.

'You are going to George De Witt.'

'What if I am? That is no concern of yours.'

'He is my cousin.'

'I wish he were a cousin very far removed from you.'

'Oh Glory! you are jesting.' He caught the side of the punt with his hand, for she made an effort to push past him. 'I shall not detain you long. Take these curlew. They are plump birds; your mother will relish them. Take them, and be damned to your pride. I shot them for you.'

'I will not have them, Elijah.'

'Then I will not either,' and he flung the dead birds into the water.

She seized the opportunity, and dipping her oars in the tide, strained at them, and shot away. She heard him curse, for his boat had grounded and he could not follow.

She laughed in reply.

In twenty minutes Mehalah ran her punt on Mersea beach. Here a little above high-water mark stood a cluster of wooden houses and an old inn, pretentiously called the 'City,' a hive of smugglers. On the shore, somewhat east, and away from the city, lay a dismasted vessel, fastened upright by chains, the keel sunk in the shingle. She had been carried to this point at spring flood and stranded, and was touched, not lifted by the ordinary tides. Mehalah's punt, drawing no draught, floated under the side of this vessel, and she caught the ladder by which access was obtained to the deck.

'Who is there?' asked George De Witt, looking over the side.

'I am come after you, George,' answered Mehalah.

'Why, Glory! what is the matter?'

'There is something very serious the matter. You must come back with me at once to the Ray.'

'Is your mother ill?'

'Worse than that.'

'Dead?'

'No, no! nothing of that sort. She is all right. But I cannot explain the circumstances now. Come at once and with me.'

'I will get the boat out directly.'

'Never mind the boat. Come in the punt with me. You cannot return by water to-night. The ebb will prevent that. You will be obliged to go round by the Strood. Tell your mother not to expect you.'

'But what is the matter, Glory?'

'I will tell you when we are afloat.'

'I shall be back directly, but I do not know how the old woman will take it.' He swung himself down into the cabin, and announced to his mother that he was going to the Ray, and would return on foot by the Strood.

A gurgle of objurgations rose from the hatchway, and followed the young man as he made his escape.

'I wouldn't have done it for another,' said he; 'the old lady is put out, and will not forgive me. It will be bad walking by the Strood, Glory! Can't you put me across to the Fresh Marsh?'

'If there is water enough I will do so. Be quick now. There is no time to spare.'

He came down the ladder and stepped into the punt.

'Give me the oars, Glory. You sit in the stern and take the lanthorn.'

'It is in the bows.'

'I know that. But can you not understand, Glory, that when I am rowing, I like to see you. Hold the lanthorn so that I may get a peep of your face now and then.'

'Do not be foolish, George,' said Mehalah. However, she did as he asked, and the yellow dull light fell on her face, red handkerchief and cap.

'You look like a witch,' laughed De Witt.

'I will steer, row as hard as you can, George,' said the girl; then abruptly she exclaimed, 'I have something for you. Take it now, and look at it afterwards.'

She drew the medal from her bosom, and passing the riband over her head, leaned forward, and tossed the loop across his shoulders.

'Don't upset the boat, Glory! Sit still; a punt is an unsteady vessel, and won't bear dancing in. What is it that you have given me?'

'A keepsake.'

'I shall always keep it, Glory, for the sake of the girl I love best in the world. Now tell me; am I to row up Mersea channel or the Rhyn?'

'There is water enough in the Rhyn, though we shall not be able to reach our hard. You row on, and do not trouble yourself about the direction, I will steer. We shall land on the Saltings. That is why I have brought the lanthorn with me.'

'What are you doing with the light?'

'I must put it behind me. With the blaze in my eyes I cannot see where to steer.' She did as she said.

'Now tell me, Glory, what you have hung round my neck.'

'It is a medal, George.'

'Whatever it be, it comes from you, and is worth more than gold.'

'It is worth a great deal. It is a certain charm.'

'Indeed!'

'It preserves him who wears it from death by violence.'

At the word a flash shot out of the rushes, and a bullet whizzed past the stern.

George De Witt paused on his oars, startled, confounded.

'The bullet was meant for you or me,' said Mehalah in a low voice. 'Had the lanthorn been in the bows and not in the stern it would have struck you.'

Then she sprang up and held the lanthorn aloft, above her head.

'Coward, whoever you are, skulking in the reeds. Show a light, if you are a man. Show a light as I do. and give me a mark in return.'

'For heaven's sake, Glory, put out the candle,' exclaimed De Witt in agitation.

'Coward! show a light, that I may have a shot at you,' she cried again, without noticing what George said. In his alarm for her and for himself, he raised his oar and dashed the lanthorn out of her hand. It fell, and went out in the water.

Mehalah drew her pistol from her belt, and cocked it. She was standing, without trembling, immovable in the punt, her eye fixed unflinching on the reeds.

'George,' she said, 'dip the oars. Don't let her float away.'

He hesitated.

Presently a slight click was audible, then a feeble flash, as from flint struck with steel in the pitch blackness of the shore.

Then a small red spark burned steadily.

Not a sound, save the ripple of the retreating tide.

Mehalah's pistol was levelled at the spark. She fired, and the spark disappeared.

She and George held their breath.

'I have hit,' she said. 'Now run the punt in where the light was visible.'

'No, Glory; this will not do. I am not going to run you and myself into fresh danger.' He struck out.

'George, you are rowing away! Give me the oars. I will find out who it was that fired at us.'

'This is foolhardiness,' he said, but obeyed. A couple of strokes ran the punt among the reeds. Nothing was to be seen or heard. The night was dark on the water, it was black as ink among the rushes. Several times De Witt stayed his hand and listened, but there was not a sound save the gurgle of the water, and the song of the night wind among the tassels and harsh leaves of the bulrushes.

'She is aground,' said De Witt.

'We must back into the channel, and push on to the Ray,' said Mehalah.

The young man jumped into the water among the roots of the reeds, and drew the punt out till she floated; then he stepped in and resumed the oars.

'Hist!' whispered De Witt.

Both heard the click of a lock.

'Down!' he whispered, and threw himself in the bottom of the punt.

Another flash, report, and a bullet struck and splintered the bulwark.

De Witt rose, resumed the oars, and rowed lustily.

Mehalah had not stirred. She had remained erect in the stern and never flinched.

'Coward!' she cried in a voice full of wrath and scorn, 'I defy you to death, be you who you may!'

CHAPTER III.

THE SEVEN WHISTLERS.

The examination of old Abraham before George De Witt did not lead to any satisfactory result. The young man was unable to throw light on the mystery. He had not been with the shepherd all the while since the sale of the sheep; nor had he seen the money. Abraham had indeed told him the sum for which he had parted with the flock, and in so doing had chinked the bag significantly. George thought it was impossible for the shot and pennypieces that had been found in the pouch to have produced the metallic sound he had heard. Abraham had informed him of the sale in Colchester. Then they had separated, and the shepherd had left the town before De Witt.

The young man had overtaken him at the public-house called the Red Lion at Abberton, half-way between Colchester and his destination. He was drinking a mug of beer with some seafaring men; and they proceeded thence together. But at the Rose, another tavern a few miles further, they had stopped for a glass and something to eat. But even there De Witt had not been with the old man all the while, for the landlord had called him out to look at a contrivance he had in his punt for putting a false keel on her; with a bar, after a fashion he had seen among the South Sea Islanders when he was a sailor.

The discussion of this daring innovation had lasted some time, and when De Witt returned to the tavern, he found Abraham dozing, if not fast asleep, with his head on the table, and his money bag in his hand.

'It is clear enough,' said the widow, 'that the money was stolen either at the Lion or at the Rose.'

'I brought the money safe here,' said Abraham sullenly. 'It is of no use your asking questions, and troubling my head about what I did here and there. I was at the Woolpack at Colchester, at the Lion at Abberton, and lastly at the Rose. But I tell you I brought the money here all safe, and laid it there on that table every penny.'

'How can you be sure of that, Abraham?'

'I say I know it.'

'But Abraham, what grounds have you for such assurance? Did you count the money at the Rose?'

'I don't care what you may ask or say. I brought the money here. If you have lost it, or it has been bewitched since then, I am not to blame.'

'Abraham, it must have been stolen on the road. There was no one here to take the money.'

'That is nothing to me. I say I laid the money all right there!' He pointed to the table.

'You may go, Abraham,' said Mehalah.

'Do you charge me with taking the money?' the old man asked with moody temper.

'Of course not,' answered the girl. 'We did not suspect you for one moment.'

'Then whom do you lay it on?'

'We suspect some one whom you met at one of the taverns.'

'I tell you,' he said with an oath, 'I brought the money here.'

'You cannot prove it,' said De Witt; 'if you have any reasons for saying this, let us hear them.'

'I have no reasons,' answered the shepherd, 'but I know the truth all the same. I never have reasons, I do not want to have them, when I know a fact.'

'Did you shake the bag and make the money chink on the way?'

'I will not answer any more questions. If you suspect me to be the thief, say so to my face, and don't go ferriting and trapping to ketch me, and then go and lay it on me before a magistrate.'

'You had better go, Abraham. No one disputes your perfect honesty,' said Mehalah.

'But I will not go, if anyone suspects me.'

'We do not suspect you.'

'Then why do you ask questions? Who asks questions who don't want to lay a wickedness on one?'

'Go off to bed, Abraham,' said widow Sharland. 'We have met with a dreadful loss, and the Almighty knows how we are to come out of it.'

The old man went forth grumbling imprecations on himself if he answered any more questions.

'Well,' asked Mehalah of De Witt, when the shepherd was gone, 'what do you think has become of the money?'

'I suppose he was robbed at one of the taverns. I see no other possible way of accounting for the loss. The bag was not touched on the table from the moment Abraham set it down till you opened it.'

'No. My mother was here all the time. There was no one else in the room but Elijah Rebow.'

'He is out of the question,' said De Witt.

'Besides, my mother never left her seat whilst he was here. Did you, mother?'

The old woman shook her head.

'What are we to do?' she asked; 'we have no money now for the rent; and that must be paid next Thursday.'

'Have you none at all?'

'None but a trifle which we need for purchases against the winter. There was more in the bag than was needed for the rent, and how we shall struggle through the winter without it, heaven alone can tell.'

'You have no more sheep to sell?'

'None but ewes, which cannot be parted with.'

'Nor a cow?'

'It would be impossible for us to spare her.'

'Then I will lend you the money,' said George. 'I have something laid by, and you shall have what you need for the rent out of it. Mehalah will repay me some day.'

'I will, George! I will!' said the girl vehemently, and her eyes filled. She took the two hands of her lover in her own, and looked him full in the face. Her eyes expressed the depth of her gratitude which her tongue could not utter.

'Now that is settled,' said De Witt, 'let us talk of something else.'

'Come along, George,' said Mehalah, hastily, interrupting him. 'If you want to be put across on Fresh Marsh, you must not stay talking here any longer.'

'All right, Glory! I am ready to go with you, anywhere, to the world's end.'

As she drew him outside, she whispered, 'I was afraid of your speaking about the two shots to-night. I do not wish my mother to hear of that; it would alarm her.'

'But I want to talk to you about them,' said De Witt. 'Have you any notion who it was that fired at us?'

'Have you?' asked Mehalah, evading an answer.

'I have a sort of a notion.'

'So have I. As I was going down the Rhyn to fetch you, I was stopped by Elijah Rebow.'

'Well, what did he want?'

'He wanted me to take some curlew he had shot; but that was not all, he tried to prevent my going on. He said that I ought not to be on the water at night alone.'

'He was right. He knew a thing or two.'

'He did not like my going to Mersea—to you.'

'I dare say not. He knew what was in the wind.'

'What do you mean, George?'

'He tried to prevent your going on?'

'Yes, he did, more than once.'

'Then he is in it. I don't like Elijah, but I did not think so badly of him as that.'

'What do you mean, George?'

As they talked they walked down the meadow to the saltings. They were obliged to go slowly and cautiously. The tide had fallen rapidly, and left the pools brimming. Every runnel was full of water racing out with the rush of a mill stream. 'You see, Glory, the new captain of the coastguard has been giving a deal of trouble lately. He has noticed the single-flashing from the Leather Bottle at the city, and has guessed or found out the key; so he has been down there flashing false signals with a lanthorn. By this means he has brought some of the smugglers very neatly into traps he has laid for them. They are as mad as devils, they swear he is taking an unfair advantage of them, and that they will have his life for it. That is what I have heard whispered; and I hear a great many things.'

'Oh, George! have you not warned him?'

'I! my dear Glory! what can I do? He knows he is in danger as well as I. It is a battle between them, and it don't do for a third party to step between. That is what we have done to-night, and near got knocked over for doing it. Captain Macpherson is about, night and day. There never was a fellow more wide awake, at least not on this station. What do you think he did the other day? A vessel came in, and he overhauled her, but found nothing; he sought for some barrels drawn along attached behind her, below water level, but couldn't find them. As he was leaving, he just looked up at the tackling. "Halloo!" said he to the captain, "your cordage is begun to untwist, suppose I have your old ropes and give you new?" He sent a man aloft, and all the ropes were made of twisted tobacco. Now, as you may suppose, the smugglers don't much like such a man.'

'But, George, he would hardly go about at night with a lanthorn in his boat.'

'That is what he does—only it is a dark lanthorn, and with it he flashes his signals. That is what makes the men so mad. It is not my doctrine to shoot a man who does his duty. If a man is a smuggler let him do his duty as one. If he is a coastguard, let him do his duty by the revenue.'

'But, George! if he were out watching for smugglers, he would not have carried his light openly.'

'He might have thought all was safe in the Rhyn.'

'Then again,' pursued Mehalah, 'I spoke, and there was a second shot after that.'

'Whoever was there waiting for the captain may have thought you were a boy. I do not believe the shot was at you, but at me.'

'But I held the light up. It would have been seen that I was a woman.'

'Not a bit. All seen would be your cap and jersey, which are such as sailor boys wear.'

Mehalah shook her head thoughtfully and somewhat doubtfully, and paced by the side of De Witt. She did not speak for some time. She was not satisfied with his explanation, but she could not state her reasons for dissatisfaction.

Presently she said, 'Do you think that it was Rebow who fired?'

'No, of course I do not. He knew you were out, and with a light; and he knows your voice.'

'But you said he was in the plot.'

'I said that I supposed he knew about it; he knew that there were men out in punts waiting for the captain, he probably knew that there was some fellow lurking in the Rhyn; but I did not say that he would shoot the captain. I do not for a moment suppose he would. He is not greatly affected by his vigilance. He gets something out of the trade, but not enough to be of importance to him. A man of his means would not think it worth his while to shoot an officer.'

'Then you conjecture that he warned me, and went home.'

'That is most likely, I would have done the same; nay more, I would not have let you go on, if I knew there were fellows about this night with guns on the lookout. He did not dare to speak plainly what he knew, but he gave you a broad hint, and his best advice, and I admire and respect him for it.'

'You and Rebow are cousins?'

'His father's sister is my mother. The land and money all went to Elijah's father who is now dead, and is now in Elijah's hands. My mother got nothing. The family were angry with her for marrying off the land on to the water. But you see at Red Hall she had lived, so to speak, half in and half out of the sea; she took to one element as readily as to the other.'

'I can trace little resemblance in your features, but something in your voice.'

'Now, Glory!' said the young man, 'here is the boat. How fast the tide ebbs here! She is already dry, and we must shove her down over the grass and mud till she floats. You step in, I will run her along.'

The wind had risen, and was wailing over the marshes, sighing among the harsh herbage, the sea-lavender, sovereign wood, and wild asparagus. Not a cloud was visible. The sky was absolutely unblurred and thick besprint with stars. Jupiter burned in the south, and cast a streak of silver over the ebbing waters.

The young people stood silent by each other for a moment, and their hearts beat fast. Other matters had broken in on and troubled the pleasant current of their love; but now the thought of these was swept aside, and their hearts rose and stretched towards each other. They had known each other for many years, and the friendship of childhood had insensibly ripened in their hearts to love.

'I have not properly thanked you, George, for the promise of help in our trouble.'

'Nor I, Mehalah, for the medal you have given me.'

'Promise me, George, to wear it ever. It saved your life to-night, I doubt not.'

'What! Does it save from death?'

'From sudden death,' answered Mehalah. 'I told you so before, in the boat.'

'I forgot about it, Glory.'

'I will tell you now all about it, my friend. The charm belonged to my mother's mother. She, as I daresay you have heard, was a gipsy. My grandfather fell in love with her and married her. He was a well-to-do man, owning a bit of land of his own; but he would go to law with a neighbour and lost it, and it went to the lawyer. Well, my grandmother brought the charm with her, and it has been in the family ever since. It had been in the gipsy family of my grandmother time out of mind, and was lent about when any of the men went on dangerous missions. No one who wears it can die a sudden death from violence—that is'—Mehalah qualified the assertion, 'on land.'

'It does not preserve one on the water then?' said George, with an incredulous laugh.

'I won't say that. It surely did so to-night. It saves from shot and stab.'

'Not from drowning?'

'I think not.'

'I must get a child's caul, and then I shall be immortal.'

'Don't joke, George,' said Mehalah gravely. 'What I say is true.'

'Glory!' said De Witt, 'I always thought you looked like a gipsy with your dark skin and large brown eyes, and now from your own lips comes the confession that you are one.'

'There is none of the blood in my mother,' said she, 'she is like an ordinary Christian. I fancy it jumps a generation.'

'Well, then, you dear gipsy, here is my hand. Tell my fortune.'

'I cannot do that. But I have given you a gipsy charm against evil men and accidents.'

'Hark!'

Out of the clear heaven was heard plaintive whistles, loud, high up, inexpressibly weird and sad, 'Ewe! ewe! ewe!' They burst shrilly on the ears, then became fainter, then burst forth again, then faded away. It was as though spirits were passing in the heavens wailing about a brother sprite that had flickered into nothingness.

'The curlew are in flight. What is the matter, Mehalah?'

The girl was shivering.

'Are you cold!'

'George! those are the Seven Whistlers.'

'They are the long-beaked curlew going south.'

'They are the Seven Whistlers, and they mean death or deathlike woe. For God's sake, George,' she threw her arms round him, 'swear, swear to me, never to lay aside the medal I have given you, but to wear it night and day.'

'There! Glory, I swear it.'

CHAPTER IV.

RED HALL.

The rent-paying day was bright and breezy. The tide was up in the morning, and Mehalah and her mother in a boat with sail and jib and spritsail flew before a north-east wind down the Mersea Channel, and doubling Sunken Island, entered the creek which leads to Salcot and Virley, two villages divided only by a tidal stream, and connected by a bridge.

The water danced and sparkled, multitudes of birds were on the wing, now dipping in the wavelets, now rising and shaking off the glittering drops. A high sea-wall hid the reclaimed land on their left. Behind it rose the gaunt black structure of a windmill used for pumping the water out of the dykes in the marsh. It was working now, the great black arms revolving in the breeze, and the pump creaking as if the engine groaned remonstrances at being called to toil on such a bright day. A little further appeared a tiled roof above the wall.

'There is Red Hall,' said Mehalah, as she ran the boat ashore and threw out the anchor. 'I have brought the stool, mother,' she added, and helped the old woman to land dry-footed. The sails were furled, and then Mehalah and her mother climbed the wall and descended into the pastures. These were of considerable extent, reclaimed saltings, but of so old a date that the brine was gone from the soil, and they furnished the best feed for cattle anywhere round. Several stagnant canals or ditches intersected the flat tract and broke it into islands, but they hung together by the thread of sea-wall, and the windmill drained the ditches into the sea.

In the midst of the pasture stood a tall red-brick house. There was not a tree near it. It rose from the flat like a tower. The basement consisted of cellars above ground, and there were arched entrances to these from the two ends. They were lighted by two small round windows about four feet from the ground. A flight of brick stairs built over an arch led from a paved platform to the door of the house, which stood some six feet above the level of the marsh. The house had perhaps been thus erected in view of a flood overleaping the walls, and converting the house for a while into an island, or as a preventive to the inhabitants against ague. The sea-walls had been so well kept that no tide had poured over them, and the vaults beneath served partly as cellars, and being extensive, were employed with the connivance of the owner as a storeplace for run spirits. The house was indeed very conveniently situated for contraband trade. A 'fleet' or tidal creek on either side of the marsh allowed of approach or escape by the one when the other was watched. Nor was this all. The marsh itself was penetrated by three or four ramifications of the two main channels, to these the sea-wall accommodated itself instead of striking across them, and there was water-way across the whole marsh, so that if a boat were lifted over the bank on one side, it could be rowed across, again lifted, and enter the other channel, before a pursuing boat would have time to return to and double the spit of land that divided the fleets. The windmill which stood on this spit was in no favour with the coastguard, for it was thought to act the double purpose of pump and observatory. The channel south of these marshes, called the Tollesbury Fleet, was so full of banks and islets as to be difficult to navigate, and more than once a revenue boat had got entangled and grounded there, when in pursuit of a smuggled cargo, which the officers had every reason to believe was at that time being landed on the Red Hall marshes, and carted into Salcot and Virley with the farmer's horses.

The house was built completely of brick, the windows were of moulded brick, mullions and drip stone, and the roof was of tile. How the name of Red Hall came to be given it, was obvious at a glance.

Round the house was a yard paved with brick, and a moat filled with rushes and weed. There were a few low outhouses, stable, cowsheds, bakehouse, forming a yard at the back, and into that descended the stair from the kitchen-door over a flying arch, like that in front.

Perhaps the principal impression produced by the aspect of Red Hall on the visitor was its solitariness. The horizon was bounded by sea wall; only when the door was reached, which was on a level with the top of the mound, were the glittering expanse of sea, the creeks, and the woods on Mersea Island and the mainland visible. Mehalah and her mother had never been at Red Hall before, and though they were pretty familiar with the loneliness of the marshes, the utter isolation of this tall gaunt house impressed them. The thorn-trees at the Ray gave their farm an aspect of snugness compared with this. From the Ray, village-church towers and cultivated acres were visible, but so long as they were in the pasture near the Hall, nothing was to be seen save a flat tract of grass land intersected with lines of bulrush, and bounded by a mound.

Several cows and horses were in the pasture, but no human being was visible. Mehalah and her mother hesitated before ascending the stair.

'This is the queerest place for a Christian to live in I ever saw,' said the widow. 'Look there, Mehalah, there is a date on the door, sixteen hundred and thirty-six. Go up and knock.'

'Do you see that little window in the sea face of the house, mother?'

'Yes. There is none but it.'

'I can tell you what that is for. It is to signal from with a light.'

'I don't doubt it. Go on.'

Mehalah slowly ascended the stair; it was without a balustrade. She struck against the door. The door was of strong plank thickly covered with nails, and the date of which the widow had spoken was made with nail-heads at the top.

Her knock met with no response, so she thrust the door open and entered, followed by her mother.

The room she stepped into was large and low. It was lighted by but one window to the south, fitted with lead lattice. The floor was of brick, for the cellarage was vaulted and supported a solid basement. There was no ceiling, and the oak rafters were black with age and smoke. The only ornaments decorating the walls were guns and pistols, some of curious foreign make.

The fire-place was large; on the oak lintel was cut deep the inscription:—

'WHEN I HOLD (1636) I HOLD FAST.'

Mehalah had scarce time to notice all this, when a trap-door she had not observed in the floor flew up, and the head, then the shoulders, and finally the entire body, of Elijah Rebow emerged from the basement. Without taking notice of his tenants, he leisurely ran a stout iron bolt through a staple, making fast the trap at the top, then he did the same with a bolt at the bottom.

At the time, this conduct struck Mehalah as singular. It was as though Rebow were barring a door from within lest he should be broken in on from the cellar.

Elijah slowly drew a leather armchair over the trap-door, and seated himself in it. The hole through which he had ascended was near the fire-place, and now that he sat over it he occupied the ingle nook.

'Well, Glory!' said he suddenly, addressing Mehalah. 'So you have not brought the rent. You have come with your old mother to blubber and beg compassion and delay. I know it all. It is of no use. Tears don't move me, I have no pity, and I grant no delay. I want my money. Every man does. He wants his money when it's due. I calculated on it, I've a debt which I shall wipe off with it, so there; now no excuses, I tell you they won't do. Sheer off.'

'Master Rebow—' began the widow.

'You may save your speech,' said Elijah, cutting her short. 'Faugh! when I've been down there.'—he pointed with his thumb towards the cellar—'I need a smoke.' He drew forth a clay pipe and tobacco-box and leisurely filled the bowl. Whilst he was lighting his pipe at the hearth, where an old pile was smouldering, and emitting an odour like gunpowder, Mehalah drew a purse from her pocket and counted the amount of the rent on the table. Rebow did not observe her. He was engaged in making his pipe draw, and the table was behind the chair.

'Well!' said he, blowing a puff of smoke, and chuckling, 'I fancy you are in a pretty predicament. Read that over the fire, cut yonder, do you see? "When I hold, I hold fast." I didn't cut that, but my fore-elders did, and we all do that. Why, George De Witt's mother thought to have had some pickings out of the marsh, she did, but my father got hold of it, and he held fast. He did not let go a penny; no, not a farthing. It is a family characteristic. It is a family pleasure. We take a pride in it. I don't care what it is, whether it is a bit of land, or a piece of coin, or a girl, it is all the same, and I think you'll find it is so with me. Eh! Glory! When I hold, I hold fast.' He turned in his chair and leered at her.

'There, there,' said she, 'lay hold of your rent, and hold fast till death. We want none of it.'

'What is that?' exclaimed Rebow, starting out of his seat, 'What money is that?'

'The rent,' said Mehalah; she stood erect beside the table in her haughty beauty, and laughed at the surprised and angry expression that clouded Rebow's countenance.

'I won't take it. You have stolen it.'

'Master Rebow,' put in the widow, 'the money is yours; it is the rent, not a penny short.'

'Where did you get the money?' he asked with a curse.

'You bid me bring the money on rent-day, and there it is,' said Mehalah. 'But now I will ask a question, and I insist on an answer.'

'Oh! you insist, do you?'

'I insist on an answer,' repeated the girl. 'How did you come to think we were without money?'

'Suppose I don't choose to answer.'

'If you don't—' she began, then hesitated.

'I will tell you,' he said, sulkily. 'Abraham Dowsing, your shepherd, isn't dumb, I believe. He talks, he does, and has pretty well spread the news all round the country how he was robbed of his money at the Rose.'

'Abraham has never said anything of the sort. He denies that he was robbed.'

'Then he says he is accused of being robbed, which is the same. I suppose the story is true.'

'It is quite true, Master Rebow,' answered the widow. 'It was a terrible loss to us. We had sold all the sheep we could sell.'

'Oh! a terrible loss, indeed!' scoffed the man. 'You are so flush of money, that a loss of ten or fifteen, or may be twenty pounds is nought to you. You have your little store in one of those cupboards in every corner of the old house, and you put your hand in, and take out what you like. You call yourself poor, do you, and think nothing of a loss like this?'

'We are very poor,' said the widow; 'Heaven knows we have a hard battle to fight to make both ends meet, and to pay our rent.'

'I don't believe it. You are telling me lies.'

He took the coin, and counted it; his dark brow grew blacker; and he ground his teeth. Once he raised his wolfish eyes and glared on Mehalah. 'That guinea is bad,' he said, and he threw it on the floor.

'It rings like a good one,' answered the girl, 'pick it up and give it to me. I will let you have another in its place.'

'Oh ho! your pocket is lined with guineas, is it? I will raise the rent of the Ray. I thought as much, the land is fatter than mine on this marsh. You get the place dirt cheap. I'll raise the rent ten pounds. I'll raise it twenty.'

'Master Rebow!' pleaded the widow, 'the Ray won't allow us to pay it.'

'Do not put yourself out, mother,' said Mehalah, 'we have a lease of twenty-one years; and there are seven more years to run, before Rebow can do what he threatens.'

'Oh, you are clever, you are, Glory! cursed clever. Now look here, Mistress Sharland, I'm going to have a rasher, and it's about dinner time, stop and bite with me; and that girl there, she shall bite too. You can't be back till evening, and you'll be perished with hunger.'

'Thank you, master,' answered the widow eagerly.

'And I'll give you a sup of the very primest brandy.'

'Mother, we must return at once. The tide will ebb, and we shall not be able to get away.'

'That's a lie,' said Elijah angrily, 'as you've got here, you can get away. There's plenty of water in the fleet, and will be for three hours. I knew you'd come and so I got some rashers all ready on the pan; there they be.'

'You're very kind,' observed the widow.

'A landlord is bound to give his tenantry a dinner on rent-day,' said Rebow, with an ugly laugh which displayed his great teeth. 'It's Michaelmas, but I have no goose. I keep plenty on the marshes. They do well here, and they pay well too.'

'I will have a witness that I have paid the rent,' said Mehalah. 'Call one of your men.'

'Go and call one yourself. I am going to fry the rashers.'

'That guinea is still on the floor,' said Mehalah.

'I have refused it. Pick it up, and give me another.'

'I will not pick it up; and I will not give you another till you have convinced me that the coin is bad.'

'Then let it lie.'

23

'Where are your men?'

'I don't know, go and find them. They're at their dinner now. I dare say near the pump.'

Mehalah left the house, but before she descended the steps, she looked over the flat. There was a sort of shed for cattle half a mile off, and she thought she saw some one moving there. She went at once in that direction.

Scarce was she gone when Elijah beckoned the widow to draw over a chair to the fire.

'You cook the wittles,' said he; 'I'm my own cook in general, but when a woman is here, why, I'm fain to let her take the job off my hands.'

The old woman obeyed with as much activity as she was mistress of. Whilst thus engaged, Elijah walked to the door, opened it, and looked out.

'She's going as straight as a wild duck,' he said, and laughed; 'she is a damned fine girl. Listen to me, mistress, that daughter of yours, Glory, is too good-looking to be mewed up on the Ray. You should marry her, and then settle yourself comfortably down for the rest of your days in your son-in-law's house.'

'Ah! Master Rebow, she is poor, she is, and now young men look out for money.'

'You don't want a very young man for such as she. Why, she is as wild as a gipsy, and needs a firm hand to keep her. He that has hold of her should hold fast.'

The widow shook her head. 'We don't see many folks on the Ray. She will have to marry a fellow on the water.'

'No, she won't,' said Rebow angrily. 'Damn her, she shall marry a farmer, who owns land and marshes, and saltings, and housen, and takes rents, and don't mind to drop some eight hundred pound on a bit of a farm that takes his fancy.'

'Such men are not easy to be got.'

'No, there you are right, mistress; but when you find one, why——' he drew his pipe over the inscription on the fireplace. 'I'm the man, and now you hold me, hold fast.'

'You, master!'

'Aye, I. I like the girl. By God! I will have Glory. She was born for me. There is not another girl I have seen that I would give an oystershell for, but she—she—she makes my blood run like melted lead, and my heart here gnaws and burns in my breast like a fiery rat. I tell you I will have her. I will.'

'If it only rested with me,' moaned the widow.

'Look here,' said Rebow. 'Lay that pan on one side and follow me. I'll show you over the house.' He caught her by the wrist, and dragged her from room to room, and up the stairs. When he had brought her back to the principal apartment in which they had been sitting, he chuckled with pride. 'Ain't it a good house? It's twenty times better than the Ray. It is more comfortable, and there are more rooms. And all these marshes and meadows are mine, and I have also some cornfields in Virley, on the mainland. And then the Ray is mine, with the saltings and all thereon;—I bought it for eight hundred pounds.'

'We are very much honoured,' said the widow, 'but you do not consider how poor Mehalah is; she has nothing.'

Elijah laughed. 'Not so very poor neither, I fancy. You lost the price of your sheep, and yet you had money in store wherewith to pay the rent.'

'Indeed, indeed we had not.'

'Where then did you get the money?'

'It was lent us.'

'Lent you, who by?' asked Elijah sharply.

'George De Witt was so good——'

Elijah uttered a horrible curse.

'Tell me,' he said furiously, coming up close to the old woman and scowling at her—into her eyes. 'Answer me without a lie; why, by what right did De Witt lend, or give you, the money? What claim had you on him?'

'Well, Elijah, I must tell you. Mehalah——'

'Here I am,' said the girl throwing open the door. 'Why am I the subject of your talk?' A couple of shepherds followed her.

'Look here,' she said, counting the coin; 'there is a guinea on the floor. Pick it up and try it, if it be good.'

'That's all right,' said one of the men, ringing the coin and then trying it between his teeth.

'This is the sum due for our half-year's rent,' she went on. 'Is it not so, Master Rebow? Is not this the sum in full?'

He sullenly gave an affirmative.

'You see that I pay this over to him. I don't want a written receipt. I pay before witnesses.'

Rebow signed to the men to leave, and then with knitted brow collected the money and put it in his pocket. The widow went on with the frying of the bacon.

'Come along with me, mother, to the boat. We cannot stay to eat.'

'You shall eat with me. You have come for the first time under my roof to-day, and you shall not go from under it without a bite.'

'I have no appetite.'

'But I have,' said the widow testily. 'I don't see why you are in such a hurry, Mehalah; and what is more, I don't see why you should behave so unpolitely to Master Rebow when he fares to be so civil.'

'Eat then, if you will, mother,' said Mehalah; 'but I cannot. I have no hunger,' after a pause, firmly, 'I will not.'

'Oh, you have a will indeed,' remarked Rebow with a growl. 'A will it would be a pleasure to break, and I'll do it.'

The bacon was fried, and the widow proceeded to dish it up. There was a rack in the next room, as Elijah told her, with plates in it, and there were knives and forks in the drawer.

Whilst the old woman was getting the necessary articles, Rebow was silent, seated in his leather chair, his elbows on his knees, with the pipe in one hand, and his head turned on one side, watching Mehalah out of his fierce, crafty eyes. The girl had seated herself on a chair against the wall, as far away from him as possible. Her arms were folded over her breast, and her head was bent, to avoid encountering his glance. She was angry with her mother for staying to eat with the man whom she hated.

During this quiet—neither speaking—a curious grating noise reached her ear, and then a clank like that of a chain. She could not quite make out whence the noise came. It was some little while before it sufficiently attracted her attention to make her consider about it; and before she had formed any conclusion, her mother returned, and spread the table, and placed the meat on a dish.

'I'll go and fetch the liquor,' said Rebow, and went away. Whilst he was absent, again the sound met the girl's ears. Neither she nor her mother had spoken, but now she said, 'Listen, mother, what is that sound?'

The old woman stood still for a moment, and then proceeded with her task.

'It is nothing,' she said indifferently, 'the sound comes up from below the floor. I reckon Master Rebow has cows fastened there.'

'By a chain,' added Mehalah, and dismissed the matter from her mind; the explanation satisfied her.

Rebow returned the next moment with a bottle.

'This is prime spirit, this is,' said he. 'You can't drink water here, it gives the fever. You must add spirits to it to make it harmless.'

'You have no beautiful spring here, as we have on the Ray,' observed the widow.

'Not likely to have,' answered the surly landlord. 'Now sit down and eat. Come, Glory.'

She did not move.

'Come, Mehalah, draw up your chair,' said her mother.

'I am not going to eat,' she answered resolutely.

'You shall,' shouted Elijah, rising impetuously, and thrusting his chair back. 'You are insulting me in my own house if you refuse to eat with me.'

'I have no appetite.'

'You will not eat, I heard you say so. I know the devilry of your heart. You will not, but I will.' In his rage he stamped on the trap-door that he had uncovered, when removing the chair. Instantly a prolonged, hideous howl rose from the depths and rang through the room. Mistress Sharland started back aghast. Mehalah raised her head, and the colour left her cheek.

'Oh ho!' roared Elijah. 'You will join in also, will you?' He drew the bolts passionately back.

'Look here,' he cried to Mehalah. 'Come here!'

Involuntarily she obeyed, and looked down. She saw into a vault feebly illuminated by daylight through one of the circular windows she had noticed on approaching the house. There she saw looking up, directly under the trap, a face so horrible in its dirt and madness that she recoiled.

'She won't eat, she won't bite with me,' shouted Rebow, 'then neither shall her mother eat, nor will I. You shall have the whole.' He caught up the dish, and threw down the rashers. The man below snapped, and caught like a wild beast, and uttered a growl of satisfaction.

Rebow flung the door back into its place, and rebolted it. Then he placed his chair in its former position, and looked composedly from the widow to Mehalah and seemed to draw pleasure from their fear.

'My brother,' he explained. 'Been mad from a child. A good job for me, as he was the elder. Now I have him in keeping, and the land and the house and the money are mine. What I hold, I hold fast. Amen.'

CHAPTER V.

THE DECOY.

There was commotion on the beach at Mersea City.

A man-of-war, a schooner, lay off the entrance to the Blackwater, and was signalling with bunting to the coastguard ship, permanently anchored off the island, which was replying. War had been declared with France some time, but as yet had not interfered with the smuggling trade, which was carried on with the Low Countries. Cruisers in the Channel had made it precarious work along the South Coast, and this had rather stimulated the activity of contraband traffic on the East. It was therefore with no little uneasiness that a war ship was observed standing off the Mersea flats. Why was she there? Was a man-of-war to cruise about the mouth of the Colne and Blackwater continually? What was the purport of the correspondence carried on between the schooner and the coastguard? Such were the queries put about among those gathered on the shingle.

They were not long left in doubt, for a boat manned by coastguards left the revenue vessel and ran ashore; the captain sprang out, and went up the beach to his cottage, followed by a couple of the crew. The eager islanders crowded round the remainder, and asked the news.

The captain was appointed to the command of the schooner, the 'Salamander,' which had come from the Downs under the charge of the first lieutenant, to pick him up. The destiny of the 'Salamander' was, of course, unknown.

Captain Macpherson was a keen, canny Scot, small and dapper; as he pushed through the cluster of men in fishing jerseys and wading boots he gave them a nod and a word, 'You ought to be serving your country instead of robbing her, ye loons. Why don't you volunteer like men, there's more money to be made by prizes than by running spirits.'

'That won't do, captain,' said Jim Morrell, an old fisherman. 'We know better than that. There's the oysters.'

'Oysters!' exclaimed the captain; 'there'll be no time for eating oysters now, and no money to pay for them neither. Come along with me, some of you shore crabs. I promise you better sport than sneaking about the creeks. We'll have at Johnny Crapaud with gun and cutlass.'

Then he entered his cottage, which was near the shore, to say farewell to his wife.

'If there's mischief to be done, that chap will do it,' was the general observation, when his back was turned.

Attention was all at once distracted by a young woman in a tall taxcart who was endeavouring to urge her horse along the road, but the animal, conscious of having an inexperienced hand on the rein, backed, and jibbed, and played a number of tricks, to her great dismay.

'Oh, do please some of you men lead him along. I daresay he will go if his head be turned east, but he is frightened by seeing so many of you.'

'Where are you going, Phoebe?' asked old Morrell.

'I'm only going to Waldegraves,' she answered. 'Oh, bother the creature! there he goes again!' as the horse danced impatiently, and swung round.

'De Witt!' she cried in an imploring tone, 'do hold his head. It is a shame of you men not to help a poor girl.'

George at once went to the rescue.

'Lead him on, De Witt, please, till we are away from the beach.'

The young man good-naturedly held the bit, and the horse obeyed without attempting resistance.

'There's a donkey on the lawn by Elm Tree Cottage,' said the girl; 'she brays whenever a horse passes, and I'm mortal afeared lest she scare this beast, and he runs away with me. If he do so, I can't hold him in, my wrists are so weak.'

'Why, Phoebe,' said De Witt, 'what are you driving for? Waldegraves is not more than a mile and a half off, and you might have walked the distance well enough.'

'I've sprained my ankle, and I can't walk. I must go to Waldegraves, I have a message there to my aunt, so Isaac Mead lent me the horse.'

'If you can't drive, you may do worse than sprain your ankle, you may break your neck.'

'That is what I am afraid of, George. The boy was to have driven me, but he is so excited, I suppose, about the man-of-war coming in, that he has run off. There! take care!'

'Can't you go on now?' asked De Witt, letting go the bridle. Immediately the horse began to jib and rear.

'You are lugging at his mouth fit to break his jaw, Phoebe. No wonder the beast won't go.'

'Am I, George? It is the fright. I don't understand the horse. O dear! O dear! I shall never get to Waldegraves by myself.'

'Let the horse go, but don't job his mouth in that way.'

'There he is turning round. He will go home again. O George! save me.'

'You are pulling him round, of course he will turn if you drag at the rein.'

'I don't understand horses,' burst forth Phoebe, and she threw the reins down. 'George, there's a good, dear fellow, jump in beside me. There's room for two, quite cosy. Drive me to Waldegraves. I shall never forget your goodness.' She put her two hands together, and looked piteously in the young man's face.

Phoebe Musset was a very good-looking girl, fair with bright blue eyes, and yellow hair, much more delicately made than most of the girls in the place. Moreover, she dressed above them. She was a village coquette, accustomed to being made much of, and of showing her caprices. Her father owned the store at the city where groceries and drapery were sold, and was esteemed a well-to-do man. He farmed a little land. Phoebe was his only child, and she was allowed to do pretty much as she liked. Her father and mother were hard-working people, but Phoebe's small hands were ever unsoiled, for they were ever unemployed. She neither milked the cows nor weighed the sugar. She liked indeed to be in the shop, to gossip with anyone who came in, and perhaps the only goods she condescended to sell was tobacco to the young sailors, from whom she might calculate on a word of flattery and a lovelorn look. She was always well and becomingly dressed. Now, in a chip bonnet trimmed with blue riband, and tied under the chin, with a white lace-edged kerchief over her shoulders, covering her bosom, she was irresistible. So at least De Witt found her, for he was obliged to climb the gig, seat himself beside her, and assume the reins.

'I am not much of a steersman in a craft like this,' said George laughing, 'but my hand is stronger than yours, and I can save you from wreck.'

Phoebe looked slyly round, and her great blue eyes peeped timidly up in the fisherman's face. 'Thank you so much, George. I shall never, never forget your great kindness.'

'There's nothing in it,' said the blunt fisherman; 'I'd do the same for any girl.'

'I know how polite you are,' continued Phoebe; then putting her hand on the reins, 'I don't think you need drive quite so fast, George; I don't want to get the horse hot, or Isaac will scold.'

'A jog trot like this will hurt no horse.'

'Perhaps you want to get back. I am sorry I have taken you away. Of course you have pressing business. No doubt you want to get to the Ray.' A little twinkling sly look up accompanied this speech. De Witt waxed red.

'I'm in no hurry, myself,' he said.

'How delightful, George, nor am I.'

The young man could not resist stealing a glance at the little figure beside him, so neat, so trim, so fresh. He was a humble fellow, and never dreamed himself to be on a level with such a refined damsel. Glory was the girl for him, rough and ready, who could row a boat, and wade in the mud. He loved Glory. She was a sturdy girl, a splendid girl, he said to himself. Phoebe was altogether different, she belonged to another sphere, he could but look and admire—and worship perhaps. She dazzled him, but he could not love her. She was none of his sort, he said to himself.

'A penny for your thoughts!' said Phoebe roguishly. He coloured. 'I know what you were thinking of. You were thinking of me.'

De Witt's colour deepened. 'I was sure it was so. Now I insist on knowing what you were thinking of me.'

'Why,' answered George with a clumsy effort at gallantry, 'I thought what a beauty you were.'

'Oh, George, not when compared with Mehalah.'

De Witt fidgeted in his seat.

'Mehalah is quite of another kind, you see, Miss.'

'I'm no Miss, if you please. Call me Phoebe. It is snugger.'

'She's more—' he puzzled his head for an explanation of his meaning. 'She is more boaty than you are—'

'Phoebe.'

'Than you are,' with hesitation, 'Phoebe.'

'I know;—strides about like a man, smokes and swears, and chews tobacco.'

'No, no, you mistake me, M——.'

'Phoebe.'

'You mistake me, Phoebe.'

'I have often wondered, George, what attracted you to Mehalah. To be sure, it will be a very convenient thing for you to have a wife who can swab the deck, and tar the boat and calk her. But then I should have fancied a man would have liked something different from a—sort of a man-woman—a jack tar or Ben Brace in petticoats, to sit by his fireside, and to take to his heart. But of course it is not for me to speak on such matters, only I somehow can't help thinking about you, George, and it worries me so, I lie awake at nights, and wonder and wonder, whether you will be happy. She has the temper of a tom cat, I'm told. She blazes up like gunpowder.'

De Witt fidgeted yet more uneasily. He did not like this conversation.

'Then she is half a gipsy. So you mayn't be troubled with her long. She'll keep with you as long as she likes, and then up with her pack, on with her wading boots. Yo heave hoy! and away she goes.'

De Witt, in his irritation, gave the horse a stinging switch across the flank, and he started forward. A little white hand was laid, not now on the reins, but on his hand.

'I'm so sorry, George my friend; after your kindness, I have teased you unmercifully, but I can't help it. When I think of Mehalah in her wading boots and jersey and cap, it makes me laugh—and yet when I think of her and you together, I'm ashamed to say I feel as if I could cry. George!' she suddenly ejaculated.

'Yes, Miss!'

'Phoebe, not Miss, please.'

'I wasn't going to say Miss.'

'What were you going to say?'

'Why, mate, yes, mate! I get into the habit of it at sea,' he apologised.

'I like it. Call me mate. We are on a cruise together, now, you and I, and I trust myself entirely in your hands, captain.'

'What was it you fared to ask, mate, when you called "George"?'

'Oh, this. The wind is cold, and I want my cloak and hood, they are down somewhere behind the seat in the cart. If I take the reins will you lean over and get them?'

'You won't upset the trap?'

'No.' He brought up the cloak and adjusted it round Phoebe's shoulders, and drew the hood over her bonnet, she would have it to cover her head.

'Doesn't it make me a fright?' she asked, looking into his face.

'Nothing can do that,' he answered readily.

'Well, push it back again, I feel as if it made me one, and that is as bad. There now. Thank you, mate! Take the reins again.'

'Halloo! we are in the wrong road. We have turned towards the Strood.'

'Dear me! so we have. That is the horse's doing. I let him go where he liked, and he went down the turn. I did not notice it. All I thought of was holding up his head lest he should stumble.'

De Witt endeavoured to turn the horse.

'Oh don't, don't attempt it!' exclaimed Phoebe. 'The lane is so narrow, that we shall be upset. Better drive on, and round by the Barrow Farm, there is not half-a-mile difference.'

'A good mile, mate. However, if you wish it.'

'I do wish it. This is a pleasant drive, is it not, George?'

'Very pleasant,' he said, and to himself added, 'too pleasant.'

So they chatted on till they reached the farm called Waldegraves, and there Phoebe alighted.

'I shall not be long,' she said, at the door, turning and giving him a look which might mean a great deal or nothing, according to the character of the woman who cast it.

When she came up she said, 'There, George, I cut my business as short as possible. Now what do you say to showing me the Decoy? I have never seen it, but I have heard a great deal of it, and I cannot understand how it is contrived.'

'It is close here,' said De Witt.

'I know it is, the little stream in this dip feeds it. Will you show me the Decoy?'

'But your foot—Phoebe. You have sprained your ankle.'

'If I may lean on your arm I think I can limp down there. It is not very far.'

'And then what about the horse?'

'Oh! the boy here will hold it, or put it up in the stable. Run and call him, George.'

'I could drive you down there, I think, at least within a few yards of the place, and if we take the boy he can hold the horse by the gate.'

'I had rather hobble down on your arm, George.'

'Then come along, mate.'

The Decoy was a sheet of water covering perhaps an acre and a half in the midst of a wood. The clay that had been dug out for its construction had been heaped up, forming a little hill crowned by a group of willows. No one who has seen this ill-used tree in its mutilated condition, cut down to a stump which bristles with fresh withes, has any idea what a stately and beautiful tree it is when allowed to grow naturally. The old untrimmed willow is one of the noblest of our native trees. It may be seen thus in well-timbered parts of Suffolk, and occasionally in Essex. The pond was fringed with rushes, except at the horns, where the nets and screens stood for the trapping of the birds. From the mound above the distant sea was visible, through a gap in the old elm trees that stood below the pool. In that gap was visible the war-schooner, lying as near shore as possible. George De Witt stood looking at it. The sea was glittering like silver, and the hull of the vessel was dark against the shining belt. A boat with a sail was approaching her.

'That is curious,' observed George. 'I could swear to yon boat. I know her red sail. She belongs to my cousin Elijah Rebow. But he can have nought to do with the schooner.'

Phoebe was impatient with anything save herself attracting the attention of the young fisherman. She drew him from the mound, and made him explain to her the use of the rush-platted screens, the arched and funnel-shaped net, and the manner in which the decoy ducks were trained to lead the wild birds to their destruction.

'They are very silly birds to be led like that,' said she.

'They little dream whither and to what they are being drawn,' said De Witt.

'I suppose some little ducks are dreadfully enticing,' said Phoebe, with a saucy look and a twinkle of the blue eyes. 'Look here, George, my bonnet-strings are untied, and my hands are quite unable to manage a bow, unless I am before a glass. Do you think you could tie them for me?'

'Put up your chin, then,' said De Witt with a sigh. He knew he was a victim; he was going against his conscience. He tried to think of Mehalah, but could not with those blue eyes looking so confidingly into his. He put his finger under her chin and raised it. He was looking full into that sweet saucy face.

'What sort of a knot? I can tie only sailor's knots.'

'Oh George! something like a true lover's knot.'

Was it possible to resist, with those damask cheeks, those red lips, and those pleading eyes so close, so completely in his power? George did not resist. He stooped and kissed the wicked lips, and cheeks, and eyes.

Phoebe drew away her face at once, and hid it. He took her arm and led her away. She turned her head from him, and did not speak.

He felt that the little figure at his side was shaken with some hysterical movement, and felt frightened.

'I have offended you, I am very sorry. I could not help it. Your lips did tempt me so; and you looked up at me just as if you were saying, "Kiss me!" I could not help it. You are crying. I have offended you.'

'No, I am laughing. Oh, George! Oh, George!'

They walked back to the farm without speaking. De Witt was ashamed of himself, yet felt he was under a spell which he could not break. A rough fisher lad flattered by a girl he had looked on as his superior, and beyond his approach, now found himself the object of her advances; the situation was more than his rude virtue could withstand. He knew that this was a short dream of delight, which would pass, and leave no substance, but whilst under the charm of the dream, he could not cry out nor move a finger to arouse himself to real life.

Neither spoke for a few minutes. But, at last, George De Witt turned, and looking with a puzzled face at Phoebe Musset said, 'You asked me on our way to Waldegraves what I was thinking about, and offered me a penny for my thoughts. Now I wonder what you are lost in a brown study about, and I will give you four farthings for what is passing in your little golden head.'

'You must not ask me, George—dear George.'

'Oh mate, you must tell me.'

'I dare not. I shall be so ashamed.'

'Then look aside when you speak.'

'No, I can't do that. I must look you full in the face; and do you look me in the face too. George, I was thinking—Why did you not come and talk to me, before you went courting that gipsy girl, Mehalah. Are you not sorry now that you are tied to her?'

His eyes fell. He could not speak.

CHAPTER VI.

BLACK OR GOLD.

When De Witt drove up to the 'City' with Phoebe Musset, the first person he saw on the beach was the last person that, under present circumstances, he wished to see—

Mehalah Sharland. Phoebe perceived her at once, and rejoiced at the opportunity that offered to profit by it.

For a long time Phoebe had been envious of the reputation as a beauty possessed by Mehalah. Her energy, determination and courage made her highly esteemed among the fishermen, and the expressions of admiration lavished on her handsome face and generous character had roused all the venom in Phoebe's nature. She desired to reign as queen paramount of beauty, and, like Elizabeth, could endure no rival. George De Witt was the best built and most pleasant faced of all the Mersea youths, and he had hitherto held aloof from her and paid his homage to the rival queen. This had awakened Phoebe's jealousy. She had no real regard, no warm affection for the young fisherman; she thought him handsome, and was glad to flirt with him, but he had made no serious impression on her heart, for Phoebe had not a heart on which any deep impression could be made. She had laid herself out to attract and entangle him from love of power, and desire to humble Mehalah. She did not know whether any actual engagement existed between George and Glory, probably she did not care. If there were, so much the better, it would render her victory more piquant and complete.

She would trifle with the young man for a few weeks or a month, till he had broken with her rival, and then she would keep him or cast him off as suited her caprice. By taking him up, she would sting other admirers into more fiery pursuit, blow the smouldering embers into flaming jealousy, and thus flatter her vanity and assure her supremacy. The social laws of rural life are the same as those in higher walks, but unglossed and undisguised. In the realm of nature it is the female who pursues and captures, not captivates, the male. As in Eden, so in this degenerate paradise, it is Eve who walks Adam, at first in wide, then in gradually contracting circles, about the forbidden tree, till she has brought him to take the unwholesome morsel. The male bird blazes in gorgeous plumage and swims alone on the glassy pool, but the sky is speckled with sombre feathered females who disturb his repose, drive him into a corner and force him to divide his worms, and drudge for them in collecting twigs and dabbing mud about their nest. The male glow-worm browses on the dewy blades by his moony lamp; it is the lack-light female that buzzes about him, coming out of obscurity, obscure herself, flattering and fettering him and extinguishing his lamp.

Where culture prevails, the sexes change their habits with ostentation, but remain the same in proclivities behind disguise. The male is supposed to pursue the female he seeks as his mate, to hover round her; and she is supposed to coyly retire, and start from his advances. But her modesty is as unreal as the nolo episcopari of a simoniacal bishop-elect. Bashfulness is a product of education, a mask made by art. The cultured damsel hunts not openly, but like a poacher, in the dark. Eve put off modesty when she put on fig-leaves; in the simplicity of the country, her daughters walk without either. The female gives chase to the male as a matter of course, as systematically and unblushingly in rustic life, as in the other grades of brute existence. The mother adorns her daughter for the war-path with paint and feathers, and sends her forth with a blessing and a smile to fulfil the first duty of woman, and the meed of praise is hers when she returns with a masculine heart, yet hot and mangled, at her belt.

The Early Church set apart one day in seven for rest; the Christian pagans set it apart for the exercise of the man hunt. The Stuart bishops published a book on Sunday amusements, and allowed of Sabbath hunting. They followed, and did not lead opinion. It is the coursing day of days when marriage-wanting maids are in full cry and scent of all marriageable men.

A village girl who does not walk about her boy is an outlaw to the commonwealth, a renegade to her sex. A lover is held to be of as much necessity as an umbrella, a maiden must not go out without either. If she cannot attract one by her charms, she must retain him with a fee. Rural morality moreover allows her to change the beau on her arm as often as the riband in her cap, but not to be seen about, at least on Sunday, devoid of either.

Phoebe Musset intended some day to marry, but had not made up her mind whom to choose, and when to alter her condition. She would have liked a well-to-do young farmer, but there happened to be no man of this kind available. There were, indeed, at Peldon four bachelor brothers of the name of Marriage, but they were grown grey in celibacy and not disposed to change their lot. One of the principal Mersea farmers was named Wise, and had a son of age, but he was an idiot. The rest were afflicted with only daughters—afflicted from Phoebe's point of view, blessed from their own. There was a widower, but to take a widower was like buying a broken-kneed horse.

George was comfortably off. He owned some oyster pans and gardens, and had a fishing smack.

But he was not a catch. There were, however, no catches to be angled, trawled or dredged for. Phoebe did not trouble herself greatly about the future. Her father and mother would, perhaps, not be best pleased were she to marry off the land, but the wishes of her parents were of no weight with Phoebe, who was determined to suit her own fancy.

As she approached the 'City,' she saw Glory surrounded by young boatmen, eager to get a word from her lips or a glance from her eyes. Phoebe's heart contracted with spite, but next moment swelled with triumph at the thought that it lay in her power to wound her rival and exhibit her own superiority, before the eyes of all assembled on the beach.

'There is the boy from the Leather Bottle, George,' said she, 'he shall take the horse.'

De Witt descended and helped her to alight, then directly, to her great indignation, made his way to Mehalah. Glory put out both hands to him and smiled. Her smile, which was rare, was sweet; it lighted up and transformed a face somewhat stern and dark.

'Where have you been, George?'

'I have been driving that girl yonder, what's-her-name, to Waldegraves.'

'What, Phoebe Musset? I did not know you could drive.'

'I can do more than row a boat and catch crabs, Glory.'

'What induced you to drive her?'

'I could not help myself, I was driven into doing so. You see, Glory, a fellow is not always his own master. Circumstances are sometimes stronger than his best purposes, and like a mass of seaweed arrest his oar and perhaps upset his boat.'

'Why, bless the boy!' exclaimed Mehalah. 'What are all these excuses for? I am not jealous.'

'But I am,' said Phoebe who had come up. 'George, you are very ungallant to desert me. You have forgotten your promise, moreover.'

'What promise?'

'There! what promise you say, as if your head were a riddle and everything put in except clots of clay and pebbles fell through. Mehalah has stuck in the wires, and poor little I have been sifted out.'

'But what did I promise?'

'To show me the hull in which you and your mother live, the "Pandora" I think you call her.'

'Did I promise?'

'Yes, you did, when we were together at the Decoy under the willows. I told you I wished greatly to be introduced to the interior and see how you lived.' Turning to Mehalah, 'George and I have been to the Decoy. He was most good-natured, and explained the whole contrivance to me, and—and illustrated it. We had a very pleasant little trot together, had we not, George?'

'Oh! this is what's-her-name, is it?' said Mehalah in a low tone with an amused look. She was neither angry nor jealous, she despised Phoebe too heartily to be either, though with feminine instinct she perceived what the girl was about, and saw through all her affectation.

'If I made the promise, I must of course keep it,' said George, 'but it is strange I should not remember having made it.'

'I dare say you forget a great many things that were said and done at the Decoy, but,' with a little affected sigh, 'I do not, I never shall, I fear.'

George De Witt looked uncomfortable and awkward. 'Will not another day do as well?'

'No, it will not, George,' said Phoebe petulantly. 'I know you have no engagement, you said so when you volunteered to drive me to Waldegraves.'

De Witt turned to Mehalah, and said, 'Come along with us, Glory! my mother will be glad to see you.'

'Oh! don't trouble yourself, Miss Sharland—or Master Sharland, which is it?'—staring first at the short petticoats, and then at the cap and jersey.

'Come, Glory,' repeated De Witt, and looked so uncomfortable that Mehalah readily complied with his request.

'I can give you oysters and ale, natives, you have never tasted better.'

'No ale for me, George,' said Phoebe. 'It is getting on for five o'clock when I take a dish of tea.'

'Tea!' echoed De Witt, 'I have no such dainty on board. But I can give you rum or brandy, if you prefer either to ale. Mother always has a glass of grog about this time; the cockles of her heart require it, she says.'

'You must give me your arm, George, you know I have sprained my ankle. I really cannot walk unsupported.'

De Witt looked at Mehalah and then at Phoebe, who gave him such a tender, entreating glance that he was unable to refuse his arm. She leaned heavily on it, and drew very close to his side; then, turning her head over her shoulder, with a toss of the chin, she said, 'Come along, Mehalah!'

Glory's brow began to darken. She was displeased. George also turned and nodded to the girl, who walked in the rear with her head down. He signed to her to join him.

'Do you know, Glory, what mother did the other night when I failed to turn up—that night you fetched me concerning the money that was stolen? She was vexed at my being out late, and not abed at eleven. As you know, I could not be so. I left the Ray as soon as all was settled, and as you put me across to the Fresh Marsh, I got home across the pasture and the fields as quickly as I could, but was not here till after eleven. Mother was angry, she had pulled up the ladder, but before that she tarred the vessel all round, and she stuck a pail of sea water atop of the place where the ladder goes. Well, then, I came home and found the ladder gone, so I laid hold of the rope that hangs there, and then souse over me came the water. I saw mother was vexed, and wanted to serve me out for being late; however, I would not be beat, so I tried to climb the side, and got covered with tar.'

'You got in, however?'

'No, I did not, I went to the public-house, and laid the night there.'

'I would have gone through tar, water, and fire,' said Glory vehemently. 'I would not have been beat.'

'I have no doubt about it, you would,' observed George, 'but you forget there might be worse things behind. An old woman after a stiff glass of grog, when her monkey is up, is better left to sleep off her liquor and her displeasure before encountered.'

'I would not tell the story,' said Mehalah; 'it does you no credit.'

'This is too bad of you, Glory! You ran me foul of her, and now reproach me for my steering.'

'You will run into plenty of messes if you go after Mehalah at night,' put in Phoebe with a saucy laugh.

'Glory!' said De Witt, 'come on the other side of Phoebe and give her your arm. She is lame. She has hurt her foot, and we are coming now to the mud.'

'Oh, I cannot think of troubling Mehalah,' said Phoebe sharply; 'you do not mind my leaning my whole weight on you, I know, George. You did not mind it at the Decoy.'

'Here is the ladder,' said De Witt; 'step on my foot and then you will not dirty your shoe-leather in the mud. Don't think you will hurt me. A light feather like you will be unfelt.'

'Do you keep the ladder down day and night?' asked Glory.

'No. It is always hauled up directly I come home. Only that one night did mother draw it up without me. We are as safe in the "Pandora" as you are at the Ray.'

'And there is this in the situation which is like,' said Phoebe, pertly, 'that neither can entice robbers, and need securing, as neither has anything to lose.'

'I beg your pardon,' answered George, 'there are my savings on board. My mother sleeps soundly, so she will not turn in till the ladder is up. That is the same as locking the door on land. If you have money in the till——'

'There always is money there, plenty of it too.'

'I have no doubt about it, Phoebe. Under these circumstances you do not go to bed and leave your door open.'

'I should think not. You go first up the ladder, I will follow. Mehalah can stop and paddle in her native mud, or come after us as suits her best.' Turning her head to Glory she said, 'Two are company, three are none.' Then to the young man, 'George, give me your hand to help me on deck, you forget your manners. I fear the Decoy is where you have left and lost them.'

She jumped on deck. Mehalah followed without asking for or expecting assistance.

The vessel was an old collier, which George's father had bought when no longer seaworthy for a few pounds. He had run her up on the Hard, dismasted her, and converted her into a dwelling. In it George had been born and reared. 'There is one advantage in living in a house such as this,' said De Witt; 'we pay neither tax, nor tithe, nor rate.'

'Is that you?' asked a loud hard voice, and a head enveloped in a huge mob cap appeared from the companion ladder. 'What are you doing there, gallivanting with girls all day? Come down to me and let's have it out.'

'Mother is touchy,' said George in a subdued voice; 'she gets a little rough and knotty at times, but she is a rare woman for melting and untying speedily.'

'Come here, George!' cried the rare woman.

'I am coming, mother.' He showed the two girls the ladder; Mrs. De Witt had disappeared. 'Go down into the fore cabin, then straight on. Turn your face to the ladder as you descend.' Phoebe hesitated. She was awestruck by the voice and appearance of

Mrs. De Witt. However, at a sign from George she went down, and was followed by Mehalah. Bending her head, she passed through the small fore-cabin where was George's bunk, into the main cabin, which served as kitchen, parlour, and bedroom to Mrs. De Witt. A table occupied the centre, and at the end was an iron cooking stove. Everything was clean, tidy, and comfortable. On a shelf at the side stood the chairs. Mrs. De Witt whisked one down.

'Your servant,' said she to Phoebe, with more amiability than the girl anticipated. 'Yours too, Glory,' curtly to Mehalah.

Mrs. De Witt was not favourable to her son's attachment to Glory. She was an imperious, strong-minded woman, a despot in her own house, and she had no wish to see that house invaded by a daughter-in-law as strong of will and iron-headed as herself. She wished to see George mated to a girl whom she could browbeat and manage as she browbeat and managed her son. George's indecision of character was due in measure to his bringing up by such a mother. He had been cuffed and yelled at from infancy. His intimacy with the maternal lap had been contracted head downwards, and was connected with a stinging sensation at the rear. Self-assertion had been beat or bawled out of him. She was not a bad, but a despotic woman. She liked to have her own way, and she obtained it, first with her husband, and then with her son, and the ease with which she had mastered and maintained the sovereignty had done her as much harm as them.

If a beggar be put on horseback he will ride to the devil, and a woman in command will proceed to unsex herself. She was a good-hearted woman at bottom, but then that bottom where the good heart lay was never to be found with an anchor, but lay across the course as a shoal where deep water was desired. Her son knew perfectly where it was not, but never where it was. Mrs. De Witt in face somewhat resembled her nephew, Elijah Rebow, but she was his senior by ten years. She had the same hawk-like nose and dark eyes, but was without the wolfish jaw. Nor had she the eager intelligence that spoke out of Elijah's features. Hers were hard and coarse and unillumined with mind.

When she saw Phoebe enter her cabin she was both surprised and gratified. A fair, feeble, bread-and-butter Miss, such as she held the girl to be, was just the daughter she fancied. Were she to come to the 'Pandora' with whims and graces, the month of honey with George would assume the taste of vinegar with her, and would end in the new daughter's absolute submission. She would be able to convert such a girl very speedily into a domestic drudge and a recipient of her abuse. Men make themselves, but women are made, and the making of women, thought Mrs. De Witt, should be in the hands of women; men botched them, because they let them take their own way.

Mrs. De Witt never forgave her parents for having bequeathed her no money; she could not excuse Elijah for having taken all they left, without considering her. She found a satisfaction in discharging her wrongs on others. She was a saving woman, and spent little money on her personal adornment. 'What coin I drop,' she was wont to say, 'I drop in rum, and smuggled rum is cheap.'

But though an article is cheap, a great consumption of it may cause the item to be a serious one; and it was so with Mrs. De Witt.

The vessel to which she acted as captain, steward, and cook, was named the 'Pandora.' The vicar was wont to remark that it was a 'Pandora's' box full of all gusts, but minus gentle Zephyr.

'Will you take a chair?' she said obsequiously to Phoebe, placing the chair for her, after having first breathed on the seat and wiped it with her sleeve. Then turning to Mehalah, she asked roughly, 'Well, Glory! how is that old fool, your mother?'

'Better than your manners,' replied Mehalah.

'I am glad you are come, Glory,' said Mrs. De Witt, 'I want to have it out with you. What do you mean by coming here of a night, and carrying off my son when he ought to be under his blankets in his bunk? I won't have it. He shall keep proper hours. Such conduct is not decent. What do you think of that?' she asked, seating herself on the other side of the table, and addressing Phoebe, but leaving Mehalah standing. 'What do you think of a girl coming here after nightfall, and asking my lad to go off for a row with her all in the dark, and the devil knows whither they went, and the mischief they were after. It is not respectable, is it?'

'George should not have gone when she asked him,' said the girl.

'Dear Sackalive! she twists him round her little finger. He no more dare deny her anything than he dare defy me. But I will have my boy respectable, I can promise you. I combed his head well for him when he came home, I did by cock! He shall not do the thing again.'

'Look here, mother,' remonstrated George; 'wash our dirty linen in private.'

'Indeed!' exclaimed Mrs. De Witt. 'That is strange doctrine! Why, who would know we wore any linen at all next our skin, unless we exposed it when washed over the side of the wessel? Now you come here. I have a bone to pick along with you, George!'

To be on a level with her son, and stare him full in the eyes, a way she had with everyone she assailed, she sat on the table, and put her feet on the chair.

'What has become of the money? I have been to the box, and there are twenty pounds gone out of it, all in gold. I haven't took it, so you must have. Now I want to know what you have done with it. I will have it out. I endure no evasions. Where is the money? Fork it out, or I will turn all your pockets inside out, and find and retake it. You want no money, not you. I provide you with tobacco. Where is the money? Twenty pounds, and all in gold. I was like a shrimp in scalding water when I went to the box to-day and found the money gone. I turned that red you might have said it was erysipelas. I shruck out that they might have heard me at the City. Turn your pockets out at once.'

George looked abashed; he was cowed by his mother.

'I'll take the carving knife to you!' said the woman, 'if you do not hand me over the cash at once.'

'Oh don't, pray don't hurt him!' cried Phoebe, interposing her arm, and beginning to cry.

'Dear Sackalive!' exclaimed Mrs. De Witt, 'I am not aiming at his witals, but at his pockets. Where is the money?'

'I have had it,' said Mehalah, stepping forward and standing between De Witt and his mother. 'George has behaved generously, nobly by us. You have heard how we were robbed of our money. We could not have paid our rent for the Ray had not George let us have twenty pounds. He shall not lose it.'

'You had it, you!—you!' cried Mrs. De Witt in wild and fierce astonishment. 'Give it up to me at once.'

'I cannot do so. The greater part is gone. I paid the money to-day to Rebow, our landlord.'

'Elijah has it! Elijah gets everything. My father left me without a shilling, and now he gets my hard-won earnings also.'

'It seems to me, mistress, that the earnings belong to George, and surely he has a right to do with them what he will,' said Mehalah coldly.

'That is your opinion, is it? It is not mine.' Then she mused: 'Twenty pounds is a fortune. One may do a great deal with such a sum as that, Mehalah; twenty pounds is twenty pounds whatever you may say; and it must be repaid.'

'It shall be.'

'When?'

'As soon as I can earn the money.'

Mrs. De Witt's eyes now rested on Phoebe, and she assumed a milder manner. Her mood was variable as the colour of the sea; 'I'm obliged to be peremptory at times,' she said; 'I have to maintain order in the wessel. You will stay and have something to eat?'

'Thank you; your son has already promised us some oysters,—that is, promised me.'

'Come on deck,' said George. 'We will have them there, and mother shall brew the liquor below.'

The mother grunted a surly acquiescence.

When the three had re-ascended the ladder, the sun was setting. The mouth of the Blackwater glittered like gold leaf fluttered by the breath. The tide had begun to flow, and already the water had surrounded the 'Pandora.' Phoebe and Mehalah would have to return by boat, or be carried by De Witt.

The two girls stood side by side. The contrast between them was striking, and the young man noticed it. Mehalah was tall, lithe, and firm as a young pine, erect in her bearing, with every muscle well developed, firm of flesh, her skin a rich ripe apricot, and her eyes, now that the sun was in them, like volcanic craters, gloomy, but full of fire. Her hair, rich to profusion, was black, yet with coppery hues in it when seen with a side light. It was simply done up in a knot, neatly not elaborately. Her navy-blue jersey and skirt, the scarlet of her cap and kerchief, and of a petticoat that appeared below the skirt, made her a rich combination of colour, suitable to a sunny clime rather than to the misty bleak east coast. Phoebe was colourless beside her, a faded picture, faint in outline. Her complexion was delicate as the rose, her frame slender, her contour undulating and weak. She was the pattern of a trim English village maiden, with the beauty of youth, and the sweetness of ripening womanhood, sans sense, sans passion, sans character, sans everything—pretty vacuity. She seemed to feel her own inferiority beside the gorgeous Mehalah, and to be angry at it. She took off her bonnet, and the wind played with her yellow curls, and the setting sun spun them into a halo of gold about her delicate face.

'Loose your hair, Mehalah,' said the spiteful girl.

'What for?'

'I want to see how it will look in the sun.'

'Do so, Glory!' begged George. 'How shining Phoebe's locks are. One might melt and coin them into guineas.'

Mehalah pulled out a pin, and let her hair fall, a flood of warm black with red gleams in it. It reached her waist, and the wind scattered it about her like a veil.

If Phoebe's hair resembled a spring fleecy cloud gilded by the sun, buoyant in the soft warm air, that of Mehalah was like an angry thunder shower with a promise of sunshine gleaming through the rain.

'Black or gold, which do you most admire, George?' asked the saucy girl.

'That is not a fair question to put to me,' said De Witt in reply; but he put his fingers through the dark tresses of Mehalah, and raised them to his lips. Phoebe bit her tongue.

'George,' she said sharply. 'See the sun is in my hair. I am in glory. That is better than being so only in name.'

'But your glory is short-lived, Phoebe; the sun will be set in a minute, and then it is no more.'

'And hers,' she said spitefully, 'hers—you imply—endures eternally. I will go home.'

'Do not be angry, Phoebe, there cannot be thunder in such a golden cloud. There can be nothing worse than a rainbow.'

'What have you got there about your neck, George?' she asked, pacified by the compliment.

'A riband.'

'Yes, and something at the end of it—a locket containing a tuft of black horsehair.'

'No, there is not.'

'Call me "mate," as you did when we were at the Decoy. How happy we were there, but then we were alone, that makes all the difference.'

George did not answer. Mehalah's hot blood began to fire her dark cheek.

'Tell me what you have got attached to that riband; if you love me, tell me, George. We girls are always inquisitive.'

'A keepsake, Phoebe.'

'A keepsake! Then I must see it.' She snatched at the riband where it showed above De Witt's blue jersey.

'I noticed it before, when you were so attentive at the Decoy.'

Mehalah interposed her arm, and placing her open hand on George's breast, thrust him out of the reach of the insolent flirt.

'For shame of you, how dare you behave thus!' she exclaimed.

'Oh dear!' cried Phoebe, 'I see it all. Your keepsake. How sentimental! Oh, George! I shall die of laughing.'

She went into pretended convulsions of merriment. 'I cannot help it, this is really too ridiculous.'

Mehalah was trembling with anger. Her gipsy blood was in flame. There is a flagrant spirit in such veins which soon bursts into an explosion of fire.

Phoebe stepped up to her, and holding her delicate fingers beside the strong hand of Mehalah, whispered, 'Look at these little fingers. They will pluck your love out of your rude clutch.' She saw that she was stinging her rival past endurance. She went on aloud, casting a saucy side glance at De Witt, 'I should like to add my contribution to the trifle that is collecting for you since you lost your money. I suppose there is a brief. Off with the red cap and pass it round. Here is a crown.'

The insult was unendurable. Mehalah's passion overpowered her. In a moment she had caught up the girl, and without considering what she was doing, she flung her into the sea. Then she staggered back and panted for breath.

A cry of dismay from De Witt. He rushed to the side.

'Stay!' said Mehalah, restraining him with one hand and pressing the other to her heart. 'She will not drown.'

The water was not deep. Several fisherlads had already sprung to the rescue, and Phoebe was drawn limp and dripping towards the shore. Mehalah stooped, picked up the girl's straw hat, and slung it after her.

A low laugh burst from someone riding in a boat under the side of the vessel.

'Well done, Glory! You served the pretty vixen right. I love you for it.'

She knew the voice. It was that of Rebow. He must have heard, perhaps seen all.

CHAPTER VII.

LIKE A BAD PENNY.

'For shame, Glory!' exclaimed De Witt when he had recovered from his surprise but not from his dismay. 'How could you do such a wicked and unwomanly act?'

'For shame, George!' answered Mehalah, gasping for breath. 'You stood by all the while, and listened whilst that jay snapped and screamed at me, and tormented me to madness, without interposing a word.'

'I am angry. Your behaviour has been that of a savage!' pursued George, thoroughly roused. 'I love you, Glory, you know I do. But this is beyond endurance.'

'If you are not prepared, or willing to right me, I must defend myself,' said Mehalah; 'and I will do it. I bore as long as I could bear, expecting every moment that you would silence her, and speak out, and say, "Glory is mine, and I will not allow her to be affronted." But not a step did you take, not a finger did you lift; and then, at last, the fire in my heart burst forth and sent up a smoke that darkened my eyes and bewildered my brain. I could not see, I could not think. I did not know, till all was over, what I had done. George! I know I am rough and violent, when these rages come over me, I am not to be trifled with.'

'I hope they never may come over you when you have to do with me,' said De Witt sulkily.

'I hope not, George. Do not trifle with me, do not provoke me. I have the gipsy in me, but under control. All at once the old nature bursts loose, and then I do I know not what. I cannot waste my energy in words like some, and I cannot contend with such a girl as that with the tongue.'

'What will folks say of this?'

'I do not care. They may talk. But now, George, let me warn you. That girl has been trifling with you, and you have been too blind and foolish to see her game and keep her at arm's length.'

'You are jealous because I speak to another girl besides you.'

'No, I am not. I am not one to harbour jealousy. Whom I trust I trust with my whole heart. Whom I believe I believe with my entire soul. I know you too well to be jealous. I know as well that you could not be false to me in thought or in act as I know my truth to you. I cannot doubt you, for had I thought it possible that you would give me occasion to doubt, I could not have loved you.'

'Sheer off!' exclaimed George, looking over his shoulder. 'Here comes the old woman.'

The old woman appeared, scrambling on deck, her cap-frills bristling about her ears, like the feathers of an angry white cockatoo.

'What is all this? By jaggers! where is Phoebe Musset? What have you done with her? Where have you put her? What were those screams about?'

'Sheer off while you may,' whispered De Witt; 'the old woman is not to be faced when wexed no more than a hurricane. Strike sail, and run before the wind.'

'What have you done with the young woman? Where is she? Produce the corpse. I heard her as she shruck out.'

'She insulted me,' said Mehalah, still agitated by passion, 'and I flung her overboard.'

Mrs. De Witt rushed to the bulwarks, and saw the dripping damsel being carried—she could not walk—from the Strand to her father's house.

'You chucked her overboard!' exclaimed the old woman, and she caught up a swabbing-mop. 'How dare you? She was my visitor; she came to sip my grog and eat my natives at my hospitable board, and you chucked her into the sea as though she were a picked cockleshell!'

'She insulted me,' said Mehalah angrily.

'I will teach you to play the dog-fish among my herrings, to turn this blessed peaceful "Pandora" into a cage of bears!' cried Mrs. De Witt, charging with her mop.

Mehalah struck the weapon down, and put her foot on it.

'Take care!' she exclaimed, her voice trembling with passion. 'In another moment you will have raised the devil in me again.'

'He don't take much raising,' vociferated Mrs. De Witt. 'I will teach you to assault a genteel young female who comes a wisiting of me and my son in our own wessel. Do you think you are already mistress here? Does the "Pandora" belong to you? Am I to be chucked overboard along with every lass that wexes you? Am I of no account any more in the eyes of my son, that I suckled from my maternal bottle, and fed with egg and pap out of my own spoon?'

'For heaven's sake,' interrupted George, 'sheer off, Mehalah. Mother is the dearest old lady in the world when she is sober. She is a Pacific Ocean when not vexed with storms. She will pacify presently.'

'I will go, George,' said Mehalah, panting with anger, her veins swollen, her eye sparkling, and her lip quivering; 'I will go, and I will never set foot in this boat again, till you and your mother have asked my pardon for this conduct; she for this outrage, you for having allowed me to receive insult, white-livered coward that you are.'

She flung herself down the ladder, and waded ashore.

Mrs. De Witt's temper abated as speedily as it rose. She retired to her grog. She set feet downwards on the scene; the last of her stalwart form to disappear was the glowing countenance set in white rays.

George was left to his own reflections. He saw Mehalah get into her boat and row away. He waved his cap to her, but she did not return the salute. She was offended grievously. George was placed in a difficult situation. The girl to whom he was betrothed was angry, and had declared her determination not to tread the planks of the 'Pandora' again, and the girl who had made advances to him, and whom his mother would have favoured, had been ejected unceremoniously from it, and perhaps injured, at all events irretrievably offended.

It was incumbent on him to go to the house of the Mussets and enquire for Phoebe. He could do no less; so he descended the ladder and took his way thither.

Phoebe was not hurt, she was only frightened. She had been wet through, and was at once put to bed. She cried a great deal, and old Musset vowed he would take out a summons against the aggressor. Mrs. Musset wept in sympathy with her daughter, and then fell on De Witt for having permitted the assault to take place unopposed.

'How could I interfere?' he asked, desperate with his difficulties. 'It was up and over with her before I was aware.'

'My girl is not accustomed to associate with cannibals,' said Mrs. Musset, drawing herself out like a telescope.

As George returned much crestfallen to the beach, now deserted, for the night had come on, he was accosted by Elijah Rebow.

'George!' said the owner of Red Hall, laying a hand on his cousin's shoulder, 'you ought not to be here.'

'Where ought I to be, Elijah? It seems to me that I have been everywhere to-day where I ought not to be. I am left in a hopeless muddle.'

'You ought not to allow Glory to part from you in anger.'

'How can I help it? I am sorry enough for the quarrel, but you must allow her conduct was trying to the temper.'

'She had great provocation. I wonder she did not kill that girl. She has a temper, has Mehalah, that does not stick at trifles; but she is generous and forgiving.'

'She is so angry with me that I doubt I shall not be able to bring her back to good humour.'

'I doubt so, too, unless you go the right way to work with her; and that is not what you are doing now.'

'Why, what ought I to do, Elijah?'

'Do you want to break with her, George? Do you want to be off with Glory and on with milk-face?'

'No, I do not.'

'You are set on Glory still? You will cleave to her till naught but death shall you part, eh?'

'Naught else.'

'George! That other girl has good looks and money. Give up Mehalah, and hitch on to Phoebe. I know your mother will be best pleased if you do, and it will suit your interests well. Glory has not a penny, Phoebe has her pockets lined. Take my word for it you can have milk-face for the asking, and now is your opportunity for breaking with Glory if you have a mind to do so.'

'But I have not, Elijah.'

'What can Glory be to you, or you to Glory? She with her great heart, her stubborn will, her strong soul, and you—you—bah!'

'Elijah, say what you like, but I will hold to Glory till death us do part.'

'Your hand on it. You swear that.'

'Yes, I do. I want a wife who can row a boat, a splendid girl, the sight of whom lights up the whole heart.'

'I tell you Glory is not one for you. See how passionate she is, she blazes up in a moment, and then she is one to shiver you if you offend her. No, she needs a man of other stamp than you to manage her.'

'She shall be mine,' said George: 'I want no other.'

'This is your fixed resolve?'

'My fixed resolve.'

'For better for worse?'

'For better for worse, till death us do part.'

'Till death you do part,' Elijah jerked out a laugh. 'George, if you are not the biggest fool I have set eyes on for many a day, I am much mistaken.'

'Why so?'

'Because you are acting contrary to your interests. You are unfit for Glory, you do not now, you never will, understand her.'

'What do you mean?'

'You let the girl row away, offended, angry, eating out her heart, and you show no sign that you desire reconciliation.'

'I have though. I waved my hat to her, but she took no notice.'

'Waved your hat!' repeated Rebow, with suppressed scorn. 'You never will read that girl's heart, and understand her moods. Oh, you fool! you fool! straining your arms after the unapproachable, unattainable, star! If she were mine——' he stamped and clenched his fists.

'But she is not going to be yours, Elijah,' said George with a careless laugh.

'No, of course not,' said Elijah, joining in the laugh. 'She is yours till death you do part.'

'Tell me, what have I done wrong?' asked De Witt.

'There—you come to me, after all, to interpret the writing for you. It is there, written in letters of fire, Mene, mene, tekel, Upharsin! Thou art weighed in the balance and found wanting, and this night shall thy kingdom be taken from thee and given to——'

'Elijah, I do not understand this language. What ought I to do to regain Mehalah's favour?'

'You must go after her. Do you not feel it in every fibre, that you must, you mud-blood? Go after her at once. She is now at home, sitting alone, brooding over the offence, sore at your suffering her to be insulted without making remonstrance. Her wrong will grow into a mountain in her heart unless it be rooted up to-night. Her pride will flame up as her passion dies away, and she will not let you speak to her another tender word. She will hate and despise you. The little crack will split into a wide chasm. I heard her call you a white-livered coward.'

'She did; you need not repeat it. She will be sorry when she is cool.'

'That is just it, George. As soon as passion abates, her generous heart will turn to self-reproach, and she will be angry with herself for what she has done. She will accuse herself with having been violent, with having acted unworthily of her dignity, with having grown in too great a heat about a worthless doll. She will be vexed with herself, ashamed of herself, unable in the twilight of her temper to excuse herself. Perhaps she is now in tears. But this mood will not last. To-morrow her pride will have returned in strength, she will think over her wrongs and harden herself in stubbornness; she will know that the world condemns her, and she will retire into herself in defiance of the world. Look up at the sky. Do you see, there is Charles' Wain, and there is Cassiopæa's Chair. There the Serpent and there the Swan. I can see every figure plain, but your landsman rarely can. So I can see every constellation in the dark heaven of Mehalah's soul, but you cannot. You would be wrecked if you were to sail by it. Now, George, take Glory while she is between two moods, or lose her for ever. Go after her at once, George, ask her forgiveness, blame yourself and your mother, blame that figure-head miss, and she will forgive you frankly, at once. She will fall on your neck and ask your pardon for what she has done.'

'I believe you are right,' said De Witt, musing.

'I know I am. As I have been working in my forge, I have watched the flame on the hearth dance and waver to the clinking of the hammer. There was something in the flame, I know not what, which made it wince or flare, as the blows fell hard or soft. So there are things in Nature respond to each other without your knowing why it is, and in what their sympathy consists. So I know all that passes in Mehalah's mind. I feel my own soul dance and taper to her pulses. If you had not been a fool, George, you would already have been after her. What are you staying for now?'

'My mother; what will she say?'

'Do you care for her more than for Glory? If you think of her now, you lose Glory for ever. Once more I ask you, do you waver? Are you inclined to forsake Mehalah for milk-face?'

'I am not,' said De Witt impatiently; 'why do you go on with this? I have said already that Glory is mine.'

'Unless death you do part.'

'Till death us do part, is what I said.'

'Then make haste. An hour hence the Ray house will be closed, and the girl and her mother in bed.'

'I will get my boat and row thither at once.'

'You need not do that. I have my boat here, jump in. We will each take an oar, and I will land you on the Ray.'

'You take a great interest in my affairs.'

'I take a very great interest in them,' said Rebow dryly.

'Lead the way, then.'

'Follow me.'

Rebow walked forward, over the shingle towards his boat, then suddenly turned, and asked in a suppressed voice, 'Do you know whither you are going?'

'To the Ray.'

'To the Ray, of course. Is there anyone on the Hard?'

'Not a soul. Had I not better go to my mother before I start and say that I am going with you?'

'On no account. She will not allow you to go to the Ray. You know she will not.'

De Witt was not disposed to dispute this.

'You are sure,' asked Rebow again, 'that there is no one on the Hard. No one sees you enter my boat. No one sees you push off with me. No one sees whither we go.'

'Not a soul.'

'Then here goes!' Elijah Rebow thrust the boat out till she floated, sprang in and took his oar. De Witt was already oar in hand on his seat.

'The red curtain is over the window at the Leather Bottle,' said George. 'No signalling to-night, the schooner is in the offing.'

'A red signal. It may mean more than you understand.'

They rowed on.

'Is there a hand on that crimson pane,' asked Rebow in a low tone, 'with the fingers dipped in fire, writing?'

'Not that I can see.'

'Nor do you see the writing, Mene, mene, tekel, Upharsin.'

'You jest, Elijah!'

'A strange jest. Perhaps the writing is in the vulgar tongue, thou art weighed and found wanting, feeble fool, and thy kingdom is taken from thee, and given to ME.'

Mehalah sat by the hearth, on the floor, in the farmhouse at the Ray. Her mother was abed and asleep. The girl had cast aside the cap and thrown off her jersey. Her bare arms were folded on her lap; and the last flicker of the red embers fell on her exposed and heaving bosom.

Elijah Rebow on the Hard at Mersea had read accurately the workings and transitions in the girl's heart. Precisely that was taking place which he had described. The tempest of passion had roared by, and now a tide of self-reproach rose and overflowed her soul. She was aware that she had acted wrongly, that without adequate cause she had given way to an outburst of blind fury. Phoebe was altogether too worthless a creature for her jealousy, too weak to have been subjected to such treatment. Her anger against George had expired. He did well to be indignant with her. It was true he had not rebuked Phoebe nor restrained his mother, but the reason was clear. He was too forbearing with women to offend them, however frivolous and intemperate they might be. He had relied on the greatness of his Glory's heart to stand above and disregard these petty storms.

She had thrown off her boots and stockings, and sat with her bare feet on the hearth. The feet moved nervously in rhythm to her thoughts. She could not keep them still. Her trouble was great. Tears were not on her cheeks; in this alone was Elijah mistaken. Her dark eyes were fixed dreamily on the dying fire—they were like the marsh-pools with the will-o'-the-wisp in each. They did not see the embers, they looked through the iron fireback, and the brick wall, over the saltings, over the water, into infinity.

She loved George. Her love for him was the one absorbing passion of her life. She loved her mother, but no one else—only her and George. She had no one else to love. She was without relations. She had been brought up without playfellows on that almost inaccessible islet, only occasionally visiting Mersea, and then only for an hour. She had seen and known nothing of the world save the world of morass. She had mixed with no life, save the life of the flocks on the Ray, of the fishes and the seabirds. Her mind hungered for something more than the little space of the Ray could supply. Her soul had wings and sought to spread them and soar away, whither, however, she did not know. She had a dim prevision of something better than the sordid round of common cares which made up the life she knew.

With a heart large and full of generous impulses, she had spent her girlhood without a recognition of its powers. She felt that there was a voice within which talked in a tongue other from that which struck her ears each day, but what that language was, and what the meaning of that voice, she did not know. She had met with De Witt. Indeed they had known each other, so far as meeting at rare intervals went, for many years; she had not seen enough of him to know him as he really was, she therefore loved him as she idealised him. The great cretaceous sea was full of dissolved silex penetrating the waters, seeking to condense and solidify. But there was nothing in the ocean then save twigs of weed and chips of shells, and about them that hardest of all elements drew together and grew to adamant. The soul of Mehalah was some such vague sea full of ununderstood, unestimated elements, seeking their several centres for precipitation, and for want of better, condensing about straws. To her, George De Witt was the ideal of all that was true and manly. She was noble herself, and her ideal was the perfection of nobility. She was rude indeed, and the image of her worship was rough hewn, but still with the outline and carriage of a hero. She could not, she would not, suppose that George De Witt was less great than her fancy pictured.

The thought of life with him filled her with exultation. She could leap up, like the whooper swan, spread her silver wings, and shout her song of rapture and of defiance, like a trumpet. He would open to her the gates into that mysterious world into which she now only peeped, he would solve for her the perplexities of her troubled soul, he would lead her to the light which would illumine her eager mind.

Nevertheless she was ready to wait patiently the realisation of her dream. She was in no hurry. She knew that she could not live in the same house or boat with George's mother. She could not leave her own ailing mother, wholly dependent on herself. Mehalah contentedly tarried for what the future would unfold, with that steady confidence in the future that youth so generally enjoys.

The last embers went out, and all was dark within. No sound was audible, save the ticking of the clock, and the sigh of the wind about the eaves and in the thorntrees. Mehalah did not stir. She dreamed on with her eyes open, still gazing into space, but now with no marsh fires in the dark orbs. The grey night sky and the stars looked in at the window at her.

Suddenly, as she thus sat, an inexpressible distress came over her, a feeling as though George were in danger, and were crying to her for help. She raised herself on the floor, and drew her feet under her, and leaning her chin on her fingers listened. The wind moaned under the door; everything else was hushed.

Her fear came over her like an ague fit. She wiped, her forehead, there were cold drops beading it. She turned faint at heart; her pulse stood still. Her soul seemed straining, drawn as by invisible attraction, and agonised because the gross body restrained it. She felt assured that she was wanted. She must not remain there. She sprang to her feet and sped to the door, unbolted it and went forth. The sky was cloudless, thick strewn with stars. Jupiter glowed over Mersea Isle. A red gleam was visible, far away at the 'City.' It shone from the tavern window, a coloured star set in ebony. She went within again. The fire was out. Perhaps this was the vulgar cause of the strange sensation. She must shake it off. She went to her room and threw herself on the bed. Again, as though an icy wave washed over her, lying on a frozen shore, came that awful fear, and then, again, that tension of her soul to be free, to fly somewhere, away from the Ray, but whither she could not tell.

Where was George? Was he at home? Was he safe? She tried in vain to comfort herself with the thought that he ran no danger, that he was protected by her talisman. She felt that without an answer to these questions she could not rest, that her night would be a fever dream.

She hastily drew on her jersey and boots; she slipped out of the house, unloosed her punt, and shot over the water to Mersea. The fleet was silent, but as she flew into the open channel she could hear the distant throb of oars on rowlocks, away in the dark, out seaward. She heard the screech of an owl about the stacks of a farm near the waterside. She caught as she sped past the Leather Bottle muffled catches of the nautical songs trolled by the topers within.

She met no boat, she saw no one. She ran her punt on the beach and walked to the 'Pandora,' now far above the water. The ladder was still down; therefore George was not within. 'Who goes there?' asked the voice of Mrs. De Witt. 'Is that you, George? Are you coming home at last? Where have you been all this while?'

Mehalah drew back. George was not only not there, but his mother knew not where he was.

The cool air and the exercise had in the mean time dissipated Mehalah's fear. She argued with herself that George was in the tavern, behind the red curtain, remaining away from his mother's abusive tongue as long as he might. His boat lay on the Hard. She saw it, with the oars in it. He was therefore not on the water; he was on land, and on land he was safe. He wore the medal about his neck, against his heart.

How glad and thankful she was that she had given him the precious charm that guarded from all danger save drowning.

She rowed back to the Ray, more easy in her mind, and anchored her punt. She returned cautiously over the saltings, picking her way by the starlight, leaping or avoiding the runnels and pools, now devoid of water, but deep in mud most adhesive and unfathomable.

She felt a little uneasy lest her mother should have awoke during her absence, and missed her daughter. She entered the house softly; the door was without a lock, and merely hasped, and stole to her mother's room. The old woman was wrapt in sleep, and breathing peacefully.

Mehalah drew off her boots, and seated herself again by the hearth. She was not sleepy. She would reason with herself, and account for the sensation that had affected her.

Hark! she heard some one speak. She listened attentively with a flutter at her heart. It was her mother. She stole back on tiptoe to her. The old woman was dreaming, and talking in her sleep. She had her hands out of bed together and parted them, and waved them, 'No, Mehalah, no! Not George! not George!' she gave emphasis with her hand, then suddenly grasped her daughter's wrist, 'But Elijah!' Next moment her grasp relaxed, and she slept calmly, apparently dreamlessly again.

Mehalah went back.

It was strange. No sooner was she in her place by the hearth again than the same distress came over her. It was as though a black cloud had swept over her sky and blotted out every light, so that neither sun, nor moon, nor star appeared, as though she were left drifting without a rudder and without a compass in an unknown sea, under murky night with only the phosphorescent flash of the waves about, not illumining the way but intensifying its horror. It was as though she found herself suddenly in some vault, in utter, rayless blackness, knowing neither how she came there nor whether there was a way out.

Oppressed by this horror, she lifted her eyes to the window, to see a star, to see a little light of any sort. What she there saw turned her to stone.

At the window, obscuring the star's rays, was the black figure of a man. She could not see the face, she saw only the shape of the head, and arms, and hands spread out against the panes. The figure stood looking in and at her.

Her eyes filmed over, and her head swam.

She heard the casement struck, and the tear of the lead and tinkle of broken glass on the brick floor, and then something fell at her feet with a metallic click.

When she recovered herself, the figure was gone, but the wind piped and blew chill through the rent lattice.

How many minutes passed before she recovered herself sufficiently to rise and light a candle she never knew, nor did it matter. When she had obtained a light she stooped with it, and groped upon the floor.

\*    \*    \*    \*    \*    \*

Mrs. Sharland was awakened by a piercing scream.

She sprang from her bed and rushed into the adjoining room. There stood Mehalah, in the light of the broken candle lying melting and flaring on the floor, her hair fallen about her shoulders, her face the hue of death, her lips bloodless, her eyes distended with terror, gazing on the medal of Paracelsus, which she held in her hand, the sea-water dripping from the wet riband wound about her fingers.

'Mother! Mother! He is drowned. I have seen him. He came and returned me this.'

Then she fell senseless on the floor, with the medal held to her heart.

CHAPTER VIII.

WHERE IS HE?

If there had been excitement on the Hard at Mersea on the preceding day when the schooner anchored off it, there was more this morning. The war-vessel had departed no one knew whither, and nobody cared. The bay was full of whiting; the waters were alive with them, and the gulls were flickering over the surface watching, seeing, plunging. The fishermen were getting their boats afloat, and all appliances ready for making harvest of that fish which is most delicious when fresh from the water, most flat when out of it a few hours.

Down the side of the 'Pandora' tumbled Mrs. De Witt, her nose sharper than usual, but her cap more flabby. She wore a soldier's jacket, bought second-hand at Colchester. Her face was of a warm complexion, tinctured with rum and wrath. She charged into the midst of the fishermen, asking in a loud imperative tone for her son.

To think that after the lesson delivered him last week, the boy should have played truant again! The world was coming to a pretty pass. The last trumpet might sound for aught Mrs. De Witt cared, and involve mankind in ruin, for mankind was past 'worriting' about.

George had defied her, and the nautical population of the 'City' had aided and abetted him in his revolt.

'This is what comes of galiwanting,' said Mrs. De Witt; 'first he galiwants Mehalah, and then Phoebe. No good ever came of it. I'd pass a law, were I king, against it, but that smuggling in love would go on as free under it as smuggling in spirits. Young folks now-a-days is grown that wexing and wicious—— Where is my George?' suddenly laying hold of Jim Morell.

The old sailor jumped as if he had been caught by a revenue officer.

'Bless my life, Mistress! You did give me a turn. What is it you want? A pinch of snuff?'

'I want my George,' said the excited mother. 'Where is he skulking to?'

'How should I know?' asked Morell, 'he is big enough to look after himself.'

'He is among you,' said Mrs. De Witt; 'I know you have had him along with a party of you at the Leather Bottle yonder. You men get together, and goad the young on into rebellion against their parents.'

'I know nothing about George. I have not even seen him.'

'I've knitted his guernseys and patched his breeches these twenty years, and now he turns about and deserts me.'

'Tom!' shouted Morell to a young fisherman, 'have you seen George De Witt this morning?'

'No, I have not, Jim.'

'Oh, you young fellows!' exclaimed the old lady, loosing her hold on the elder sailor, and charging among and scattering the young boatmen. 'Where is my boy? What have you done with him that he did not come home last night, and is nowhere wisible?'

'He went to the Mussets' last evening, Mistress. We have not set eyes on him since.'

'Oh! he went there, did he? Galiwanting again!' She turned about and rushed over the shingle towards the grocery, hardware, drapery, and general store.

Before entering that realm of respectability, Mrs. De Witt assumed an air of consequence and gravity.

She reduced her temper under control, and with an effort called up an urbane smile on her hard features when saluting Mrs. Musset, who stood behind the counter.

'Can I serve you with anything, ma'am?' asked the mother of Phoebe, with cold self-possession.

'I want my George.'

'We don't keep him in stock.'

'He was here last night.'

'Do you suppose we kept him here the night? Are you determined to insult us, madam? You have been drinking, and have forgot yourself and where you are. We wish to see no more of your son. My Phoebe is not accustomed to demean herself by association with cannibals. It is unfortunate that she should have stepped beyond her sphere yesterday, but she has learned a lesson by it which will be invaluable for the future. I do not know, I do not care, whether the misconduct was that of your son or of your daughter-in-law. Birds of a feather flock together, and lambs don't consort with wolves. I beg, madam, that it be an understood matter between the families that, except in the way of business, as tobacco, sugar, currants, or calico, intimacy must cease.'

'Oh indeed!' exclaimed Mrs. De Witt, the colour mottling her cheek. 'You mean to insinuate that our social grades are so wery different.'

'Providence, madam, has made distinctions in human beings as in currants. Some are all fruit, and some half gravel.'

'You forget,' said Mrs. De Witt, 'that I was a Rebow—a Rebow of Red Hall. It was thence I inherit the blood in my weins and the bridge of my nose.'

'And that was pretty much all you did inherit from them,' observed Mrs. Musset. 'Much value they must be to you, as you have nothing else to boast of.'

'Oh, indeed, Mistress Musset!'

'Indeed, Mistress De Witt!' with a profound curtsey.

Mrs. De Witt attempted an imitation, but having been uninstructed in deportment as a child, and inexperienced in riper years, she got her limbs entangled, and when she had arrived at a sitting posture was unable to extricate herself with ease.

In attempting to recover her erect position she precipitated herself against a treacle barrel and upset it. A gush of black saccharine matter spread over the floor.

'Where is my son?' shouted Mrs. De Witt, her temper having broken control.

'You shall pay for the golden syrup,' said Mrs. Musset.

'Golden syrup!' jeered Mrs. De Witt, 'common treacle, the cleanings of the niggers' feet that tread out the sugar-cane.'

'It shall be put down to you!' cried the mistress of the store, defying her customer across the black river. 'I will have a summons out against you for the syrup.'

'And I will have a search-warrant for my son.'

'I have not got him. I should be ashamed to keep him under my respectable roof.'

'What is this disturbance about?' asked Mr. Musset, coming into the shop with his pipe.

'I want my son,' cried the incensed mother. 'He has not been seen since he came here last night. What have you done to him?'

'He is not here, Mistress. He only remained a few minutes to enquire after Phoebe, and then he left. We have not seen him since. Go to the Leather Bottle; you will probably find him there.'

The advice was reasonable; and having discharged a parting shot at Mrs. Musset, the bereaved mother departed and took her way to the quaint old inn by the waterside, entitled the Leather Bottle.

Mrs. De Witt pushed the door open and strode in. No one was there save the host, Isaac Mead. He knew nothing of George's whereabouts. He had not seen him or heard him spoken of. Mrs. De Witt having entered, felt it incumbent on her to take something for the good of the house.

The host sat opposite her at the table.

'Where can he be?' asked Mrs. De Witt. 'The boy cannot be lost.'

'Have you searched everywhere?'

'I have asked the lads; they either know nothing, or won't tell. I have been to the Musset's. They pretend they have not seen him since last night.'

'Perhaps he rowed off somewhere.'

'His boat is on the Hard.'

'Do not bother your head about him,' said the host with confidence, 'he will turn up. Mark my words. I say he will certainly turn up, perhaps not when you want him, or where you expect him, but he assuredly will reappear. I have had seven sons, and they got scattered all over the world, but they have all turned up one after another, and,' he added sententiously, 'the world is bigger than Mersea. It is nothing to be away for twelve or fourteen hours. Lads take no account of time, they do not walue it any more than they walue good looks. We older folks do; we hold to that which is slipping from us. When we was children, we thought we could deal with time as with the sprats. We draw in all and throw what we can't consume away. At last we find we have spoiled our fishing, and we must use larger meshes in our net. I will tell you another thing, Mistress,' continued the host, who delighted to moralise, 'time is like a clock, when young it goes slow, and when old it gallops. When you and I was little, we thought a day as long as now we find a year. As we grew older years went faster; and the older we wax the greater the speed with which time spins by; till at last it passes with a whisk and a flash, and that is eternity.'

'He cannot be drowned,' said Mrs. De Witt. 'That would be too ridiculous.'

'It would, just about.' After a moment's consideration Isaac added, 'I heard that Elijah Rebow was on the Hard last night, maybe your George is gone off with him.'

'Not likely, Isaac. I and Elijah are not on good terms. My father left me nothing. Elijah took all after his parents, and I did not get a penny.'

'You know we have war with foreigners,' observed the publican. 'Now I observe that everything in this world goes by contraries. When there's peace abroad, there is strife at home, and vice versâ. There was a man-of-war in the bay yesterday. I should not wonder if that put it into George's head to be a man-of-peace on land. When you want to estimate a person's opinions, first ask what other folks are saying round him, and take the clean contrary, and you hit the bull's-eye. If you see anything like to draw a man in one direction, look the opposite way, and you will find him. There was pretty strong intimation of war yesterday with the foreigners, then you may be dead certain he took a peaceful turn in his perwerse vein, and went to patch up old quarrels with Elijah.'

'It is possible,' said Mrs. De Witt. 'I will row to Red Hall and find out.'

'Have another glass before you go,' said the landlord. 'Never hurry about anything. If George be at his cousin's he will turn up in time. There is more got by waiting than by worrying.'

'But perhaps he is not there.'

'Then he is elsewhere.'

'He may be drowned.'

'He will turn up. Drowned or not, he will turn up. I never knew boys to fail. If he were a girl it would be different. You see it is so when they drown. A boy floats face upwards, and a girl with her face down. It is so also in life. If a girl strays from home, she goes to the bottom like a plummet, but a boy on the contrary goes up like a cork.'

Mrs. De Witt so far took Isaac Mead's advice that she waited at her home till afternoon. But as George did not return, she became seriously uneasy, not so much for him as for herself. She did not for a moment allow that any harm had befallen him, but she imagined this absence to be a formal defiance of her authority. Such a revolt was not to be overlooked. In Mrs. De Witt's opinion no man was able to stand alone, he must fall under female government or go to the dogs. Deliberate bachelors were, in her estimation, God-forsaken beings, always in scrapes, past redemption. She had ruled her husband, and he had submitted with a meekness that ought to have inherited the earth. George had been always docile. She had bored docility into him with her tongue, and hammered it into him with her fist.

The idea came suddenly on her,—What if he had gone to the war schooner and enlisted? but was dismissed as speedily as impossible. Tales of ill-treatment in the Navy were rife among the shoremen. The pay was too small to entice a youth who owned a vessel, a billyboy, and oyster pans. He might do well in his trade, he must fare miserably in the Navy. Captain MacPherson had indeed invited George and others to follow him, but not one had volunteered.

She determined at last, in her impatience, to visit Red Hall, and for that purpose she got into the boat. Mrs. De Witt was able to row as well as a man. She did not start for Red Hall without reluctance. She had not been there since her marriage, kept away by her resentment. Elijah had made no overtures to her for reconciliation, had never invited her to revisit her native place, and her pride prevented her from making first advances. She had been cut off by her father, the family had kept aloof from her, and this had rankled in her heart. True, Elijah's father and mother were dead, and he was not mixed up in the first contentions; but he had inherited money which she considered ought to have fallen to her.

She was, however, anxious to see the old place again. Her young life there had not been happy; quite the reverse, for her father had been brutal, and her mother Calvinistic and sour. Yet Red Hall was, after all, her old home; its marshes were the first landscape on which her eyes had opened, its daisies had made her first necklaces, its bulrushes her first whips, its sea-wall the boundary of her childish world. It was a yearning for a wider, less level world, which had driven her in a rash moment into the arms of Moses De Witt.

The tide was out, so Mrs. De Witt was obliged to land at the point near the windmill. She walked thence on the sea-wall. She knew that wall well, fragrant with sovereign wood in summer, and rank with sea spinach. The aster blooming time was past, and the violet petals had fallen off, leaving only the yellow centres.

There, before her, like a stranded ark, was the old red house, unaltered, lonely, without a bush or tree to screen it.

The cattle stood browsing in the pasture as of old. In the marsh was a pond, a flight of wild fowl was wheeling round it, as in the autumns long ago. There was the little creek where her punt had lain, the punt in which she had been sometimes sent to Mersea to buy groceries for her mother.

The hard crust about the heart of Mrs. De Witt began to break, and the warm feeling within to ooze through. Gentler sentiments began to prevail. She would not take her son by the ears and bang his head, if she should find him at Red Hall. She would forgive him in a Christian spirit, and grant his dismissal with an innocuous curse.

She walked straight into the house. Elijah was crouched in his leather chair, with his head on one side, asleep. She stood over him and contemplated his unattractive face in silence, till he suddenly started, and exclaimed, 'Who is here? Who is this?'

Next moment he had recognised his visitor.

'So you are come, Aunt. You have not honoured me before. Will you have some whisky?'

'Thank you, Elijah, thank you. I am dry with rowing. But how come you to be asleep at this time of day? Were you out after ducks last night?'

'No, I was not out. I lay abed. I went to bed early.'

'Elijah, where is my son?'

He started, and looked at her suspiciously.

'How am I to know?'

'I cannot find him anywhere,' said the mother. 'I fear the boy has levanted. I may have been a little rough with him, but it was for his good. You cannot clean a deck with whiting, you must take holystone to the boards, and it is so with children. If you are not hard, you get off no edges, if you want to polish them, you must be gritty yourself. I doubt the boy is off.'

'What makes you think so?'

'I have not seen him. Nobody at Mersea has seen him. Have you?'

'Not since last night.'

'You saw him then?'

'Yes, he was on the beach going to Mehalah.'

'Galiwanting!' exclaimed Mrs. De Witt. 'Oh, what wickedness comes of galiwanting!' Then, recovering herself, 'But how could he get there? His boat was left on the Hard!'

'I suppose he went by land. He said something to that effect. You see the tide would have been out if he purposed to stay some time.'

'But what should make him go to the Ray? He had seen Mehalah on his boat.'

'He said there had been a quarrel, and he was bent on making it up. Go and look for him on the Ray. If he is not back on your boat already, you will find him, or hear of him, there.'

'Oh, the worries to parents that come of galiwanting!' moaned Mrs. De Witt, 'none who have not experienced can tell. Do not stay me, Elijah. Dear sackalive; I must go home. I dare say the boy is now on the "Pandora," trying to look innocent.' She rubbed her hands, and her eyes glistened. 'By cock!' she exclaimed, 'I would not be he.' She was out of the room, without a farewell to her nephew, down the steps, away over the flat to the sea-wall and her boat, her heart palpitating with anger.

It was late in the afternoon before Mrs. De Witt got back to Mersea. She ascended her ladder and unlocked the hatches. She looked about her. No George was on deck. She returned to the shore and renewed her enquiries. He had not been seen. No doubt he was still galivanting at the Ray. The uncertainty became unendurable. She jumped into her boat once more, and rowed to the island inhabited by Glory and her mother.

With her nose high in the air, her cap-frills quivering, she stepped out of the skiff. She had donned her military coat, to add to her imposing and threatening aspect.

The door of the house was open. She stood still and listened. She did not hear George's voice. She waited; she saw Mehalah moving in the room. Once the girl looked at her, but there was neither recognition nor lustre in her eyes. Mrs. De Witt made a motion towards her, but Glory did not move to meet her in return.

As she stepped over the threshold, Mrs. Sharland, who was seated by the fire, turned and observed her. The widow rose at once with a look of distress in her face, and advanced towards her, holding out her hand.

'Where is George?' asked Mrs. De Witt, ignoring the outstretched palm, in a hard, impatient tone.

'George!' echoed Mehalah, standing still, 'George is dead.'

'What nonsense!' said Mrs. De Witt, catching the girl by the shoulder and shaking her.

'I saw him. He is dead.' She quivered like an aspen.

The blood had ebbed behind her brown skin. Her eyes looked in Mrs. De Witt's face with a flash of agony in them.

'He came and looked in at the window at me, and cast me back the keepsake I had given him, and which he swore not to part with while life lasted.'

'Dear sackalive!' exclaimed Mrs. De Witt; 'the girl is dreaming or demented. What is the meaning of all this, Mistress Sharland?'

'Last night,' explained the widow, 'as Mehalah was sitting here in the dark, some one came to the window, stove it in—look how the lead is torn, and the glass fallen out—and cast at the feet of Mehalah a medal she had given George on Thursday. She thinks,' added the old woman in a subdued tone, 'that what she saw was his spirit.'

Mrs. De Witt was awed. She was not a woman without superstition, but she was not one to allow a supernatural intervention till all possible prosaic explanations had been exhausted.

'Is this Gospel truth?' she asked.

'It is true,' answered the widow.

'Did you see the face, Glory? Are you sure that what you saw was George?'

'I did not see the face. I saw only the figure. But it was George. It could have been no other. He alone had the medal, and he brought it back to me.'

'You see,' explained the widow Sharland, 'the coin was an heirloom; it might not go out of the family.'

'I see it all,' exclaimed Mrs. De Witt. 'Galiwanting again! He came to return the keepsake to Mehalah, because he wanted to break with her and take on with another.'

'No, never!' exclaimed Mehalah vehemently. 'He could not do it. He was as true to me as I am to him. He could not do it. He came to tell me that all was over.'

'Dear sackalive!' said Mrs. De Witt, 'you don't know men as I do. You have had no more experience of them than you have of kangaroos. I will not believe he is dead.'

'He is dead,' Mehalah burst forth with fierce vehemence. 'He is drowned, he is not false. He is dead, he is dead.'

'I know better,' said Mrs. De Witt in a low tone to herself as she bit her thumb. 'That boy is galiwanting somewhere; the only question to me is Where. By cock! I'd give a penny to know.'

CHAPTER IX.
IN MOURNING.

A month passed, and no tidings whatever of George De Witt had reached his mother or Mehalah. The former constantly expected news of her son. She would not believe in his death, and was encouraged in her opinion by Isaac Mead. But Mehalah had never entertained hope; she did not look for news, she knew that George was drowned.

His body had not been found. His disappearance had been altogether mysterious. Mrs. De Witt used every effort to trace him, but failed. From the moment the door of the Mussets had closed upon him, no one had seen him. With the closing of that door the record of his life had closed. He had passed as completely beyond pursuit as though he had passed through the gate of death.

There was but one possible way of accounting for his disappearance, and it was that at which public opinion arrived. He had gone round by the Strood from Mersea to reach the Ray, which was on that side accessible, but with difficulty, and occasionally only by land, had lost his way among the saltmarshes in the night, had fallen into one of the myriad creeks that traverse this desolate region, and had been engulfed in the ooze. The sea will give up her dead after a storm and with the tide, but the slime of the marshes never.

Mehalah made no attempt to account for the disappearance of George; it was sufficient for her that he was lost to her for ever. But his mother made enquiries when selling shrimps along the Colchester road, and on the island. He had nowhere been seen. He had not visited the Rose.

It was Elijah Rebow who finally brought Mrs. De Witt to admit that her son was entirely lost to her.

He visited her in November. She was surprised and pleased to see him. Since the disappearance of George, Mrs. De Witt had taken more vigorously than before to grog. Her feelings needed solace, and she found it in her glass. Perhaps the presence of George had acted as a restraint on his mother. She had not wished him to suppose her a habitual tippler. Her libations had been performed when he was away, or under the excuse of stomachics. On the subject of her internal arrangements, discomforts, and requirements, Mrs. De Witt had afforded her son information more copious than interesting. Her digestion sympathised with all the convulsions then shaking Europe. Revolutions were brought about there by the most ordinary edibles, and were always to be reduced by spirituous drinkables.

The topic of her internal economy, when introduced by Mrs. De Witt, always prefaced a resolve to try a drop of cordial. Now that George was gone, Mrs. De Witt brooded over her loss at home, stirring her glass as if it were the mud of the marshes, and she hoped to turn George up out of the syrup of the dissolving sugar.

Mrs. De Witt had laid aside her red coat, as inappropriate to her forlorn condition. The month of October had seen a sad deterioration in the mistress of the 'Pandora.' Her funds had been fast ebbing. The bread-winner was gone, and the rum-drinker had obtained fresh excuse for deep potations. There were fish in the sea to be caught, but he that had netted them was now under the mud. Things could not go on thus for ever.

Mrs. De Witt was musing despondingly over her desperate position, when Elijah appeared above the hatchway and descended to the cabin.

Mrs. De Witt had stuck a black bow in her mob cap, as a symbol of her woe. She hardly needed to hang out the flag, for her whole face and figure betokened distress. It cannot be said that her maternal bowels yearned after her son out of love for him so much as out of solicitude for herself. She naturally grieved for her 'poor boy,' but her grief for him was largely tinctured with anxiety for her own future. How should she live? On what subsist? She had her husband's old hull as a home, and a fishing smack, and a rowing boat. There was some money in the box, but not much. 'There's been no wasteful outlay over a burying,' said Mrs. De Witt. 'That is a good job.'

But, as already said, Mrs. De Witt only yielded reluctantly to the opinion that her boy was drowned. She held resolutely in public to this view for reasons she confided to herself over her rum. 'It is no use dropping a pint of money in dragging for the body, and burying it when you've got it. To my notion that is laying out five pound to have the satisfaction of spending another five. George was a gentleman,' she said with pride. 'If he was to go from his pore mother, he went as cheap from her as a lad could do it.'

Another reason why she refused to believe in his death was characteristic of the illogicality of her sex. This she announced to Rebow. 'You have it in a nutshell. How can the poor boy be drowned? For, if so, what is to become of me, and I a widow?'

'Mrs. De Witt,' said Rebow, helping himself to some rum, 'you may as well make your mind easy on this point. If George be not dead where can he be?'

'That I do not take on myself to say.'

'He is nowhere on Mersea, is he?'

'Certainly not.'

'He did not go along the Colchester road beyond the Strood?'

'No, or I should have heard of him.'

'Moreover, he told me he purposed going to the Ray.'

'To be sure he did.'

'And he never reached the Ray.'

'No, for certain.'

'Then it is obvious he must have been lost between Mersea and the Ray.'

'There is something in what you say, Elijah; there is what we may term argument in it.'

'There was a reason why he should go to the Ray.'

'I suppose there was.'

'He had quarrelled with Glory, and desired to make it up that night.'

'I know there had been a squall.'

'Then do not flatter yourself with false hopes. George is gone past recall; you and Glory must give him up for ever.'

Mrs. De Witt shook her head, wiped her eyes with the frill of her cap, looked sorrowfully into her glass and said, 'Pore me!'

'You are poor indeed,' said Elijah, 'but how poor I suspect rather than know. What have you got to live upon?'

'That is just it,' answered Mrs. De Witt; 'my head has been like the Swin light, a rewolving and a rewolving. But there is this difference, the Swin rewolves first light and then dark alternately, whereas in my head there has been naught rewolving but warious degrees of darkness.'

'What do you propose doing?'

'Well, I have an idea.' Mrs. De Witt hitched her chair nearer to her nephew, and breathed her idea and her spirit together into his ear. 'I think I shall marry.'

'You——!'

'Yes, I. Why not? There is the billyboy running to waste, rotting for want of use, crying out for a master to take her out fishing. There are as many fisher-boys on shore as there are sharks in the ocean, ready to snap me up were I flung to them. I have felt them. They have been a-nibbling round me already. Consider, Elijah! there is the "Pandora," good as a palace for a home, and the billyboy and the boat, and the nets, and the oyster garden, and then there is my experience to be thrown in gratis, and above all,' she raised herself, 'there is my person.'

Rebow laughed contemptuously.

'What have these boys of their own?' asked Mrs. De Witt, laying down the proposition with her spoon. 'They have nothing, no more than the sea-cobs. They have naught to do but swoop down on whatever they can see, sprats, smelt, mullet, whiting, dabs, and when there is naught else, winkles. Their thoughts do not rise that proudly to me, and I must stoop to them. I tell you what, Elijah, if I was to be raffled for, at a shilling a ticket, there would be that run among the boys for me, that I could make a fortune. But I won't demean myself to that. I shall choose the stoutest and healthiest among them, then I can send him out fishing, and he can earn me money, as did George, and so I shall be able to enjoy ease, if not opulence.'

'But suppose the lads decline the honour.'

'I should like to see the impertinence of the lad that did,' said Mrs. De Witt firmly. 'I have had experience with men, and I know them in and out that familiarly that I could find my way about their brains or heart, as you would about your marshes, in the dark. No, Elijah, the question is not will they have me, but whether I will be bothered with any more of the creatures. I will not unless I can help it. I will not unless the worst comes to the worst. But a woman must live, Elijah.'

'How much have you got for current expenses?'

'Only a few pounds.'

'There are five and twenty pounds owed you by the Sharlands. You are not going to let them have it as a present?'

'No, certain, I am not.'

'Do you expect to get it by waiting for it?'

'To tell you the truth, Elijah, I hadn't given that five and twenty pounds a thought. I will go over to the Ray and claim the money.'

'You will not get it.'

'I must have it.'

'They cannot possibly pay.'

'But they shall pay. I want and will have my money.'

'Mehalah will pretend that George gave her the money.'

'No, she will not. She acknowledged the debt to me before George's face. She promised repayment as soon as she had sufficient.'

'If you do not seize on their goods, or some of them, you will never see the colour of the coin again.'

'I must and will have it.'

'Then follow my advice. Put in an execution. I will lend you my men. All you have to do is to give notice on this island when the sale is to be, get together sufficient to bid and buy, and you have your money. You must have an auction.'

'Can I do so, Elijah?'

'Of course you can. Go over to the Ray at once and demand your money. If they decline to pay, allow them a week's grace, more if you like. I'll go with you, when the sale is to take place, and perhaps bid. We will have a Dutch auction.'

'By cock! I'll do it. I will go there right on end.'

At once, with her natural impetuosity, the old woman started. Before departing, however, to heighten her importance, and give authority and sternness to her appearance, she donned her red coat. In token of mourning she wrapped a black rag round her left arm. Over her cap she put a broad-brimmed battered straw hat, in front of which she affixed with a hair-pin the large black bow that had figured on her cap. Thus arrayed she entered her boat and rowed to the Ray.

The demand for the money filled Mrs. Sharland with dismay. It was a demand as unexpected as it was embarrassing. She and Mehalah were absolutely without the means of discharging the debt. They had, indeed, a few pounds by them, which had been intended to serve to carry them through the winter, and these they offered Mrs. De Witt, but she refused to receive a portion on account when she wanted the whole of the debt.

Mrs. Sharland entreated delay till spring, but Mrs. De Witt was inexorable. She would allow no longer than a week. She departed, declaring that she would sell them up, unless the five and twenty pounds were produced.

Since the death or disappearance of George De Witt, Mehalah had gone about her usual work in a mechanical manner. She was in mourning also. But she did not exhibit it by a black bow on her cap or a sable rag round her arm, like the mother of the lost lad. She still wore her red cap, crimson kerchief and blue jersey. But the lustre was gone from her eyes, the bloom from her cheek, animation from her lips. There was no spring in her step, no lightness in her tone. The cow was milked as regularly as usual, and foddered as attentively as before. The house was kept as scrupulously clean, Mrs. Sharland ministered to with the same assiduity, but the imperiousness of Mehalah's nature had gone. The widow found to her astonishment that she was allowed to direct what was to be done, and that her daughter submitted without an objection.

It is the way with strong natures to allow their griefs no expression, to hide their sorrows and mask their wounds. Glory did not speak of George. She did not weep. She made no lamentation over his loss; more wonderful still in her mother's eyes, she uttered no reproaches against anyone for it. A weak nature always exhausts its troubles in reproaches of others; a strong one eats out its own heart. Mehalah listened with a dull ear to her mother's murmurs, and made no response. Mrs. Sharland set her down as unfeeling. A feeble querulous woman like her was quite unable to measure the depth of her daughter's heart, and understand its working. The result was that she read them wrong, and took false soundings.

When her mother was in bed and asleep, then Mehalah sat at the hearth, or leaned at the window looking at the stars, hour by hour, immovable, uttering no sound, not building castles in the clouds, not weaving any schemes for her future, not hoping for anything, not imagining anything, but exhaling her pain. As the turned earth after the plough may be seen in a sudden frost to smoke, so was it with that wounded heart, it smoked, gave up its fever heat, and in silence and solitude cooled. There was something, which yet was no thing, to which her weary soul stretched, in dim unconsciousness. There was a communing without words, even without the thoughts which form into words, with that Unseen which is yet so surely felt. It was the spirit—that infinite essence so mysteriously enclosed within bounds, in strange contradiction to its nature, asserting its nature and yearning for Infinity.

The human heart in suffering is like the parched soil in summer; when its sky is overcast and it cannot see beyond the cloud that lies low over it, then it must harbour its heat, and gape with fever. But, should a rent appear in the earthborn vaporous veil, through which it can look into unfathomable space, at once it radiates the ardour that consumes it, casts off the fever that consumes it, and drinks in, and is slaked by, the dew of heaven.

CHAPTER X.
STRUCK COLOURS.

Woman is the natural enemy of woman. When one woman is over thirty or plain, and the other is young or beautiful, the enmity on one side is implacable and unqualified by mercy. A woman can be heroically self-sacrificing and behave with magnificent generosity towards man, but not towards one of her own sex. She is like the pillar that accompanied the Israelites and confounded the Egyptians; she is cloud and darkness to these, but light and fire to those. She will remorselessly pursue, and vindictively torment a sister who offends by having a better profile and less age. No act of submission will blunt her spite, no deed of kindness sponge up her venom. There is but one unpardonable sin in the sight of Heaven; there are two in the eyes of a middle-aged woman, youth and beauty. She is unconscious of fatigue in the pursuit, and without compunction in the treatment of the member of her sex who has sinned against her in one particular or other. The eternal laws of justice, the elementary principles of virtue, are set aside as inappropriate to the world of women. Generosity, charity, pity are unknown quantities in the feminine equation. As the Roman tyrant wished that mankind had but one neck which he might hack through, so woman would like that womankind had but one nose which she might put out of joint. Every woman is a kill-joy to every other woman, a discord in the universal harmony. Her ideal world is that of the bees, in which there is but one queen, and all other shes are stung to death. Eve was the only woman who tasted of happiness unalloyed, because in Eden she had no sisters.

The iron maid of Nuremberg was sweet and smiling externally, but a touch revealed the interior bristling with spikes, and the victim thrust into her embrace was only released a corpse to drop into an oubliette. All women are Nuremberg maidens, with more or fewer spikes, discovered perhaps by husbands, unsuspected by the rest of men, but known to all other women, who are scarred from their embraces.

Mehalah knew that no leniency was to be looked for in Mrs. De Witt. She thought that lady exceptionally rigorous and exacting; she thought so because she knew nothing of the world. Her mother spent her breath in repinings that could not help, and in hopes which must be frustrated. The extremity of the danger roused Mehalah from her dreams. There was no pity to be expected from the creditor, and there was no means that she could see of defraying the debt. She considered and tried to find some road out of the difficulty, but could discover none. Now more than ever did she need the advice, if not the help, of him who was gone. There was nothing on the farm that could be sold without leaving them destitute of means of carrying it on and defraying the next half-year's rent. The cow, the ewes, her boat, were necessary to them. The furniture in the house was of little value, and it was impossible for her to transport it to Colchester for sale.

She sat thinking of the situation one evening over the fire opposite her mother, without uttering a word. Her hands with her knitting needles lay in her lap; she could not work, she was too fully engrossed in the cares which pressed on her.

Presently her mother roused her from her reverie, by saying, 'There is no help for it, Mehalah, you must go to Wyvenhoe, and find out my cousin, Charles Pettican. He is my only relative left;—at least as far as I know, and him I have not seen for fifteen or sixteen years. I do not even know if he be yet alive. We haven't had a chance of meeting. I go nowhere, I am imprisoned on this island, and he is cut off from us by the river Colne. I see no way out of our trouble but that of borrowing money from him. He was a kind-hearted lively fellow when young, but what he is now that he is old I cannot tell. You must go and try what you can do with him. He is well off, and would not miss twenty pounds more than twenty pence.'

Mehalah greatly disliked the idea of going to a stranger, to one who, though a connection, was quite unknown to her, and begging a loan of him. It galled her pride and wounded her independence. It lowered her in her own eyes. She would rather have worked her fingers to the bone than so stoop, but no work of hers could raise twenty pounds in a week. The thought was altogether so intolerable to her, that she fought against it as long as she could. She would herself cheerfully have gone out of her home and left the farm rather than do this, but she was obliged to consider her mother. She yielded at last most reluctantly; and with tears of mortification filling her eyes, and her cheeks burning with shame, she threw aside her customary costume, and dressed herself in dark blue cloth gown, white kerchief, and a bonnet, and took her way to Wyvenhoe. She had to walk some seven miles. Her road led her to the top of high ground overlooking the mouth of the Colne.

The blue water was dotted with sails. Beyond the river on a height rose from above trees the lofty tower of Brightlingsea. Up a winding creek she looked, and at the head could distinguish the grey priory of St. Osyth, then the seat of the Earl of Rochford, at the entrance to a noble park. She descended the hill, and by a ferry crossed the river to the village of Wyvenhoe.

On her walk she had mused over what she should say to Mr. Charles Pettican, without coming to any determination. Her mother had let fall some hints that her cousin had once been her fond admirer, but that they had been parted by cruel parents. Mrs. Sharland's reminiscences were rather vague, and not much reliance could be placed on them; however, Mehalah hoped there might be some truth in this, and that old recollections might be stirred in the breast of Mr. Pettican, and stimulate him to generosity. The river was full of boats, and on the landing were a number of people. 'We're lively to-day,' said the ferryman who put her over, 'the regatta is on. It is late this season, but what with one thing and another, we couldn't have it earlier no way.'

'Will Mr. Pettican be there?'

'Lor bless you, no,' answered the man, 'that's impossible.'

Glory asked her way to the house of her mother's cousin. He was, or rather had been, a shipbuilder. He occupied a little compact wooden house painted white, on the outskirts of the village. It was a cheerful place. The shutters were after the French fashion, external, and painted emerald green. The roof was tiled and looked very red, as though red ochred every morning by the housemaid after she had pipeclayed the walls. Over the door of the house was a balcony with elaborate iron balustrades gilt; against these leaned two figureheads, females, with very pink and white complexions, and no expression in their faces.

There was a sanded path led from the gate to the door, and there were two green patches of turf, one on each side of it. In the centre of that on the left was another figure-head—a Medusa with flying serpent locks, but with a face as passionless and ordinary as that of a milliner's block. In the midst of the other plot rose a mast. On this day, when all Wyvenhoe was en fête, a flag ought properly to be flying from the mast. Every other in the village and on the water was adorned with its bunting, but that of Mr. Pettican alone ignored the festival.

As Mehalah ascended the walk, a gull with its wings clipped uttered a fierce scream, and rushing across the garden with outspread pinions, dashed at her foot with his sharp beak, and then falling back, threw out his breast, elevated his bill, and broke into a long succession of discordant yells, whoops, and gulps.

At the same moment one pane in the window on the right of the door opened, a little dry face peered through and nodded.

'If you're going to knock, don't. Come in, and make no noise about it. It's very kind. She's out.'

The gull made a second assault at Mehalah's foot.

'Kick him,' said the face; 'don't fear you will hurt him. He is as good as a watch dog. Open the door, and when you are in the hall turn to the right-hand.'

Then the pane was slammed to, and Mehalah turned the handle of the front door. She found herself in a narrow passage with a flight of very steep stairs before her, and a door on each hand. Over each of these on a bracket stood a ship fully rigged, with all her sail on.

She entered the room on the right as directed, and found herself in a little parlour with very white walls, and portraits of ships, some in worsted work on canvas, others painted in oils, others again in water-colours, covering the walls.

In the window, half sat, half reclined, an old man, with a scrubby grey head, a pair of very lively eyes, but with a trembling feeble mouth.

He wore very high shirt-collars, exceedingly stiff, and thick folds of black silk round his neck. His blue coat had a high black velvet collar. The little man seemed to draw his head in between his blinkers and beneath his coat-collar, and lose his face in his cravat, then at will to project his head from them, as though he were a tortoise retiring into or emerging from his shell.

As Glory came in, the little wizened face was scarce perceptible, save that the bright eyes peeped and twinkled at her from somewhere in a chaos of black velvet, blue cloth, white linen, and black silk; then all at once the head shot forward, and a cheery voice said, 'I can't rise to meet you, Mary,' he made at the same time a salutation with his hand, 'or I would throw myself at your feet. Glad to see you. How are you, Lizzy, my dear.'

'My name is neither Mary nor Lizzy, but Mehalah.'

'Let it be Methuselah or Melchisedek, or what you like, it is all one to me. I don't care for the name you give a wine when it is good, I drink it and smack my lips, whether you call it Port, or Tarragona, or Roussillon; and I don't bother about a girl's name. If she is sweet and sunny, and bright and pretty as'—he made a little bow and a great flourish of his hand as a salute—'as you are, I see her and listen to her, and admire her.'

'My name's——'

'I have told you it don't matter. I never yet met with a girl's name that wasn't pretty, except one, and I thought that pretty once.'

'What name?'

'Admonition.'

'Why do you not like it?'

The little man looked out of the window, along the walls, then turned his head round and sighed. 'Never mind. Do you see that figure-head out there? It belonged to a wessel I built; she was called the "Medusa." Bad luck attended her. She was always fouling other wessels. She ran down a Frenchman once, but that was no matter, and she did the same by a Dutchman. Well, at last she got such a character that I was forced to change her head and her name, but then she fared worse than before. Changing their names don't always mend wessels and women. Well!' with another sigh, 'we will leave unpleasant topics, and laugh and be jolly while we may. You haven't told me how you are. This is very kind of you to drop in on me. It is like old times; my halcyon days, as I think they call 'em. I haven't had such a wisit since,' he waved towards his flagstaff, 'since I lowered my flag.'

'But, sir,' said Mehalah, 'you must let me explain my purpose in coming here; and to do that, I must tell you who I am, and whence I come.'

'I don't want to hear it. I don't care a bit about it. Be jolly and gather the rosebuds while you may. She ain't out for long, and we must be joyful at such opportunities as are afforded us. I know as well as you do why you have come. You have come in the goodness of your female heart to cheer a poor crippled wretch like me.'

'I did not know you were a cripple, sir!'

'You didn't. Give me my crutches. Look at this.' He placed his crutches under his arms, swung himself dexterously off his chair, and stumped round the room, dragging his lower limbs behind him, as though they did not belong to him. They were lifeless. When he returned to his seat he threw himself down. 'Now, Jemima, put up my legs on that chair. I can't stir them myself. I couldn't raise them an inch if you was to promise me a kiss for my pains. There, thank ye; now sit down and be jolly.'

'Sir,' said Mehalah, 'you remember my mother, Mistress Sharland.'

'What! Liddy Vince, pretty cousin Liddy! I should think I did remember her. Why, it is only the other day that she married.'

'I am her daughter, and my age is nineteen.'

'I haven't seen her for—well, never mind how many years. Years don't tell on a man as they do on a woman; they mellow him, but wither her. So you are her daughter, are you? Stand round there by my feet where I can see you.'

He drew his head down among his clothes and peered at her from between his tall white collars. 'You are an uncommon fine girl,' he said, when his observation was completed, 'but not a bit like Liddy. You are more like her mother—she was the deuce of a splendid woman, such eyes, such hair—but she was a——' he hesitated, his courtesy forbade his saying what rose to the tongue.

'A gipsy;' Mehalah supplied the words.

'Well, she was, but she couldn't help it, you know. But that is not what I was about to say. I intended to observe that she was a—little before my time. She was old when I knew her, but I've heard what a beauty she was, and her eyes always remained large and noble, and her hair luxuriant. But women don't improve with age as does good port, and as do men. Well, now, tell me your name.'

'Mehalah.'

'A regular Essex marshland name. I hope I shall remember it. But I have to carry so many names of nice-looking girls in my head, and of ships I have built, that they run one another down, and I cannot be sure to recall them. My memory is not going. Don't suppose that. Why, bless your dear heart, I can remember everything your mother and I said to one another when we were sweet upon each other. That don't look like a failing memory, does it? But you see, as we go on in life, every day brings something more to remember, and so this head gets choke full. A babe a year old has some three hundred and sixty-five things to recollect, that is if he remembers only one thing per diem, and a man of fifty has over eighteen million of things stuffed away in this little warehouse,' tapping his head; 'so he has to rummage and rout before he can find the particular article he wants. His memory don't go with age, but gets overchoked. Now, to change the topic, why haven't you been to see me before?'

'Sir! I could not. I did not know you, and you live a long way from the Ray. Mother cannot walk so far.'

'And I can't neither, but not from age but from accident. So your mother can't walk a matter of seven miles. Dear me! How women do deteriorate either with age or with marriage! I could; I would think nothing of it but for my accident. Now tell me what has brought you here, Mehalaleel?'

'I have come,' answered Mehalah, looking down, 'because driven by necessity to apply to you, as our only relative.'

'Bless my soul! Want my help! How? I wish I could as easily apply for yours. My dear girl, I am past help. I've hauled down my flag. All is up with me. I'm drawn up on the mud and put to auction. They are breaking me up. Tell your mother so. Tell her that time was—but let bygones be bygones. How is she looking? Are the roses altogether faded?'

'She is very feeble and suffering. She is greatly afflicted with ague.'

'She had it as a girl. One day as I was courting her and whispering pretty things in her ear, she was going to blush and smile, when all at once the fit of shivers came on her, and she could do nought but chatter her teeth and turn green and stream with cold sweat. So she is very feeble, is she?'

'She is weak and ailing.'

'Women never do improve, like men, by ripening,' said Mr. Pettican. 'Girls are angels up to one and twenty, some a little bit later, but after that they deteriorate and become old cats. They are roses up to marriage and after that are hips, with hard red skins outside and choke and roughness within. Men are quite the reverse. They are louts to twenty-five, as unformed in body as young colts, and in mind as young owls; after that they begin to ripen, and the older they get the better they grow. A man is like a medlar, only worth eating when rotten. A young man is raw and hard and indigestible, but a man of forty is full of juice and sweetness. Now don't tell your mother what I have said about old women.'

'I will not.'

'Sit ye down, sit ye down, and be jolly. Don't stand. It does not fare to be comfortable.'

'Sir, I must mention the object of this visit.'

'All in good time. But first let us be jolly. Give me some fun, I haven't had any since—since,' he pointed sadly to his flagless staff and shook his head. 'It is all up with me, save when a stray gleam of liveliness and mirth shoots athwart my gloomy sky. But that is rarely the case now.'

'Thank you, sir,' said Mehalah, taking a chair. 'Now to the point.'

'First be jolly. I have enough of mouths drawn down at the corners—but never mind now. Begone dull care, thou canker. Come! I should like your mother to know all about me. You will tell her how young I am looking. You will say that I would be sure to come tripping over to see her but for my accident.'

'I will tell her how I have seen you.'

'You needn't dwell on the crutches; but she knows, she has heard of that affliction of mine, it was the talk of the county, thousands of tender hearts beat in sympathy with me. My accident is one of long standing. I won't say when it happened. I have not a good head for dates, but anyhow it was not quite last year, or the year before that. It has told on me. I look older than I really am, and yet I am hearty and well. I have such an appetite. Just pull me up, dear, in the chair, and I will tell you what I eat. I had a rasher of bacon and a chop for breakfast, and a pewter of homebrewed beer; that don't look like a failing digestion, does it. And I shall eat,—Lord bless you! You would laugh to see me at my dinner, I eat like a ploughboy. That is not like the decay of old age attacking the witals, is it, my pretty? Now listen to me, and I will tell you all about it. Do you chance to notice here and there a little grey in my hair? Just as though a few grains of salt had dropped among black pepper? They come of care, dearest, not of years. I never had a grizzled hair on my head till—till I struck my colours. Now I'll tell you all about it, and you tell your mother. She will pity me. One day in my yard I stumbled over a round of timber and fell on my back on it, and hurt my spine, and I've been a cripple ever since. It is a sad pity— such a fine, strapping, manly fellow as I, in the prime of age, to be laid by like an old condemned wessel! Well! here I have had to lie in my window, looking out, and not seeing much to interest me. But the girls of Wyvenhoe, bless their kind hearts,—they are angels up to one and twenty—used to come to the window, and wish me a good day, and ask after my health, and have pleasant little gossips, and be altogether jolly. Next, whenever they could, some one or two would bring her knitting or needlework, and come in, and sit here and spend an hour or so, talking, laughing and making fun. That was pleasant, wasn't it? It is wonderful what a lot those dear girls had to say for themselves; they became quite confidential with me, and told me all their love affairs, and how matters stood, and who their sweethearts were. It was worth while being ill and laid on one's back to enjoy such society. Whenever I was dull and wanted some chat, I sent my man to hoist the flag, and the next girl that went by, "Ah!" said she, "there's that poor fellow would like my society," and in she came and sat talking with me as long as she was able. Then sometimes I had a dish of tea brought in, or some cakes, or fruit. It was a pleasant time. I wish it were to come over all again. Tell your mother all this. I was quite the pet of all the kind-hearted young folks in Wyvenhoe. Now that is over. I'll tell you about it.' He sighed and passed a shaking hand over his bright, twinkling eyes. 'You must explain it all to your mother— Liddy that was. You see, I don't forget her name. Now tell me yours again; it is gone from me.'

'Mehalah.'

'I'll write it down in my note-book and then I shall remember it. My memory is overstocked, and it takes me a deal of time to find in it what I want. But your mother's name don't get buried, but lies at hand on the top. You'll tell her so. Now about my troubles. There was one damsel, who was called Admonition; and she was very particularly pleasant and attentive to me, and many a little teasing and joking I had with her about her name. She was the girl fullest of fun, she regularly brimmed over with it, and it ran down her sides. She was a milliner, and had to work for her living. She had no relations and no money of her own. It is curious what a lot of cousins she has now, mostly in the sea-faring line, and all young. Then she was always ready for a chat. She would bring her needlework and sit with me by the hour. I thought it vastly pleasant, and how much more pleasant it would be if she were always by my side to keep me laughing and chirpy. I must tell you that I go down some degrees when alone,—not that my spirits fail me with age,—it is constitutional. I was so as a boy.—Bless me! it seems to me only the other day when I was a romping lout of a lad—I'm crisp and crackly like seaweed in an East wind when I am in female society, that is, female society up to one and twenty— but I'm like the same seaweed in a Sou'wester when I'm alone. One day the flag was flying, but no visitor came except Admonition. It was the day of the Regatta. She said, and the tears came into her eyes, that she was a lone girl, with no one to accompany her, so she had come to sit with me. She tried to cheer up and laugh, but she felt her loneliness so that my heart was touched, and I proposed and we were married.' There ensued a long pause. Mr. Pettican looked out of the window. 'I had a queer sort of premonitory feeling when I said, "I take thee Admonition to my wedded wife," but it was too late then to retract. Now the flag that has braved a thousand breezes is down. It has not flown since that day.'

'Where is Mrs. Pettican now?' asked Mehalah.

'At the Regatta,' answered the cripple. 'You'll tell your mother how I am situated. She will drop a tear for poor Charlie. I will tell you what, Me———' he looked at his note-book, 'Mehalah; men fancy all girls sultana raisins, but when they bite them they get very hard pips between their teeth. There's a Methodist preacher here has been haranguing on conversion, and persuading Admonition that she is a new creature. I know she is. She was converted on the day of the marriage ceremony; but the conversion was not something to boast of. Matrimony with women is what jibbing is with ships, they go through a movement of staggering and then away they start off on a tack clean contrary to the course they were sailing before. Marriage, Mehalah, is like Devonshire cream; it is very rich and tasty, but it develops a deal of bile. Look here, my pretty!' In a moment he was off his chair, stumping in his crutches round the room, dragging his paralysed limbs after him. He returned to his chair. 'Put up my legs, dear,' he begged; then said, 'That is the state of my case; my better half is Admonition, the poor paralysed, helpless, dead half is me.'

He did not speak for some moments, but brushed his eyes with his feeble hand. At last he said, 'I've unburdened my soul. Tell your mother. Now go ahead, and let me know what you want.'

Mehalah told Mr. Pettican the circumstances. She said that her mother wanted a loan of fifteen or twenty pounds. If she could not procure the sum, she would have her cow taken from her, then they would be unable to pay the rent next Lady Day, and be without milk for the winter. They would be turned out of the little farm on which her mother had lived so long, in quiet and contentment, and this would go far to break her mother's heart. She told him candidly that the loan could only be repaid in instalments.

The old man listened patiently, only passing his hand in an agitated manner across his face several times.

'I wish I could help you,' he said, when she had done; 'I have money. I have laid by some. There is plenty in the box and more at the bank, but I can't get at it.'

'Sir!'

'Before I struck my colours, Mehalah, I did what I liked with my money; on market days my man went into Colchester, and I always gave him a little sum to lay out in presents for my kind visitors. Bless you; a very trifle pleased them. It is different now. I don't spend a penny myself. The money is spent for me. I don't keep the key of my cashbox. Admonition has it.'

'Then,' said Mehalah, rising from her seat, 'all is over with us. My mother, your cousin, will in her old age be cast destitute into the world. But, if you really wish to help her, be a man, use your authority, and do what you choose with your own.'

'Bless me!' exclaimed Mr. Pettican touching his brow with his trembling hand, 'I will be a man. Am I not a man! If I don't exert my authority, people will say I am in my dotage. I—I—in my flower and cream of my age—in the dotage! Go, Me———' he looked in his note-book, 'Mehalah, fetch me my cashbox, it is in the bedroom cupboard upstairs, on the right, over this. Bring the box down. Stay though! Before you come down just feel in my wife's old dress pocket. She may have forgotten to take her keys with her to the Regatta. It is just possible.'

'I cannot do that.'

'Well, no, perhaps you had better not. Do you happen to have a bunch of keys with you?'

'No, sir.'

'Well, never mind. Bring me the case. I will be a man. I will show the world I am not in my dotage. I will be of the masculine gender, dative case, if it pleases me, and Admonition may lump it if she don't like it.'

Mehalah obeyed. She found the box, which was of iron, brought it downstairs, and placed it on the table by Mr. Pettican. 'I've been turning the matter over in my mind,' said he, 'and I see a very happy way out of it without a row. Give me the poker. You will find a cold chisel in that drawer.'

'I will tell you my idea. Whilst I am left here all alone, burglars have broken into the house, knowing my helpless condition, and have ransacked the place, found my cashbox and broken it open.' He chuckled and rubbed his hands. 'I shall be able accurately to describe the ruffians. One has a black moustache, and the other a red beard, and they look like foreigners and speak a Dutch jargon.'

He put the chisel to the lid, and struck at it with the poker, starting the hinges by the blow.

At that moment the door was flung wide, and in swam a dashing young woman in very gay colours, on the arm of a yachtsman.

'Charles!' she cried; 'what are you after?' then turning abruptly on Mehalah, 'And pray what are you doing here, in my house?' Mr. Pettican's head, which had been craned forward in eagerness over the box, retreated amidst the collar and cravat, and almost disappeared.

'Who are you?' she asked of Mehalah, with an insulting air. 'Out of this house with you at once!'

'My dear Monie!' pleaded Mr. Pettican, lifting his shaking hands into an attitude of prayer.

'No "My dears" and "Monies" to me,' said the wife. 'I want to know what you are after with my cashbox? Ho, ho! trying to prize it open and squander my little sums laid aside for household expenses on—Heaven knows whom.'

'Mr. Pettican is my mother's cousin,' said Mehalah.

'Cousin, indeed! never heard Mr. Pettican speak of you. Cousins are sure to turn up when money is wanted.'

'Mr. Pettican,' said Mehalah, refusing to notice the insolent woman, 'be a man and let me have the money you promised.'

'I should like to be a man, oh! I wish I were a man! But I can't, I can't indeed, dear. I haven't been myself since I hauled down my flag.'

'Charles, hold out your hand, and invite my cousin Timothy to dinner. He has kindly consented to stay a fortnight with us.'

'Timothy!' echoed Mr. Pettican, 'I did not know you had such a cousin.'

'Do you think you know anything of my relations?' exclaimed Admonition; 'I should hope not, they are a little above your sphere. There are lots more cousins!'

The poor little man sat shrinking behind his blinkers, peering piteously now at Mehalah, and then at his wife.

'Be a man,' said Mehalah, grasping him by both hands. 'Save us from ruin.'

'Can't do it, Pretty, can't. I have struck my colours.'

## CHAPTER XI

## A DUTCH AUCTION.

Mehalah returned sadly to the Ray. The hope that had centred in help from Wyvenhoe had been extinguished.

Her mother was greatly disappointed at the ill-success of the application, but flattered at her cousin's recollection of her.

'If it had not been for that woman's coming in when she did, we should have had the money,' said Mrs. Sharland. 'What a pity she did not remain away a little longer. Charles is very well disposed, and would help us if he could pluck up courage to defy his wife. Suppose you try again, Mehalah, some other day, and choose your time well.'

'I will not go there again, mother.'

'If we do get turned out of this place we might settle at Wyvenhoe, and then choose our opportunity.'

'Mother, the man is completely under his wife's thumb. There is no help to be found there.'

'Then, Mehalah, the only chance that remains, is to get the money from the Mersea parson.'

'He cannot help us.'

'There is no harm trying.'

The day on which Mrs. De Witt had threatened to come had passed, without her appearing. True it had blown great guns, and there had been storms of rain. Mrs. Sharland hoped that the danger was over. The primitive inhabitants of the marshes had dwelt on piles, she built on straws. Some people do not realise a danger till it is on them and they cannot avert it. Mrs. Sharland was one of these. She liked her grievance, and loved to moan over it; if she had not a real one she invented one, just as children celebrate funerals over dolls. She had been so accustomed to lament over toy troubles that when a real trouble threatened she was unable to measure its gravity.

She was a limp and characterless woman. Mehalah had inherited the rich red blood of her grandparents, and Mrs. Sharland had assimilated only the water, and this flowed feebly through her pale veins. Her nature was parasitic. She could not live on her own root, but must adhere to a character stronger than herself. She had hung on and smothered her husband, and now she dragged at her daughter. Mehalah must stand upright or Mrs. Sharland would crush her to the ground. There are women like articles of furniture that will 'wobble' unless a penny or a wedge of wood be put under their feet. Mrs. Sharland was always crying out for some trifle to steady her.

Mehalah did not share her mother's anticipations that the danger had passed with the day, that Mrs De Witt's purpose had given way to kinder thoughts; she was quite sure that she would prove relentless and push matters to extremities. It was this certainty which drove her to act once more on her mother's suggestion, and go to the Mersea Rectory, to endeavour to borrow the sum of money needed to relieve them from immediate danger.

She found the parson in his garden without his coat, which hung on the hedge, making a potatoe pie for the winter.

He was on all fours packing the tubers in straw. His boots and gaiters were clogged with clay.

'Hallo!' he exclaimed as Mehalah came up. 'You are the girl they call Glory? Look here. I want you to see my kidneys. Did you ever see the like, come clean out of the ground without canker. Would you like a peck? I'll give them you. Boil beautiful.'

'I want to speak with you, sir.'

'Speak then by all means, and don't mind me. I must attend to my kidneys. A fine day like this is not to be wasted at this time of the year. Go on. There is an ashtop for you. I don't care for the potatoe as a potatoe. It don't boil all to flour as I like. You can have a few if you like. Now go on.'

Down went his head again, and was buried in a nest of straw. Mehalah waited. She did not care to address his back and legs, the only part of his person visible.

'You can't be too careful with potatoes,' said the parson, presently emerging, very red in the face, and with a pat of clay on his nose. 'You must make them comfortable for the winter. Do to others as you would they should do to you. Keep them well from frost, and they will boil beautiful all the winter through. Go on with your story. I am listening,' and in went the head again.

Mehalah lost heart. She could not begin thus.

'Pah! how I sweat,' exclaimed the parson, again emerging. 'The sun beats down on my back, and the black waistcoat draws the heat. And we are in November. This won't last. Have you your potatoes in, Glory?'

'We have only a few on the Ray.'

'You ought to have more. Potatoes like a light soil well drained. You have gravel, and with some good cow-dung or sheep-manure, which is better still, with your fall, they ought to do primely. I'll give you seed. It is all nonsense, as they do here, planting small whole potatoes. Take a good strong tuber, and cut it up with an eye in each piece; then you get a better plant than if you keep the little half-grown potatoes for seed. However, I'm wasting time. I'll be back in a moment. I must fetch another basket load. Go on with your story all the same: I can hear you. I shall only be in the shed behind the Rectory.'

Parson Tyll was a curate of one parish across the Strood and of the two on the island. The rector was non-resident, on the plea of the insalubrity of the spot. He had held the rectory of one parish and the vicarage of the other thirty years, and during that period had visited his cures twice, once to read himself in, and on the other occasion to exact some tithes denied him.

'All right,' said Mr. Tyll, returning from the back premises, staggering under a crate full of roots. 'Go on, I am listening. Pick up those kidneys which have rolled out. Curse it, I hate their falling and getting bruised; they won't keep. There now, you never saw finer potatoes in your life than these. My soil here is the same as yours on the Ray. Don't plant too close, and not in ridges. I'll tell you what I do. I put mine in five feet apart and make heaps round each. I don't hold by ridges. Hillocks is my doctrine. Go on, I am listening. Here, lend me a hand, and chuck me in the potatoes as I want them. You can talk all the same.'

Parson Tyll crept into his heap and seated himself on his haunches. 'Chuck away, but not too roughly. They mustn't be bruised. Now go on, I can stack the tubers and listen all the same.'

'Sir,' said Mehalah, out of heart at her reception, 'we are in great trouble and difficulty.'

'I have no doubt of it; none in the world. You don't grow enough potatoes. Now look at my kidneys. They are the most prolific potatoes I know. I introduced them, and they go by my name. You may ask for them anywhere as Tyll's kidneys. Go on, I am listening.'

'We owe Mrs. De Witt a matter of five and twenty pounds,' began Mehalah, red with shame; 'and how to pay her we do not know.'

'Nor I,' said the parson. 'You have tried to go on without potatoes, and you can't do it. Others have tried and failed. You should keep geese on the saltings, and fowls. Fowls ought to thrive on a sandy soil, but then you have no corn land, that makes a difference. Potatoes, however, especially my kidneys, ought to be a treasure to you. Take my advice, be good, grow potatoes. Go on, I am listening. Chuck me some more. How is the stock in the basket? Does it want replenishing? Look here, my lass, go to the coach-house and bring me some more. There is a heap in the corner; on the left; those on the right are ashtops. They go in a separate pie. You can talk as you go, I shall be here and harkening.'

Mehalah went sullenly to the place where the precious roots were stored, and brought him a basketful.

'By the way,' said the parson, peeping out of his mole-hill at her, 'it strikes me you ought not to be here now. Is there not a sale on your farm to-day?'

'A sale, sir?'

'A sale, to be sure. Mrs. De Witt has carried off my clerk to act as auctioneer, or he would be helping me now with my potatoes. She has been round to several of the farmers to invite them to attend and bid, and they have gone to see if they can pick up some ewes or a cow cheap.'

Mehalah staggered. Was this possible?

'Go on with your story, I'm listening,' continued the parson, diving back into his burrow, so that only the less honourable extremity of his vertebral column was visible. 'Talk of potatoes. There's not one to come up to Tyll's kidneys. Go on, I am all attention! Chuck me some more potatoes.'

But Mehalah was gone, and was making the best of her way back.

Parson Tyll was right. This fine November day was that which it had struck Mrs. De Witt was most suitable for the sale, that would produce the money.

Mehalah had not long left the Strood before a strange procession began to cross the Marshes.

Mrs. De Witt sat aloft in a tax-cart borrowed of Isaac Mead, the publican, by the side of his boy who drove. Behind, very uncomfortably, much in the attitude of a pair of scissors, sat the clerk, folded nearly double in the bottom of the cart; his head reclined on Mrs. De Witt's back and the seat of the vehicle, his legs hung over the board at the back, and swung about like those of a calf being carried to market or to the butcher's. Mrs. De Witt wore her red coat, and a clean washed or stiffly starched cap. She led the way. The road over the Marshes was bad, full of holes, and greasy. A recent tide had corrupted the clay into strong brown glue.

The farmers and others who followed to attend the sale had put up their gigs and carts at the cottage of the Strood keeper, and pursued their way on foot. But Mrs. De Witt was above such feebleness of nerve. She had engaged the trap for the day, and would take her money's worth out of it. The boy had protested at the Strood that the cart of his master could not go over the marshes, that Isaac Mead had not supposed it possible that it would be taken over so horrible and perilous a road. Mrs. De Witt thereupon brought her large blue gingham umbrella down on the lad's back, and vowed she would open him like an oyster with her pocket-knife unless he obeyed her. She looked quite capable of fulfilling her threat, and he submitted.

The cart jerked from side to side. The clerk's head struck Mrs. De Witt several sharp blows in the small of her back. She turned sharply round, pegged at him with the umbrella, and bade him mind his manners.

'Let me get out. I can't bear this, ma'am,' pleaded the man.

'It becomes you to ride to the door as the officer of justice,' answered she. 'If I can ride, so can you. Lie quiet,' and she banged at him with the umbrella again.

At that moment there came a jolt of a more violent description than before, and Mrs. De Witt was suddenly precipitated over the splash-board, and, after a battle in the air, on the back of the prostrate horse, with her feet, hands and umbrella she went into a mud hole. The horse was down, but the knees of the clerk were up far above his head. He struggled to rise, but was unable, and could only bellow for assistance.

Mrs. De Witt picked herself up and assisted the boy in bringing the horse to his feet again. Then she coolly pinned up her gown to her knees, and strode forward. The costume was not so shocking to her native modesty as might have been supposed, nor did it scandalise the farmers, for it was that adopted by the collectors of winkles on the flats. The appearance presented by Mrs. De Witt was, however, grotesque. In the mud her legs had sunk to the knees, and they looked as though she wore a pair of highly polished Hessian boots. The skirt and the red coat gave her a curious nondescript military cut, as half Highlander. Though she walked, she would not allow the clerk to dismount. She whacked at the pendant legs when they rose and protested, and bade the fellow lie still; he was all right, and it was only proper that he, the functionary on the occasion, should arrive in state, instead of on his own shanks.

'If you get up on the seat you'll be bobbed off like a pea on a drum. Lie in the bottom of the cart and be peaceful, as is your profession,' said Mrs. De Witt, with a dig of the umbrella over the side.

They formed a curious assemblage. There were the four brothers Marriage of Peldon, not one of whom had taken a wife. Once, indeed, the youngest, Herbert, had formed matrimonial schemes; but on his ventilating the subject, had been fallen on by his three brothers and three unmarried sisters who kept house for them, as though he had hinted the introduction of a cask of gunpowder into the cellars. He had been scolded and lectured, and taunted, as the apostate, the profligate, the prodigal, who was bent on the ruin of the family, the dissipation of the accumulated capital of years of labour, the introducer of discord into a united household. And yet the household was only united in theory, in fact the brothers were always fighting and swearing at one another about the order of the work to be executed on the farm, and the sisters quarrelled over the household routine.

There was Joshua Pudney, of Smith's Hall, who loved his bottle and neglected his farm, who grew more thistles than wheat, and kept more hunters than cows, a jolly fat red-faced man with white hair, always in top boots. Along with him was Nathaniel Pooley, who combined preaching with farming, was noted for sharp practice in money matters, and for not always coming out of pecuniary transactions with clean hands. Pudney cursed and Pooley blessed, yet the labourers were wont to say that Pudney's curses broke no bones, but Pooley's blessings did them out of many a shilling. Pudney let wheat litter in his stubble, and bid the gleaners go in and be damned, when he threw the gate open to them. Pooley raked the harvest field over thrice, and then opened the gleaning with an invocation to Providence to bless the widow, the fatherless, and the poor who gathered in his fields.

Farmer Wise was a gaunt, close-shaven man, always very neatly dressed, a great snuff-taker. He was a politician, and affected to be a Whig, whilst all the rest of his class were Tories. He was argumentative, combative, and cantankerous, a close, careful man, and reported a miser.

A dealer, riding a black pony, a wonderful little creature that scampered along at a flying trot, came up and slackened rein. He was a stout man in a very battered hat, with shabby coat; a merry man, and a good judge of cattle.

The proceedings of the day were, perhaps, hardly in accordance with strict English law, but then English law was precisely like Gospel precepts, made for other folk. On the Essex marshes people did not trouble themselves much about the legality of their proceedings; they took the law into their own hands. If the law suited them they used it, if not they did without it. But, legally or not legally, they got what they wanted. It was altogether inconvenient and expensive for the recovery of a small debt to apply to a solicitor and a magistrate, and the usual custom was, therefore, to do the thing cheaply and easily through the clerk of the parish constituted auctioneer for the occasion, and the goods of the defaulter were sold by him to an extemporised assembly of purchasers on any day that suited the general convenience. The clerk so far submitted to legal restrictions that he did not run goods up, but down; he began with an absurdly high figure, instead of one preposterously low.

When the cart and its contents and followers arrived at the Ray, the horse was taken out, and the vehicle was run against a rick of hay, into which the shafts were deeply thrust, so as to keep the cart upright, that it might serve as a rostrum for the auctioneer.

'We'll go and take stock first,' said the clerk; 'we've to raise twenty-five pounds for the debt and twenty shillings my costs. What is there to sell?'

'Wait a bit, gaffer,' said the cattle jobber; 'you're a trifle too quick. The old lady must demand the money first.'

'I'm agoing to do so, Mr. Mellonie,' said Mrs. De Witt; 'you teach your grandmother to shell shrimps.' Then, looking round on about twenty persons who had assembled, she said, 'Follow me. Stay! here comes more. Oh! it is Elijah Rebow and his men come to see fair play. Come by water have you, Elijah? We are not going to sell anything of yours, you needn't fear.'

She shouldered her umbrella like an oar, and strode to the house door. Mrs. Sharland was there, white and trembling.

'Have you got my money?' asked Mrs. De Witt.

'Oh, mistress,' exclaimed the unfortunate widow, 'do have pity and patience. Mehalah has just gone to get it.'

'Gone to get it?' echoed Mrs. De Witt. 'Why, where in the name of wonder does she expect to get it?'

'She had gone to Parson Tyll to borrow it.'

'Then she won't get it,' said the drover. 'There's no money to be wrung out of empty breeches pockets.'

'Let me into the house,' said Mrs. De Witt. 'Let us all see what you have got. There's a clock. Drag it out, and stick it up under the tree near the cart. That is worth a few pounds. And take that chair.'

'It is my chair. I sit in it, and I have the ague so bad.'

'Take the chair,' persisted Mrs. De Witt, and Rebow's men carried it forth. 'There's some good plates there. Is there a complete set?'

'There are only six.'

'That is better than none. Out with them. What have you got in the corner cupboard?'

'Nothing but trifles.'

'We'll sell the cupboard and the dresser. You can't move the dresser, Elijah. We'll carry it in our heads. Look at it,' she said to the clerk; 'see you don't forget to put that up. Now shall we go into the bedrooms, or go next to the cowhouse?'

'Leave the bedroom,' said Mellonie, 'you can't sell the bed from under the old woman.'

'I can though, if I don't raise enough,' said Mrs. De Witt. 'I've slept on a plank many a time.'

'Oh dear! Oh dear!' moaned the widow Sharland; 'I wish Mehalah had returned; perhaps she has the money.'

'No chance of that, mistress,' said Rebow. 'You are sold up and done for past escape now. What will you do next, you and that girl Glory, I'd like to know?'

'I think she will get the money,' persisted the widow.

Elijah turned from her with a sneer.

'Outside with you,' shouted Mrs. De Witt. 'The sale is going to begin.'

The men—there were no women present except Mrs. De Witt—quickly evacuated the house and pushed into the stable and cowhouse.

There was no horse, and only one cow. The sheep were on the saltings. There was no cart, and very few tools of any sort. The little farm was solely a sheep farm, there was not an acre of tillage land attached to it.

The clerk climbed up into the cart.

'Stop, stop, for Heaven's sake!' gasped Mehalah dashing up. 'What is this! Why have we not been warned?'

'Oh yes! forewarned indeed, and get rid of the things,' growled Mrs. De Witt. 'But I did tell you what I should do, and precious good-natured I was to do it.'

Mehalah darted past her into the house.

'Tell me, tell me!' cried the excited mother, 'have you the money?'

'No. The parson could not let me have it.'

'Hark! they have begun the sale. What is it they are crying now?'

'The clock, mother. Oh, this is dreadful.'

'They will sell the cow too,' said the widow.

'Certain to do so.'

'There! I hear the dresser's put up. Who has bought the clock?'

'Oh never mind, that matters nothing. We are ruined.'

'Oh dear, dear!' moaned Mrs. Sharland, 'that it should come to this! But I suppose I must, I must indeed. Run, Mehalah, run quick and unrip the belt of my green gown. Quick, fetch it me.'

The girl hastily obeyed. The old woman got her knife, and with trembling hand cut away the lining in several parts of the body. Shining sovereigns came out.

'There are twenty here,' she said with a sigh, 'and we have seven over of what George let us have. Give the wretches the money.'

'Mother, mother!' exclaimed Mehalah. 'How could you borrow! How could you send me——!'

'Never mind, I did not want to use my little store till every chance had failed. Run out and pay the money.'

Mehalah darted from the door.

The clerk was selling the cow.

'Going for twenty-five pounds. What? no one bid, going for twenty-five pounds, and dirt cheap at the money, all silent! Well I never, and such a cow! Going for twenty-three——'

'Stop!' shouted Mehalah. 'Here is Mrs. De Witt's money, twenty-five pounds.'
'Damnation!' roared Elijah, 'where did you get it?'
'Our savings,' answered Mehalah, and turned her back on him.

## CHAPTER XII.
## A GILDED BALCONY.

Mehalah was hurt and angry at her mother's conduct. She thought that she had not been fairly treated. When the loss sustained presumably by Abraham Dowsing's carelessness had been discovered, Mrs. Sharland had not hinted the existence of a private store, and had allowed De Witt to lend her the money she wanted for meeting the rent. Glory regarded this conduct as hardly honest. It jarred, at all events, with her sense of what was honourable. On the plea of absolute inability to pay the rent, they had obtained five and twenty pounds from the young fisherman. Then again, when Mrs. De Witt reclaimed the debt, Mehalah had been subjected to the humiliation of appealing to Mr. Pettican and being repulsed by Admonition. She had been further driven to sue a loan of the parson; she had not, indeed, asked him for the money, but that was only because he avoided, intentionally or not she could not say, giving her the chance. She had gone with the intention of begging, and his manner, and the accidental discovery that the sale was already taking place, had alone prevented her from undergoing the shame of asking and being refused.

She did not like to charge her mother with having behaved dishonourably, for she felt instinctively that her mother's views and hers were not coincident. Her brow was clouded, and an unpleasant gleam flickered in her eyes. She resisted the treatment she had been subjected to as unnecessary. It was only justifiable in an extreme emergency, and no such emergency had existed. Her mother would rather sacrifice her daughter's self-respect than break in on the little hoard.

'Charles said he had money in the bank, did he?' asked Mrs. Sharland.

'Yes.'

'To think of that! My cousin has an account in the bank, and can write his cheques, and one can cash cheques signed Charles Pettican! That is something to be proud of, Mehalah.'

'Indeed, mother?'

'And you say he has a beautiful house, with a verandah. A real gilt balcony. Think of that! And Charles is my cousin, the cousin of your own mother. There's something to think of, there. I couldn't sleep last night with dreaming of that house with its green shutters and a real balcony. I do believe that I shall die happy, if some day I may but see that there gilded—you said it was gilded—balcony. Charles Pettican with a balcony! What is the world coming to next! A real gilded balcony, and two figureheads looking over—there's an idea! Did you tell me there was a sofa in his sitting-room; and I think you said the dressing-table had a pink petticoat with gauze over it. Just think of that. I might have been Mrs. Charles Pettican, if all had gone well, and things had been as they should have, and then I should have had a petticoat to my dressing-table and a balcony afore my window. I am glad you went, it was like the Queen of Sheba visiting Solomon and seeing all his glory, and now you've come back into your own land, and filled me with your tidings.'

Mehalah let her mother meander on, without paying any attention to what she said. Mrs. Sharland had risen some stages in her self-importance since she had heard how prosperous in a pecuniary sense her relation was. It shed a sort of glory on her when she thought that, had fate ruled it so, she might have shared with him this splendour, instead of being poor and lonely on the desolate Ray. Mrs. Sharland would have loved a gossip, but never got a chance of talking to anyone with a similar partiality. Had she married Mr. Charles Pettican she would have been in the vortex of a maelstrom of tittle-tattle. It was something to puff her up to think that if matters had taken another turn this would have been her position in Wyvenhoe.

'I don't think Mrs. De Witt had any notion how rich and distinguished my relatives are, when she came here asking for her five and twenty pounds. I'll take my oath on it, she has no cousin with a balcony and a sofa. I don't suppose we shall be troubled much now, when it is known that my cousin draws cheques, and that the name of Charles Pettican is honoured at the bank.'

'You forget we got, and shall get, no help from him.'

'I do not forget it, Mehalah. I remember perfectly how affably he spoke of me—his Liddy Vince, his pretty cousin. I do not forget how ready he was to lend the money. Twenty pounds! if you had asked fifty, he'd have given it you as readily. He was about to break open his cash-box, as he hadn't the key by him, and would have given me the money I wanted, had not a person who is no relation of mine interposed. That comes of designing women stepping in between near relatives. Charles Pettican is my cousin, and he is not ashamed to acknowledge it; why should he? I have always maintained myself respectable, and always shall.'

'Mother,' said Mehalah, interrupting this watery wash of vain twaddle, 'you should not have borrowed the money of George De Witt. That was the beginning of the mischief?'

'Beginning of what mischief?'

'The beginning of our trouble.'

'No, it was not; Abraham's carelessness was the beginning.'

'But, mother, I repeat it, you did wrong in not producing your hidden store instead of borrowing.'

'I did not borrow. I never asked George De Witt for his money, he proposed to let us have it himself.'

'That is indeed true; but you should have at once refused to take it, and said it was unnecessary for us to be indebted to him, as you had the sum sufficient laid by.'

'That is all very well, Mehalah, but when a generous offer is made me, why should I not accept it? Because there's still some milk of yesterday in the pan, do you decline to milk the cow to-day? I was glad of the opportunity of keeping my little savings untouched. Besides, I always thought George would make you his wife.'

'I thought so too,' said Mehalah in a low tone, and her face became sad and blank as before; she went off into a dream, but presently recovered herself and said, 'Then, when Mrs. De Witt asked for her money, why did you not produce it, and free us of her insults and annoyance?'

'I did not want to part with my money. And it has turned out well. If I had done as you say, we should not have revived old acquaintance, and obtained the valuable assistance of Charles Pettican.'

'He did not assist us.'

'He did as far as he was able. He would have given us the money, had not untoward circumstances intervened. He as good as let us have the twenty pounds. That is something to be proud of—to be helped by a man whose name is honoured at the bank—at the Colchester Bank.'

'But, mother, you have given me inexpressible pain!'

'Pained you!' exclaimed Mrs. Sharland. 'How could I?'

Her eyes opened wide. Mehalah looked at her. They had such different souls, that the girl saw it was of no use attempting to explain to her mother what had wounded her; her sensations belonged to a sense of which her mother was deprived. It is idle to speak of scarlet to a man who is blind.

'I did it all for you,' said Mrs. Sharland reproachfully. 'I was thinking and caring only for you, Mehalah, from beginning to end, from first to last.'

'Thinking and caring for me!' echoed Glory in surprise.

'Of course I was. I put those gold pieces away, one a quarter from the day you were born, till I had no more savings that I could put aside. I put them away for you. I thought that when I was gone and buried, you should have this little sum to begin the world upon, and you would not say that your mother died and left you nothing. Nothing in the world would have made me touch the hoard, for it was your money, Mehalah—nothing but the direst need, and you will do me the justice to say that this was the case to-day. It would have been the worst that could have happened for you to-day had the money not been paid, for you would have sunk in the scale.'

'Mother!' exclaimed Mehalah, intensely moved, 'you did all this for me; you thought and cared for me—for me!'

The idea of her mother having ever done anything for her, ever having thought of her, apart from herself, of having provided for her independently of herself, was too strange and too amazing for Mehalah to take it in at once. As long as she remembered anything she had worked for her mother, thought for her, and denied herself for her, without expecting any return, taking it as a matter of course that she should devote herself to her mother without the other making any acknowledgment.

And now the thought that she had been mistaken, that her mother had really cared for and provided for her, overwhelmed her. She had not wept when she thought that George De Witt was lost to her, but now she dropped into her chair, buried her face in her arms, and burst into a storm of sobs and tears.

Mrs. Sharland looked at her with a puzzled face. She never had understood Mehalah, and she was content to be in the dark as to what was passing in her breast now. She settled back in her chair, and turned back to the thoughts of Charles Pettican's gilt balcony, and petticoated dressing-table.

By degrees Mehalah recovered her composure, then she went up to her mother and kissed her passionately on the brow.

'Mother dear,' she said in a broken voice, 'I never, never will desert you. Whatever happens, our lot shall be cast together.'

Then she reared herself, and in a moment was firm of foot, erect of carriage, rough and imperious as of old.

'I must look after the sheep on the saltings,' she said. 'Abraham's head is turned with the doings here to-day, and he has gone to the Rose to talk and drink it over. The moon is full, and we shall have a high tide.'

Next moment Mrs. Sharland was alone.

The widow heaved a sigh. 'There is no making heads or tails of that girl, I don't understand her a bit,' she muttered.

'I do though,' answered Elijah Rebow at the door. 'I want a word with you, mistress.'

'I thought you had gone, Elijah, after the sale.'

'No, I did not leave with the rest. I hung about in the marshes, waiting a chance when I might speak with you by yourself. I can't speak before Glory; she flies out.'

'Come in, master, and sit down. Mehalah is gone down to the saltings, and will not be back for an hour.'

'I must have a word with you. Where has Glory been? I saw her go off t'other day in gay Sunday dress towards Fingringhoe. What did she go after?'

Mrs. Sharland raised herself proudly. 'I have a cousin lives at Wyvenhoe, and we exchange civilities now and then. I can't go to him and he can't come to me, so Mehalah passes between us.'

'What does she go there for?'

'My cousin, Mr. Charles Pettican—I dare say you have heard the name, it is a name that is honoured at the bank———' she paused and pursed up her lips.

'Go on, I have heard of him, an old shipbuilder.'

'He made his fortune in shipbuilding,' said Mrs. Sharland. 'He has laid by a good deal of money, and is a free and liberal man with it, among his near relatives.'

'Curse him,' growled Elijah, 'he let you have the money?'

'I sent Mehalah to my cousin Charles, to ask him to lend me a trifle, being for a moment inconvenienced,' said Mrs. Sharland with stateliness.

'She—Glory—went cringing for money to an old shipbuilder!' exclaimed Rebow with fury in his face.

'She did not like doing so,' answered the widow, 'but I entreated her to put her prejudices in her pocket, and do as I wished. You see, Master Rebow, this was not like asking strangers. Charles is my cousin, my nearest living relative, and some day, perhaps, there is no knowing———' she winked, and nodded, and ruffled up in her pride. 'We are his nearest of kin, and he is an old man, much older than I am. I am young compared to him, and he is half-paralysed.'

'He gave the money without any difficulty or demur?' asked Elijah, his face flaming.

'He was most willing, anxious, I may say, to help. You see, Master Rebow, he is well off, and has no other relatives. He is a man of fortune, and has a gilt balcony before his house, and a real sofa in his sitting-room. His name is engraved on brass on a plate on the door, it commands respect and receives honour at the Colchester Bank.'

'So you are fawning on him, are you?' growled Elijah.

'He has real oil-paintings on his walls. There's some in water-colours, and some in worsted work, but I make no count of them, but real oils, you know; there's something to think of in that. A man don't break out into oil unless he has money in the bank at command.'

Mrs. Sharland was delighted with the opportunity of airing her re-discovered cousin, and exalting his splendour before some one other than her daughter.

'A valance all round his bed—there's luxury!' said the widow, 'and that bed a whole tester. As for his dressing-table, it wears a better petticoat than I, pink calico that looks like silk, and over it gauze, just like a lady at an assembly ball, a real quality lady. My cousin is not one to see his Liddy—he calls me his pretty cousin Liddy—my name before I was married was Vince, but instead of Sharland it might have been Pettican, if all had been as it ought. I say cousin Charles is not the man to see his relatives sold up stick and stock by such as Mrs. De Witt.'

'You think if you can't pay me my rent, he will help you again?'

'If I feel a little behind-hand, Master Rebow, I shall not scruple sending Mehalah to him again. Charles is a man of kind and generous heart, and it is touching how he clings to his own flesh and blood. He has taken a great affection for Mehalah. He calls her niece, and wants her to look on him as an uncle, but you know that is not the real relationship. He was my mother's only brother's son, so we was first cousins, and he can only be a cousin of some sort to Mehalah, can he?'

'Oh curse your cousinships!' broke in Elijah angrily. 'To what an extent can you count on his help?'

'To any amount,' said the widow, too elated to care to limit her exaggeration.

'How is Mehalah? Is she more inclined to think of me?'

Mrs. Sharland shook her head.

'She don't love me?' said Elijah with a laugh.

'I fear not, Elijah.'

'She won't be disposed to take up her quarters at Red Hall?'

Mrs. Sharland sighed a negative.

'Nor to bear with me near her all day?'

'No, Elijah.'

'No, she won't,' said he with a jerky laugh, 'she won't till she is made to. She won't come to Red Hall till she can't help it. She won't live with me till I force her to it. Damn that cousin! He stands in my path. I will go see him. There comes Mehalah, back from the saltings. I must be off.'

'My cousin is a man of importance,' observed Mrs. Sharland, bridling up at Elijah's slighting remark. 'He is not accustomed to be cursed. Men with names that the bank honours, and who have gilded balconies over their doors, don't like it, they don't deserve it.'

CHAPTER XIII.

THE FLAG FLIES.

A month after the interrupted auction, Elijah Rebow appeared one day before Mr. Pettican's door at Wyvenhoe. The gull was screaming and flying at his feet. His stick beat a loud summons on the door, but the noise within was too considerable for the notices of a visitor to be heard and responded to.

Elijah remained grimly patient outside, with a sardonic smile on his face, and amused himself with tormenting the gull.

Presently the door flew open, and a dashing young woman flung out, with cherry-coloured ribands in her bonnet, and cherry colour in her cheeks.

'All right, Monie?' asked a voice from the balcony, and then Elijah was aware of a young man in a blue guernsey and a straw hat lounging over the balustrade, between the figureheads, smoking a pipe.

'He has learned his place at last,' answered Admonition; 'I never saw him so audacious before. Come along, Timothy.' The young man disappeared, and presently emerged at the door. At the same time a little withered face was visible at the window, with a dab of putty, as it seemed, in the middle of it, but which was probably a nose flattened against the glass. Two little fists were also apparent shaken violently, and a shrill voice screamed imprecations and vowed vengeance behind the panes, utterly disregarded by Admonition and Timothy, who stared at Elijah, and then struck down the gravelled path without troubling themselves to ask his business.

The door was left open, and Elijah entered, but stood on the threshold, and looked after the pair as they turned out of the garden-gate, and took the Colchester road, laughing and talking, and Admonition tossing her saucy head, in the direction of the face at the window, and then taking the sailor's arm.

A wonderful transformation had taken place in Mrs. Pettican's exterior as well as in her manner since her marriage.

She had been a soft demure little body with melting blue eyes and rich brown hair very smoothly laid on either side of her brow—a modest brow with guilelessness written on it—and the simplest little curls beside her round cheeks. She wore only black, in memory of a never-to-be-forgotten mother, and a neat white cap and apron. If she allowed herself a little colour, it was only a flower in her bosom. Poor Charles Pettican! How often he had supplied that flower!

'I can't pick one myself, Admonition,' he had said; 'you go into my garden and pluck a rose.'

'But you must give it me,' she had invariably said on such occasions, with a shy eye just lifted, and then dropped again.

And of course Mr. Pettican had presented the flower with a compliment, and an allusion to her cheek, which had always deepened the modest flush in it.

Now Admonition affected bright colours—cherry was her favourite. She who had formerly dressed below her position, now dressed above it; she was this day flashing through Wyvenhoe in a straw broad-brimmed hat with crimson bows, lined with crimson, and in a white dress adorned with carnation knots, and a red handkerchief over the shoulders worn bare in the house. There was no doubt about it, that Admonition looked very well thus attired, better even than in her black.

Her hair was now frizzled over her brow, and she wore a mass of curls about her neck, confined in the house by a carnation riband. The soft eyes were now marvellously hard when directed upon the husband, and only retained their velvet for Timothy. The cheek now blushed at nothing, but flamed at the least opposition.

'I married one woman and got another,' said Charles Pettican to himself many times a day. 'I can't make it out at all. Marriage to a woman is, I suppose, much like a hot bath to a baby; it brings out all the bad humours in the blood. Young girls are as alike as flour and plaster of Paris, and it is not till you begin to be the making of them that you find the difference. Some make into bread, but others make into stone.'

When Elijah Rebow entered the little parlour, he found Mr. Pettican nearly choked with passion. He was ripping at his cravat to get it off, and obtain air. His face was nearly purple. He took no notice of his visitor for a few moments, but continued shaking his fist at the window, and then dragging at his neckcloth.

Being unable to turn himself about, the unfortunate man nearly strangled himself in his inability to unwind his cravat. This increased his anger, and he screamed and choked convulsively.

'You will smother yourself soon,' observed Elijah dryly, and going up to Mr. Pettican, he loosened the neckcloth.

The cripple lay back and panted. Presently he was sufficiently recovered to project his head towards Rebow, and ask him what he wanted, and who he was.

Elijah told him his name. Charles Pettican did not pay attention to him; his mind was engrossed by other matters.

'Come here,' said he, 'here, beside me. Do you see them?'

'See what?' asked Elijah in return, gruffly, as Pettican caught his arm, and drew him down, and pointed out of the window.

'There they are. Isn't it wexing to the last degree of madness?'

'Do you mean your daughter and her sweetheart?'

'Daughter!' echoed the cripple. 'Daughter! I wish she was. No, she's my wife. I don't mean her.'

'What do you mean then?'

'Why, my crutches. Don't you see them?'

'No, I do not,' answered Rebow looking round the room.

'They are not here,' said Pettican. 'Admonition flew out upon me, because I wouldn't draw more money from the bank, and she took away my crutches, to confine me

76

till I came into her whimsies. There they are. They are flying at the mast-head. She got that cousin of hers to hoist them. She knows I can't reach them, that here I must lie till somebody fetches them down for me. You should have heard how they laughed, those cousins as they call themselves, as my crutches went aloft. Oh! it was fun to them, and they could giggle and cut jokes about me sitting here, flattening my nose at the pane, and seeing my crutches hoisted. They might as well have robbed me of my legs—better, for they are of no use, and my crutches are. Fetch me them down.'

Elijah consented, chuckling to himself at the distress of the unfortunate shipbuilder. He speedily ran the crutches down, and returned them to Pettican.

'Turning me into fun before the whole town!' growled Pettican, 'exposing my infirmity to all the world! It was my wife did it. Admonition urged on her precious cousin Timothy to it. He did fare to be ashamed, but she laughed him into it, just as Eve jeered Adam into eating the apple. She has turned off my servant too, and here am I left alone and helpless in the house all day, whilst she is dancing off to Colchester market with her beau—cousin indeed! What do you think, master—I don't know your name.'

'Elijah Rebow, of Red Hall.'

'What do you think, Master Rebow? That cousin has been staying here a month, a whole calendar month. He has been given the best room, and there have been junketings without number; they have ate all the oysters out of my pan, and drank up all my old stout, and broken the necks of half the whisky bottles in my cellar, and smoked out all my havannahs. I have a few boxes, and indulge myself occasionally in a good cigar, they come costly. Well, will you believe me! Admonition routs out all my boxes, and gives her beau a havannah twice a day or more often, as he likes, and I haven't had one between my lips since he came inside my doors. That lot of old Scotch whisky I had down from Dundee is all drunk out. Before I married her, Admonition would touch nothing but water, and tea very weak only coloured with the leaf; now she sucks stout and rum punch and whisky like a fish. It is a wonder to me she don't smoke too.'

The cripple tucked his recovered crutches under his arms, rolled himself off his chair, and stumped vehemently half a dozen times round the room. He returned at length, out of breath and very hot, to his chair, into which he cast himself.

'Put up my legs, please,' he begged of Elijah. 'There!' he said, 'I have worked off my excitement a little. Now go into the hall and look in the box under the stairs, there you will find an Union Jack. Run it up to the top of the mast. I don't care. I will defy her. When that girl who came here the other day—I forget her name—sees the flag flying she will come and help me. If Admonition has cousins, so have I, and mine are real cousins. I doubt but those of Admonition are nothing of the sort. If that girl——'

'What girl?' asked Rebow gloomily, as he folded his arms across his breast, and scowled at Charles Pettican.

'I don't know her name, but it is written down. I have it in my note-book—Ah! Mehalah Sharland. She is my cousin, her mother is my cousin. I'll tell you what I will do, master. But before I say another word, you go up for me into the best bed-room—the blue room, and chuck that fellow's things out of the window over the balcony, and let the gull have the pecking and tearing of them to pieces. I know he has his best jacket on his back; more's the pity. I should like the gull to have the clawing and the beaking of that, but he can make a tidy mess of his other traps; and will do it.'

'Glory——' began Elijah.

'Ah! you are right there,' said Pettican. 'It will be glory to have routed cousin Timothy out of the house; and if the flag flies, my cousin—I forget her name—Oh! I see, Mehalah—will come here and bring her mother, and before Master Timothy returns with

Admonition from market—they are going to have a shilling's worth on a merry-go-round, I heard them scheme it—my cousins will be in possession, and cousin Timothy must content himself with the balcony, or cruise off.'

'Glory—or Mehalah, as you call her.'

'I'll not listen to another word, till you have chucked that fellow's trape overboard. There's a portmantle of his up there, chuck that over with the rest, and let the gull have the opening and examination of the contents.'

There was nothing for it but compliance, if Elijah wished to speak on the object of his visit. The old man was in an excited condition which would not allow him to compose his mind till his caprices were attended to, and his orders carried out. Rebow accordingly went upstairs and emptied the room of all evidences of its having been occupied. There was a discharge of boots, brush, clothes, pipes, into the garden, at which Pettican rubbed his hands and clucked like a fowl.

Rebow returned to the parlour, and the old shipbuilder was profuse in his thanks. 'Now,' said he, 'run the flag up. You haven't done that yet. Then come and have a glass of spirits. There is some of the whisky left, not many bottles, but there is some, and not locked up, for Admonition thought she had me safe when she hoisted my crutches up the mast-head. Go now and let the bunting float as of old in my halcyon days.' This was also done; the wind took, unfurled, and flapped the Union Jack, and the old man crowed with delight, and swung his arms.

'That is right. I haven't seen it fly for many months; not since I was married. Now that girl, I forget her name, oh! I have it here—Mehalah—will see it, and come to the rescue. Do you know her?'

'What, Glory?'

'That ain't her name. Her name is—is—Mehalah.'

'We call her Glory. She is the girl. I know her,' he laughed and his eyes glittered. He set his teeth. Charles Pettican looked at him, and thought he had never seen a more forbidding countenance. He was frightened, and asked hastily,

'Who are you?'

'I am Elijah Rebow, of Red Hall.'

'I don't know you or the place.'

'I am in Salcott and Virley. You know me by name.'

'Oh! perhaps I do. My memory is not what it once was. I get so put out by my wife's whimsies that I can't collect my faculties all at once. I think I may have heard of you, but I haven't met you before.'

'I am the landlord of Glory—Mehalah, you call her. The Ray, which is their farm, belongs to me, with all the marshes and the saltings, and all that thereon is. I bought it for eight hundred pounds. Glory and her mother are mine.'

'I don't understand you.'

'I bought the land, and the farm, and them, a job lot, for eight hundred pounds.'

'I remember, the girl—I forget her name, but I have it here, written down——'

'Glory!'

'No, not that, Mehalah. I wish you wouldn't call her what she is not, because it confuses me; and I have had a deal to confuse me lately. Marriage does rummage a man's hold up so. Mehalah came here a few weeks back to ask me to lend her some money, as her mother could not pay the rent. Her mother is my cousin, Liddy Vince that was, I used to call her "Pretty Liddy," or Lydia Languish, after a character in a play, because of her ague, and because she sort of languished of love for me. And I don't deny it, I was sweet on her once, but the ague shivers stood in the way of our love waxing wery hot.'

78

'You lent her the money.'

'I—I——' hesitated Mr. Pettican. 'You see how I am circumstanced, my wife——'

'You lent her the money. Mistress Sharland told me so.'

'She did!' exclaimed Pettican in surprise.

'Yes, she did. Now I want to know, will you do that again? I am landlord. I bought the Ray for eight hundred pounds, and I don't want to drop my money without a return. You understand that. A man doesn't want to give his gold away, and be whined out of getting interest for it by an old shivering, chattering woman, and flouted out of it by a devil of a girl.' His hands clenched fiercely.

'Of course, of course,' said the cripple. 'I understand you. You think those two can't manage the farm, and were better out of it.'

'I want to be sure of my money,' said Elijah, knitting his dark brows, and fixing his eyes intently on Pettican.

'I quite understand,' said the latter, and tapping his forehead, he added, 'I am a man of business still. I am not so old as all that, whatever Admonition may say.'

'Now what I want to know,' pursued Elijah, 'is this—for how long are you going to pay your cousin's rent? For how long is that Glory to come to me and defy me, and throw the money down before me?'

'I don't quite take you,' said Pettican.

'How many times will you pay their rent?' asked Rebow.

'Well!' said the cripple, passing his hand over his face. 'I don't want them to stay at your farm at all. I want them to come here and take care of me. I cannot defend myself. If I try to be a man—that girl, I forget her name, you confuse me about it—told me to be a man, and I will be a man, if she will back me up. I have been a man somewhat, have I not, master, in chucking cousin Timothy's traps to the gull—that I call manly. You will see the girl——Mehalah—I have the name now. I will keep my note-book open at the place. Mehalah, Mehalah, Mehalah, Mehalah.'

'I want to know——' broke in Elijah.

'Let me repeat the name ten times, and then I shall not forget it again.' Pettican did so. 'You called her something else. Perhaps we are not speaking of the same person.'

'Yes, we are. I call her Glory. I am accustomed to that name. Tell me what you want with her.'

'I want her and her mother to come and live with me, and take care of me, and then I can be a man, and make head against the wind that is now blowing in my teeth. Shall you see them?'

'Yes.'

'To-day?'

'Perhaps.'

'Then pray make a point of seeing the girl or her mother, in case she should not notice the flag, and say that I wish them to come here at once; at once it must be, or I shall never have courage to play the man again, not as I have to-day. They did put my monkey up by removing my crutches and hoisting them to the masthead, leaving me all by myself and helpless here. I should wish Mehalah to be here before Admonition and her beau return. They won't be back till late. There's a horsemanship at Colchester as well as a merry-go-round, and they are going to both, and perhaps to the theatre after that. There'll be junketings and racketings, and I—poor I—left here with no one to attend to me, and my crutches at the mast-head. You will tell the girl and her mother that I expect their help, and I will be a man, that I will. It would be something to boast of, would it not, if Timothy were to return and find his room occupied and his baggage picked to rags, and if Admonition were to discover that I have cousins as well as she?'

'You are bent on this?'

'I rely on you. You will see them and tell them to come to me, and I will provide for them whilst I am alive, and afterwards—when I am no more—we won't talk or think of such an eventuality. It isn't pleasant to contemplate, and may not happen for many years. I am not so old as you might think. My infirmity is due to accident; and my digestion is, or rather was, first-rate. I could eat and drink anything before I was married. Now I am condemned to see others eat and drink what I have laid in for my own consumption, and I am put off with the drumstick of the fowl, or the poorest swipes of ale, whilst the others toss off my stout—bottled stout. I will not endure this any longer. Tell that girl—I forget her name—and her mother that they must come to me.'

'But suppose they will not come.'

'They will, I know they will. The female heart is tender and sympathetic, and compassionates misery. My suffering will induce them to come. If that will not, why then the prospects of being comfortably off and free from cares will make them come. I have plenty of money. I won't tell you, I have not told Admonition, how much. I have money in the Colchester Bank. I have South Sea shares, and insurances, and mortgages, and I shall not let Admonition have more money than I can help, as it all goes on cousin Timothy, and whirligigs and horsemanships, or regattas, and red ribands, and what not; none is spent on me. No, no. The Sharlands shall have my money. They are my cousins. I have cousins as well as Admonition. I will be a man and show that I have courage too. But I have another inducement that will be sure to bring them.'

'What is that?'

'I have observed,' said Pettican, with a hiccuppy giggle, 'that just as tom-cats will range all over the country in search of other tom-cats, just for the pleasure of clawing them and tearing out their hair, so women will hunt the whole country-side for other women, if there be a chance of fighting them. Tell my cousin Liddy that Admonition is game, she has teeth, and tongue, and nails, and sets up her back in a corner, and likes a scrimmage above everything, and my word for it, Liddy—unless the ague has taken the female nature out of her—will be here before nightfall to try her teeth, and tongue, and nails on Admonition. It is said that if on a May morning you rub your eyes with cuckoo spittle, you see things invisible before, the fairies in the hoes dancing and feasting, swimming in eggshells on the water to bore holes in ships' sides, milking the cows before the maids come with the pail, and stealing the honey from the hives. Well, marriage does much the same sort of thing to a man as salving his eyes in cuckoo spittle; it affords him a vision of a world undreamt of before; it gives him an insight into what is going on in the female world, and the workings and brewings and the mischief in women's hearts. Tell Liddy Sharland about my Admonition, and she will be here, with all her guns run out and ready charged, before nightfall.'

Rebow shook his head. 'Mistress Sharland and Glory won't come.'

'Don't say so. They must, or I shall be undone. I cannot live as I have, tyrannised over, insulted, trampled on by Admonition and her cousin. I will no longer endure it. The flag is flying. I have proclaimed my independence and defiance. But, as you see, I am unable to live alone. If Liddy and her daughter will not come to me, I shall be driven to do something desperate. My life has become intolerable, I will bear with Admonition no longer.'

'What will you do?' asked Elijah with a sneer.

'I tell you, I do not care. I am reckless, I will even fire the house, and burn it over their heads.'

'What good would that do?'

'What good would it do?' repeated Pettican. 'It would no longer be a shelter for Admonition and that beau Timothy. I am not going to be trifled with, I have endured too much. I will be a man. I shouldn't mind a bit smoking them out of this snug lair.'

'And what about yourself?'

'Oh, as for me, I could go to the Blue Anchor, and put up there for the rest of my days. I think I could be happy in a tavern, happier than here, and I should have the satisfaction of thinking I had shaken the weevils out of the biscuit.'

Elijah started, and strode up and down the room, with head bent, and his eyes fixed on the floor. His hands were clenched and rigid at his side.

'You will tell Liddy,' said the cripple, watching him.

'Smoke them out! Ha! ha! that is a fine idea!' burst forth from Elijah, with a laugh.

'You will tell Liddy,' repeated Charles Pettican. 'You must, you know, or I am lost. If Admonition were to return with Timothy at her heels, and were to find the flag flying, and me alone——' he passed his agitated hand over his face, and his lips trembled.

'I see,' said Rebow. 'You would then cease to be a man.'

It was late when Admonition and her cousin returned from the market. It was so dark that they did not see the flag. But as Admonition put her hand on the gate it was grasped.

'Stop,' said Elijah. 'A word with you.'

'Who are you?' asked Mrs. Pettican in alarm, and Timothy swaggered forward to her defence.

'Never mind who I am. I have waited here some hours to warn you. Was there a girl, a handsome girl, a glorious girl, here to see that man, your husband, a month ago? You need not answer. I know there was. She is his cousin. He lent her money.'

'No, he did not. I stopped that, didn't I, Tim?'

'He lent her money. You think you stopped that, but you did not. He let her have the money, twenty pounds, how I know not. She had his money, and she will have more, all, unless you keep a sharp watch on him.'

'Tim! do you hear this?' asked Admonition.

'He will send for his cousin to live in the house with him, and to support him against you.'

'Oh, oh! That's fine, isn't it, Tim?'

'If they come, your reign is at an end. That girl, Glory, has a head of iron and the heart of a lion. No one can stand against her but one. There is only one in all the world has dared to conquer her, and he will do it yet. Don't you think you will be able to lift a little finger against her will. She will be too strong for you and a hundred of your Timothys.'

Admonition laughed. 'My little mannikin daren't do it. He is under my thumb.'

'The flag is flying,' sneered Elijah.

At that moment the faint light of evening broke through the clouds and Admonition saw the Union Jack at the mast-head.

'He is right. There is audacity! Run, Tim, haul it down, and bring it me. It shall go into the kitchen fire to boil the water for a glass of grog.'

CHAPTER XIV.

ON THE BURNT HILL.

It was Christmas Eve. A hard frost had set in. The leaves which had hung on the thorn trees on the Ray rained off and were whirled away by the wind and scattered over the rising and falling waters in the Rhyn. On the saltings were many pools, filled from below, through crab burrows, from the channels; when the tide mounted, the water squirted up through these passages and brimmed the pools, and when the tide fell, it was sucked down through them as if running out of a colander. Now a thin film of ice was formed about the edges of these pondlets, and the marsh herbs that dipped in them were encased in crystal. The wild geese and ducks came in multitudes, and dappled the water of Mersea channel.

'There's four gone,' said Abraham Dowsing in a sulky voice to Mehalah.

'Four what?'

'Four ewes to be sure, of what else have we more than one?'

'Where are they?'

'That is what I should like to know. Two went yesterday, but I said nothing about it, as I thought they might be found, or that I hadn't counted aright; but there's two more missing to-day.'

'What can have become of them?'

'It's no use asking me. Is it like I should know?'

'But this is most extraordinary. They must have wandered off the saltings, on to the causeway, and so away.'

'That is likely, ain't it,' said Abraham. 'It is like the ways of sheep, to scatter, and two or three to go off and away from all the flock. I'll believe that when sheep change their nature.'

'They must have fallen into a pool and been drowned.'

'Then I should find their carcases; but I haven't. Perhaps there has been a spring tide at the wrong time of the year and overflowed and drowned them. That's likely, isn't it?'

'But, Abraham, they must be found.'

'Then you must find 'em yourself.'

'Where can they be?'

'I've told you it is no use asking me.'

'Can they have been stolen?'

'I reckon that is just about it.'

'Stolen!' exclaimed Mehalah, her blood flashing to her face and darkening cheek and brow. 'Do you mean to tell me that some scoundrel has been here in the night, and carried off four of our ewes?'

Abraham shrugged his shoulders; 'Mud tells tales at times.'

Mehalah trembled with anger.

'Some boat was here last night, and night afore, and the keel marks remain. I saw them, and I saw footprints of sheep too, near them.'

'When?'

'The tide is up, and you can't see. Near the Burnt Hill.'

'Abraham, this is not to be borne.'

'Who is to help it?'

'I will. I will watch,' she stamped her foot fiercely on the red glasswort; 'I will kill the cowardly sneaking thief who comes here to rob the widow and the orphan.'

'You must see him first,' said Abraham, 'and sheep-stealers don't generally let themselves be seen.'

'A man who steals sheep can be hung for it.'

'Yes.'

'I'll catch him,' she laughed, 'and the gallows will be set up on the Burnt Hill, and then he shall dangle till his bones drop away into the ooze.'

'You must catch him first,' said the shepherd, and shrugged his shoulders again.

Mehalah strode up and down in the marsh, her brows knit, and the veins swollen on her temples. She breathed fast and her blood sang in her ears. To be robbed in this cowardly manner! The thought was maddening. Hitherto she and her mother had deemed themselves perfectly safe on the Ray: nothing had ever been taken from them; the ooze and the sea water walled them in. The Ray was a trap from which there was no escape save by boat. It was said that once a deserter found his way into Mersea Isle and lingered about the marshes for many days. He dared not return by the causeway, thinking it would be watched and he would be secured, and he had no money wherewith to bribe a boatman to put him across elsewhere. One evening he lit on a farmer with a spade over his shoulder going to the sea-wall to block a rent against an expected tide. He fell on the man from behind, wrenched away his spade and cut his head open with it, then turned out his pockets in search of coin, but found none. The man was taken. He could not escape, and was hung on the marshes where the murder was done, by the mouth of the Pyefleet.

If Mersea was a trap, how much more so the Ray. The Sharlands had not even a lock to their door. No one was ever seen on the island after dark save those who dwelt there, for the hill was surrounded on all sides, save where girt by the sea, by a labyrinth of creeks and pools. A robber there would be like a fly in a cobweb, to be caught at once. The sheep were allowed to ramble all over the marsh and saltings, they could thread their way; and it was only when the moon was full or new, and the wind in the south-east, that the shepherd drove them into fold till the waters subsided. There were times—such as the coincidence of a peculiar wind with an equinoctial tide—when to leave the sheep on the marsh would be to ensure their being drowned. This was so well known, that precaution was always taken against the occasion.

The sense of being treated unjustly, of being cruelly wronged, of advantage being taken of their feebleness, filled Mehalah's heart with bitterness, with rage. An overmastering desire for revenge came upon her. She, a girl, would defend her property, and chastise the man who injured her. She gave up all thought of obtaining the assistance of Abraham, if it ever entered her mind. The old man was too slow in his movements, and dull of sight and hearing, to be of use. As likely as not, moreover, he would refuse to risk himself on the saltings at night, to expose himself to the ague damp or the bullet. What could he, a feeble old loon, do against a sturdy sheep-stealer?

'Whom do you suspect?' asked Glory abruptly.

He drew up his shoulders.

'Come, tell me.'

'An empty belly.'

'Abraham! one man cannot have taken four sheep for himself.'

Another shrug.

There was nothing to be got out of the dogged rustic. Mehalah waited till evening, then she wrapped a cloak round her, put her pistol in her belt, and walked through the marsh to the point indicated by the shepherd as the Burnt Hill.

Through all the low flat coast land of this region, above the saltings, or pasture overflowed by high tides occasionally, are scattered at irregular intervals large broad circular mounds of clay burned to brick red, interspersed with particles of charcoal. A few fragments of bone are found in them, relics of the meals of those who raised these heaps, but they cover no urns, and enclose no cists, they contain no skeletons. They were never intended as funeral monuments, and are quite different from the hoes or barrows which stand on high land, and which were burial mounds. The burnt or red hills are always situate at high-water mark; near them, below the surface of the vegetable deposit, are multitudes of oyster shells. Near them also are sometimes found, sunk in the marsh, polished chert weapons. Who raised these mounds? For what purpose were they reared? These are questions that cannot be answered satisfactorily. One thing is certain. An immense amount of wood must have been consumed to burn such a mass of clay, and the country must then have been more overgrown with timber than at present. Many of the mounds are now enclosed in fields by sea-walls which hold out the tide, the plough has been drawn over them, and the spade has scattered them over the surface, colouring a whole field brick red, and making it rich for the production of corn. There is no better manure than a red hill.

But why were these mounds so laboriously raised? The tradition of the marsh-dwellers is that they were platforms for huts, the earth burned as a prevention to ague. It is curious that in the marshy regions of Central Africa the natives adopt a precisely similar method for their protection from miasma. But why men dwelt in such numbers on the saltings remains undetermined. Whether they lived there to burn the glasswort for nitre, or to steam the sea water for salt, or to take charge of oyster grounds, is uncertain. Fragments, very broken, of pottery are found in these heaps, scattered throughout them, but not a specimen of a perfect vessel. The burnt hills are built up on the old shingle of the shore, with no intervening line of vegetable matter, the growth of the marsh has been later and has risen about their bases and has partly buried them.

Glory reached the Burnt Hill, and stood on it. A cold east wind wailed over the waste; a white fog like curd lay on the water, and the surface of the saltings, clinging to the surface and rising scarce above three feet from it. Here and there it lifted itself in a vaporous column, and moved along in the wind like a white spectral woman, nodding her head and waving her arms cumbered with wet drapery. Above, the sky was clear, and a fine crescent moon sparkled in it without quenching the keenness of the stars. Cassiopeia was glorious in her chair, Orion burned sideways over Mersea Isle. No red gleam was visible to-night from the tavern window at the City, the veil of fog hung over it and curtained it off. To the north-west was a silvery glow at the horizon, then there rose a pure ray as of returning daylight, it was answered by a throb in the north-east, then it broke into two rays, and again united and spread, and suddenly was withdrawn. Mehalah had often seen the Aurora, and she knew that the signals portended increased cold or bad weather.

She seated herself on the mound, and drew her cloak about her more closely, the damp cold bit into her flesh; she knew she was safe from ague on the burnt earth.

Her anger subsided, not that she resented the wrong the less, but that her mind had passed to other contemplations. She was thinking of George, of her dead hopes, of the blankness of the future before her. A little sunlight had fallen on her sad and monotonous life, but it had been withdrawn, and had left her with nothing to live for, save her mother. Her heart had begun to expand as a flower, and a frost had fallen on it, and blackened its petals. She brooded now on the past. She wished for nothing in the future. She had no care for the present. It was all one to her what befell her, so long as her mother were cared for. She had no one else to love. She was without a friend. She would resent an injury, and fight an enemy. George might have introduced her into a new world of gentleness, and pity, and love. Now the door to that world was shut for ever, and she must beat her way through a world of hard realities, where every man's hand was lifted against his brother, and where was hate and resentment, and exacting of the uttermost farthing. She had gone forth seeking help, and except from George, had found none. Mrs. De Witt, Phoebe Musset, Admonition, such were the women she had met; and the men were selfish as Parson Till, fools as Charles Pettican, surly as Abraham Dowsing, or brutal as Elijah Rebow.

Hark!—She caught the dip of an oar.

She drew in her breath and raised her head. Then she saw a boat shoot out of the mist, white and ghost-like as the mist forms that stalked over the water, and in the boat a man.

There he was! The sheep-stealer, come once more to rob her mother and herself. At once her furious passion boiled up in her veins. She saw before her the man who had wronged her; she thought nothing of her own weakness beside his strength, of there being no one within call to come to her aid, should his arm be stouter than hers. She sprang to her feet with a shout, such as an Indian might utter on leaping on his foe, and rushed to the water's edge, just as the man had landed, and had her hands at his throat in a moment.

'You coward, you thief!' she cried shaking him savagely.

'Glory!'

In an instant a pair of stronger hands had wrenched her hands away and pinioned them.

'By heaven! you wild cat, what are you flying at me like that for? What has brought you here at this time of night?'

Mehalah was abashed. Her rage sank. She had mistaken her man. This was no sheep-stealer. She could not speak, so great was her agitation. She writhed to free herself, but writhed in vain. Elijah laughed at her attempts.

'What are you here for?' he asked again. 'Can you not answer my question?'

'Some one has been stealing our ewes,' she said.

'And you took me for the thief,' said Rebow. 'Much obliged for the compliment. Me—the owner of Red Hall, and the man that purchased the Ray, the farm house, and the marshes and the saltings and all that thereon is for eight hundred pounds, to be taken and hanged for sheep-lifting! A likely story, Glory. You must manage better another time.'

'What brings you here?' asked Mehalah sullenly, angry with herself and with him.

'That is the question I asked of you, and you return it. I will tell you. I am out duck-shooting, but the mist lies so thick on the water, and eats into the marrow of the bones. I could see no ducks, and I was freezing in my punt; so I have come to lie with my gun on the Burnt Hill awhile till the fog clears, as it will in an hour, when I shall return.'

'Were you here yesterday night?'

'No, I was not; I was up Tottesbury creek and got a dozen pair of wild duck. Will you have some? I have a pair or two in the punt.'

'I have refused them before, and I refuse them again.'

'Why do you ask me if I were here yesternight?'

'Because then two sheep were taken. Were you here the night before?'

'No, I was then on Abbots' Hall marshes. Do you suspect me still of sheep-stealing?' he asked scoffingly.

'I do not, but I thought had you been here you might have seen some signs of the villains who have robbed us.'

'Come here, Glory! out of the fog on to the Burnt Hill.'

'I am going home.'

'You are not, till I have said what I have to say. Come out of the ague damps.'

'I am going home, now.'

He held her by both wrists. She was strong, but her strength was nothing to his. She made no great effort to get away. If he chose to speak to her, she would listen to him. If she struggled in his grasp, it would make him think she feared him. She would not allow him to suppose himself of such importance to her. If he insulted her, she had her pistol, and she would not scruple to defend herself.

He drew her to the top of the mount; there they were clear of the mist, which lay like snow below and round them, covering the morass and the water. The clear cut crescent moon hung over a clump of pines on Mersea. Rebow looked at it, then waved an arm in the direction.

'Do you see Grim's Hoe yonder?—That great barrow with the Scotch pines on top? Do you know how it comes there? Have you heard the tale?'

Mehalah was silent.

'I will tell you, for I often think of it, and so will you when you have been told the tale. In the old times when the Danes came here, they wintered on Mersea Isle, and in the summer they cruised all along the coast, burning and plundering and murdering. There were two chiefs to them, brothers, who loved one another, they were twins, born the same hour, and they had but one heart and soul; what one willed that willed the other, what one desired that the other desired also. One spring they sailed up the creek to St. Osyth's, and there they took Osyth and killed her. She had a sister, very beautiful, and she fell to the lot of the brothers. They brought her back to Mersea, and then each would have her for his own. So the brothers fell out whose she should be, and all their love turned to jealousy, and their brotherhood to enmity, and it came about that they fought with their long swords who should have the maid. They fought, and smote, and hacked one another till their armour was broken, and their flesh was cut off, and their blood flowed away, and by nightfall they were both dead. Thereupon the Danes drew their ship up to the top of the hill just above the Strood, and they placed the maid in the hold with a dead brother on either side of her, in his tattered harness, sword in hand, and they heaped a mountain over them and buried them all, the living and the dead together.'

Rebow paused, and pointed to the moon hung over the hoe.

'When the new moon appears, the flesh grows on their bones, and the blood stanches, and the wounds close, and breath comes back behind their ribs. When the moon is full they rise in the ship's hold and fall on one another, and if you listen at full moon on the hoe you can hear the brothers fighting below in the heart of the barrow. You hear them curse and cry out, and you hear the clash of their swords. But when the moon wanes the sounds grow fainter, their armour falls to bits, their flesh drops away, the blood oozes out of all the hacked veins, and at last all is still. Then, when there is no moon, you can hear the maid mourning and sobbing: you can hear her quite distinctly till the new moon reappears, and then she is hushed, for the brothers are recovering for a new fight. This will go on month after month, year after year, till one conquers the other and wins the maid; but that will never be, for the brothers are of the same age, and equally strong, and equally resolute.'

'Why have you told me this?' asked Mehalah.

'Why have I told you this, Glory?' repeated Rebow; 'because you and I are like those brothers, only they began with love and ended with fighting, and you and I begin with fighting and must and shall end with love. I love you, Glory, and yet, at times, I almost hate you.'

'And I,' broke in Mehalah, 'hate you with my whole heart, and never, never can love you.'

'You have a strong spirit, so have I,' said Elijah; 'I like to hear you speak thus. For long you have let me see that you have hated me: you have fought me hard, but you shall love me yet. We must fight, Glory; it is our destiny. We were made for one another, to love and fight, and fight and love, till one has conquered or killed the other. How can you live at the Ray, and I at Red Hall, apart? You know, you feel it, that we must be together to love and fight, and fight and love, till death. What is the use of your struggling against what must come about? As soon as ever I saw you I knew that you were ordained for me from the moment you were born. You grew up and ripened for me, for me, and no one else. You thought you loved George De Witt. I hated you for loving him. He was not worthy of you, a poor, foolish, frightened sop. You would have taken him and turned him inside out and torn him to pieces, in a week, disgusted with the fellow that made calf-love to you, when you had sounded his soul and found a bottom as soon as the lead went out of your hand. You thought George De Witt would belong to you. It could not be. You cannot oppose your destiny. A strong soul like yours must not mate but with a strong soul like mine. Till I saw you I hated women, poor, thin-headed, hollow-souled toys. When I saw you I saw the only woman who could be mine, and I knew, as the pointers yonder know the polestar, that you were destined to me. You hate me because you know this as well as I do. You know that there is no man on earth who can be yours save me, but you will play and fight with your destiny. Sooner or later you must bend to it. Sooner or later you must give way. You thought of George De Witt, and he is swept out of your path. You may fancy any other man, and he will go this way or that, and nothing will prosper till you set your face in the direction whither your destiny points. You can take no other than me, however much you may desire it. You need me and I need you. You may hate me and go on hating me and fighting me to the last, but you cannot escape me.

'Elijah,' said Mehalah, 'escape you I will. Since I have known you, you have been mixed up with all the ills that have come upon us, I do not know how; but I seem to feel that you are like an evil wind or a blighting cloud passing over my life. I would look up and laugh, but I cannot, I turn hard, and hate the world—only because you are in it. It would be another world without you.'

'Why do you turn hard and hate the world? Because you are on a wrong road, you are battling against your destiny. All goes across with you, because you are across your proper path. Why do you hate me? Because you feel in your soul that you must sooner or later be mine, and your haughty will rebels against having your future determined for you. Yet I know it. The time is at hand when you will take me for better, for worse, for all life. We cannot live a moment the one without the other. If I were to die you would die too, you would rage and writhe against death, but it would come. I know it. Our lives are bound up together in one bundle, and the knife that cuts one string cuts the other also. Our souls are twins to love and to hate, to fondle and fight, till death us do part! Till death us do part!' repeated Rebow scornfully, 'Death can no more part us than life. We will live together and we will die together, and moulder away in one another's arms. The worm that gnaws me shall gnaw you. I think of you night and day. I cannot help it: it is my fate. I knew it was so the moment I saw you. I came here. I cannot keep away till you come to me to Red Hall.'

'I shall never go there again,' said Mehalah sullenly,

'Not before New Year?'

'Never.'

He laughed. 'She would swear to it, and yet at the New Year she will be there. And she will take me and be mine. For me she must and will love. It is her fate; she cannot oppose that for ever. For me she would even give up George De Witt.'

'George De Witt is dead.'

'I say, were it to come to this, George or Elijah, one or the other, you would fly to Elijah and cast George off.'

'Let me go. I will have no more of this mad babble,' said Mehalah, wrenching her hands out of his grasp. She would not run away. She was too proud. She folded her arms on her breast and confronted him.

'Hark!' she said, 'the Christmas bells.'

Faint and far off could be heard the merry pealing of the Colchester bells. The wind had shifted.

'Peace on earth and good will to men,' muttered Elijah; 'but to them that fight against their destiny fury and hate.'

'Go back, Elijah, and speak to me no more on this matter. I will not hear you again. I have but endured it now.'

'This is Christmas Eve,' said Rebow. 'In eight days is the New Year, and then you will be in Red Hall, Glory!'

'Listen to me, Elijah,' exclaimed Mehalah passionately. 'If you find me there, then you may hope to see your other fond dream fulfilled. Destiny will have been too strong for me.'

'Farewell.'

'May we not meet again.'

'We shall. It cannot be helped. I feel it coming. You may fight against it; you cannot escape. Destiny must fulfil itself. We must fight and love, and love and fight in life, in death, and through eternity, like the old warriors in Grim's Hoe.'

'Farewell.'

'Till this day sen'night.'

CHAPTER XV.

NEW YEAR'S EVE.

No more sheep were stolen; but then the moon was filling her horns, and a robbery could not be committed without chance of detection. But though nothing further had been taken, Mehalah was uneasy. Some evilly-disposed person had visited the Ray and plundered her and her mother of four ewes; others, or the same, might attempt the house, in the hopes of finding money there. The auction had shown people that Mistress Sharland was not without money.

On New Year's Eve Mehalah went to Colchester to make some purchases for the New Year. The kalends of January and not the Nativity of Christ is the great winter festival among the Essex peasantry on the coast. They never think of wishing one another a Happy Christmas, but only a Merry New Year. No yule log is burnt, no mummers dance, no wassail bowl is consumed at Christmas, but each man who can afford it deems himself bound to riot and revel, to booze and sing, to wake the death of the old year, and baptise the new with libations of brandy or ale.

When Mehalah returned, she brought with her a new lock and key for the house-door. There had been once a lock there, but it had been broken many years ago, and had never been repaired. On the Ray no lock was needed, it had been supposed. Mehalah was of a different opinion now. The short day had closed some time ago; she had seen it die over Bradwell from Abberton Hill, but the full moon was rising, and she knew her way over the marshes, she could thread the tangle easily by moonlight. She reached the Ray, threw open the door, and strode in. Her mother was by the fire, with her head on the table. Mehalah's heart stood still for a moment, and then her face flushed. The smell of spirits in the close room, the attitude of her mother, the stupefied eyes which opened on her, and then closed again without recognition, convinced her that her mother had been drinking.

Mehalah was angry as well as distressed. This was a new trouble, one to which she was quite unaccustomed. She knew that her mother had taken a little rum-and-water against her ague, and she had not grudged it her. But of late there had been something more than this. Since Rebow had supplied Mrs. Sharland with spirits, the old woman had been unable to resist the temptation of going to her keg whenever she felt lonely or depressed. Mehalah had insisted on her mother receiving no more from Elijah Rebow, but she was by no means certain that the widow had complied with her desire. The sight of her mother in this condition angered Mehalah, for she was sure now that a fresh supply had been obtained, and was secreted somewhere. She was angry with her mother for deceiving her and with Rebow for tempting the old woman and laying her under an obligation to him. She was angry with herself for not having watched her mother more closely, and explored the places of concealment which abounded in the old house.

She stood over her mother for some moments with folded arms and bowed head, her brows knit, and a gloomy light in her eyes. Then she shook her roughly and spoke harshly to her.

'Mother! answer me. You have received more from Rebow?'

'It was very kind, very kind indeed,' stuttered the old woman. 'Capital for ague shivers and rheumatic pains in the bones.'

'Has Elijah been here again?'

'He's wery civil; he knows what suits old bones.'

'Has he brought you another keg?'

'It is stowed away,' said the widow drowsily. 'Quite comfortable. Go to bed, Mehalah, it's time to get up.'

The girl drew back in disgust and wrath. Elijah was making her own mother despicable in her eyes. She was quite resolved what to do. She thrust open the door to the cellar, and behind a heap of faggots found a fresh keg, evidently recently brought, and quite full. She drew it forth into the front room and held it up.

'Mother!' she shouted.

'I am here, Mehalah. The ague isn't on me yet.'

'Do you see this little cask? It is full, quite full.'

'Don't do that, child, you may drop it.'

'I shall dash it to pieces,' said the girl, and she flung it with her whole force on the bricks. A stave was broken: the precious liquor spurted out. Some flew into the fire and flashed into blue flame up the chimney. In a moment the floor was swimming, and the thirsty bricks were sucking in the spirit. The old woman was too besotted with drink to understand what was done. Mehalah's bosom heaved with passion and excitement.

'I have done with that,' she said; 'I said that I would, and I have kept my word. Never, never shall my poor mother be like this again. He did it.' She knit her hands, and a fire flickered in her eye, like that of the burning spirit in the chimney.

'Now come to bed, mother.' She drew or carried the old woman out of the room, undressed her, and put her in bed. Mrs. Sharland made no resistance. She submitted drowsily, and her head was no sooner on the pillow than she fell asleep.

Mehalah returned to the front room. She got out some tools and set herself to work at once to fasten on the lock. She was accustomed to doing all sorts of things herself; she could roughly carpenter, she had often patched her boat. The old farmhouse was in a decayed condition and needed much mending, and for several years she had done what was required to it. To put on a lock was a trifle; but the old nails that had fastened the former lock remained in the wood, and had to be punched out, and the keyhole was not quite in the right place when the lock was first put on, and had to be altered. At length the lock was fast, a strong lock, strong for such a worm-eaten door.

Mehalah went to her mother's room and looked at the old woman. She slept heavily, unlike her usual sleep, which would be broken at once by the entry of her daughter with a light.

Mehalah returned to the kitchen and seated herself at the hearth. How long had this keg of spirits been in the house? She had paid no attention to the introduction of spirits since George's death, her mind had been occupied with other matters. Her mother and Rebow had taken advantage of this. How was it that Rebow came to the house when she was away? He never came when she was present, at least not since the night when the money was stolen; but she was sure that he visited her mother during her absence, from little things let drop by the old woman.

How did he manage to time his visits so as not to meet her? She would find out when he was last at the Ray Farm. She sprang up, and went out of the door, unlocking it to let herself go forth; and she called Abraham. There was no answer. The old man was already turned into his loft over the cowhouse, and asleep.

She called him again, but with equal want of success. Not a thunderbolt falling on the thorns beside the house would rouse him. Mehalah knew that, and went back to her seat by the fire, relocking the door. 'I will ask him in the morning. He must know.'

She drew off her shoes, and put her bare feet on the warm hearth. She was without her guernsey and cap, for she did not wear them when she went to Colchester.

She fell, as was her wont, to thinking. Since the death of George, she had been accustomed to sit thus over the fire, after her mother had retired. She was not thinking of him now, she was thinking of Elijah. His words, his strange, mad, fierce words, came back to her. Was there a destiny shaping her life against her will, and forcing her into his arms? She shuddered at the thought. To hate and love, and love and hate, year out, year in, that was what they were fated to do, according to him. That he was drawn towards her by some attractive power exercised against her will, she knew full well, but she would not allow that he exercised the least attraction on her. Yet she did feel that there was some sort of spell upon her. Hate him as she did and would, she knew that she could not altogether escape him, she had an instinctive consciousness that she was held by him, she did not understand how, in his hands. Perhaps it was her destiny to hate and fight him; for how long? Love him she never could, she never would. There was an assurance in his manner and tone which impressed her against her better judgment. He spoke as though it were but a matter of time before she yielded herself wholly to him, and came under his roof and joined her lot with his, for life and for death. What right had he to assume this? What grounds had he for this confidence? None but a blind, dogged conviction in his own mind that destiny had ordained them for each other. Then she thought of the story of Grim's Hoe, of the two who loved and hated, embraced and fought eternally therein, those two destined from their mother's womb to be together in life and death, with twin souls and bodies, who had they lived in love might have rested in death, but as they fought must fight on. There they were, in the old hollow womb of the ship down in the earth in darkness, loving one another as brothers, fighting each other as rivals; the conflict lasting till one shall master the other, a thing that never can be, for both were born with equal strength, and equal purpose, and equal stubbornness of will. The fumes of the spilled spirits hung in the air, and stimulated Mehalah's brain. Instead of stupefying, they quickened her mind into activity. Her heart beat. She felt as if she were in the ship hold watching the eternal conflict, and as if she must take a part with one or the other; as if her so doing would determine the victory. But which should she will to conquer, when each was the counterpart of the other? She could not bear this thought, she could not endure the fumes of the spirit, it suffocated her. She sprang up. The full moon was glaring in at the window from a cloudless sky.

She opened the door. The air was cold, but there was little wind. She could see on the south-east horizon, at the highest point of the island, the great Hoe crowned with black pines.

The moon was at full. The old warriors were now hewing at one another, and the dim, frightened captive maid looked on with her hands on her heart, her great eyes gleaming like glow-worms in the decaying ship hold. Ha! at each sword stroke the sparks flashed. Ha! the cut flesh glimmered like phosphorescent fish, and the blood ran like blue fire. Was the story true? Could anyone hear the warriors shout and smite, who chose to listen at the full of the moon? The distance to Grim's Hoe was not over two miles. Mehalah thought she must go there and listen with her own ears. She would go.

Once more she returned to her mother's room, and saw that Mrs. Sharland was asleep. Then she drew on her shoes, her guernsey, and her red cap, went out, locked the door, and put the key in her pocket.

'Who went there?' She started. She thought she saw something—some one, move; but then laughed. The moon was so bright that it cast her shadow on the wall, distinct and black as if it were a palpable body. She stood still, listened, and looked round. She could see the stretch of the saltings as distinctly as if it were day, only that the shadows were inky black, not purple as by sunlight. Not a sound was to be heard.

'I will go,' she said, and she strode off towards the causeway.

The path over the marshes was perfectly distinct. She walked fast, the earth crackled under her feet, the frost was keen. Her eyes rose ever and anon to Grim's Hoe. The pines on it did not stir, they stood like mourners above a grave.

The Mersea channel gleamed like a belt of silver, not a ripple was on the water on the west side of the causeway, and but slight flapping wavelets, driven by the north-east wind, played with the tangles on the piles on the other side of the Strood.

She reached the island of Mersea by the causeway, now dry, and began to ascend the hill. Once she turned and looked back. She could see the Ray rising above the marshes, bathed in moonlight, patched with coal black shadows cast by the ancient thorn trees, and the farm buildings.

Before her rose the great barrow, partly overgrown with shrubs, but bare on the north-west towards the Strood. It was a bell-shaped mound rising some thirty feet above the surface of the ground. She paused a moment at the foot and listened. Not a sound. She must then climb the tumulus, and lie on the top between the pines, and lay her ear to the ground. She stepped boldly up the little path trodden by children and sheep, and in a few moments was at the top. She stopped to breathe, to look up at the wan white moon that gazed down on her, and then she cast herself on the ground, with her face to the north-west.

What was that? A fir cone fell beside her. There was no sound. Hist! a stoat ran past and disappeared in a hole. Then she heard screams. A poor rabbit was attacked and its blood sucked. She lifted her head, and then laid it on the ground again. Her eyes were fixed on the distance.

What was that? In a moment she was on her feet.

What was that red spot over the marshes, on the Ray, among the trees? What was that leaping, dancing, lambent tongue, shooting up and recoiling? What was that white rising cloud above the thorns?

Before she knew where she was, Mehalah was flying down the hill towards the Strood, the dead Danish warriors forgotten in the agony of her fear. As she ran on, her eyes never left the Ray, and she saw the red light grow in intensity and spread in body. The farm was on fire. The house was on fire, and her mother was in a dead sleep within—locked in—and the key was in her pocket.

O God! what had she done? Why had she gone? Had not the spilled spirits caught fire and set the house in flames! Why had she locked her mother in? a thing never done before. Mehalah ran, terror, horror, anguish at her heart. She did not look at her path, she took it instinctively, she did not heed the rude bridges, she dashed across them, and one broke under her hasty foot, and fell away after she had passed. The flames were climbing higher. She could see them devouring the wooden tarred walls. Then came a great burst of fire, and a rushing upwards of blazing sparks. The roof had fallen in. A pillar of blue and golden light stood up and illumined the whole Ray. The thorn trees looked now like wondrous, finely-ramified, golden seaweeds in a dim blue sea. Mehalah would not pause to look at anything, she saw only flames leaping and raging where was her home, where lay her mother. How could she reach the place before the house was a wreck, and her dear mother was buried beneath the burned timbers of the roof, and the hot broken tiles?

She was there at last, before the great blaze; she could see that some one or two men were present.

'My mother, my mother!' she gasped, and fell on her knees.

'Be still, Glory, she is safe, no thanks to you.'

Mehalah lost consciousness for a few moments. The revulsion of feeling was so great as to overcome her. When she recovered, she was still unable for some time to gather all her faculties together, rise, look round, and note what had taken place.

The whole farmhouse was on fire, every wall was flaming, and part of the roof had fallen in. If once the house were to catch fire it was certain to go like tinder. A spout of flame came out of her mother's bed-room window. The fire glowed and roared in the old kitchen sitting-room.

'Where is my mother?' asked Mehalah abruptly.

'She is all safe,' answered Abraham Dowsing, who was dragging some saved bedding out of reach of the sparks. 'She is in the boat.'

'The cow?' asked Mehalah.

'She is all right also. The fire has not caught the stable.'

'Who got my mother out?'

'I did, Glory!' answered Elijah Rebow. 'You owe her life to me. Why were you not here? Fighting your destiny, I suppose.'

Several articles were scattered about under the trees. The Sharlands had not many valuables; such as they had seemed to have been saved.

'Where is my mother? Lead me to her.'

'She is in the boat, Glory!' said Rebow. 'Come with me. The fire must burn itself out. There is nothing further to be done; we must put your mother at once under shelter. There is a cruel frost, and she will suffer.'

'Where is she? What have you done with her?' again asked Mehalah, still hardly collected and conscious of what she said.

'She is safe in my boat, well wrapped up. Come with me. You shall see her. Abraham and my man shall stay and watch till the fire dies out, and see that no further harm is done, and then follow in your boat.'

'Where are you going?'

'I am going to place your mother under cover, at once, or the cold will kill her. Come on, Glory!'

Elijah led the way down the steep gravelly slope to the Rhyn. There floated his boat—his large two-oared boat, and in the stern half lay, half crouched, Mrs. Sharland, amidst blankets and bedding.

'Joseph!' shouted Elijah to one of the men by the fire, 'follow us as soon as you can, and bring Abraham Dowsing with you. We will fetch away the traps to-morrow.'

Mrs. Sharland was wailing and wringing her hands.

'Oh Mehalah! this is dreadful! too dreadful!'

'Step in and take the oar,' said Elijah impatiently. 'We must get off, and house the old woman as soon as possible, or she will be death-struck.'

The flames were reflected in the water about the boat, it seemed to float in fire.

'Take the oar!' ordered Elijah gruffly.

Mehalah obeyed mechanically. He thrust the boat off, and cast himself in.

No word was spoken for some time, Mehalah's eyes were fixed on her burning home, with despair. Her brain was numb, her heart oppressed. Mrs. Sharland wailed and wept, and uttered loud reproaches against Mehalah, which the girl heard not. She was stunned, and could not take in the situation.

The boat shot past the head of the Ray.

There stood the low broad bulk of the Burnt Hill. Mehalah roused herself.

Elijah looked over his shoulder and laughed.

'Up Salcot Fleet!' he said shortly.

'What!' suddenly exclaimed Mehalah, as a pang shot through her heart. 'Whither are we going?'

'To Red Hall,' answered Elijah.

'I will not go there!' exclaimed the girl in a tone of despair, as she drew her hands sharply from the oar, and the boat swung round.

'Take the oar again,' ordered Elijah. 'Where else can your mother go? You must think of her. She cannot be left to die of cold on the marshes, this night.'

A groan escaped Mehalah's breast. She resumed the oar. 'Hold hard!' shouted Elijah after a row of half-an-hour. He sprang into the water, and drew the boat ashore.

'Give your mother a hand and help her to land,' he said peremptorily. Mehalah obeyed without a word.

Rebow caught the girl by both hands as she stepped on shore.

'Welcome, Glory! welcome to Red Hall! The new year sees you under the roof where you shall rule as mistress; your destiny is mightier than your will.'

CHAPTER XVI.

IN NEW QUARTERS.

When the boat reached the landing place for Red Hall, Mrs. Sharland was found to have been so overcome with terror, and numbed with frost, as to be unable to walk. She moaned under her blankets, but made no effort to rise. Elijah was obliged to carry her out of the boat upon the sea-wall, and then with the assistance of Mehalah she was conveyed to the house in their arms. Neither spoke, and Mrs. Sharland's lamentations, over various articles she had prized, and which she feared were lost or destroyed, remained unattended to.

The old woman was wrapped up from the cold in a blanket that enfolded her entire person and head, and she kept working an aperture for her face, whilst being carried, not so much to obtain air, as to give vent to queries.

'My green bombazine,—where is it?'

The folds of the blanket closed over the face. The fingers worked at them, till they had made a gap.

'Is the toad-jug saved?' at the same time a point of a nose and a thin finger emerged from the wraps.

'There was a dozen of Lowestoft soup-dishes!' A jerk as she was being lifted over a rail sent her head and shoulders deeper into the blanket, and it was some minutes before she had grubbed a hole for herself again.

'The warming-pan! I can't go to bed unless I have the sheets aired.'

A spring across a dyke buried the old woman again 'in woollen.' She emerged only as the house was reached to exclaim 'My rum!'

'You've come where there's lots of that,' said Elijah, and he indicated with his chin to Mehalah to carry her up the steps into the hall.

A red fire was glowing and painting the walls. The great room was warm, and Mrs. Sharland battled out of her envelopes as soon as she became aware that she was under cover.

'Take me to bed,' she said; 'my legs are frozen. I can't go a step. Oh! is the toad-jug saved?'

'I will carry her now,' said Elijah. 'You light a candle, Glory, and follow me.'

He took the old woman over his shoulder, and led the way up the stairs. Mehalah followed with a light she had kindled at the hearth. He conducted into a bed-room, comfortably furnished, with white curtains to the windows, and a low tester bed in the corner.

'Light the fire,' he ordered, and Mehalah applied the candle to the straw and chips in the grate. Presently the flames were dancing up the chimney, and making the whole chamber glow. The old woman was laid on the bed.

'This looks comfortable,' said she; 'just as if you was prepared for us.'

'I was prepared for you. Everything was ready. Glory knows that I have been expecting you and her. I told her she must come, sooner or later. Sooner or later the same roof must cover both, as sooner or later the same grave will hold us both. She would fight me, and would not come to me, but her destiny is stronger than her will. My will is the destiny of her life. It shapes and directs it.'

Mehalah did not speak. She could not speak. She was stunned. A belt of iron bound her heart and restrained its free bounds, a weight of lead crushed her brain and killed its independence of action. She, who had been hitherto a law to herself, whose will had been unfettered, now discovered herself a captive under the thraldom of a will mightier, or more ungovernable, than her own. She had no time or power to think how to escape, and free herself from the situation in which she was placed. All her thoughts that she could collect must be about her mother. She must think of herself when she had more leisure. But though she could not think of herself, she could feel that she was conquered, and a captive, and that escape would not be easy.

'There,' said Elijah, indicating a door, 'there is another little room for you and your mother to put away what you like. If you want anything, come downstairs.'

Elijah went heavily down the stairs and out at the door. Mehalah looked from the window, and saw him on his way to the boat. He was going back to the Ray. She could still see a red cloud hanging over her burnt home. The tears rose in her heart at the sight, but would not well out at her eyes. She stood and looked long at the dying fire, drawing the window curtain behind her to screen from her the light of the room. Her mother lay quiet, evidently pleased at having got into such comfortable quarters, and exhausted with her alarm. By degrees she dozed off into unconsciousness of her loss and of her situation, and Mehalah remained at the window looking moodily over the fens and the water, at the ruby spark that marked her old home.

She was standing in the same place when the boats arrived, bringing portions of their goods to Red Hall. She heard the voices of Rebow and other men below. She opened the door and listened. He was giving them something to eat and drink. Abraham Dowsing was there. She could distinguish his voice.

'If I hadn't turned you out, you'd have been burnt,' said Rebow.

'A good job for mistress we saved the cowhouse,' answered Abraham, with sulky unwillingness to admit that he was indebted to Elijah for anything.

'Don't you think you owe me your life?' asked Rebow.

'The cowhouse didn't burn.'

'No. But it would have, had not we been there to keep the flames off,' observed one of the men.

'Good job for mistress I wasn't burnt. I don't know how she'd got along without me.'

'It did not matter particularly to yourself then, Abby?'

'Don't know as it did. A man must die some time, and I've always heard as smothering is a nice quiet sort of death—better than being racked with cramps and tormented with rheumatics and shivered into the pithole with agues.' After a pause Abraham's voice was heard to add, 'Besides, I should have woke, myself, with the fire and smoke.'

'Not you. And if you had, what could you have done to save the old woman? She'd have been burnt to a cinder before you woke.'

'That's mistress' matter, not mine,' answered Dowsing.

'You could not have got the things out of the house.'

'They are not mine,' retorted Abraham angrily. 'You are not going to make a merit to me of saving what are the belongings of other folk?'

'They belong to your mistress.'

'Well, so they do, that is, they don't belong to me; so none of your boasting to me, as if I owed you anything.' This ungracious remark, but one not unnatural for a rude peasant jealous lest an obligation should place him in a position of disadvantage, was followed by silence, during which the party ate.

Presently Abraham asked, 'How came you to be there?'

'Master sent Jim out with me in the big boat after ducks, and he was in the punt,' answered one of the men. 'He bade us lie by at the mouth of the Rhyn, while he went on to drive the birds our way; there was a lot, and we thought to pepper into a whole flight. He was not long away—not above an hour—when we saw the Ray house afire, and heard him shouting to us to come on, so we rowed as hard as hard, and by the time we landed he had broke open the door, and got the old lady out. We helped as best we might, and saved a deal of things.'

'They ain't worth much,' said Abraham. 'There's nothing in the house worth five pound,—take the whole lot. The cow was the only thing would pay for saving, and she was safe. I slept in the loft over her.'

'The life of your mistress was worth something, I hope, Abby.'

'Don't know that. Not to me, anyhow. She's not mistress; it is Mehalah that orders, and does everything. I don't reckon an old woman's life is worth a crown, not to nobody but herself, may be; but that is her concern not mine. She was an ailing aguish body. Why!' exclaimed Abraham banging his can of ale on the table, 'when you've saved an old woman who is nought but a trouble to everybody as does with her, of what wally is it?

They might have paid you to let her alone, but not to lug her out of the fire. Now, Mehalah, she was another sort. But you didn't save her.'

'Where was she? She was not in the house.'

'How am I to know? I don't spy after her. Others may,' he gave a sly, covert look at Elijah, 'I don't. But I reckon she was out on the saltings watching for the sheep-stealers.'

'Have you had sheep-stealers on the Ray?'

'Aye, we have.'

'Did you watch for them at night?'

'I!' with a grunt. 'They were not my sheep. No, thank you. Let them that wallys the sheep watch 'em. I do what I'm paid to do, and I don't do more.'

Mehalah did not listen to the whole of this conversation. She had satisfied herself that Abraham was there, and had heard how Rebow and his men came to be on the spot when the fire broke out; she then closed the door again, and returned to the window. She did not leave her station till dawn, except to attend to the fire, to make it up from the heap stacked by the side of the chimneypiece. When day began to break, she seated herself on a stool by the bed, and laying her head on the mattress fell asleep, and slept for an hour or two, uneasily, troubled by dreams and the discomfort of her position.

When she awoke the house was quiet. She went downstairs, with reluctance, and found no one stirring, but the fire made up and a kettle boiling over it, the table spread with everything she could desire for breakfast. Elijah, Abraham, and the other men were gone. There was a canister with tea on the board. Mehalah made her mother some, and took it up to her.

The old woman was awake, and drank the tea with eagerness.

'I don't think I can get out of bed to-day, Mehalah!' she said. 'I feel my limbs all of an ache; the cold has got into the marrow of my bones, and I feel as if the frost were splitting them, as at times it will split pipes. I must lie abed till the thaw comes to them.'

'Can you eat anything?'

'I think I can.'

'Mother, how long are we going to remain here?'

'It is wery comfortable, I am sure.'

'But we cannot stay in this house.'

'Where else can we go?'

'I will get into service somewhere.'

'You cannot leave me. Where shall I go? I cannot leave my bed, and I don't think the frost will get out of my bones for a week or more.'

'I can not, I will not, remain here.'

'Where can we go?'

Mehalah put both her hands to her brow. She could not answer this question. Were she alone, she could get a situation in a farmhouse, perhaps; but with a sick mother dependent on her, this was not possible. No farmer would take them both in for the sake of her services.

'Where else can we go?' again asked Mrs. Sharland; then in a repining voice, 'If Master Rebow houses us for a while, it is very good of him, and we must be thankful, for we have no chance of shelter elsewhere. Where is the money to pay for rebuilding the farmhouse? Do you think my cousin, Charles Pettican———'

'No, no,' exclaimed Mehalah, 'not a word about him.'

'He spoke up and promised most handsomely,' said Mrs. Sharland.

'He can do nothing, mother, I will not ask him.'

'A man that has a gilded balcony to his house wouldn't miss a few pounds for running up a wooden cottage.'

'I will not go to him again.'

'My dear child,' said Mrs. Sharland, 'I don't doubt he would take us in on a visit for a while, when we are forced to leave Red Hall.'

'You think we shall not be obliged to remain here?'

'I don't see how we can. It is very good of Master Rebow to house us for a bit, but I doubt we can't stick as fixtures. I only wish we could. Anyhow stay here a bit we must. We have nowhere else to go to, except to my cousin Charles.'

Mehalah knew what this alternative was worth. It was a relief to her to hear her mother speak of their stay in Red Hall as only temporary. She could not endure to contemplate the possibility of its being permanent. She formed a hope that she would be able to find work somewhere, and hire a small cottage; she was strong enough to do as much as a man.

During the day, everything that had been rescued from the fire on the Ray was brought to Red Hall, even the cow, which was driven round by land, a matter of eleven miles. The old clock arrived, and was set up in the large room below, an old cypress chest or 'sprucehutch' as Mrs. Sharland called it, covered with curious shallow carvings picked out with burnt umber, representing a hawking party, that contained her best clothes, and was a security against moth, was conveyed into her bedroom. It weighed half a ton. The old Lowestoft dishes she valued were placed in the rack in the hall along with the ware that belonged to Elijah. The toad-jug, a white jug with a painted and glazed figure of a toad squatting inside it in the neck, was also brought to Red Hall, so even were two biscuit-china poodles with shaven posteriors and with manes and tufted tails, that had stood on the chimneypiece at the Ray. The warming-pan of brass with a stamped portrait of H.M. George I. on it was likewise transported to Red Hall, and hung up in the little oak-panelled parlour behind the entrance hall generally occupied by Rebow.

By degrees most of the property of Mrs. Sharland was brought to the house, and the small oak parlour was furnished with it. Her arm-chair of leather with high back was placed in the hall by the great fireplace that bore the inscription, 'When I hold, I hold fast.' There were also some things belonging specially to Glory that had been saved, and these were put in the oak parlour. The satisfaction of Mrs. Sharland at finding herself surrounded by her goods was extreme. She did not leave her bed, but she insisted on her daughter bringing her up everything that could be carried, that she might turn it about, and inspect it minutely and rejoice over what was uninjured, and bewail what had suffered. One of the poodles had lost an ear and part of its tail. The old woman cried and grumbled and scolded about this injury, as though it were on a level with the destruction of the house. She would see the men Jim and Joe who had brought it from the Ray in the boat; she catechised them minutely, she insisted on knowing which had brought the dog out of the burning house, where it had been placed till removal, and fretted, till they promised to examine the spot beneath the thorn tree where the china brute had spent the night, and also the bottom of the boat, for the missing tail tuft and ear tip.

'You know,' she said, 'if I boil them in milk with the dog, I can get them to stick on.'

Among certain persons, the mind is destitute of perspective, and consequently magnifies trifles and disregards great evils. Mrs. Sharland had a mind thus constituted. She harped all day on the battered biscuit-china dog, because it was placed on the mantelpiece of her bedroom, and was under her eyes whenever she turned her head that way. The farmhouse was almost forgotten in her distress about the tail; her flaming home formed but a red background to the mutilated white poodle.

Mehalah saw nothing of Elijah Rebow all day. He was several times in the house; directly her foot sounded on the stairs, however, he disappeared. But she saw and felt that he was considering her; his care to recover all the little treasures and property on the Ray evinced this; and in the house he provided everything she could need; he placed meat on the table in the hall for her dinner, and had boiled potatoes over the fire. They were set ready for her, she had only to take them out. Her mother ate heartily, and was loud in expressions of satisfaction at the comfort that surrounded them.

'I hope, Mehalah, we shan't have to leave this in a hurry.'

Glory did not answer.

Towards evening Abraham Dowsing arrived with the cow. The girl heard the low, and ran down—she could not help it—and threw her arms round the neck of the beast. There was a back stair leading to the kitchen and yard, by which she could descend without entering the hall, and by this means she avoided Elijah, who, she was aware, was there.

Elijah, however, came to the top of the steps after she had descended, and looked into the yard where she was. Mehalah at once desisted from lavishing her tenderness on the animal.

Abraham stood sulkily by.

'I've had a long bout,' he said.

'I dare say you have, Abraham,' she answered.

'I want something to eat and drink, I haven't bit nought since morning. There's nothing but ashes on the Ray now, and they are red-hot. You don't expect me to fill my belly on them.'

Mehalah put her hand to her mouth and checked her tongue, as she was about to tell him to go indoors and get some supper. She had now nothing to give the old man. She lived on the bounty of Rebow.

'I cannot go without my wittles,' persisted Abraham. 'Now I want to know where my wittles are to come from. I paid fourpence at the Rose for some bread and cheese, and you owes me that.'

'There is the money,' said Mehalah producing the coin.

'Ah! that is wery well. But where am I to get my wittles now? Am I your servant or ain't I? If I am,—where's my wittles?'

'Come here, Abraham,' said Elijah, from the kitchen door. 'There is bread and cold potatoes and meat here. You shall have your supper, and you can sleep in the loft.'

'Look here, master,' pursued the sullen old man, 'I want to know further where I'm to look for my wages.'

'To me,' said Rebow. 'I take you on.'

'Where am I to work?'

'Here, or on the Ray, looking after the sheep.'

'The sheep are not yours, they are hers,'—pointing to Mehalah with his thumb.

'The Ray and Red Hall are one concern,' answered Rebow. 'You look to me as your master, and to her as your mistress;' then he entered and slammed the door.

Abraham shrugged his shoulders. He leered at Mehalah, who had put her hands to her forehead.

'When are you going to church? Eh, mistress? I thought it was coming to this. But I don't care so long as I gets my wittles and wage.'

Abraham went slowly into the cattlehouse with the cow. Mehalah remained rooted to the spot, pressing her brow.

This was more than she could endure. She ran up the steps, she would speak to Rebow while her heart was full. She dashed through the kitchen and into the hall. He was not there. As she ran on, she tripped and almost fell; and recovered herself with horror. She had almost precipitated herself through the trap into the vault beneath. The door was thrown back, her foot had caught this. Faugh! an odour rose from the cellar as from the lair of a wild beast. She looked in, there was the maniac racing up and down in the den fastened by his chain, jabbering and uttering incoherent cries. He was almost naked, covered with filthy rags, and his hair hung over his face so that she could distinguish no features by the dim light that strayed down from the trap, and from the horn lanthorn that Elijah had placed on the steps. Rebow had a pitchfork, and he was tossing fresh straw to his brother, and raking out the sodden and crushed litter of the wretched man.

Mehalah could not bear the sight; she withdrew. She needed a little while by herself to consider what was best to be done, to think of what had taken place. She opened the front door, and descended by the long flight of steps over the arch. Then she saw that a shutter covered the circular window that in summer lighted the den of the maniac. This was now closed to shut out the cold of winter. There was a door. As she looked, Rebow opened it from within, and appeared, raking out the litter and the gnawed bones, the relics of his brother's repasts. He did not notice her, or he pretended not to do so, and she shrank back. Her wish to speak with him had gone from her. She was not equal to an interview till she had been alone for a while, and had gathered up her strength. An interview with him must be a contest. It was clear to her that he was resolved that she should stay at Red Hall. She was equally determined not to do so. But how to get away and remove her mother was more than she could discover.

She left the house and the garden round it, and walked through the meadow till she reached the sea-wall. She ascended that, and went along it to the spot where the Red Hall marsh divided the Tollesbury Fleet from the Virley and Salcott Creeks.

Then she threw herself beneath the windmill, the mill that pumped the water out of the dykes, and worked day and night whenever there was wind to move the sails. The mill was now at work. The wings rushed round, and the pump painfully creaked, and after every stroke sent a dash of water into the sea over the wall.

Mehalah hoped that here, away from her mother and Rebow, and the sights and sounds of Red Hall, she might be able to think. But it was not so. Her numbed head was unable to form any plans. She looked out at sea, it was leaden grey, ruffled with angry waves, and the mews screamed and dipped in them. The sky overhead was overcast. The Bradwell shore looked grey and bleak and desolate; there was not a sail in the offing. The fancy took her to sit and wait, and if she saw a ship pass to take it as a good omen, a promise of escape from her present perplexity.

She sat and waited. The sea darkened to a more sullen tint. The mews were no longer visible. Mersea with its trees and church tower disappeared. Bradwell coast loomed black as pitch against the last lingering light of day. Not a sail appeared.

Far away, out to sea, as the darkness deepened, gleamed a light. It gleamed a moment, then grew dim and disappeared in the blackness. A minute, and then it waxed, but waned again, and once more all was night. So on, in wearisome iteration. What she saw was the revolving Swin light fifteen miles from land, a floating Pharos. She thought of Elijah's words, she thought of the horrible iterations in the barrow on the hill, the embracing and fighting, embracing and fighting, loving and hating, loving and hating, till one should conquer of the twin but rival powers.

CHAPTER XVII.
FACE TO FACE.

Mehalah returned slowly to the house, her spirits oppressed with gloom. It was night without and within, before her face, and in her soul. The wind sighed and sobbed among the rushes and over the fen, in a disconsolate, despairing manner, and the breath of God within—the living soul—sighed and sobbed like His breath that blew over the wintry marsh without. Not a star looked down from His heaven above, and none looked up from His heaven below in the little confines of a human heart. Mehalah could scarce see her way in the fen, among the dykes and drains; she was as unable to find a path in the level of her life.

She reached Red Hall at last, and mounted the front stairs to the principal door. She would see Elijah now. It were better to speak with him and come to some understanding at once. It was intolerable to allow the present position to remain unexplained, and the future undetermined. She hesitated at the door. It was not without a struggle that she could open it and go in and face the man whose hospitality she was receiving and yet whom she abhorred. She knew that she was greatly indebted to him. He had saved her mother's life, he had secured from destruction a large amount of their property; yet she could not thank him. She resented his intrusion into their affairs, when anyone else would have been unobjectionable. She disliked him all the more because she knew she was heavily in his debt; it galled her almost past endurance to feel that she and her mother were then subsisting on his bounty.

'Come in, Glory!' shouted Elijah from within, as she halted at the door.

She entered. He was seated by the fire with his pipe in his hand; he had heard her step on the stairs, and had paused in his smoking, and had waited in a listening, expectant attitude.

He signed her to take a chair—her mother's chair—on the other side of the hearth. She paid no attention to the sign, but stood in the middle of the room, and unconsciously covered her eyes with her hands. Her pulses quivered in her temples. Her heart grew cold, and a faintness came over her.

'The light is not too strong to dazzle you,' said Elijah, 'put your hands down, I want to see your face.'

She made an effort to retain them where they were, but could not; they fell.

'Sit down.'

She shook her head.

'Sit down.'

'I want to speak with you, Elijah, for a moment. I must speak with you.' Her heart palpitated, her breast heaved. She could only utter short sentences.

'Sit down there!' he beckoned with the stalk of his pipe.

She still refused to obey. Her power was slipping from her. The exhaustion after the excitement she had gone through had affected even her stout will. She resolved to oppose him in this trifling matter, but knew that her resolution was infirm. She clung desperately to what remained to her of power.

'I will not listen to a word you say unless you sit down.'

He paused, and looked at her; then he said, 'Go to your mother!' and continued his smoking, with face averted.

'Elijah, I know what you have done, and are doing now for my mother.'

He sprang from his seat, and strode up and down the room, turning and glowering at her, sucking at his pipe, and making it red and angry like his eyes in the firelight. He walked fast and noisily on the brick floor, with his high shoulders up and his head down. She watched him with painful apprehension; he reminded her of the mad brother pacing in the vault below. She could not speak to him whilst he persisted in this irritating, restless tramp. There was no help for it. She dropped into her mother's leather chair.

'There!' said he, and he flung a ring with some keys attached to it, into her lap. 'Take them. They are yours now. The keys of everything in the house, except of——' he jerked his pipe towards the den beneath.

'I cannot take them,' she said, and let them slide off her lap upon the floor.

'Pick them up!' he ordered.

'No,' she said firmly, 'I will not. Elijah, we must come to an understanding with each other.'

'We already understand each other,' he said, pausing in his walk. 'We always did. I can read your heart. I know everything that passes there, just as if it was written in red letters on a page. I understand you, and there's nobody else in the world that can. I was made to read you. I heard a Baptist preacher say one day that God wrote a book, and then He created mankind to read it. You are a book, and God made me to read you. I can do it. That wants no scholarship, it comes by nature to me. Others can't. They might puzzle and rack their heads, they'd make nothing of you. But you are clear as light of day to me. You understand me?'

'I do not.'

'You will not. You set your obstinate, wicked mind against understanding me. I heard a preacher once say—I went to chapel along of my mother when I was a boy; I goes nowhere now but to the Ray after you—What is God? It is that as makes a man, and keeps him alive, and gives him hopes of happiness, or plunges him in hell. Every man has his own God; for there is something different makes and mars each man. What do I want but you, Glory? It is you that can make and keep me alive, and you are my happiness or my hell.'

'But,' said he standing still again, and flourishing his hand and pipe, 'as I was saying, I heard a preacher say once, that God made every man of a lump of clay and a drop of spittle, and that He made always two at a time. He couldn't help it. He has two hands and ain't right and left handed as we, but works with both, and then He casts about the men He has made, anywhere. Hasn't He made all things double? Have not you two hands and two feet and two eyes? Is there not a sun and a moon, are there not two poles to the earth, and two sexes, and day and night, and winter and summer? and—' he went up before Mehalah, and with a burst of passion—'and you and me?' Then he recommenced his pacing, but slower, and continued, 'Wherever those two are that God made with His two hands, they must come together. It don't matter where they be, if one is in Mersea, and t'other is in Asia, or Africa, or China, or America, or London, it don't matter, soon or late, they must come together, and when they come together then they are in heaven. Now if a man takes some other left-handed figure—it was the left hand made woman—then it don't matter, he can't go against his destiny. He has taken the wrong woman, and he is not happy. He knows it all along, and he feels restless and craving in his soul, and if he does not find the proper one in this world when he goes out of it, he waits and wanders, till the proper one dies and begins to hunt about for her right-hand man. That is what makes ghosts to ramble. Ghosts are those that have married the wrong ones, wandering and waiting, and seeking for their right mates. Do you hear the piping and the crying at the windows of a winter night? That is the ghosts looking in and sobbing because they are out in the cold shivering till they meet their mates. But when they meet, then that is heaven. There's a heaven for everyone, but that is only once for all when the two doubles find each other, and if that be not in this life, why it is after. And there is a hell too, but that isn't reserved for all, and it does not last for ever and ever, but is only when one has taken the wrong mate and has found it out.' He stopped. He had become very earnest and excited by what he had said. He came again over against Mehalah. 'Glory!' he continued, 'don't you see how the moon goes after the sun and cannot come to him? She is his proper mate and double, and the sun don't know, and won't have it, and so day and night, and winter and summer, and waxing and waning goes on and on. But that won't go on for ever. The sun will grow sad at heart, and wane for want of the moon some day, and then there will be a great flare and blaze and glory, and they will be in heaven. And now the two poles of the earth are apart, and so long as they keep apart, the world rolls on in misery and pain, and that is what makes earthquakes, and volcanoes, and great plagues—the poles are apart which ought to be together. But they are drawing gradually nearer each other. The seasons now are not what they used to be, and that is it. The poles are not where they were, they are straining to meet. And some day they will run into one, and that will be the end. I've heard say that in the Bible it is spoken that there'll be an end of this world. I could have known that without the Bible. The poles must come together some day, and be one. Glory!' he went on, 'you and I are each other's doubles, you was made with God's left hand, and I with his right, at the same moment of time, and He cast you into the Ray, and me to Red Hall. There was not much space between, only some water and ooze and marsh, and we've been drawing and drawing nearer and closer for ever so long, and now you are here, under my roof. You can't help it. You cannot fight agin it. You was made for me and I for you, and you'll have a life of hell unless you take me now. I must be yours. You thought you'd resist and take George De Witt. It might have been. Suppose you had, and I had died years before you. You would have heard me crying at your window and beating at your door, and you would have felt me drawing and drawing of you, whether you chose or not, taking the heart away from your George, and bringing it to me. Then at last, you'd have died, and then, then, you'd have been mine, and you would have found our heaven after thirty, forty, fifty years of hell.'

The terrible earnestness of the man imposed on Mehalah. He spoke what he believed. He gave utterance, in his rude fierce way, to what he felt. She, untaught, full of dim gropings after something higher, vaster, than the flat, narrow life she led, was startled.

'Heaven with you!' she cried, drawing back; 'never! never!'

'Heaven with me, and with none but me. You can't get another heaven but in my arms, for you was made for me by God. I told you so, but you would not believe it. Try, if you like, to find it elsewhere. God didn't make you and George De Witt out of one lump. He couldn't have done it—You, Glory! strong, great, noble, with a will of iron, and that weak, helpless, vulgar lout, tied to his mother's apron. He couldn't have done it. He made, like enough, Phoebe Musset and George De Witt out of one piece, but you and me was moulded together at the same time, out of the same clay, and the same breath is in our hearts, and the same blood in our veins. You can't help it, it is so. You can not, you shall not, escape me. Soon or late you must find your proper mate, soon or late you must seek your double, soon or late find your heaven.'

He came now quietly and seated himself in his chair opposite Mehalah.

'What did you fare to say, Glory?' he asked. 'I interrupted you.'

'I must thank you first for what you have done for my mother.'

'I have done nothing for her,' said Elijah sharply.

'You drew her out of the burning house. You saved her goods from the flames. You have sheltered her here.'

'I have done nothing for her,' said Elijah again. 'Whatever I have done, I did for you. But for you she might have burned, and I would not have put out a finger to help her. What care I for her? She is naught to me. She wasn't destined for me; that was you. I saved her because she was your mother. I collected your things from the blazing house. I have taken you in. I take her in only as I might take in your shoe, or your cow, because it is yours. She is naught to me. I don't care if I never saw or heard her again.'

He got up and went to the window, took a flask thence; then brought his gun from a corner, and began to polish the brass fittings with rag, having first put on the metal some of the vitriol from the bottle.

'Look at this,' he said, dropping some of the acid on the tarnished brass. 'Look how it frets and boils till it has scummed away the filth, and then the brass is bright as gold. That's like me. I'm fretted and fume with your opposition, and I dare say it is as well I get a little. But after a bit it will bring out the shining metal. You will see what I am. You don't like me now, because I'm not shapely and handsome as your George De Witt. But there is the gold metal underneath; he was but gilt pinchbeck—George De Witt!' he repeated. 'That was a fancy of yours, that he was your mate! You could not have loved him a week after you'd known what he was. Marriage would have rubbed the plating off, and you would have scorned and cast him aside.'

'Elijah!' said Mehalah, 'I cannot bear this. I loved once, and I shall love for ever,—not you!—you—never,' with gathering emphasis, 'George, only George, none but George.'

'More fool you,' said Rebow sulkily. 'Only I don't believe it. You say so to aggravate me, but you don't think it.'

She did not care to pursue the subject. She had spoken out her heart, and was satisfied.

'Well, what else had you to say? I didn't think you was one of the bread and butter curtsey-my-dears and thanky, sirs! That is a new feature in you, Glory! It is the first time I've had the taste of thanks from you on my tongue.'

'You never gave me occasion before.'

'No more I did,' he answered. 'You are right there. And I don't care for thanks now. I'd take them if I valued them, but I don't. I don't care to have them from you. I don't expect thanks from my body when I feed it, nor from my hands when I warm 'em at the fire; they belong to me, and I give 'em their due. What I do for you I do for myself, for the same reason. You belong to me.'

'I must speak,' said Mehalah. 'This is more than I can endure. You say things of me, and to me, which I will not suffer. Do you mean to insult me? Have I ever given you the smallest reason to encourage you to assume this right?'

'No. But it must be. You can't always go against fate.'

'I do not believe in this fate, this destiny, of which you talk,' said the girl gathering up her strength, as her indignation swelled within her. 'You have no right over me whatever. I have been brought here against my will, but at the same time I cannot do other than acknowledge your hospitality. Had you not given us a shelter, I know not whither we should have gone. I ask you to let us shelter here a little longer, but only a little longer, till I have found some situation where I can work, and support my mother. We must sell our little goods, our sheep and cow, and with the proceeds——'

'With the proceeds you will have to pay the rent of the Ray to Lady Day.'

'You cannot be so ungenerous,' gasped Mehalah, flashing wrathfully against him. 'This undoes all your kindness in housing us. But if it must be, so be it. We will sell all, and pay you every penny; yes, and for our keep in this house, as long as we are forced to remain.'

'Not so fast, Glory,' said Elijah composedly. 'There are various things to be considered first. You can't find a situation—no one would take you in along of an old bedridden mother.'

'I can but try.'

'Aye, try; try by all means, and then come back to me. You have tried a deal of tricks to escape me, but you can't do it. You tried by borrowing money of George De Witt, you tried by going to that old palsied shipbuilder, you tried at Parson Tyll's, you tried, I don't know how at last, and you got the money; but yet you couldn't escape me. You tried to get George De Witt as your husband, to keep you from me in life, but it came to naught. He's gone out of the path that leads from you to me. You may heap up what you will, but the earth will open, and swallow all obstructions, and leave the way smooth and open. Did you ever see the old place—they call it the Devil's Walls—by Payne's? No, I dare say you don't know thereabouts. Well, I'll tell you how that spot lies waste, and covered with brambles and nettles now. The old lords D'Arcy thought to build a castle there. Then the Salcott creek ran up so far, and they could row and sail right up to their gates, were the mansion built. But it could not be. The masons built all day, and at night the earth sucked the walls in. They worked there a whole year, and they brought stones from Kent, and they poured in boulders, and they laid bricks, but it was all of no good, the earth drank in everything they put on it, as water. At last they gave it up, and they built instead on the hill where stands Barn Hall. It will be the same with you. You may build what you like, and where you like, it will go; it cannot stand, it will be swallowed up; you can only build on me.'

'Elijah! I insist on your listening to me. I will not hear this.'

'You will not? I do not care, you must. My will will drink in yours. But go on; say what you wish.'

'I am going to propose this. Pay me a wage, and I will work here. I will attend to the house and the cows, and do anything you require of me. You have no servant, and you need one. You shall let me be your servant. I shall not be ashamed to be that, but I will not remain here unless my place be determined and recognised.'

'You shall be the mistress.'

'I do not want, I do not choose to be anything else in this house but your hired servant. Pay me a wage, and I will remain till I can find some other situation; refuse, and, if I have to leave my mother, I will go out of this house to-night.'

'If you leave your mother, I will throw her out.'

'I would fetch her away. I would carry her in my arms. I will not stay here on any other terms.'

'I will humour you. You shall be paid. I will give you five shillings a week. Is that enough?'

'More than enough, with my keep and that of my mother. I thank you now. In future speak of me to the men as their fellow-servant, and not as you did recently to Abraham as their mistress.'

'I shall speak to them as I like. Am I to be controlled by you?'

'Then I will leave. I will carry my mother to the inn at Salcott, and rest there till I can find some other shelter.'

'Now look here, Glory,' said Elijah. He put his gun aside, and leaned his elbows on his knees, and faced her. 'It is of no use your talking of running away from me. You may run, but I can draw you back. I sit here of a night brooding over my fire, I begin thinking of you. I think, I think, and then a spirit takes me as it were, and fills me with fierce will, to bring you here. I feel I have threads at every finger and threads to my knees and to my feet, all fast to you, and if I stir, I move you. I lift my finger, and you raise yours. I wave my hand up, and you throw up yours. You don't know it. I do. I know that I have but to rise up from my chair, and I lift you up wherever you may be, in your bed, in your grave, and then, if I draw in with my will, I wind up these threads, and you come, you come, from wheresoever you are, out of your bed in your smock, out of your grave in your shroud; doors are nothing, my will can burst them open; locks are naught, my will can wrench them off; the screws in the coffin lid and five feet of earth are nothing, I could draw you through all. I could draw you over the ooze, and you would not be sucked in by it. I could draw you over the water, and you would not wet your foot. I could draw you through the marsh and you would not break a bullrush; look there—' he waved his arm towards the door. 'That door would fly open, and there you would stand, like one dreaming, with your eyes wide open as they are now, with your cheek colourless as now, with your lips parted as now, helpless, unable to stir a finger, or utter a sound, against my will, and you would rush into my arms, and fall on my heart. I can do all that. I feel it. I know it. I have sat here and wanted to do it, but I have not. I would not have you come to me in that way, but come of your own free will. You must come to me one way or other. Look here!' he raised his hand, and involuntarily, unconsciously, she lifted hers.

'Pick up the keys.'

She stooped and took them up.

'One day,' he said, 'you refused to take a piece of money that fell, when I bade you. Now you are more compliant. My will is gaining over yours. Your will is stout and rebellious, but it must bend and give way before mine. Go; I have done with you for the present.'

CHAPTER XVIII.

IN A COBWEB.

A month passed. Mrs. Sharland recovered, as far as recovery was possible to one of her age and enfeebled constitution, much shaken by the events of the night that saw the destruction of her home and the abrasion of the ear and tail of her biscuit-china poodle. After remaining in bed for more than a week, Mehalah almost by force obliged her to get up and descend. When once she had taken this step and found that her leather high-backed chair was before the fire in the hall, she showed no further desire to spend her days upstairs. Her life resumed the old course it had run at the Ray, but she sat more by the fire, and did less in the house than formerly. She devolved most of the domestic work on her daughter. That she had declined in strength of late was obvious. Old people will go on from year to year without any visible alteration, till some shock, or change in their surroundings takes place, when they drop perceptibly a stage, and from that moment declension becomes rapid.

Mrs. Sharland was unmistakably contented with her position at Red Hall. She enjoyed comforts which were not hers at the Ray. She saw more people, some gossip reached her ears. There was a village, Salcotty within two miles, and the small talk of a village will overflow its bounds, and dribble into every house in its neighbourhood. Every little parish throws up its coarse crop of vulgar tittle-tattle, on which the inhabitants feed, and which is exactly adapted to their mental digestion. Human characters as well as skins are subject to parasitic attacks, but human beings are the vermin which burrow their heads into, and blow themselves out on the blood of moral life. There are certain creatures which will lie shrivelled up on their backs, and endure flood and frost and burning sun, without its killing them, with suspended animation, till the animal on which they feed chances to come that way, when they leap into activity and voracity at once. Mrs. Sharland had been laid aside on the Ray, without neighbours, and therefore without matter of interest and objects of attack. She was now within leaping, lancing, and sucking distance of fresh life, and she rejoiced in renewed vigour, not of body, but of mind, if mind that can be called which has neither thought nor instinct, but only a certain gravitation which sets the tongue in motion. The brain of the rustic is as unlike the brain of the man of culture as the maggot is unlike the butterfly; the one is the larva of the other. They feed, live, move in different spheres; one chews cabbage, the other sips honey; one crawls on the earth, the other flies above it; one is clumsy in all its motions, the other agile; one is carnal, the other is spiritual. And yet—wondrous thought! the one is the parent of the other.

Mehalah had a great deal to do, and that work of a sort she had not been much engaged on at the Ray. No female hand had been employed at Red Hall since the death of Elijah's mother, and everything was accordingly falling out of repair and into disorder. She saw nothing of Rebow except at meals, and not always then, for he was often away with beasts at market, or at sales making purchases.

The rich marshes of Red Hall were unrivalled for the grazing of cattle, and the rearing of young stock.

As Mehalah was well occupied, her mind was taken off from herself, and she was for a while satisfied with her position. Rebow had not spoken to her in the manner she so disliked, and she had small occasion to speak with the men. Her mother, on the contrary, seized every occasion to entangle them in talk, or to initiate a conversation with Rebow. He maintained a surly deference towards her, and condescended at times to answer her queries and allow himself to be drawn into talk by the old woman. When that was the case, Mehalah found excuse to leave the room and engage herself in the kitchen or among the cows.

Abraham Dowsing saw much less of her than formerly. The old man, with all his sulky humour and selfish greed, had got a liking for the girl. He was much at the Ray, but often about Red Hall, where he got his food.

If he went after the sheep for the day, Mehalah provided him with 'baggings,' provision during his absence.

Lambing time was at hand, when he would be away for some weeks, returning only occasionally. Mehalah noticed that the shepherd hesitated each time he received his food, as though he desired to speak to her, but put off the occasion. At last, one day at the beginning of February, when he was about to depart for the Ray, and would be absent some days, he said to her in a low dissatisfied tone, 'I suppose, when I come back after the lambing, you'll have been to church with him.'

'What do you mean?'

'What do I mean?' repeated Abraham, 'I mean what I say. I ain't one of those that says one thing and means another. Nobody can accuse me of that.'

'I do not understand you, Abraham.'

'There's none so dull as them that won't take,' he pursued.

'I don't hold, myself, that much good comes of going to church with a man, except this, that you fasten him, and he can't cast you off when he's tired of you.'

Mehalah flushed up.

'Abraham,' she said angrily, 'I will not allow you to speak thus to me. I understand you now, and wish I did not.'

'Oh! you do take at last! That's well. I'd act on it if I was you. A man, you see, don't make no odds of taking up with a girl, and then when he's had a bit of her tongue and temper, he thinks he'd as lief be without her, and pick up another. He'd ring a whole change on the bells, he would, if it warn't for churches. That is my doctrine. Churches was built, and parsons were made, for tying up of men, and the girls are fools who let the men make up to them, and don't seize the opportunity to tie them.'

'Abraham, enough of this.'

'It is no odds to me. I don't care so long as I has my wittles and my wage. Only I'd rather see you mistress here than another. I'd get my wittles more regular and better, because you know me and my likings, and a new one wouldn't. That's all. Every man for himself, is my doctrine.'

'I forbid this for once and all. I am servant on wage here just as you are; I am that, and I shall never be anything else.'

'Oh, there you think different from most folks. You don't think according to your interests; and mistress, let me tell you, you don't talk as does the master.'

He went away mumbling something about it being no concern of his, and if some people did not know how to eat their bread and butter when they had it in their hands it was no odds to him.

Mehalah was hurt and incensed. She went to her mother.

'Mother,' she said, 'when will you be able to move? I shall look out for a situation elsewhere.'

'What, my dear child! Move from here, where I am so comfortable! You can not. Elijah won't hear of it. He told me so. He told me you was to remain here, and I should spend the rest of my days here in quiet. It is a very pleasant place, and more in the world than was the Ray. I am better off here than I was there. Now we get everything for nothing, we don't lay out a penny, and you get wage beside.'

'Mother, Abraham has been speaking to me. He has hinted, what I do not like, that I ought to marry Elijah——'

'So you ought,' said the widow. 'Elijah, I am sure, is willing. It is what he has been wishing and hoping for all along, but you have been so stubborn and set against him. After all he has done for us you might yield a bit.'

'I will never marry him.'

'Don't say that. You will do anything to secure a comfortable home for me. It may not be long that I may have to trouble you,—I know you look on me as a trouble, I know that but for me you would feel free, and go away into the world. You think me a burden on you, because I can do nothing: you are young and lusty. But I bore with you, Mehalah, when you was young and feeble, and I laid by for you money that would have been very acceptable to me, and bought me many little comforts that I forbore, to save for you——'

The old woman with low cunning had discovered the thread to touch, to move her daughter.

'Say no more, say not another word, mother,' exclaimed Mehalah. 'You know that I never, never will forsake you, that you are more to me a thousand times than my own life. But there is one thing I never will do for you. I never will marry Elijah.'

'I am afraid, Mehalah, that folks will talk.'

'I fear so too, but they have no occasion. I will show them that. I will find a situation elsewhere.'

'You shall not, Mehalah!'

'I must, mother.'

She thought for some time what she should do, and then put on her bonnet, and walked into Salcott. She had not been into the village since her arrival at Red Hall.

Salcott is a small village of old cottages at the head of a creek that opens out of the Blackwater. It has a church with a handsome tower built of flints, but with no chancel. Within a bowshot, across the creek, connected with it by a bridge, is Virley church, a small hunchbacked edifice in the last stages of dilapidation, in a graveyard unhedged, unwalled; the church is scrambled over by ivy, with lattice windows bulged in by the violence of the gales, and a bellcot leaning on one side like a drunkard. Near this decaying church is a gabled farm, and this and a cottage form Virley village. The principal population congregates at Salcott, across the wooden bridge, and consisted—a hundred years ago—of labourers, and men more or less engaged in the contraband trade. Every house had its shed and stable, where was a donkey and cart, to be let on occasion to carry smuggled goods inland. At the end of the village stands a low tavern, the Rising Sun, a mass of gables; part of it, the tavern drinking-room, is only one storey high, but the rest is a jumble of roofs and lean-to buildings, chimneys, and ovens, a miracle of picturesqueness. Mehalah walked into the bar, and found there the landlady alone.

'I have come here, mistress,' she said abruptly, 'in search of work. I am strong and handy, and will do as much as a man. I will serve you faithfully and well if you will engage me. I have an infirm mother who must be lodged somewhere, so I ask for small wage.'

'Who are you? Where do you come from?' asked the landlady eyeing her with surprise.

'My name is Mehalah Sharland. I lived on the Ray till the house was burned down. Since then I have been at Red Hall.'

'Oh!' exclaimed the woman, her countenance falling. 'You are the young woman, are you, that I heard tell of?'

'I am the young woman now in service there, but wanting to go and work elsewhere.'

'I've heard tell of you,' said the landlady dryly.

'What have you heard of me?'

The woman looked knowingly at her, and smiled.

'Pray what does Master Rebow say to your leaving him? You and he have fallen out, have you?' said the hostess knowingly. 'You'll come together all the faster for it. There's nothing like a good breeze for running a cargo in.'

'Can you give me work?'

'I dursn't do it.'

'Have you need of anyone now?'

'Well,' with a cough, 'if Master Rebow were agreeable, I might find such a girl as you wery handy about the house. I've lost the last girl I had; she's took with the small-pox. You could have her bed, and her work, and her wage, and welcome. But unless the master gave his consent,' she began to dust the table, 'I dursn't do it.'

'Is he your landlord?'

'No, he is not.'

'Then why need you doubt about taking me?'

'Because Rebow wouldn't allow of it.'

'He could not stop me. I am not engaged to him for any time.'

'I dursn't do it. How long have you been with Rebow?'

'A little more than a month.'

'You've never gone against him perhaps. If you had, you wouldn't ask me the reason why I dursn't stand in his way.'

Mehalah considered. She had opposed Elijah from the very beginning.

'There's no one would dare to do it,' continued the landlady. 'If you want to get from Master Rebow, you must go farther inland; but I doubt if you'll escape him. However,' and she tossed her head, 'you only want to make him fast. If a girl gives way at once, she's cheap.'

'You mistake me, you altogether mistake me,' said Mehalah indignantly. 'I will not remain in his house any longer; I must and I will go elsewhere.'

'If Elijah Rebow was to take the purse out of my pocket, or the bed from under me, if he was to take my daughter from my side, I dursn't say nay. If you think to escape against the will of the master, you are mistaken.'

'I shall.'

'Look here,' said the landlady; 'take my advice and go back and be mum. I won't say another word with you, lest I get into trouble.' She turned and left the bar.

Mehalah went out, more determined than ever to break away from Red Hall, whether her mother desired it or not.

She crossed the creaking rude wooden bridge to Virley. The churchyard and the farmyard seemed all one. The pigs were rooting at the graves. A cow was lying in the porch. An old willow drooped over a stagnant pool beneath the chancel window. Shed roof-tiles and willow leaves lay mouldering together on the edge of the pond. The church of timber and brick, put up anyhow on older stone foundations, had warped and cracked; the windows leaned, fungus growths sprouted about the bases of the timbers. Every rib showed in the roof as on the side of a horse led to the knackers.

The farm was but little more prosperous in appearance than the church. Patched windows and broken railings showed a state of decline. Mehalah walked into the yard, where she saw a man carrying a pitchfork.

'Who is the master here?' she asked.

'I am.'

'Is there a mistress?'

'Yes. What have you to say to her?'

Mehalah told her story as she had told it to the landlady of the Rising Sun. 'I will work for my keep and that of my mother, and work harder than any man on your farm.'

'Where do you come from?'

'Red Hall.'

'Oh!' said the farmer, with a whistle, 'Rebow's girl, eh?'

'I am working for him now.'

'Working for him, come now that's fine.'

'I am working for him,' repeated Mehalah with clouding brow.

'And you want to come here. You think my missus would let you, do you? Now tell me, what put you on to coming to me? Has Elijah picked a quarrel with me, that he sends you here? Does he want occasion against me? Do you think I want to run any risks with my barns and my cattle and my life? No, thank you. I dursn't do it.'

'Tell me, where can I find work?'

'You must go out of the reach of Rebow's arm, if you find it.'

'You won't give me any?'

He shook his head. 'For my life, I dursn't do it.' He laughed and put out his hand to chuck her under the chin, she struck his fingers up with her fist. 'There ain't a better judge of beasts in all the marshes than Rebow, nor in horse-flesh neither. You ain't a bad bit of meat neither. I approve his taste.'

Mehalah wrenched the pitchfork out of his hand. Her eyes flamed. She would have struck him; but was suddenly assailed from behind by the farmer's wife.

'Now then, hussy, what are you up to?'

The girl could not answer; her anger choked the words in her throat.

'She's that wench of Rebow's, you know,' said the farmer. 'I guess it is cat and dog in that house.'

'Get you gone,' shouted the woman, 'go out of my premises, hussy! I don't want my place to be frequented by such as you. Get you gone at once, or I will loose the mastiff.'

Mehalah retired with bowed head, and her arms folded on her bosom. She halted on the bridge, and kicked fragments of frozen earth and gravel into the water. A woman going by looked at her.

'Where is the parson?' asked Mehalah.

'Yonder, you go over the marsh by the hill with the windmill on it, and you come to a road, you'll find a blacksmith's shop, and you must ask there. He's the curate, there's no rector hereabouts. They keep away because of the ague.'

Mehalah cross the fen indicated, passed beside the windmill and the blacksmith's shop, and found the cottage occupied by the curate, a poor man, married to a woman of a low class, with a family of fourteen children, packed in the house wherever they could be stowed away. The curate was a crushed man, his ideas stunned in his head by the uproar in which he dwelt. His old scholarship remained to him in his brain like fossils in the chalk, to be picked ont, dead morsels. There was nothing living in the petrified white matter that filled his skull.

Mehalah knocked at the door. The parson opened it, and admitted her into his kitchen. As soon as the wife heard a female voice, she rushed out of the back kitchen with her arms covered with soap suds, and stood in the door. A little-minded woman, she lived on her jealousy, and would never allow her husband to speak with another woman if she could help it.

'What do you want, my dear?' asked the curate.

'Ahem!' coughed the wife. 'Dear, indeed! Pray who are you, miss?'

Mehalah explained that she sought work, and hoped that the parson would be able to recommend her.

'You don't, you don't——' faltered he.

'You don't suppose I'd take you on here,' said the parson's wife. 'You're too young by twenty years. I don't approve of young women; they don't make good servants. I like a staid matronly person of forty to fifty, that one can trust, and won't be gadding after boys or——' she shook her suds at her husband. 'But I don't at present want any servant. We are full.'

'We don't keep any,' said the pastor.

'Edward! don't demean us, we do keep servants—occasionally. You know we do, Edward. Mrs. Cutts comes in to scour out and clean up of a Saturday. You forget that. We pay her ninepence.'

'Who are you, my dear—I mean, young woman?' asked the curate.

'Yes, who are you?' said his better half. 'We must know more of you before we can recommend you among our friends. Our friends are very select, and keep quite a better sort of servants, they don't pick up anybody, they take so to speak the cream, the very purest quality.'

Mehalah gave the required information. Mrs. Rabbit bridled and blew bubbles. The Reverend Mr. Rabbit became depressed, yet made an effort to be confidential. 'You'd better—you'd better marry him,' he hinted. 'It would be a satisfaction on all sides.'

'What is that? What did you say, Edward? No whisperings in my house, if you please. My house is respectable, I hope, though it mayn't be a lordly mansion. I do drive a conveyance,' she said, 'I hire the blacksmith's donkey-cart when I go out to make my calls, and drop my cards. So I leave you to infer if I'm not respectable. And Miss—Miss—Miss—' with a giggle and a curtsey, 'when may I have the felicity of calling on you at Red

Hall, and of learning how respectable that establishment has become? There's room for improvement,' she said, tossing her nose.

At that moment a rush, a roar, an avalanche down the narrow stairs, steep as a ladder. In a heap came the whole fourteen, the oldest foremost, the youngest in the rear.

'We've got him, we're going to drown him.'

'What is it?' feebly enquired the father, putting his hands to his ears.

'We'll hold him to the fire and pop his little eyes.'

'No, they're too small.'

'Into the water-butt with him!'

A yell.

'He's bitten me. Drown him!'

'What is it?' shouted the mother.

'A bat. Tommy found him in the roof. We're going to put him in the butt, and see if he can swim.'

The whole torrent swept and swirled round Mehalah, and carried her to the front door.

The curate stole out after her.

'My good girl,' he whispered, 'botch it up. Marry. Most marriages hereabouts are botches.'

'Edward!' shouted Mrs. Rabbit, 'come in, no sneaking outside after lasses. Come back at once. Always wanting a last word with suspicious characters.'

'Marry!' was the pastor's last word, as he was drawn back by two soapy hands applied to his coat tails, and the door was slammed.

Mehalah walked away fast from the yelping throng of children congregated about the water-butt, watching the struggles of the expiring bat. She took the road before her, and saw that it led to Peldon, the leaning tower of which stood on a hill that had formed the northern horizon from the Ray. There was a nice farm by the roadside, and she went there, and was met with excuses. The time was not one when a girl could be engaged. There was no work to be done in the winter. The early spring was coming on, she urged, and she would labour in the fields like a man. Then the sick mother was mentioned as an insuperable objection. 'We can't have any old weakly person here on the premises,' said the farmer's wife. 'You see if she was to die, you've no money, and we should be put to the expense of the burying; anyhow there'd be the inconvenience of a corpse in the house.'

Mehalah went on; and now a hope dawned in her. Another two miles would bring her to the Rose, the old inn that stood not far from the Strood. There she was known, and there she was sure, if possible, she would be accommodated and given work.

She walked forward with raised head, the dark cloud that had brooded on her brow began to rise, the bands about her heart that had been contracting gave way a little. There was the inn, an old-fashioned house, with a vine scrambling over the red tile roof, and an ancient standard sign before the door, on the green, bearing a rose, painted the size of a gigantic turnip.

Mehalah walked into the bar. The merry landlord and his wife greeted her with delight, with many shakes of the hands, and much condolence over the disasters that had befallen her and her mother.

'Well, my dear,' said the landlady, confidentially, 'you're well out of it, if you come here. To be sure we'll take you in, and I dare say we'll find you work; bring your mother also. It ain't right for a handsome wench like you to be living all along of a lone man in his farm. Folks talk. They have talked, and said a deal of things. But you come here. What day may we expect you?'

'I must bring my mother by water. The tide will not suit for a week. It must be by day, my mother cannot come in the boat if there be much rain; and we shall not be able to come—at least there will be a difficulty in getting away—should Rebow be at home. Expect us some day when the weather is favourable and there be an afternoon tide.'

'You will be sure to come?'

'Sure.'

## CHAPTER XIX.
## DE PROFUNDIS.

Mehalah's heart was lighter now than it had been for many a week. She had secured her object. She could be out of the toils of Rebow, away from his hateful presence.

She had worked hard and conscientiously at Red Hall, and felt that she had to some extent cancelled the obligation he had laid on her. Her proud spirit, lately crushed, began to arise; her head was lifted instead of being bowed.

Rebow remarked the change in her, and was satisfied either that she had reconciled herself to her position, or that she meditated something which he did not understand.

Mrs. Sharland did not share in her daughter's exultation. She grumbled and protested. She was very comfortable at Red Hall, she was sure Elijah had been exceedingly kind to them. They had wanted nothing. The house was much better than the old ramshackle Ray, and their position in it superior to any they could aspire to at the Rose. This was a hint to Mehalah, but the girl refused to take it. As for Elijah, what was there to object to in him? He was well off, very well off, a prosperous man, who spent nothing on himself, and turned over a great deal of money in the year. He was not very young, but he was a man who had seen the world and was in his prime of strength and intelligence. Mrs. Sharland thought that they could not do better than settle at the Red Hall and make it their home for life, and that Mehalah should put her foolish fancies in her pocket and make the best of what offered.

But Mehalah's determination bore down all opposition.

St. Valentine's Day shone bright with a promise of spring. The grey owls were beginning to build in the hayrick, the catkins were timidly swelling on the nut bushes; in the ooze the glasswort shot up like little spikes of vitriol-green glass. A soft air full of wooing swept over the flats. The sun was hot.

The tide flowed at noon, and Elijah was absent.

Mehalah, deaf to her mother's remonstrances, removed some of their needful articles to the boat, and at last led her mother, well wrapped up, to the skiff.

When the girl had cast loose, and was rowing on the sparkling water, her heart danced and twinkled with the wavelets; there was a return of spring to her weary spirit, and the good and generous seeds in her uncultivated soul swelled and promised to shoot. She was proud to think that she had carried her point, that in spite of Rebow, she had established her freedom, that her will had proved its power of resistance. She even sang as she rowed, she,—whose song had been hushed since the disappearance of George. She had not forgotten him, and cast away her grief at his loss, but the recoil from the bondage and moral depression of Red Hall filled her with transient exultation and joyousness.

The row was long.

'O mother!' she said, as she passed under the Ray hill, 'I must indeed run up and look at the place. I cannot go by.'

'Do as you will,' said Mrs. Sharland. 'I cannot control you. I don't pretend to. My wishes and my feelings are nothing to you.'

Mehalah did not notice this peevish remark, she was accustomed to her mother's fretfulness. She threw the little anchor on the gravel at the 'hard,' and jumped on shore. She ascended the hill and stood by the scorched black patch which marked her old home. The house had burned to the last stick, leaving two brick chimneys standing gauntly alone. There was the old hearth at which she had so often crouched, bare, cold, and open. A few bricks had been blown from the top of the chimney, but otherwise it was intact.

As she stood looking sadly on the relics, Abraham Dowsing came up.

'What are you doing here?'

'I have come away from Red Hall, Abraham,' she said gaily, 'I do not think I have been so happy for many a day.'

'When are you going back?'

'Never.'

'Who then is to prepare me my wittles?' he asked sullenly. 'I ain't going to be put off with anything.'

'I do not know, Abraham.'

'But I must know. Now go back again, and don't do what's wrong and foolish. You ought to be there, and mistress there too. Then all will run smooth, and I'll get my wittles as I like them.'

'You need not speak of that, Abraham, I shall never return to Red Hall. I have quitted it and I hope have seen the last of the hateful house and its still more hateful master.'

'I wonder,' mused the shepherd, 'whether I could arrange with Rebow to get my wittles from the Rose.'

'That is where I am going to.'

'Oh!' his face lightened, 'then I don't mind. Do what you think best.' His face darkened again. 'But I doubt whether the master will keep me on when you have left. I reckon he only takes me because of you; he thinks you wouldn't like it, if I was to be turned adrift. No. You had better go back to Red Hall. Make yourself as comfortable as you can. That's my doctrine.'

Presently the old man asked, 'I say, does the master know you have left?'

'No, Abraham.'

'Are you sure?'

'I never told him.'

'Did your mother know you had made up your mind to leave?'

'Yes, I told her so a week ago.'

'And you suppose she has kept her mouth shut? She couldn't do it.'

'If Elijah had suspected we were going to-day,' said Mehalah, 'I do not think he would have left home; he would have endeavoured to prevent me.'

'Perhaps. But he's deep.'

'Good day, Abraham!' She waved him a farewell with a smile. She knew, and made allowance for the humours of the old man. In a moment she was again by her mother, at the oar, and speeding with the flowing tide up the Rhyn to the 'hard' at its head belonging to the Rose Inn.

'Have you brought the toad-jug with you, Mehalah?'

'No, mother.'

'Nor the china dogs?'

'No, mother.'

'It is of no use, I will not live at the Rose. I will not get out of the boat. I must have all my property about me.'

'I will fetch the other things away. When you are housed safely, then I shall not care. I will go back and bring away all our goods.'

'You are so rough. I won't let anyone handle the china but myself. Last time the poodles were moved, you know one lost a ear and a bit of its tail. There is no one fit to touch such things but me. Those rough-handed fellows, Jim and Joe, what do they know of the value of those dogs? You will promise me, Mehalah, to be gentle with them. Put them in the foot of a pair of stockings and wrap the legs round them, and then perhaps they will travel. I wouldn't have them lose any more of their precious persons,—no, not for worlds,—not for worlds.'

'I will take heed, mother.'

'And mind and stuff my old nightcap,—the dirty one, I mean—and my bedsocks into the toad-jug, then it won't break. You'll promise me that, won't you; if that were injured, I'd as soon die as see it.'

'I will use the utmost precaution with it.'

'Then there are the soup plates, of Lowestoft. I had them of my father, and he had them of his grandmother; there's a dozen of them, and not a chip or a crack. True beauties as ever you saw, I think you'd best put them in the folds of some of my linen. Put them between the sheets, wide apart, in the spruce hutch.'

'All right, mother; now hold hard, here we are.'

The boat grated on the bottom, and then it was drawn up by a firm hand. Mehalah looked round and started.

Elijah and two other men were there. Elijah had stepped into the water, and pulled the boat ashore.

'Here we are, Glory!' he said, 'waiting ready for you. The sheriff's officer with his warrant, all ready. You haven't kept us waiting long.'

'What is that? What is that?' screamed Mrs. Sharland.

'Step out, Glory! step out, mistress!' said Elijah.

'What is the meaning of this?' asked Mehalah, a cloud suddenly darkening her sky and quenching the joy of her heart.

'I've a warrant against you, madam,' said the man who stood by Rebow. 'Please to read it.' He held it out.

'What is this?' screamed Mrs. Sharland, rising in the boat and staggering forwards. Mehalah helped her on shore.

'This is what it is,' answered Rebow. 'You and Glory there are my tenants for the Ray. The farm is mine, with the marshes and the saltings. I gave eight hundred pounds for it. You've burnt down my premises, between you, you and Glory there. You've robbed me of a hundred or two hundred pounds worth of property with your wilfulness or carelessness. Now, I want to know, how is it you have not built up my farmhouse again?'

'I can't do it. I haven't the money!' wailed Mrs. Sharland. 'I am sure, Master Rebow, there was nothing but pure accident in the fire. I never thought——'

'Pure accident!' scoffed Elijah. 'Do you call that pure accident, soaking the whole chamber in spirits, with a fire burning on the hearth, and dashing the cask staves here and there, on the fire and off it.'

Mehalah looked at him.

'Ah, ha! Glory! You think I don't know it. You think I didn't see you! Why, I was at the window. I saw you do it. Tell me, mother, did not Glory smash the keg I had just given you?'

'I believe she did, Elijah! I am very sorry. I did my best to stop her, but she is a perverse, rebellious girl. You must forgive her, she intended no harm.'

'If you saw me do it, why did you let the house catch fire?' asked Mehalah, looking hard in Rebow's face.

'Could I help it?' he asked in reply. 'There you sat by the hearth, and no harm came of it. At last you went out, and locked and double-locked the door. I went down to my boat. I tell you, I was uneasy, and I looked back, and I saw by the light in the room that the spirit had caught. I ran back and tried to get in. The floor was flaming.'

'The floor was of brick,' said Mehalah.

'The door was fast locked. You know best why you locked it. It never was fastened before that night. You screwed on the lock, then you went out of the place yourself, leaving the room on fire, and fastened the door that none might get in.'

'A lie!' exclaimed the girl.

'Is it a lie? I don't think it. I can't cipher out your doings any other way. I tried to break open the door, but you had put too stout a fastening on. Then I burst open the window, and when the wind got in, it made the fire rage worse. So I ran and shouted to my men in the big boat, and I got a balk and I stove the door in, and then it was too late to do more than save your mother and her goods. As for you, you left her and them to burn together; you wanted to be off and free of her. I know you.'

'Oh, Master Rebow! I know I'm a burden to her, but she would not do that!' put in Mrs. Sharland.

'Why did you watch me?' asked Mehalah, and then regretted that she had put the question.

'You see,' said Elijah turning to the officer, 'she didn't think anyone was near to give evidence against her.'

'Here I am,' said Mehalah, 'put me in prison, do with me what you will. I am innocent of all intent to burn the farm.'

'I could hang you for it,' laughed Elijah. 'That pretty neck where the red handkerchief hangs so jauntily would not look well with a hemp rope round it. You'd dangle on the Ray, where the house stood. You'd have a black cap then pulled over those dark eyes and brown skin, not a red one, not a red one, Glory!' he rubbed his hands.

'I have no warrant against you,' said the bailiff to Mehalah. 'You stand charged with nothing. The warrant is against your mother.'

'Against me? What will you do with me?' cried the old woman.

'You must go to prison if you cannot build the house up again, and restore it as good as it was to the landlord. He can't be at a loss by your neglect.'

'I cannot do it. I have not the money.'

'Then you must go to prison till you get it.'

Mrs. Sharland sank on the gravel. She wept and wrung her hands. This was worse than the burning of the house, worse even than the lesion of the ear and tail of the poodle.

'I won't go. I can't go!' she sobbed. 'I've the ague so bad. I suffer from rheumatism in all my bones. Let me alone,' she pleaded, 'and I promise I'll go to bed and never get out of it again.'

'You'll suffer in prison, I can promise you,' said Elijah exultingly. 'You'll have no bed to crawl into, unless you can pay for it; you'll have no blankets to wrap round you in the cold frosty night, if you can't pay for them; you'll have no fire to shiver by when there is ice on the ponds, if you haven't money to pay for it. The frost in your bones will make you shriek and jabber in prison.'

'I have no money. I gave the last to pay off Mrs. De Witt,' wailed the wretched woman. 'But there are the sheep.'

115

'They go to pay your rent up to Lady Day, aye, and till Michaelmas. I haven't had notice yet that you are about to quit. You can't give up the farm without, and I will exact every penny of my rent.'

'Then I am at your mercy,' sobbed Mrs. Sharland. She turned to Mehalah and pleaded, 'Haven't you a word to say, to save me?'

The girl was silent. What could she say?

'Come along, madam, it is of no use. The warrant is here, and come along you must.'

'I will not go to prison. I will not. I shall die of cold and ague and rheumatics there. My bones will burst like water-pipes, and I'll shiver the teeth out of my jaws and the nails off my fingers and toes. I won't go!' she screamed. 'You must carry me, I can't walk. I'm a dying old woman.'

'Would you like to go back to Red Hall?' asked Elijah gravely.

'Oh! Master Rebow, if I might! I could shiver in comfort.'

'You and Glory! You and Glory!' He looked from one to the other. 'I don't take back one without the other.'

'Take me back!' wailed Mrs. Sharland. 'I know you won't be so cruel as to send me to prison. Let me go back to my armchair; Mehalah! promise him everything.'

'I will promise him nothing,' she said gloomily. 'If ever I hated this man, I hate him now.'

'Then she must go to prison,' growled Rebow. 'Now look you here, Glory! I don't ask much. I only ask you to go back with your mother, and work for me as you have worked hitherto. I do not say a word about anything else. You thought to escape me. You cannot. I have told you all along that it is impossible. As for the future, let the future determine. I wish to let you take your own course. I will not say another word about my wishes, till you come to me, of your own accord, and say that you will be mine. There! I promise you that. I will not force you any further; but I will not allow you to leave my house. There you must remain till you come to me and bid me take you, till you come and give yourself freely into my hands. Do you hear me, Glory?'

'Mehalah, save me,' pleaded Mrs. Sharland. 'Do what you can to save me from prison. Did I not lay by for you when I was a widow and needy? And will you refuse me this?'

'One thing or another,' said Rebow. 'Either your mother rots in prison, with no escape possible till she goes out to her grave in a pauper's shell, or you and she return at once to Red Hall, on the same conditions as you have been there hitherto, on the conditions you proposed yourself.'

Mehalah trembled.

'Let us go back,' said Mrs. Sharland. 'Help me into the boat. He couldn't have spoken more fair. You see, Mehalah, the Ray house is a great loss to him, and he gave eight hundred pounds for it.'

'And the marshes, and the saltings, and for you and Glory, and all things,' put in Rebow.

Mehalah held out her arms. Her head swam; she stood as though balancing herself on a high wall. Then she clasped her hands over her forehead, and burst into a storm of tears.

'Jim!' said Elijah, 'get the old doll into the stern, and you row her back to Red Hall. Take her under your arm and chuck her in anyhow.'

He looked at the convulsed girl with an ugly smile of triumph.

'Give me the warrant, bailiff!' He took the paper, held it under Mehalah's eyes and tore it in pieces, and scattered them over the water.

'Shove off, Jim. Row the old bundle back quick. Glory and I are going to drive home.'

Mehalah looked up, with a gasp as though stung.

'Yes, Glory! To-day is Valentine's Day. Valentine's Day it is. I have my little gig here. It accommodates two beautifully. I am going to take you up by my side, and drive you home, home, to your home and mine, Glory, in it; and all along the road, here at the Rose where the horse is standing, at Peldon, at Salcott and Virley,—all along the road,—at the parson's, at the Rising Sun, at Farmer Goppin's,—everywhere I'll let them see that I'm out a-junketing to-day along with my Valentine.'

All power of resistance was gone from Mehalah. The landlady at the Rose looked at her with pitying eyes, as she was helped up into the gig.

'I thought you was coming to us,' said the woman.

'You thought wrong,' answered Elijah with a boisterous laugh. 'Glory is coming back to me. We've had a bit of a tiff, but have made it up. Haven't we, Glory?'

The girl's head fell in shame on her bosom. She could not speak, but the tears rolled out of her eyes and streaked the 'Gloriana' on her breast.

He did not say a word to her as he drove home; but he stopped wherever she had halted a few days before. At Peldon farm he drew up, and struck at the door. He asked if there was a bullock there to be sold. The woman came into the garden with him.

'Out a Valentining along with my lass,' he said, indicating Mehalah with his whip over his shoulder.

He arrested his horse at the parson's cottage, and shouted till the door opened, and Mr. Rabbit appeared, with Mrs. Rabbit behind his back, peeping over his shoulder.

'I say,' roared Rebow, 'one of those cursed brats of yours has been on my marshes plaguing my cows, and has run two of them lame. Let him try it on again, let him put his foot on my ground, and I'll cut it off, and send him limping home.'

He stopped at the Rising Sun and called for spirits, and offered some to Mehalah. She turned aside her head in disgust; he drove up to Virley Hall farm, and into the yard, and called forth Farmer Goppin and his wife.

'I tell you,' he said, 'one of my cattle has been straying, I don't suppose she has done damage; she got into this here yard, I'm told. You turned her out. I'm a man of few words, but I thank ye. I am carrying her home before she is pounded.'

And then he drove straight to Red Hall.

Mehalah descended, crushed, broken, no more herself, the bold haughty girl of the Ray. She crept upstairs, took off her red cap and tore it with her hands and teeth. Her liberty was for ever gone from her.

Her mother was in their common bedroom, the boat had returned before the cart, for the way by water was the shortest, and tide had favoured. The old woman babbled about her grievances, and rejoiced at Rebow's magnanimity. She was busy replacing all the little articles that had been carried away, and were now brought back.

Mehalah could not endure the thrumming of her talk, and she hid herself in a corner of the little inner apartment, an empty room lighted by a small triangular window. There she crouched in the corner, on the ground, with her head on her knees and her hands in her hair behind. She sat there motionless. The fountain of her tears was dried up. The hectic flames burned in her cheeks, but all the rest of her face was deadly in its pallor. She could not think, she could not feel. She had experienced but one such another period of agony, that when the medal was restored and she knew that George was lost to her. That moment was sweet to this. That was one of pure pain, this of pain and humiliation, of crushed pride, of honour trampled and dragged in the dirt. Her self-respect had had its death-wound, and she sat and let her heart bleed away. Once or twice she put her hand on the floor. She thought that that must have been flooded with blood and tears, as if, when she took her hand up, it must be steeped red. It was not so.

But the soul has its ichor as well as the heart, and when it is cut deep into it also drains away, and is left empty, pulseless, pallid. Mrs. Sharland came in and spoke to her daughter, but got no answer. Mehalah looked up at her, but there was no expression in her eyes, she did not hear, or if she heard, did not understand what was said to her. The old woman went away muttering.

The evening fell, and Mehalah still sat crouched in her corner. The golden triangle which had stood on the wall opposite her had moved to her side, turned to silver, and now was but a nebulous patch on the white plaster. With the death of the day some abatement came to Mehalah's distress. She moved her cramped limbs. She rose to her knees, and fixed her eyes on the sky that glimmered grey through the triangular window. A star was hanging there. She saw it, and looked at it long, it shone through her eyes and down into the dark abyss in her soul. By little her ideas began to shape themselves; recollections of the past formed over that despairing gulf; she could not think of the present; she had not the power or the will to look into the future.

A year had passed since, on such an evening as this, looking on that star, she had stood with George de Witt on the Ray beneath the thorn trees, and he had gaily called her his Valentine, and given her in jest a picture of the Goddess of Liberty as proclaimed in Paris, wearing the bonnet rouge. She a goddess! She who was now so weak. Her power was gone. Liberty! She had none. She was a slave.

She drew herself up on her knees, and strained her united fingers, with the palms outward, towards that glittering star, and moaned, 'My Valentine! My George, my George!'

Suddenly, as if in answer to that wail from her wounded heart, there came a crash, and then loud, pealing, agonising, a cry from below out of the depths, and yet in the air about—'Glory! Glory! Glory!'

## CHAPTER XX.
## IN PROFUNDUM.

The cry roused Mehalah, as a step into cold water is a shock bringing a somnambulist instantly to full consciousness.

In a minute she was outside the house, looking for the person whose appeal had struck her ear. She saw the wooden shutter that had closed the window of the madman's den broken, hanging by one hinge. Two bleached, ghostly hands were stretched through the bars, clutching and opening.

At his door, above the steps, stood Elijah.

'Hah! Glory!' he said, 'has the crazed fool's shout brought you down?'

She was stepping towards the window. Rebow ran down before her.

'Go in!' he shouted to his brother. 'Curse you, you fool! breaking the shutter and yelling out, scaring the whole house.' He had a whip, a great carter's whip in his hand, and he smacked it. The hands disappeared instantly.

'Bring me a hammer and nails,' ordered Rebow. 'You will find them in the window of the hall.'

Mehalah obeyed. Rebow patched up the shutter temporarily. There were iron bars to the window. The wooden cover had a small hole in it to admit a little light. During the summer the shutter was removed. It was used to exclude the winter cold.

'Why did he call me?' asked Mehalah.

'He did not.'

'I heard his cry. He called me thrice, Glory! Glory! Glory!'

'He was asking for his victuals,' said Rebow, with a laugh. 'Look you here, Glory! I have been alone in this house so long, and have thought of you, and brooded on you, and had none to speak to about you. At last I took to teaching my brother your name. I wouldn't give him his food till he said it. I taught him like a parrot. I made him speak your name, as you make a dog sit up and beg for a bit of bread. I've been about on the road all day, on account of your perversity and wilfulness, and so forgot to give my brother his food. But I don't care. He had no right to smash the shutter and yell out the way he has. I'll punish him for it. I'll lay into him with the whip, so as he shall not forget. He'll be quieter in future.'

'Do not,' said Mehalah. 'It is a shame; it is wicked to treat a poor afflicted wretch thus.'

'Oh! you are turned advocate, are you? You take the side of a madman against the sane. That is like a perverse creature such as you. What has he done for you, that you should try to save his back?'

'No mercy is to be looked for at your hands,' said Mehalah sullenly.

'Look you here, Glory! the moon is full, and that always makes him madder. I have to keep him short of food, and strap his shoulders, or he would tear the walls down in his fury.'

'Let me attend to him,' asked Mehalah.

'You'd be afraid of him.'

'I should pity him,' said the girl. 'He and I are both wretched, both your victims, both prisoners, wearing your chains.'

'You have no chains round you, Glory.'

'Have I not? I have, invisible, may be, but firmer, colder, more given to rust into and rub the flesh than those carried by that poor captive. I have tried to break away, but I cannot. You draw me back.'

'I told you I could. I have threads to every finger, and I can move you as I will. I can bring you into my arms.'

'That—never,' said Mehalah gloomily and leisurely.

'You think not?'

'I am sure not. You may boast of your power over me. You have a power over me, but that power has its limits. I submit now, but only for my mother's sake. Were she not dependent wholly on me, were she dead, I would defy you and be free, free as the gull yonder.'

Elijah put his hand inside his door, drew out his gun, and in a moment the gull was seen to fall.

'She is not dead,' said Mehalah, with a gleam of triumph in her sad face.

'No, but winged. The wretch will flutter along disabled. She will try to rise, and each effort will give her mortal agony, and grind the splintered bones together and make the blood bleed away. She will skim a little while above the water, but at length will fall into the waves and be washed ashore dead.'

'Yes,' said Mehalah; 'you will not kill, but wound—wound to the quick.'

'That is about it, Glory!'

'Let me repeat my request,' she said; 'allow me to attend to your brother. I must have someone, some thing, to pity and minister to.'

'You can minister to me.'

'So I do.'

'And you can pity me.'

'Pity you!' with scorn.

'Aye. I am to be pitied, for here am I doing all I can to win the heart of a perverse and stubborn girl, and I meet with nothing but contempt and hate. I am to be pitied. I am a man; I love you, and am defied and repulsed, and fled from as though I had the pestilence, and my house were a plague hospital.'

'Will you let me attend to your brother?'

'No, I will not.'

The shutter was dashed off its hinges, flung out into the yard, and the two ghastly hands were again seen strained through the bars. Again there rang out in the gathering night the piteous cry, 'Glory! Glory! Glory!'

'By God! you hound,' yelled Elijah, and he raised his whip to bring it down in all its cutting force on the white wrists.

'I cannot bear it. I will not endure it!' cried Mehalah, and she arrested the blow. She caught the stick and wrenched it out of the hand of Rebow before he could recover from his surprise, and broke it over her knee and flung it into the dyke that encircled the yard. There was, however, no passion in her face, she acted deliberately, and her brown cheek remained unflushed. 'I take his cry as an appeal to me, and I will protect him from your brutality.'

'You are civil,' sneered Elijah. 'What are you in this house? A servant, you say. Then you should speak and act as one. No, Glory! you know you are not, and cannot be, a servant. You shall be its mistress. I forgive you what you have done, for you are asserting your place and authority. Only do not cry out and protest if in future I speak to the workmen of you as the mistress.'

A hard expression settled on Mehalah's brow and eyes. She turned away.

'Are you going? Have you not a parting word, mistress?'

'Go!' she said, in a tone unlike that usual with her. 'I care for nothing. I feel for no one. I am without a heart. Do what you will with that brother of yours. I am indifferent to him and to his fate. Everything in the world is all one to me now. If you had let me think for the poor creature and feed him, and attend to him, I might have become reconciled to being here; I could at least have comforted my soul with the thought that I was ministering to the welfare of one unhappy wretch and lightening his lot. But now,' she shrugged her shoulders. 'Now everything is all one to me. I can laugh,' she did so, harshly. 'There is nothing in the world that I care for now, except my mother, and I do not know that I care very much for her now. I feel as if I had no heart, or that mine were frozen in my bosom.'

'You do not care now for your mother!' exclaimed Rebow. 'Then leave her here to my tender mercy, and go out into the world and seek your fortune. Go on the tramp like your gipsy ancestry.'

'Leave my mother to your mercy!' echoed Mehalah. 'To the mercy of you, who could cut your poor crazed brother over the fingers with a great horsewhip! To you, who have stung and stabbed at my self-respect till it is stupefied; who have treated me, whom you profess to love, as I would not treat a marsh briar.[1] Never. Though my heart may be stunned or dead, yet I have sufficient instinct to stand by and protect her who brought me into the world and nursed me, when I was helpless. As for you, I do not hate you any more than I love you. You are nothing to me but a coarse, ill-conditioned dog. I will beat you off with a hedge-stake if you approach me nearer than I choose. If you keep your distance and keep to yourself, you will not occupy a corner of my thoughts. I take my course, you take yours.' She walked moodily away and regained her room.

[1] Horse-fly.

120

Mrs. Sharland began at once a string of queries. She wanted to know who had cried out and alarmed them, what Mehalah had been saying to Rebow, whether she had come to her senses at last, how long she was going to sulk, and so on.

Mehalah answered her shortly and rudely; that the cry had come from the madman, that he meant nothing by it, he had been taught to yell thus when he wanted food, that he had been neglected by his brother and was distressed; as for her mother's other questions, she passed them by without remark, and brushing in front of the old woman, went into the inner chamber.

'Mehalah!' called Mrs. Sharland. 'I will not have you glouting in there any longer. Come out.'

The girl paid no attention to her. She leaned her head against the wall and put her hands to her ears. Her mother's voice irritated her. She wanted quiet.

'This is too much of a good thing,' said the old woman, going in after her. 'Come away, Mehalah, you have your work to do, and it must be done.'

'You are right,' answered the girl in a hard tone, 'I am a servant, and I will do my work. I will go down at once.' She knitted her brows, and set her teeth. Her complexion was dull and dead. Her hair was in disorder, and fell about her shoulders. She twisted it up carelessly, and tied it round her head with George's handkerchief.

When she returned, her mother was in bed, and half-asleep. Mehalah went to the window, the window that looked towards the Ray, and drawing the curtains behind her, remained there, her head sunk, but her eyes never wavering from the point where her home had been when she was happy, her heart free, and her self-respect unmangled. So passed hour after hour. There was full moon, but the sky was covered with clouds white as curd, scudding before a north-west wind. The moon was dulled but hardly obscured every now and then, and next moment glared out in naked brilliancy.

Everything in the house was hushed. Elijah had gone to bed. Mehalah had heard his heavy tread on the stair, and the bang of his door as he shut it; it had roused her, she turned her head, and her face grew harder in the cold moonlight. Then she looked back towards the Ray.

Her mother was asleep. The starlings and sparrows who had worked their way under the eaves, and were building nests between the ceiling and the tiles, stirred uneasily; they were cold and hungry and could not sleep. Anyone not knowing what stirred would have supposed that mice were holding revel in the attics. There yonder on the marsh was something very white, like paper, flapping and flashing in the moonlight. What could it be? It moved a little way, then blew up and fell and flapped again. Was it a sheet of paper? If so how came it not to be swept away by the rushing wind. No, it was no sheet of paper. Mehalah's curiosity was roused. She opened the window and looked out. At the same moment it rose, fluttered nearer, eddied up, and fell again. A cloud drifted over the moon and made the marsh grey, and in the shadow the restless object was lost, the flash of white was blotted over. When the moon gleamed out again, she saw it once more. It did not move. The wind tore by, and shook the casement in her hand, but did not lift and blow away that white object. Then there was a lull. The air was still for a moment. At that moment the white object moved again, rose once more and fluttered up, it was flying, it was nearing,—it fell on the roof of the bakehouse under the window. Now Mehalah saw what this was. It was the wounded gull, the bird Rebow had shot.

The miserable creature was struggling with a broken wing, and with distilling blood, to escape to sea, to die, and drop into the dark, tossing, foaming waves, to lose itself in infinity. It could not expire on the land, it must seek its native element, the untamed, unconfined sea; it could not give forth its soul on the trampled, reclaimed, hedged-in earth.

Was it not so with Glory? Could her free soul rest where she now was? Could it endure for ever this tyranny of confinement within impalpable walls? She who had lived, free as a bird, to be blown here and there by every impulse, when every impulse was fresh and pure as the unpolluted breath of God that rushes over the ocean. Was she not wounded by the same hand that had brought down the white mew? There she was fluttering, rising a little, again falling, her heart dim with tears, her life's vigour bleeding away, the white of her bosom smeared with soil that adhered, as she draggled in the mire, into which he had cast her. Whither was she tending? She turned her face out to sea—it lay stretched before her ink-black. Red Hall and its marshes were to her a prison, and freedom was beyond its sea-wall.

She was startled by a sound as of bricks falling. She listened without curiosity. The sound recurred again, and was followed after a while by a grating noise, and then a rattle as of iron thrown down. She heard nothing further for a few minutes, and sank back into her dull dream, and watching of the poor mew, that now beat its wings on the roof, and then slid off and disappeared. Was it dead now? It did not matter. Mehalah could not care greatly for a bird. But presently from out of the shadow of the bakehouse floated a few white feathers. The gull was still wending its way on, with unerring instinct, towards the rolling sea. Just then Mehalah heard a thud, as though some heavy body had fallen, accompanied by a short clank of metal. She would have paid it no further attention had she not been roused by seeing the madman striding and then jumping, with the chain wound round one arm. He looked up at the moon, his matted hair was over his face, and Mehalah could not distinguish the features. He ran across the yard, and then leaped the dyke and went off at long bounds, like a kangaroo, over the pasture towards the sea-wall.

Mehalah drew back. What should she do? Should she rouse Elijah, and tell him that his brother had wrenched off the grating of his window and worked his way out, and was now at large in the glare of moon on the marshes, leaping and rejoicing in his freedom? No, she would not. Let the poor creature taste of liberty, inhale the fresh, pure air, caper and race about under no canopy but that of God's making. She would not curtail his time of freedom by an hour. He would suffer severely for his evasion on the morrow, when Elijah would call out his men, and they would hunt the poor wretch down like a wild beast. She could see Rebow stand over him with his great dog-whip, and strike him without mercy. She rouse Rebow! She reconsign the maniac to his dark dungeon, with its dank floor and stifling atmosphere! The gull was forgotten now; its little strivings overlooked in anxiety for the mightier strivings of the human sufferer. Yet all these three were bound together by a common tie! Each was straining for the infinite, and for escape from thraldom; one with a broken wing, one with a broken brain, one with a broken heart. There was the wounded bird flapping and edging its way outwards to the salt sea. There was the dazed brain driving the wretched man in mad gambols along the wall to the open water. There was the bruised soul of the miserable girl yearning for something, she knew not what, wide, deep, eternal, unlimited, as the all-embracing ocean. In that the bird, the man, the maid sought freedom, rest, recovery.

She could not go to bed and leave the poor maniac thus wandering unwatched. She would go out and follow him, and see that no harm came to him.

She took off her shoes, shut the window. Her mother was sleeping soundly. She undid the door and descended the stairs. They creaked beneath her steps, but Rebow, who had slept through the noise made by his brother in effecting his escape, was not awakened by her footfall. She unlocked the back door, closed it, and stole forth.

As she passed the bakehouse she lit on the wounded bird. In a spasm of sympathy she bent and took it up. It made a frantic effort to escape, and uttered its wild, harsh screams; but she folded her hands over the wings and held the bird to her bosom and went on. The blood from the broken bone and torn flesh wet her hand, and dried on it like glue. She heeded it not, but walked forward. By the raw moonlight she saw the madman on the wall. He had thrown down his chain. He heeded it not now. There had been sufficient intelligence or cunning in his brain to bid him deaden its clanking when making his escape from the house.

He sprang into the air and waved his arms; his wild hair blew about in the wind, it looked like seaweed tangles. Then he sat down. Mehalah did not venture on the wall, but crept along in the marsh. He had got a stone, and was beating at his chain with it upon the stone casing of the wall on the sea face. He worked at it patiently for an hour, and at last broke one of the links. He waved the chain above his head with a shout, and flung it behind him into the marsh. He ran on. Mehalah stole after him. He never looked back, always forwards or upwards. Sometimes he danced and shouted and sang snatches to the moon when it flared out from behind a cloud. Once, when at a bend of the wall, his shadow was cast before him, he cowered back from it, jabbering, and putting his hands supplicatingly towards it; then he slipped down the bank, laughed, and ran across the marsh, with his shadow behind him, and thought in his bewildered brain that he had cunningly eluded and escaped the figure that stood before him to stop him. He reached the mill that worked the pump. He must have remembered it: it was mixed up somehow with the confused recollections in his brain, for it did not seem to startle or frighten him. He scarcely noticed it, but, uttering a howl, a wild, triumphant shout, sprang upon a duck punt hauled up on the wall. It was Elijah's punt, left there occasionally, quite as often as at the landing near the house, a small, flat-bottomed boat, painted white, with a pair of white, muffled oars in it.

In a moment, before Mehalah had considered what to do, or whether she could do anything, he had run the punt down into the water, and had seated himself in it, and taken the oars and struck out to sea, out towards the open, towards the unbounded horizon.

He rowed a little way, not very far, and then stood up. He could not apparently endure to face the land, the place of long confinement, he must turn and look out to sea.

Mehalah stood on the sea-wall. The waves were lapping at her feet. The tide had turned. It flowed at midnight, and midnight was just past. She had forgotten the gull she bore, in her alarm for the man, she opened her arms, and the bird fluttered down and fell into the water.

The moon was now swimming in a clear space of sky free of cloudfloes. In that great light the man was distinctly visible, standing, waving his arms in the white punt, drifting, not rapidly, but steadily outwards. In that great light went out also, on the same cold, dark water, the dying bird, that now stirred not a wing.

Mehalah watched motionless, with a yearning in her heart that she could not understand, her arms extended towards that boundless expanse towards which the man and the bird were being borne, and into which they were fading. He was singing! Some old, childish lay of days that were happy, before the shadow fell.

There stood Glory, looking, indistinctly longing, till her eyes were filled with tears. She looked on through the watery vail, but saw nothing. When she wiped it away she saw nothing. She watched till the day broke, but she saw nothing more.

CHAPTER XXI.
IN VAIN!

Mrs. De Witt was not happy, taken all in all. There were moments indeed of conviviality when she boasted that she was now what she had always wanted to be, independent, and with none to care for but herself, 'none of them bullet-headed, shark-bellied men to fuss and worrit about.' But she laboured, like the moon, under the doom of passing through phases, and one of these was dark and despondent. As she lay in her bunk of a raw morning, and contemplated her toes in the grey light that fell through the hatches, she was forced to admit that her financial position was not established on a secure basis. It reposed on smelt, shrimps, dabs and eels, a fluctuating, an uncertain foundation. She strode about the island and the nearest villages on the mainland, with a basket on her arm, containing a half-pint measure, and a load of shrimps, or swung a stick in her hand from which depended slimy eels. She did a small trade at the farm-houses, and reaped some small retail profits. The farmers' wives were accustomed to see her in sunshine habited in scarlet more or less mottled with crimson, in storm wearing a long grey military great coat. In summer a flapping straw hat adorned her head; in winter a fur cap with a great knob at the top, and fur lappets over her ears. In compliment to her condition of mourner a big black bow was sewn to the summit of the knob, and she looked like a knight helmeted, bearing as crest a butterfly displayed, sable. It was seldom that she was dismissed from a farmhouse without having disposed of a few shrimps, or some little fish; for if she were not given custom regularly, she took huff and would not call with her basket again, till an apology were offered, and she was entreated to return.

The profits of the trade were not however considerable, and such as they were underwent reduction on all her rounds. She consumed the major part of them in her orbit at the 'Fountain,' the 'Fox,' the 'Leather Bottle' or the 'Dog and Pheasant.' In the bar of each of these ancient taverns, Mrs. De Witt was expected and greeted as cordially as at the farm-kitchen. There she was wont to uncasque, and ruffle out her white cap, and turn out her pockets to count her brass. There also this brass underwent considerable diminution. The consumption of her profits generally left Mrs. De Witt in a condition rather the worse than the better. She was a sinking fund that sucked in her capital. However cheery of face, and crisp of gathers, Mrs. De Witt may have started on her mercantile round, the close saw her thick of speech, leery of eye, festoony of walk, vague in her calculations, reckless of measurement with her little pewter half-pint, and generally crumpled in cap and garment. If she were still able to rattle a few coppers in her pocket when she stumbled up the ladder, toppled down into the hold, and tumbled into her bunk, she was happy. She was her own mistress, she had no helpless, foolish man, husband or son, to consider, and before whom to veil her indiscretions; she pulled up the ladder as soon as she was home; and, as she said, sat up for no one but herself.

She had not quite reconciled her smoking to her conscience, when she had a son to set a model of life to, before whom to posture as the ideal of womanhood and maternity; then when his foot was heard on the ladder she would slip her clay into the oven, and murmur something about a pinch out of her snuff-box having fallen on the stove, or about her having smoked her best gown as a preventive to moth. Now she smoked with composure, and turned over in her mind the various possibilities that lay before her. Should she bow to the hard necessity of leading about a tame man again, or should she remain in her present condition of absolute freedom? The five-and-twenty pounds had nearly disappeared, and she was not certain that she could live in comfort on her gains by the trade in shrimps and eels.

Mrs. De Witt was a moralist, and when nearly drunk religious. She was not a church-goer, but she was fond of convivial piety. Over her cups she had a great deal to say of her neighbours' moral shortcomings and of her own religious emotions. When in a state of liquor she was always satisfied that she was in a state of grace. In her sober hours she thought of nothing save how to make both ends meet. She mused on her future, and hovered in her choice, she feared that sooner or later she must make her election, to take a man or to do without one. The eagle can gaze on the sun without blinking, but Mrs. De Witt could not fix her eye on matrimony without the water coming into it. That was a step she would not take till driven to it by desperation. The Pandora's bottom was not all that could be wished, it was rotten. Mrs. De Witt saw that the repair of the Pandora was a matter she could not compass. When she let in water, Mrs. De Witt would admit a husband. Whilst a plank remained impervious to the tide, so would her breast to matrimonial dreams.

The spring tides came, and with them seawater oozing in at the rotted joints of the vessel. Mrs. De Witt was well aware of the presence of bilgewater in the bottom. Bilgewater has the faculty of insisting on cognisance being taken of its presence. Whenever she returned to the Pandora, the odour affected her with horror, for it assured her that her days of independence were numbered. But all at once a new light sprang up in the old lady's mind, she saw a middle course open to her; a way of maintaining a partial independence, on a certainty of subsistence.

She had not returned the call made her by her nephew Elijah Rebow. Half a year had elapsed, but that was no matter. Etiquette of high life does not rule the grades to which the Rebows and De Witts belonged. Why should not she keep house for her nephew? He was well off, and he was little at home; his house was large, she would have free scope in it for carrying on her own independent mode of life, and her keep would cost her nothing. That house had been her home. In it she had been born and nurtured. She had only left it to be incumbered with a husband and a son. Now she was free from these burdens, what more reasonable than that she should return? It was the natural asylum to which she must flee in her necessity.

It was true indeed that Rebow had taken in Mrs. Sharland and Glory, but what ties attached them to him equal to hers of flesh and blood. Was she not his aunt?

Now that Mrs. De Witt saw that it was clearly in her interest to disestablish the Sharlands and install herself in their place, she saw also, with equal clearness, that morality and religion impelled her to take this course. What was Elijah's connection with Glory? Was it not a public scandal, the talk of the neighbourhood? As aunt of Rebow was she not in duty bound to interfere, to act a John the Baptist in that Herod's court, and condemn the intimacy as improper?

Mrs. De Witt pulled herself up, morally as well as physically, and in habit also. That is, she was sitting on her military coat tails, and with a gathering sense of her apostleship of purity she shook them out, she drew in at the same time the strings of her apron and of her cap, tightened and lifted her bustle, so that the red military tails cocked in an audacious and defiant—if not in an apostolic and missionary manner. She ran her fingers through the flutings of her frills, to make them stand out and form a halo round her face, like the corolla of white round the golden centre of the daisy. Then she drank off a noggin of gin to give herself courage, and away she started, up the companion, over the deck, and down the ladder, to row to Red Hall with her purpose hot in her heart.

After the disappearance of the madman, Mehalah had returned to the house and to her room. She said nothing next day of what she had seen. Elijah and his men had searched the marshes and found no trace of the man save the broken chain. That Rebow took back, and hung over his chimney-piece. He enquired in Salcott and Virley, but no one there had seen anything of the unfortunate creature. It was obvious that he had not gone inland. He had run outward, and when it was found that the punt was gone, the conclusion arrived at was that the madman had left the marshes in it.

Elijah rowed to Mersea, and made enquiries without eliciting any information. He went next to Bradwell on the south coast of the great Black water estuary, there his punt had been found, washed ashore; but no traces of the man were to be discovered. That he was drowned admitted of no doubt. Rebow satisfied himself that this was the case, and was content to be thus rid of an encumbrance. Mehalah's knowledge of the matter was unsuspected, and she was therefore not questioned. She did not feel any necessity for her to mention what she had seen. It could be of no possible advantage to anybody.

Her life became monotonous, but the monotone was one of gloom. She had lost every interest; she attended to her mother without heart; and omitted those little acts of tenderness which had been customary with her, or performed them, when her mother fretted at the omission, in a cold, perfunctory manner. Mrs. Sharland had been accustomed to be overruled by her daughter, but now Mehalah neither listened to nor combated her recommendations. She rarely spoke, but went through the routine of her work in a mechanical manner. Sometimes she spoke to her mother in a hard, sharp tone the old woman was unused to, and resented; but Mehalah ignored her resentment. She cared neither for her mother's love nor for her displeasure.

When she met the men about the farm, if they addressed her, she repelled them with rudeness, and if obliged to be present with them for some time, did not speak.

Neither had she a word for Rebow. She answered his questions with monosyllables, or not at all, and he had often to repeat them before she condescended to answer. He spoke at meal times, and attempted to draw her into conversation, but she either did not listen to him, was occupied with her own thoughts, or she would not appear to hear and be interested in what he said.

A morose expression clouded and disfigured her countenance, once so frank and genial. Joe remarked to Jim that she was growing like the master. Jim replied that folks who lived together mostly did resemble one another. He knew a collier who had a favourite bull-dog, and they were as alike in face as if they were twins.

Mehalah avoided Abraham, she rarely spoke to him, and when he attempted to open a conversation with her she withdrew abruptly. When all her work was done, she walked along the sea-wall to the spit of land, and, seating herself there, remained silent, brooding, with dull, heavy eyes looking out to sea at the passing sails, or the foaming waves.

She did not think, she sat sunk in a dull torpor. She neither hoped anything nor recalled anything. As she had said to Elijah, she neither loved nor hated; she did not fear him or desire him. She disliked to be in his presence, but she would not fix her mind on him, and concern herself about him. Her self-respect was sick, and till that was recovered nothing could interest and revive her.

Mehalah was seated under the windmill when Mrs. De Witt drew to land. That lady was on her war-path, and on seeing the person whom she designed to attack and rout out of her shelter, she turned the beak of her boat directly upon her, and thrust ashore at Mehalah's feet.

The sight of Mrs. De Witt in her red coat roused the girl from her dream, and she rose wearily to her feet and turned to walk away.

'Glory!' shouted the fishwife after her. 'Sackalive! I want to speak to you. Stop at once.'

Mehalah paid no attention to the call, but walked on. Mrs. De Witt was incensed, and, after anchoring her boat, rushed after and overtook her.

'By Cock!' exclaimed the lady, 'here's manners! Didn't you hear me hollering to you to hold hard and heave to?' She laid her hand on Mehalah's shoulder. The girl shook it off.

'Sackalive!' cried Mrs. De Witt. 'We are out of temper to-day. We have the meagrims. What is all this about? But I suppose you can't fare to look an honest woman in the face. The wicious eye will drop before the stare of wirtue!'

'What have you to say to me?' asked Mehalah moodily.

'Why, I want to speak along of you about what concerns you most of all. Now his father and his mother are dead, who's to look after Elijah's morals but me, his aunt? Now I can't stand these goings on, Glory! Here are you living in this out-of-the-way house with my nephew, who is not a married man, and folks talk. My family was always respectable, we kept ourselves up in the world. My husband's family I know nothing about. He was a low chap, and rose out of the mud, like the winkles. I took him up, and then I dropped him again; I was large and generous of heart when I was young—younger than I am now. I wouldn't do it again, it don't pay. The man will raise the woman, but the woman can't lift the man. He grovels in the mud he came out of. She may pick him out and wipe him clean a score of times, but when she ain't looking, in he flops again. I have had my experience. Moses was a good-looking man, but he looked better raw than cooked, he ate tougher than he cut. He wasn't the husband that he seemed to promise as a bachelor. George was another; but he was an advance on Moses, he had a little of me in him. There was Rebow mixed with De Witt; he was a glass of half and half, rum and water. But this is neither here nor there. We are not talking of my family, but of you. I'm here for my nephew's welfare and for yours. Glory! you ain't in Red Hall for any good. Do you think my nephew can take in an old woman that is not worth sixpence to bait lines with, and feed her and find her in liquor for nothing! Everybody knows he's after you. He's been after you ever so long. Everybody knows that. He had a hankering after you when George was a galliwanting on the Ray. That's known to all the world. Well, you can't live in the house with him and folks not talk.'

'Do you dare to believe——'

'Glory! I always make a point to believe the worst. I'm a religious person, and them as sets up to be religious always does that. It is part of their profession. When I buy fish of the men, I say at once, it stinks, I know it ain't fresh! when I take shrimps I say, they're a week out of the water, and they won't peel nicely. So I look upon you and everyone else, and then it's a wery pleasing surprise when I find that the stale fish turns out fresh. But it ain't often that happens. It may happen now and then, just as now and then a whale is washed up on Mersea Island. Now look you here, Glory! don't you believe that Elijah will marry you and make an honest woman of you. He won't do it. He don't think to do it. He never did intend it. He belongs to a better family than yours. You have gipsy blood in your veins, and he knows it; that's as bad as having king's evil or cancer. I made a mistake and looked below me. He won't do it. He knows that I made a mistake, he won't do the same. There's as much difference in human flesh as there is in that of flat-fish, some is that of soles, other is that of dabs; some is fresh and firm as that of small eels, other is coarse and greasy as that of conger. The Rebows belong to another lot from you altogether. Elijah knows it. He never thought to marry you. He couldn't do it.'

Mehalah, stung even through the hard panoply of callousness in which she had encased herself, turned surlily on the woman.

'You lie! It is I who will not marry him.'

'There's an Adam and Eve in every brown shrimp,'[1] said Mrs. De Witt sententiously; 'and there's wigour and weakness in every human creature. It is possible that at a time when Eve is up in Elijah he may have proposed such a foolish thing as to marry you, and it is possible that, at a time when Adam was the master in you, you may have refused him. I don't deny it. But I do say that Elijah will never marry you in cold blood. And I'll tell you what—you won't stand out against him for long. He has too much of the Adam, and you too little for that. You may set up your pride and self-will against him, but you will give way in the end—your weakness will yield to his strongheadedness. What he purposes he will carry out; you cannot oppose Elijah; the Adam in his heart is too old and wigorous and heady.'

[1] Children find in the front paddles of the brown shrimp, when pulled out, two quaint little figures which they call Adam and Eve.

Mehalah made no answer. Sunk in her dark thoughts she strode on, her arms folded over her heart, to still and crush it; her head bowed.

'Now Glory!' pursued Mrs. De Witt; 'I've a bit of a liking for you, after all, and I'm sorry for what I was forced to do about that five and twenty pounds. I tell you, I am sorry, but I couldn't help it. I couldn't starve, you know—I was a lone widow without a son to help me. As I said, I've a sort of a liking for you, for you was the girl my George——' Mehalah's breast heaved, she uttered an ill-suppressed cry, and then covered her face.

'My poor George,' went on the old woman, aware that she had gained an advantage. 'He was wery fond of you. Sackalive! how he would love to talk of you to me his doting old mother, and scheme how you was to live in love together! That boy's heart was full of you, full as——' she cast about for a simile, 'as a March sprat is full of oil. Now I know, my George—he was a good lad! and more like me in features than his father, but he hadn't the soul of a Rebow!—My George, I feel sure, couldn't rest in his grave, if he'd got one, knowing as how tongues were going about you, and hearing what wicked things was said of your character. A woman's good name is like new milk. If it once gets turned there's no sweetening it after, and I can tell you what, Glory! your name is not as fresh as it was; look to it before it is quite curdled and sour.'

'I can do nothing! I can do nothing!' moaned the despairing girl.

'Look you here, Glory!' said Mrs. De Witt. 'I'm the aunt of the party, and I must attend to his morals. I'll go in and see him and I'll manage matters. He's my nephew. I can do anything with him. Trust me with men, girl. I know 'em. They are like nettles. Grasp 'em and they are harmless; touch 'em trembling, and they sting you. They are like eels, try to hold them where you will and they wriggle away, but run a skewer through their gills and you have them.'

'What are you here for, talking to my girl?' asked Rebow, suddenly coming from behind the house, which Mrs. De Witt had now reached.

'Sackalive!' exclaimed his aunt, 'how you flustered me. We was just talking of you when you appeared. It is wonderful how true proverbs are; they are the Bible of those that don't read, a sort of scripture written in the air. But I want a talk along of you, Elijah, that is what I'm come after, I your precious aunt, who loves you as the oyster loves his shell, and the crab its young that it cuddles.'

'What do you want with me?'

'Come, Elijah, let us go indoors. To tell you Gospel truth, I'm dry after my row and want a wet. As I wet I will talk. I've that to say to you that concerns you greatly.'

'Follow me,' he said surlily, and led the way up the steps. Mehalah turned back, but walked not to the point where she had been sitting before, lest she should be again disturbed on the return of Mrs. De Witt to her boat. She went instead to the gate at the bridge over the dyke, that led towards Salcott. There was no real road, only a track through the pasture land. She leaned her hands on the bar of the gate and laid her weary head on her hands. Outside the gate was a tillage field with green wheat in it glancing in the early summer air. Aloft the larks were spiring and caroling. In the ploughed soil of Mehalah's heart nothing had sprung up,—above it no glad thought soared and sang. Her head was paralysed and her heart was numb. The frost lay there, and the clods were as iron.

In the meantime Mrs. De Witt was in the hall with her nephew, endeavouring to melt him into geniality, but he remained morose and unimpressionable.

By slow approaches she drew towards the object of her visit.

'I have been very troubled, nephew, by the gossip that goes about.'

'Have you?' asked he, 'I thought you were impervious to trouble short of loss of grog.'

'You know, Elijah, that your character is precious to me. I wally it, for the honour of the family.'

'What are you driving at?' he asked with an oath. 'Speak out, and then take your slimy tongue off my premises.'

'This is my old home, Elijah, the dear old place where I spent so many happy and innocent days.'

'Well, you are not likely to spend any more of either sort here now. Say what you have to say, and begone.'

'You fluster me, Elijah. When I have a glass of rare good stuff such as this, I like to sit over it, and talk, and sip, and relax.'

'I don't,' he said; 'I gulp it down and am off. Come, say your say, and be quick about it. I have my affairs to attend to and can't sit here palavering with an old woman.'

'Oh!' exclaimed Mrs. De Witt, in rising wrath, 'if I were young it would be different, if I were not a moral and religious character it would be different, if I were not a Rebow, but half gipsy, half boor, it would be different!'

'If you allude to Glory, with that sneer,' said he, 'I tell you, it would be different.'

'I dare say!' exclaimed Mrs. De Witt tossing her head. 'Blood and kinship are all forgot.'

'You forgot them fast enough when you ran after Moses De Witt.'

'I did demean myself, I admit,' said she; 'but I have repented it since in dabs and sprats, and I don't intend to do it again. Listen to me, Elijah. Once for all, I want to know what you mean by keeping this girl Glory here?'

'You do, do you?—So do I. I wonder; she defies and hates me, yet I keep her. I keep her here, I can do no other. I would to God I could shake free of her and forget her, forget that I had ever seen her, but I can't do it. She and I are ordained for one another.'

'Parcel of stuff!' exclaimed his aunt. 'You send her packing, her and her old fool of a mother, and I will come and keep house for you.'

'Pack Glory off!' echoed Elijah.

'Yes, break this wretched, degrading tie.'

'I couldn't do it!' he said. 'I tell you again, I would if I could. I know as well as if it were written in flames on the sky that no good can come of her being here, but for better for worse, for well or for woe, here we two are, and here we remain.'

'You love her??

'I love her and I hate her. I love her with every fibre and vein, and bone and nerve, but I hate her too, with my soul, because she does not love me, but hates me. I could take her to my heart and keep her there,' his breast heaved and his dark eyes flared, 'and kiss her on her mouth and squeeze the breath out of her, and cast her dead at my feet. Then perhaps I might be happy. I am now in hell; but were she not here, were I alone, and she

129

elsewhere, it would be hell unendurable in its agonies, I should go mad like my brother. She must be mine, or my fate is the same as his.'

'Are you going to marry her?'

'She will not marry me. Believe what I say. That girl, Glory, is the curse and ruin of me and of this house. I know it, and yet I cannot help it. She might have made me happy and built up my prosperity and family. Then I should have been a good and a glad man, a man altogether other from what I am now. But your son came in the way. He marred everything. Glory still thinks of him, it does not matter that he be gone. She will cling to him and keep from me. Yet she is destined for me. She never was for George. If he were to turn up—I don't say that it is possible or even probable, but suppose he were—she would fly to him. I might chain her up, but she'd break away. There is nothing for it,' he pursued, drooping into a sullen mood. 'We must battle it out between us. None can or must intervene; whoever attempts it shall be trampled under our feet. We must work out our own fate together; there is no help for it. I tell you, if I were born again, and I knew that this were before me, I'd fly to the Indies, to Africa, anywhere to be from her, so as never to see her, never to know of her, and then I might jog on through life in quiet, and some sort of happiness. But that is not possible. I have seen her. I have her here under my roof, but we are still apart as the poles. Go away, aunt, it is of no good your interfering. No one comes here, she and I must work the sum out between us. There's a fate over all and we cannot fight against it, but it falls on us and crushes us.'

Mrs. De Witt was awed. She rose. She knew that her mission was fruitless, that there was no possibility of her gaining her point.

She opened the door, and started back before an apparition in carnation and white.

'Whom have we here?'

'Mrs. Charles Pettican, madam,' said the apparition with a stately curtsey.

CHAPTER XXII.

THE LAST STRAW.

Mehalah was lost to consciousness, leaning on the gate, her aching brow and leaden eyes in her hand. She did not hear the larks that sang above her, nor saw the buttercups and daisies that smiled to her from below. By the gate was a willow covered with furry flower now ripe and shedding its golden pollen. The soft air scattered the delicate yellow dust over the girl's hair and neck and shoulders, a minute golden powder, but she noticed it not. The warm air played caressingly with some of her dark hair, and the sun brought out its copper glow—she was unaware of all.

A little blue butterfly flickered above her and lighted on her head, it lay so still that the insect had no fear.

Then a hand shook the gate.

'Gone to sleep, girl?' asked a female voice.

Mehalah looked up dreamily.

A young, handsome, and dashing lady before her, in white and carnation, a crimson feather in her hat, and carmine in her cheeks. Mehalah slowly recognised Admonition.

Mrs. Pettican looked curiously at her.

'Who are you?—Oh! I know, the girl Sharland!' and she laughed.

Mehalah put her hand to the latch to open the gate.

'You need not trouble,' said Admonition: 'I want nothing from you. I have heard of you. You are the young person,' with an affected cough, 'whom Master Rebow has taken to live with him I think. You had the assurance once to come to my dear husband, and to pester him.'

'He was kind to me,' said Mehalah to herself.

'Oh yes, he was very kind indeed. He did not know much of you then. Report had not made him familiar with your name.'

Mehalah looked moodily at her. It was of no use pretending to misunderstand her. It was of no use resenting the insinuation. She sullenly bore the blow and suffered.

'I have come here on your behalf,' said Admonition, speaking to her across the gate. She had the gate half open, and kept it between them.

'You have nothing to do with me, or I with you,' said Mehalah.

'Oh! nothing, I am respectable. I keep myself up, I look after my character!' sneered Mrs. Pettican. 'Nevertheless I am here with an offer from my husband. He is ready to receive your mother into his house; I do not approve of this, but he is perverse and will have his way. He will take her in and provide for her.'

'Mehalah looked up. A load was being lifted from her heart. Were her mother taken in by Mr. Pettican, then she could leave, and leave for ever, Red Hall.

'Yes. He admits his relationship,' said Admonition. 'I would not, were I he, now that the name is—well—not so savoury as it was. But he is not particular. Men are not. I have been brought up, I am thankful to say, with very strict ideas, and have been formed in a school quite other from that of Mr. Pettican. However, as I was observing—you need not come near me—keep the gate between us, please.'

'You were saying,' anxiously repeated Mehalah, who had stepped forward in her eagerness.

'I was saying that Mr. Pettican will overlook a great deal, and will receive your mother into his house, and provide her with all that is necessary. But you——'

'I,' repeated Mehalah, breathlessly.

'You must never, never set foot within my doors. I could not allow it. I am a person of respectability, I value proprieties. I could not allow my house to be spoken of as one which admitted—' with a contemptuous shrug.

Mehalah took no notice of the insult. She looked hard at Admonition, and said gravely, 'You will shelter and care for my mother, on condition that I never go near her.'

'Yes.'

'I may never see her, never speak to her, never kiss her again.'

'No, I could not suffer you to enter my respectable house.'

'Not even if she were dying?'

'My character would not allow of it. The respectability of my house must be maintained.'

Mehalah thought for awhile.

'I cannot make up my mind at once,' she said.

'It will be a great relief to you to get rid of your mother.'

'Yes, immeasurable.'

'I thought as much!' with a toss of the head, and curl of the lip.

Mehalah did not give attention to these marks of contempt. Presently she asked, 'And who will attend to my mother?'

'I will.'

'You!' exclaimed Glory, with a flash of her old indignation. 'You, who neglect and illtreat the husband who lifted you out of the gutter. You who have not gratitude and generosity to the man to whom you owe your position and comforts! How would you treat a poor, helpless, aged woman trusting to your mercy unconditioned, when the man who bound you to him by most solemn and sacred promises is insulted, and neglected, and degraded by you? No, never. My mother shall never, never be left to you of all women in the world. Never, never, never!' she beat her hand on the gate. 'Let me bear my burden, let it crush me, but she shall not be taken from me and die of neglect and cruel treatment. I can bear!' she raised herself with a poor effort of her old energy, 'I will bear all for her. She once bore with me.'

'Drab!' hissed Admonition, and she flung past her, shaking the gate furiously as she went by.

It was with carnation in her cheek as well as in her dress and hat that she appeared before Mrs. De Witt and Elijah Rebow.

Mrs. De Witt drew back to let Mrs. Pettican in.

'I think you was passing out,' said the latter; 'madam, your servant.'

'Your servant, madam,' from Mrs. De Witt, still lingering.

'Now then, one at a time. Aunt, go out and shut the door,' said Rebow peremptorily, and the old woman was obliged to obey.

'What has brought you here?' asked Elijah surlily.

Mrs. Pettican looked round, then drew nearer. 'I think,' she said, 'you once advised me something, but I don't know how far your interest is the same as it was.'

'What do you mean?'

'I don't know whether you would be satisfied to get Mehalah Sharland off your hands now, or keep her here.'

'She remains here, she never shall leave it.'

'It is just this,' said Admonition. 'My husband has of late been plucking up a little courage, or showing obstinacy. My cousin Timothy—I don't know what to make of him—he is not what he was. He is always making some excuse or other to get away, and I find he goes to Mersea. He hasn't been as dutiful and amiable to me of late, as I have a right to expect, considering how I have found him in food and drink and tobacco, the best of all, and no stint. There's some game up between him and my husband, and I believe it is this, I know it is this. Charles is bent on getting Mrs. Sharland and her daughter, the latter especially, to come and live with him and take care of him. He dares to say I neglect him. He reckons on pitting that girl against me, he thinks that she would be more than a match for me.'

'He thinks right,' burst in Rebow with a laugh.

'I won't have her in the house. I don't mind taking in the old woman, but the daughter I will not admit.'

'You are right. She'd master you and make you docile or drive you out,' jeered Rebow.

'She shall not come. I have told her so. I will not be opposed and brow-beaten in my own house. I will not have the care of my husband wrested from me.'

'Have you come here to tell me this?'

'I know that Charles and Timothy have put their heads together. They are both up in rebellion against me, and Timothy has walked over to Mersea to get a boat and row here to invite that girl to come with her mother to Wyvenhoe, and take up their abode with my husband. Charles promises if they will do so to provide for them and leave them everything in his will, so as to make them independent at my cost. When I got wind of this—I overheard the scheme by the merest accident—I got a gig and was driven over to Salcott, and the boy has put up the horse at the inn, and I walked on. I will stop this little game. The girl shall not come inside the house. If she puts in her little finger, her fist will follow, and I will be driven out, though I am the lawful wife of Charles Pettican. I don't know what Timothy means by aiding and abetting him in this. I will have it out with him, and that very soon. I want to know what are your views. I have been pretty plain with mine. You may help me or hinder me, but I hope I shall be able to keep my door locked against such as that girl, and if Timothy thinks to flirt along with her under my roof, and before my face, he is vastly mistaken. That husband of mine is deeper than I suspected, or he would not have come over Timothy and got him to aid him in this. But I see it all. Timothy thinks if the girl gets there, and is to have Charles' money, he will make up to her, marry her, and share the plunder. If that be his game he has left me out of his calculations. Timothy is a fool, or he would not have gone over from me to Charles. I'll have the matter out here———'

'Not in this room,' said Elijah. 'There's rows enough go on in here without your making another. Set your mind at rest: Glory does not leave this house. But I advise you to see your cousin, and, if possible, prevent him from making the proposal. If she hears it, she will be off to-morrow, and carry her mother with her; and then there may be trouble to you and me to get her back.'

'She shall not come across my doorstep.'

'I tell you if once she hears that the chance is given her, she will go, and not you nor a legion of such as you could keep her out. Go upstairs and go straight on till you come to a door. Go in there; it is the bedroom of Glory and her mother. Never mind the old fool—she is sick and in bed. You will find a small room or closet beyond, with a three-cornered window in it. Look out of that. It commands the whole bay, and you will see a boat, if it approaches the Hall. There's Sunken island and Cobb marsh between you and Mersea City. You will see a boat creep through one of the creeks of Cobb marsh into Virley flat, and that will be the boat with your cousin in it. If you come down then you will meet him as he lands.'

As soon as Admonition had rushed past Mehalah the girl walked away from the gate and ascended the sea-wall. She could obtain peace nowhere. She could hide nowhere, be nowhere without interruption. She saw Mrs. De Witt depart, and thought that now she could sit on the wall and remain unmolested. But again was she disturbed, this time by old Abraham. He was at the near landing-stage, just come from the Ray—the landing-place employed when tides were full. 'Hark ye, mistress,' said the shepherd. 'I've had much on my tongue this many a day, but you haven't given me the chance to spit it out. I won't be put off any longer.'

She did not answer or move away. The reaction after the momentary kindling of hope and burst of passion had set in, and she had relapsed into her now wonted mood.

'It is of no use, mistress, your going on as you are,' continued the old man. 'Wherever he is, the master speaks of you as no man ought to speak save of his wife; and all the world knows you are not that. What are you, then? You are in a false position, and that is one of your own making.'

'You know it is not, Abraham.'

'I know it is one you could step out of to-morrow if you chose,' he said. 'The master has offered you your right place. As long as you refuse to take it so long everybody will be turned against you, and you against everybody. You keep away from everybody because you shame to see them and be seen by them. I know you don't like the master, but that's no reason why you shouldn't take him. Beggars mustn't be choosers. He is not as young and handsome as George De Witt, but he is not such a fool, and he has his pockets well lined, which the other had not.'

'It is of no use your saying this to me, Abraham,' said Mehalah sadly.

'No, it is not,' pursued the dogged old man. 'Here you must stick as long as your mother lives, and she may live yet a score of years. Creaky gates last longest. Why, she ain't as old as I, and there's a score of years' work in me yet. How can you spend twenty years here along of the master, with all the world talking? It will shame you to your grave, or brazen you past respect. This state of things can't do good to anybody. You must take him, and set yourself right with the world, or go from here.'

'I cannot get away. Would to heaven I could!'

'Then you must marry him. There is no escape from it, for your own sake. Why, girl,' the shepherd went on, 'if you was his wife you would have a lawful right and place here—this house, these marshes, these cattle would be yours. You would not be dependent on him for anything; you would hold them as a right. Now he can have you and your mother in prison at any time, for you are still his tenants and owe him rent for the Ray. But if you marry him, you cut away his power: he can't proceed against you and your mother for one penny. You would cancel the debt, do away with the obligation. If you was to marry him, and saw your way clear, I fancy you might go away at any time, and he would have no hold on you. Now he has you fast by this claim. And now your character is being ruined by association with him. There,' continued the old man, 'I doubt I never said so much afore; but I have known you since you was a girl, and I no more like to see you going to the bad than I like to see a field that has been well tilled allowed to be overrun with thistles, or a sheep lie down in the fen and die of rot that might have been saved with a little ointment stuck on in proper time.'

Mehalah made no response.

'I dare say it stings.' said Dowsing. 'I've seen sheep jump with pain when the copperas comes against a raw; but that's better than to lie down and rot away without an effort, and without a word, as you are doing now.' He gave her a nod, and went on his way.

Mehalah stepped into his boat and seated herself in her usual manner, with her head in her arms, and sank into her wonted torpor.

'Now, then, young woman!'

Again interrupted, again aroused. There was no rest for her that day.

'Jump on land, will you, young woman, and let this lass step into your boat and get ashore without having to go into the mud.'

'Timothy! that is Mehalah!' exclaimed Phoebe Musset. She was in the boat with Admonition's cousin. 'I'd rather you carried me. I do not want to be obliged to her for anything.'

Mehalah stepped from her boat upon the turf, and held out her hand mechanically to assist the girl.

'Don't hold out your hand to me!' screamed Phoebe. 'I wouldn't touch it. Keep to yourself, if you please, and let me pass.'

'Why, Phoebe!' exclaimed Timothy, 'what is the matter? I have come here to see this girl.'

'What!—to see Mehalah—or Glory, as you sailor and fisher fellows like to call her?'

'Yes.'

'Then I'm ashamed to have come with you,' said Phoebe, pouting. 'You offered me a nice little row on the water, and the sun was so bright, and the air so warm, and you were so agreeable, that I ventured; but I would not have stepped into the boat had I known you were coming to visit another young woman, and she one of so smirched a character.'

'Phoebe! For shame!'

'For shame!' repeated the girl turning on Timothy. 'For shame to you, to bring me here with you when you are visiting this——' She eyed Mehalah from head to foot with studied insolence, and sniffed. 'I know her. A bad, spiteful cat! always running after fellows. She tried to wheedle poor George De Witt into marrying her. When he was lost, she burnt her house and flung herself on the mercy, into the arms, of Rebow. Now, I suppose, she is setting her red cap at you. Oh! where is the cap gone, eh?' turning to Mehalah as she skipped ashore.

Timothy was fastening the boat to that of Dowsing.

Mehalah's wrath was rising. She had endured much that day—more than she could well bear. The impertinence of this malicious girl was intolerable altogether. She turned away to leave her.

'Stop! stop!' shouted Timothy. 'I have come here with a message to you. I have come here expressly to see you. I picked up Miss Musset on the way——'

'You picked me up just to amuse me till you found Glory!' screamed Phoebe. 'Now you pitch me overboard, as that savage treated me once. I will not stand this. Timothy, come back this instant! Row me back to Mersea. I have not come here to be insulted. I will not speak another word with you unless you——'

'For heaven's sake,' cried Timothy, tearing down the sea-wall and jumping into the boat, 'come in, Phoebe, at once, or I shall be off and leave you!'

'What is the matter now?'

He had his knife out, and was hacking through the cord that attached his boat to Dowsing's. In another moment he was rowing as hard as he could down the creek.

Admonition appeared on the wall. Timothy had detected her crossing the marsh, and fled.

She turned in fury on Phoebe.

Mehalah withdrew to the windmill, away from their angry voices, and remained sitting by the sea till the shadows of evening fell.

Then she returned, a fixed determination in her face, which was harder and more moody than before.

She walked deliberately to the hall, opened the door, and stepped in. Elijah was there, crouched over the empty hearth, as though there was a fire on it. He looked up.

'Well, Glory?'

Her bosom heaved. She could not speak.

'You have something to say,' he proceeded. 'Won't the words come out? Do they stick?' His wild dark eye was on her.

'Elijah,' she said, with burning brow and cheek, 'I give up. I will marry you.'

He gave a great shout and sprang up.

'Listen patiently to me,' she said, with difficulty controlling her agitation. 'I will marry you, and take your name, but only to save mine. That is all. I will neither love you, nor live with you, save as I do now. These are my terms. If you will take them, so be it. If not, we shall go on as before.'

He laughed loudly, savagely.

'I told you, Glory, my own, own Glory, what must be. You would not come under my roof, but you came. You would not marry me—now you submit. You will not love me—you must and shall. Nothing can keep us apart. The poles are drawing together. Perhaps there may be a heaven for us both here. But I do not know. Anyhow the sum is nearer the end than it was. Glory, this day week you shall be my wife.

CHAPTER XXIII.

BEFORE THE ALTAR.

Virley Church has been already described, as far as its external appearance goes. The interior was even less decent.

It possessed but one bell, which was tolled alike for weddings and for funerals; there was a difference in the pace at which it went for these distinct solemnities, but that was all. The bell produced neither a cheerful nor a lugubrious effect on either occasion, as it was cracked. The dedication of Virley Church is unknown—no doubt because it never had a patron; or if it had, the patron disowned it. No saint in the calendar could be associated with such a church and keep his character. St. Nicholas is the patron of fishers, St. Giles of beggars, but who among the holy ones would spread his mantle over worshippers who were smugglers or wreckers? When we speak of worshippers we use an euphemism; for though the church sometimes contained a congregation, it never held one of worshippers. Salcott and Virley, the Siamese-twin parishes, connected by a wooden bridge, embraced together five hundred souls. There were two churches, but few churchgoers.

On the day of which we write, however, Virley Church was full to overflowing. This is not saying much, for Virley Church is not bigger than a stable that consists of two stalls and a loose box, whereof the loose box represents the chancel. When the curate in charge preached from the pulpit—the rectors of the two parishes were always non-resident—they kept a curate between them—he was able to cuff the boys in the west gallery who whispered, cracked nuts, or snored.

The bellringer stood in the gallery, and had much ado to guard his knuckles from abrasion against the ceiling at each upcast of the rope. He managed to save them when tolling for a burial, but when the movement was double-quick for a wedding his knuckles came continually in contact with the plaster; and when they did an oath, audible throughout the sacred building, boomed between the clangours of the bell.

Virley Church possessed one respectable feature, a massive chancel-arch, but that gaped; and the pillars slouched back against the wall in the attitude of the Virley men in the village street waiting to insult the women as they went by.

On either side of the east window hung one table of the Commandments, but a village humourist had erased all the 'nots' in the Decalogue; and it cannot be denied that the parishioners conscientiously did their utmost to fulfil the letter of the law thus altered.

The congregation on Sundays consisted chiefly of young people. The youths who attended divine worship occupied the hour of worship by wafting kisses to the girls, making faces at the children, and scratching ships on the paint of the pews. Indeed, the religious services performed alternately at the two churches might have been discontinued, without discomposure to any, had not traditional usage consecrated them to the meeting of young couples. The 'dearly beloveds' met in the Lord's house every Lord's day to acknowledge their 'erring and straying like lost sheep' and make appointments for erring and straying again.

The altar was a deal table, much wormeaten, with a box beneath it. The altar possessed no cover save the red cotton pocket-handkerchief of the curate cast occasionally across it. The box contained the battered Communion plate, an ironmoulded surplice with high collar, a register-book, the pages glued together with damp, and a brush and pan.

The Communion rails had rotted at the bottom; and when there was a Communion the clerk had to caution the kneelers not to lean against the balustrade, lest they should be precipitated upon the sanctuary floor. No such controversy as that which has of late years agitated the Church of England relative to the position of the celebrant could have affected Virley, for the floor in the midst, before the altar, had been eaten through by rats, emerging from an old grave, and exposed below gnawed and mouldy bones a foot beneath the boards.

A marriage without three 'askings' was a novelty in Salcott and Virley sufficient to excite interest in the place; and when that marriage was to take place between one so well known and dreaded as Elijah Rebow and a girl hardly ever seen, but of whom much was spoken, it may well be supposed that Virley Church was crowded with sightseers. The gallery was full to bursting. Sailor-boys in the front amused themselves with dropping broken bits of tobacco-pipe on the heads below, and giggling at the impotent rage of those they hit.

There was a sweep in Salcott, who tenanted a tottering cottage, devoid of furniture. The one room was heaped with straw, and into this the sweep crept at night for his slumbers. This man now appeared at the sacred door.

'Look out, blackie!' shouted those near; 'we are not going to be smutted by you.'

'Then make way for your superiors.'

'Superiors!' sneered a matron near.

'Well, I am your superior,' said the sweep, 'for my proper place is poking out at the top of a chimney, and yours is poking into the fire at the bottom. Make way. I have a right to see as well as the best of you.'

The crowd contracted on either side in anxiety for their clothes, and the sweep worked his way to the fore.

'I'll have the best place of you all,' he said, as the gods in the gallery received him with ironical cries of 'Sweep! sweep!'

He charged into the chancel, and sent his black legs over the Communion rails.

At some remote period the chancel of Virley had fallen, and had been rebuilt, with timber and bricks on the old walls left to the height of two feet above the floor. As the old walls were four feet thick, and the new walls only the thickness of one brick, the chancel was provided with a low seat all round it, like the cancellæ of an ancient basilica. The sweep, with a keen eye peering through his soot, had detected this seat and seen that it was unappropriated. He was over the altar with a second jump, and had seated himself behind it, facing west, in the post of dignity occupied in the Primitive Church by the bishop, with his legs under the table, and his elbows on it, commanding the best view attainable of everything that went on, or that would go on, in the church.

His example was followed at once. A rush of boys and men was made for the chancel; the railings fell before them, and they seized and appropriated the whole of the low seat that surrounded the sanctuary.

'I've the best place now, you lubbers,' said the sweep. 'I shall have them full in face, and see the blushes of the bride.'

'They are a-coming! they are a-coming!' was repeated through the church. A boy peering out of the window that lighted the gallery had seen the approach of the procession from Red Hall over the wooden bridge.

In came the Reverend Mr. Rabbit, very hot and sneezy—he laboured under hay fever all the blooming time of the year. He got to the altar. The clerk dived into the box and rose to the surface with the register-book and the surplice.

'Where is the ink?'

'Here is a pen,' said the clerk, producing one with nibs parted like the legs of the Colossus of Rhodes.

'But we shall want ink.'

'There is a bottle somewhere in the box,' said the clerk.

'Never mind if there ain't,' observed one of the elders seated by the table; 'there is the sweep here handy, and you have only to mix a bit of his smut with the tears of the bride.'

'Shut that ugly trap of yours,' said the chimney-cleaner.

'It may be ugly,' retorted the humourist, 'but it is clean.'

'Here they are!' from the gallery.

'Make way!' shouted Mrs. De Witt, battering about her with her umbrella. 'How are people to get married if you stuff up the door, as though caulking a leak?'

She drove her way in.

'Now, then,' said she, 'come on, Mistress Sharland. Dear soul alive! how unmannerly these Virley people are! They want some of us from Mersea to come and teach them manners. Now, then, young Spat!' she shouted to a great boy in a fishing guernsey, 'do you want your head combing? Do you see what you have done to my best silk gown? What do you mean coming to a house of worship in mud-splashers?[1] Are you come here after winkles?'

[1] Wooden paddles, worn by those who go out 'winkling' in the mud, to prevent their sinking.

'I ain't got my splashers on,' said the boy.

'Then you have feet as big and as dirty as paddles. You have trodden on my best silk and took it out at the gathers.' Then, turning and looking through the door behind her, she waved her umbrella with a proud flourish. 'Come on, hearties! I've cleared the way.'

She put her shoulder to the crowd and wedged her way further ahead. 'Ah!' she said, 'here are a lot of sniggering girls. If all was known what ought to be known some of you ought to be getting married to-day. Leave off your laughing up there!' gesticulating towards the boys in the loft. 'Don't you know yet how to behave in a place of worship? I have a great mind to draw my Pandora up at Virley hard and settle here and teach you.'

Mehalah came in, pale, with sunken eyes, that burned with feverish brightness. A hectic flush dyed her cheeks. Her lips were set and did not tremble.

After having given her promise, under conditions, to Rebow she had neither slept nor eaten. She had abandoned her habit of retiring to the shore to sit and brood, and maintained instead incessant activity. When she had done what was necessary for others she made work for herself.

Mrs. Sharland had forgotten her ague and left her bed in the excitement and pleasure of her daughter's submission. She had attempted several times to speak to Mehalah of her approaching marriage, but had not been able to wring a word out of her. From the moment Glory gave her consent to Rebow she said not another syllable on the subject to him or to anyone. She became more taciturn and retiring, if possible, than before. Abraham Dowsing had saluted her and attempted a rough congratulation. She had turned her back and walked away.

Elijah's conduct was the reverse of Glory's. His gloom was gone, and had made way for boisterous and demonstrative joy. His pride was roused, and he insisted on the marriage preparations being made on a liberal scale. He threw a purse into Mrs. Sharland's lap, and bade her spend it how she liked on Mehalah's outfit and her own. The old woman had been supremely happy in arranging everything, her happiness only dashed by the unsympathetic conduct of one chief performer in the ceremony, her daughter, whom she could not interest in any point connected with it.

There had been a little struggle that morning. Mehalah had drawn on her blue 'Gloriana' jersey as usual, and Mrs. Sharland had insisted on its coming off. The girl had submitted after a slight resistance, and had allowed herself passively to be arrayed as her mother chose.

Elijah was dressed in a blue coat, with brass buttons, and knee-breeches. No one had seen him so spruce before.

'I say, dame,' whispered Farmer Goppin to his wife, 'the master of Red Hall is turning over a new leaf to-day.'

'Maybe,' she answered, 'but I doubt it will be a blank one. Look at the girl. It won't be a gay[2] for him.'

[2] Essex for 'Picture.'

'Move on!' said Mrs. De Witt. 'I'll keep the road.'

Mrs. De Witt had come at Rebow's special request. She had put on for the occasion her silk dress, in which she had gone from home and been married. Her figure had altered considerably through age and maternity, and the dress was now not a little too tight for her. Her hooking together had been a labour of difficulty, performed by Mrs. Sharland at Red Hall; it had been beyond her own unassisted powers, in the Pandora, when she drew on the ancient dress.

'Dear Sackalive!' exclaimed Mrs. De Witt when she extracted the garment from the lavender in which it had lain, like a corpse in balm, for some five-and-twenty years, 'I was a fool when I last put you on; and I won't fit myself out in you again for the same purpose, unless I am driven to it by desperate circumstances.'

Unable to make the body meet, she had thrown a smart red coat over it; and having engaged a boy to row her to Red Hall, sat in the stern, with her skirt pinned over her head, as though the upper part of her person were enveloped in a camera lucida; in which she was viewing in miniature the movements of the outer world. On reaching Red Hall she had thrown off the scarlet, and presented her back pleadingly to Mrs. Sharland.

'I ought not to have done it, but I did,' said she in a tone of confidence. 'I mean I oughtn't to have put this gown on, last time I wore it,' she explained when Mrs. Sharland inquired her meaning. 'It was thus it came about: I was intimate with the sister of Moses De Witt, and one Mersea fair I went over to the merrymakings, and she inwited me to take a mouthful with her and her brother on board the Pandora. I went, and I liked the looks of the wessel, and of Moses, so I said to him, "You seem wery comfortable here, and I think I could make myself comfortable here too. So, if you are noways unobjectionable, I think I will stay." And I did. I put on my silk gown, and was married to Moses, in spite of all my parents said, and I turned the sister of De Witt out and took her place.'

Mrs. De Witt felt great restraint in the silk gown. Her arms were like wings growing out of her shoulderblades. She was not altogether satisfied that the hooks would hold, and therefore carried to church with her the military coat, over her arm. She wore her hair elaborately frizzled. She had done it with the stove poker, and had worn it for some days in curl-papers. Over this was a broad white chip hat, tied under her chin with skyblue ribands, and she had inserted a sprig of forget-me-nots inside the frizzle of hair over her forehead. 'Bless my soul,' she said to herself, 'the boys will go stark staring mad of love at the sight of me. I look like a pretty miss of fifteen—I do, by Cock!'

Mrs. De Witt succeeded in bringing her party before the altar, at which still sat the sweep, deaf to the feeble expostulations of the curate, which he had listened to with one eye closed and his red tongue hanging out of the corner of his mouth.

Mr. Rabbit was obliged to content himself with a protest, and vest himself hastily for the function.

'Look here,' said Mrs. De Witt, who took on herself the office of master of the ceremonies: 'I am not going to be trodden on and crumpled. Stand back, good people; stand back, you parcel of unmannerly cubs! Let me get where I can keep the boys in order and see that everything gives satisfaction. I have been married; I ought to know all the ways and workings of it, and I do.'

She thrust her way to the pulpit, ascended the stair, and installed herself therein.

'Oh, my eye!' whispered the boys in the gallery. 'The old lady is busted all down her back!'

'What is that?' asked Mrs. De Witt in dismay. She put her hands behind her. The observation of the boys was just. Her efforts to clear a way had been attended with ruin to the fastenings of her dress, and had brought back her arms to their normal position at the expense of hooks-and-eyes.

'It can't be helped,' said Mrs. De Witt, 'so here goes!' And she drew on her military coat to hide the wreck.

'Now, then, parson, cast off! Elijah, you stand on the right, and Glory on the left.'

The curate sneezed violently and rubbed his nose, and then his inflamed eyes. The dust of the flowering grass got even into that mouldy church, rank with grave odours and rotting timber. He began with the Exhortation. Mrs. De Witt followed each sentence with attention and appropriate gesture.

'"Is not to be enterprised nor taken in hand unadvisedly, lightly, or wantonly,"' she repeated, with solemn face and in an awestruck whisper; then, poking the boys in the gallery with her umbrella, 'Just you listen to that, you cubs!' Then she nodded and gesticulated at the firstly, secondly, and thirdly of the address to those whom she thought needed impressing with the solemn words. Elijah answered loudly to the questions asked him whether he would have the girl at his side to be his wedded wife. Her answer was faint and reluctantly given.

'"Who giveth this woman to be married to this man?"'

There was a pause.

'Speak up, Mistress Sharland, speak up!' said Mrs. De Witt in a tone of authority. 'Or, if you don't speak, curtsey.'

The curate was affected with a violent sneezing fit. When he recovered he went on. Rebow clasped Mehalah's hand firmly, and firmly repeated the sentences after the priest.

'"I, Elijah, take thee———"' began the curate; then asked, in a whisper, 'What is the bride's name?'

'Mehalah,' answered the mother.

'"I, Elijah, take thee, Mehalah, to my wedded wife,"' began the curate.

'"I, Elijah, take thee, Glory, to my wedded wife,"' repeated Rebow.

'That is not the name,' protested Mr. Rabbit.

'I marry Glory, and no one else; I take her by that name and by none other,' said Rebow. 'Go on.'

'Say the words after me,' the curate whispered to Mehalah, who began to tremble. She obeyed, but stopped at the promise 'to love, cherish, and to obey.' The curate repeated it again.

'"To obey,"' said Mehalah.

Mr. Rabbit looked uncertain how to act.

'"To love, cherish, and obey,"' he suggested faintly.

'Go on,' ordered Rebow. 'Let her obey now; the rest will come in due season.'

The priest nervously submitted.

'Now for the ring,' said the clerk. 'Put it on the book.'

Rebow was taken by surprise. 'By heaven!' he said, 'I forgot all about that.'

'You must have something to use for the purpose,' said the curate. 'Have you no ring of your own?'

'No. Am I like to have?'

'Then let her mother lend her her own marriage-ring.'

'She shall not,' said Rebow angrily. 'No, no! Glory's marriage with me is not a second-hand affair, and like that of such fools as she,' pointing to Mrs. Sharland. 'No, we shall use a ring such as has never been used before, because our union is unlike all other unions. Will this do?' He drew the link of an iron chain from his pocket.

'This is a link broke off my brother's fetters. I picked it up on the sea-wall this morning. Will it do?'

'It must do for want of a better,' said the curate.

Elijah threw it on the book; then placed it on Mehalah's finger, with a subdued laugh. 'Our bond, Glory,' he said, in a low tone, 'is not of gold, but of iron.'

## CHAPTER XXIV.
### THE VIAL OF WRATH.

Elijah Rebow, in the pride and ostentation of his heart, had invited the curate, the clerk, Mrs. De Witt, Farmer Goppin, Reuben Grout, innkeeper of the 'Rising Sun,' and several others to eat and drink with him and his bride at Red Hall after the ceremony. The marriage had taken place in the afternoon. The law in Marshland was flexible as osier—it must bend to man's convenience, not man submit to law.

Mrs. De Witt took the management of everything out of the hands of the feeble Mrs. Sharland. 'You're not up to the job,' she said. 'It wants some one with eyes in her elbows and as many legs as a crab.'

Mrs. De Witt was everywhere, in the kitchen, the hall, the oak parlour. She had pinned up her silk dress about her, so that it might take no harm.

'There,' said she to the assembled guests, as she brought in a pail full of shrimps and set it on the table. 'Stay your appetites on them, and imitate the manners of high society, which always begins with fish and works up to solids. I brought them myself as my contribution to the feast. Do you, Elijah, hand a wet round: if the others be like me they are dry. Marriage, as I always found it, is a dry job.'

'Where is Glory?' asked Elijah.

'Oh, yes!' exclaimed Mrs. De Witt. 'That is like you, Elijah, shouting, "Where is Glory?" Do you think she is to come here toozling about among the wittles in her best gown? She is upstairs getting her dress changed.'

He was pacified.

Mrs. Sharland passed here and there, eager to be supposed useful, actually getting across Mrs. De Witt's path and interfering with her proceedings.

'I can't stand this,' said the fishwife. 'You go upstairs and see after Mehalah. I am going to dish up the pudding.'

'I will take the gravy in the sauceboat,' said Mrs. Sharland.

'Don't get your shivers on at the time, then, and send the grease over everyone,' advised Mrs. De Witt.

'There now, Elijah!' exclaimed she, full of pride, when the table was spread. 'Do look at them dumplings. They are round, plump, and beautiful as cherubs' heads on monuments.'

'Where is Glory?' asked Rebow.

'Run up,' said Mrs. De Witt to the mother, 'tell the girl we are waiting for her. Bid her come at once before the gravy clots.'

An Essex dinner begins with dumplings soused in gravy. When these have been demolished the flesh follows.

The guests sat, with black-handled knives and forks in hand, mouths and noses projected, and eyes riveted on the steaming puddings, ready to cut into them the moment the signal was given.

Mrs. Sharland was slow of foot. Every step was taken leisurely up the stairs and along the passage.

'I'm afeared,' said Farmer Goppin, 'the outer edge of the pudding, about an inch deep all round, is getting the chill.'

'And there is a scum of fat forming on the gravy, said Reuben Grout, 'just like cat-ice on my duck-pond, or like mardlins[1] in spring on a ditch. Had not I better set the gravy against the fire till the good lady comes down?'

[1] 'Mardlins' are duckweed.

'She is coming,' said Rebow; and then he drummed on the table with his knife. Mrs. Sharland leisurely returned. She was alone.

'Well?' from Rebow.

'Mehalah is not in her room.'

'Curse it!' said Elijah. 'Where is she, then? Go and fetch her.'

'I do not know where she is.'

'She will be here directly,' said Rebow, controlling himself. 'You may fall to, neighbours.'

At the word every fork was plunged into the puddings, and every knife driven into their hearts. Each sought who could appropriate to himself the largest block of pudding. Then there ensued a struggle for the gravy, and great impatience was manifested by those who had to wait till others had well drenched their hunches of dough in the greasy liquor.

Rebow leaned back in his chair, holding knife and fork erect on the table. 'Why is she not here? She ought to be here.'

'Take some dumpling, Elijah?'

'I won't eat till my Glory comes.'

'Lord preserve you!' exclaimed Mrs. De Witt, slapping his back. 'Go on and eat. You don't understand girls, as you do calves, that is a fact. Why, a girl on her marriage-day is shamefaced, and does not like to be seen. In high society they hide their heads in their wails all day. That is what the wails are for. I was like that. You may look at me, but it is true as that every oyster wears a beard. When I was married to Moses I was that kittle, coy young bird I would have dived and hid among the barnacles on the keel of the wessel, had I been able to keep under water like a duck.'

'Where is she?'

'How do I know? Never fear; she is somewhere—gone out to get a little fresh air. It was hot and stank in that hold of an old church. What with the live corpses above in the pews and the dead ones below deck, it gave me a headache, and you may be sure Mehalah was overcome. I saw she did not look well. The pleasure, I suppose, has been too much for her. A wery little tipple of that topples some folks over.'

'You think so?'

'I am sure of it. Have I not been a bride myself? I know about those sort of things by actual experience. I've gone through the operation myself. It is wery like being had up before the magistrate and convicted for life.'

Elijah was partly satisfied, and he began to eat; but his eyes turned restlessly at intervals to the door.

'Don't you put yourself out,' murmured Mrs. De Witt as she leaned over his shoulder and emptied his glass of spirits. 'Girls are much like scallops. If you want to have them tender and melting in your mouth, you must treat them with caution and patience. You take the scallops and put them first in lukewarm water, working up into a gentle simmer, and at last, but not under two hours, you toast them, and pepper and butter them, and then they are scalding and delicious. But if you go too fast to work with them, they turn to leather, and will draw the teeth out of your gums if you bite into them. Girls must be treated just similarly, or you spoil them. You wouldn't think it, looking at me, but my Moses, with all his faults, knew how to deal with me, and he got me that soft and yielding that he could squeeze me through his fingers like Mersea mud. True as gospel. Fill your glass, Elijah; it don't look hospitable to allow it to stand empty.'

When the lady in her red coat entered, holding triumphantly above her head a leg of boiled mutton, there was a general burst of delight.

'A hunter's dinner!' said Goppin.

'But where is the bride?' asked Grout. 'I want to drink health and a long family to her.'

'Glory ought to be here. Go up, Mistress Sharland, and bring her down. She has returned by this time,' said Rebow.

'I don't think she has,' said the old woman.

'I am sure of it; go and look.'

The widow revisited the bedroom.

When she returned she said, 'No, Elijah; Mehalah has not come back. She has taken off her bridal dress and laid it on the bed, and has put on her blue jersey, and I see she has taken with her a red cap.'

'She tore that to pieces.'

'She has been knitting a new cap this week,' said Mrs. Sharland.

'I like that! She has done it to please me,' said Elijah, his eye twinkling. 'I loved her in that; and I hate to see her as she was tricked out to-day.'

'We are waiting for you to carve,' said Goppin.

'Don't forget we like fat,' said Grout.

'I say,' murmured Jabez Bunting, a storekeeper, 'look at the gravy, how it oozes out; I'm fit to jump at the sight. Don't think we eat like ladies of quality, Rebow. Give us good large helpings, and the redder and rawer the better.'

'Some one,' said Elijah, 'tell Abraham Dowsing to go on the sea-wall and look out for Glory, and bring her home.'

'There's the boy what rowed me here,' said Mrs. De Witt. 'He is sitting outside on the step, and I'm throwing him the bits of skin and fat and gristle. I'll send him.'

'Really,' observed the Rev. Mr. Rabbit, after a fit of sneezing, 'the circumstance reminds the student of Holy Writ somewhat of Queen Vashti.'

'What do you mean?' asked Elijah abruptly.

'No offence, no offence meant,' gasped the curate, waxing very red; 'I only thought your good lady was to-day like Queen Vashti.'

'Glory is like nobody,' said Rebow, with some pride. 'There never was, there never can be, another Glory. I don't care who or what your Vashti was—Was she beautiful?' shortly interrupting himself.

'Did she bring property into the family!' asked Mrs. De Witt, leaning over Elijah's shoulder and emptying his tumbler. 'Elijah! you must replenish. Look hospitable, and keep the liquor flowing.'

'I really don't know,' said Mr. Rabbit.

'Then what do you mean by saying she was like my Glory?' asked Rebow angrily.

'I—I only suggested that there was a faint similarity in the circumstances, you know. King Ahasuerus made a great feast—as you have done.'

'Was there boiled mutton at it?' asked Grout.

'I really cannot say. It is not recorded.'

'Give me boiled mutton, a little underdone, and I ask for nothing more,' said Goppin.

'And,' went on the curate, 'he naturally wished his wife to be present. He wanted her to come down to be seen of his lords and princes.'

'Go on! Damn your sneezing. Put it off till you're preaching, and then no one will care,' said Rebow.

'But,' pursued the parson, when he had wiped his nose and eyes, and recovered breath after the fit, 'Queen Vashti refused to come down.'

'Well, what did the husband say to that?' asked Elijah.

'If he was a sensible man,' said Goppin, 'he cut into the mutton, and didn't bother about she.'

'You don't know, neighbour, that it was a leg of mutton,' said Grout. 'It might have been sirloin.'

'Sirloin!' exclaimed Bunting; 'I wouldn't go ten yards to taste sirloin. There's not enough on the bone, except fat.'

'Go on,' said Elijah to the curate. 'How did the man—king, was he—take it?'

'He dismissed Vashti, and took Esther to be his queen. But then,' put in the frightened curate, thinking he had suggested a startling precedent, 'Ahasuerus was not a Christian, and knew no better.'

'Do you think,' laughed Rebow, 'that I would cast off my Glory for any other woman that ever was born? No, I would not. Let her do what she likes. She don't care to associate with such as you. She holds herself above you. And she's right. She is one the like of whom does not exist. She has a soul stronger and more man-like than anyone of you. If she don't choose to come and guzzle here along of you, she's right. I like her for it.'

He flung himself back in his chair and drained his full glass.

'I ask you, Goppin! Did you ever see the equal of my Glory?'

'I can't say as ever I did, Rebow,' answered the farmer.

'I took the liberty to chuck her under the chin, and she up with the pitchfork out of my hand, and had like to have sent me to kingdom come, had not my good woman been nigh to hand, and run to the rescue. I hope you'll find her more placable when you come to ask a kiss.'

Elijah rubbed his hands, and laughed boisterously.

'Ha!' shouted he, 'that is my Glory! I tell you, Goppin, she'd have drove the prongs of the fork into your flesh as I dig this into the meat,' and he stabbed at the joint fiercely with his carving fork.

'I dare say,' grumbled the farmer, wincing and rubbing his leg. 'I'd for my part rather have a more peaceable mate; but there's no choosing fat beasts for others, as the saying goes.'

'What do you think of her?' asked Rebow, turning round with exultation on Bunting and Grout.

'She came to my old woman,' said the latter, 'and asked her to take her in and give her work. She wanted to leave you.'

'She did,' exclaimed Rebow. 'And what did your old woman say to that?'

'She said she durstn't do it. She durstn't do it.'

'She durstn't do it!' echoed Elijah with a great laugh. 'That was fine. She durstn't do it!'

'No,' pursued Grout, 'without your leave.'

'And you wouldn't have dared to do it neither,' turning to Bunting, who shook his head.

'No, you would not dare. I'd like to see the man or woman in Salcott or Virley as would dare. I reckon there is none that knows me would make the venture. By God!' he burst forth. 'Where is the girl? I will have her here; and I'm cursed if you shall not all stand on your legs, and drink to her health and happiness as the most splendid woman as ever was or shall be.'

'Abraham Dowsing is at the door,' said Mrs. Sharland.

'Come in, and say what you have to say before us all,' called Elijah. 'If it be anything about my Glory, say it out.'

'She is gone off in her boat,' said the old man; 'I saw her.'

'Why did you not stop her then?' asked Mrs. De Witt.

'I stop her!' repeated Abraham. 'She is my mistress, and I a servant.'

'That is right,' said Elijah, 'if she had taken a whip and lashed your back till it was raw, you couldn't stop her. Where is she gone to?'

Abraham drew up his shoulders. 'That's her concern. It's no odds to me. But I tell ye what, Master. Here are you feasting here, and we han't had nothing extra with our wittles. I ask that we may eat and drink prosperity to you both, to her and you.'

'You shall,' said Elijah.

'Stay,' put in Mrs. De Witt. 'What do you mean, you old barnacle, you? Let your superiors eat their fill first, and then you and the other men shall have what's over. That's fair. I shall manage for you. Go, Abraham.'

The supper drew to a close. Elijah drank a great deal. He was fretted, though he tried not to show it, by the absence of Glory. As more spirits were drunk and pipes were lighted in the hall, whilst the men of the farm fed in the kitchen, several of those present repeated their regret that she in whose honour they were assembled, the new mistress of the house in which they had met, had not deigned to show herself, and receive their good wishes and congratulations.

Rebow gulped down the contents of glass after glass.

Mrs. De Witt had seated herself with the rest, and was doing her best to make up for lost time, with the bottle.

'Elijah!' said she, 'one or other must establish the mastery, either you or Glory. I did think she were a bit shy at first to come among us; but now the night is coming on and still she is away. I don't deny that this ain't civil. But then, she has lived all her life on the Ray, and can't know the fashions of high society; and again, poor thing, it's her first experience of matrimony. She will do better next time. Let us drink!' said she, holding up her brimming glass, 'to her profiting speedily by her experience, and next time we have all of us the honour of attending at her wedding, may she do us the favour to respond.'

'Amen!' said the clerk, who was present.

'Go out some one, and see if she is coming,' said Rebow, his dark face burning with anger and drink. He could not, however, wait till the messenger returned, but left his guests, and went forth himself. He mounted the sea-wall, and turned his eyes down the creek; nothing was visible. He stood there, bareheaded, cursing, for a quarter of an hour, and then went back with knitted brows.

He found his guests preparing to depart.

'Go along!' he said; 'I want no congratulations; say nothing. Glory and I have a marriage different from other folks, as she and I are not like other folks, We must fight it out between us.'

He waved his guests away, with a rude impatient gesture.

Mrs. De Witt roused her boat-boy by kicking him off the steps—he had gone to sleep there—and then tumbling on top of him. She staggered up, tucked the lad under her arm, and marched off.

'If I meet Glory by the way, I'll send her home, I'll be sure and mind it,' said she to Rebow as she departed.

He went in. He ordered Mrs. Sharland to go to her bed. The charwoman, had in for the day, cleared the table of all the glasses, save that of Elijah, and retired. He was left alone. He went to the back door and fastened it. Glory should not slink home that way without facing him. He seated himself in his armchair, and refilled his tumbler with spirits and water. He was very angry. She had deliberately insulted him before his guests, defied him in the face of the principal people of the parish. It would be spoken of, and he would be laughed at throughout the neighbourhood.

The black veins in his brow puffed out. A half-drunken, half-revengeful fire smouldered in his deep-set eyes. There was no lamp or candle burning in the room, but the twilight of midsummer filled it with a grey illumination.

He walked to the door, opened it, and looked out. The gulls were crying over the marsh, and the cattle were browsing in it. No Mehalah was to be seen.

'On my wedding day!' he muttered, and he resumed his seat. 'On that for which I have worked, to which I have looked, for which I have thought and schemed, she flies in my face, she scorns me, she shows everyone that she hates me!'

His pipe was out, he threw it impatiently away.

'She does not know me, or she would not dare to do it. There is no one in all the neighbourhood dare defy me but she. Everyone fears me but she, for everyone knows me but she. Know me she must, know me she shall. There will be no wringing love out of her till she bends under me and fears me. She will never fear me till she knows all. She shall know that; by God!' he cried aloud, 'I will tell her that which shall make her shrink and fall, and whine at my feet; and then I shall take her up, and drag her to my heart, and say, "Ah, ha! Glory! think what a man you have gotten to-day, a man whom none can withstand. There is none like me, there is none will dare what I will dare. You and I, I and you, are alone in the world. One must submit or there is no peace. You must learn to cower beneath me, or we shall fight for ever."'

He went out again upon the sea-wall, but saw nothing, and came back more angry. As he stood on his steps he heard from the path to Salcott a burst of merriment. He swore an ugly oath. Those men, rolling home, were ridiculing him, keeping his marriage feast without the presence of his bride!

He flung himself again into his chair, and rocked himself in it. He could not sit there, tortured with auger and love, in the gloaming, doing nothing. He emptied the bottle, there was not a drop more in it, and he cast it in the hearth. Then he fetched down his old musket mounted in brass, and getting the vitriol bottle from the window, began to rub and polish the metal.

He wearied of that in the end. His mind could not be drawn off Glory, and wondering where she was, and why she had thus gone away.

'I love her,' he muttered, as he replaced his gun on the nails above the chimney-piece, 'but yet I hate her. My very heart is like Grimshoe with love and hate warring together, and neither gets the mastery. I could clasp her to my breast, but I could tear out her heart with my nails, because it will not love me.' He rocked himself in his seat savagely, and his breath came fast: 'We must work the riddle out between us. We can get no help, no light from any others; she and I, and I and she, are each other's best friends and worst foes.'

A firm hand was on the door, it was thrown open, and in the grey light stood Mehalah.

'Where have you been?' asked Elijah, hardly able to speak, so agitated with fury and disappointed love was he.

'I have been,' she said composedly, 'on the Ray, sitting there and dreaming of the past.'

'Of the past!' shouted Rebow. 'You have been dreaming of George?'

'Yes, I have.'

'I thought it, I knew you were,' he yelled. 'Come here, my wife.'

'I am not your wife. I never will be your wife, except in name. I told you so. I can not, and I will not love you. I can not, and I will not, be aught to you but a housekeeper, a servant. I have taken your name to save mine, that is all.'

'That is all because you love George De Witt.'

'George De Witt is dead.'

'I don't care whether he be dead or not, you think that he is your double. I tell you, as I have told you before, he is not. I am.'

'I will not listen to more of this,' she said in a hard tone. 'Let me pass, let me go to my room.'

'I will not let you pass,' he swore; the breath came through his nostrils like the snorting of a frightened horse; 'I will not. Hear me, Glory, my own Glory! hear me you shall.' He grasped her arms between the elbow and shoulder with his iron hands, and shook her savagely.

'Listen to me, Glory, you must and shall. You do not love me, Glory, because you do not fear me. The dog whom I beat till it howls with torture creeps up to me and licks my hand. A woman will never love her equal, but she will worship her superior. You have shown me to-day that you think yourself on a level with me. You have donned again your cap of liberty,' he raised one hand to her head, plucked off the cap and cast it on the floor, 'thinking that now you have taken me before the world, you have broken my power over you. You do not know me, Glory! you do not know me. Listen to me!' Through the twilight she could see his fierce eyes flaring at her, her hair was disturbed by the hot blasts of his labouring lungs. His fingers that held her twitched convulsively as he spoke.

'Listen to me, Glory! and know me and respect me. I am no more to be escaped from than fate. I am mighty over you as a Providence. You may writhe and circumvent, but I meet you at every turn, and tread you down whenever you think to elude me. Listen to me, Glory!' He paused, and drew a long breath; 'Listen, I say, to me. Glory! how did you lose your money that night that Abraham Dowsing sold your sheep? I feel you stirring and starting in my hands. Yes, I took it. You went out with George De Witt, and left the purse on the table. When your mother left the room, I took the money. You may have it back now when you like, now that I have you. I took it—you see why. To have you in my power.'

'Coward and thief!' gasped Mehalah.

'Ah! call me names if you like; you do not know me yet, and how impossible it is to resist me. You thought when you had got the money again, from George, that you had escaped me.'

'Stay!' exclaimed Mehalah. 'It was you,' with compressed scorn, 'that fired on George and me in the marsh.'

'I fired at him, not at you; and had you not changed the place of the lanthorn in the boat, I should have shot him.'

The girl shuddered in his hands.

'I feel you,' he said with savage exultation. 'You are beginning to know me now, and to tremble. When you know all, you will kneel to me as to your God, as almighty over your destiny, irresistible, able to crush and kill whom I will, and to conquer where I will. George De Witt stood in my way to you.'

Mehalah's heart leaped and then stood still. Her pulse ceased to beat. She seemed to be hanging in space, seeing nothing, feeling nothing, hearing only, and only the words of the man before her.

'He left Mersea City one night. He left it in my boat with me.'

'He paused, rejoicing in her horror at this revelation of himself to her.

'Have you not a question to ask me, "Where he now is? What I know of him?"'

No—she could not speak, she could not even breathe.

'Do you remember when you came on Michaelmas Day to pay me my rent, how you heard and saw my mad brother in the cell there below?'

He paused again, and then chuckled. 'The poor wretch died and I buried him there. I brought George here, I made him drunk, and chained him in my brother's place, and he went mad with his captivity in darkness and cold and nakedness.'

The blood spouted from her heart through every artery. She tried to cry but could not, she strove to escape his hands, she was unable. She panted, and her eyes stood open, fixed as those of a corpse, staring before her.

'You lost your sheep,' he went on, with exultation. 'I took them. I took them to rob you of every chance of paying me, and keeping clear of me.'

She did not hear him. She cared nothing about sheep. She was thinking of George, of his imprisonment and madness.

'At last, when I feared that after all you might slip from me by means of that cripple at Wyvenhoe, I did more. I watched you on New Year's Eve; I waited for you to go to sleep, that I might fire your house. You did better than I had thought, you went out; and then I set the Ray Farm in flames. What cared I for the loss? It was nothing. By it I gained you, I secured you under my roof, by burning you out of the shelter of your own.' He swelled with pride. 'You know me now, Glory! Now think you that escape from me is possible? No, you do not, you cannot. I hedge you in, I undermine the ground you tread. I saw away the posts that hold up the roof above your head. You know now what I am, irresistible, almighty, as far as you are concerned, your fate incarnate. And I know you. I know that you are one who will never yield till you have found a man who is mightier in will and in power than you; those who have fought are best friends after the struggle, when each knows his own strength and the full measure of the resistance of the other. We have had one wrestle, and I have flung you at every round; you in your pride have stood up again, and wiped the blood from your heart, and the tears from your eyes, and tried another fall with me; but now, Glory, you have tried your last. Hitherto you fought not knowing the extent of my power, thinking that I put forth my full might when I spoke, but that I had no strength to act. Now you see what I can do, and what I have done, and you will abandon the fruitless battle. Glory! Glory! Come to my heart. You fear me now, and fear is the first step leading to love. Glory! my own Glory!' his voice faltered, and his fingers worked, 'I love you madly. I will do and dare all for you. I will live for you and for nothing in the world but you. Never till this day in the church have I so much as held your hand. Never till this moment, Glory! have I held you to my heart, never till this moment have I felt it bounding against mine, never till this moment have I kissed those dear, dear lips, as I shall now.'

He drew her to him. He unloosed his hands to throw his arms round her. She felt them closing on her like a hoop of iron, she felt his heart beating like the strokes of a blacksmith with his hammer; his burning breath was on her cheek. He! He kiss her! She lie on that heart which had schemed and carried out the destruction of her George!

She cried out. She found her tongue. 'Let go! I hate you as I never hated you before! I hate you as a mad dog, as a poisonous adder! Let go!' She writhed and slipped partly away.

'Never till I have held you to my breast and kissed you,' he said.

'That never, never!' she gasped. She got her hands on his breast and forced his arms asunder behind her.

'Ha, ha! strong,' he laughed, 'but not strong as I.' He gripped her wrists and bent her arms back. She threw herself on the ground, he drew her up. She flung herself against the chair, crushing his hand against the chimney-piece, so that he let go with it for an instant. She groped about with her free hand, in the dark, for some weapon, she grasped something. He cursed her for the pain she had given him, and attempted again to seize her hand. In a moment she had struck him—him the coward assailant, him the thief, him the murderer—between the brows with the weapon her hand had taken. It was a blow with her whole force. There followed a crash of glass, then a sense as of her hand being plunged into fire. Then a shriek loud, tearing through roof and wall, loud, agonised, as only a man or a horse can utter in supreme moments of torture; and Rebow fell on the floor, writhing like a worm, with his hands over his face and eyes.

CHAPTER XXV.
IN THE DARKNESS.

Day by day Elijah Rebow lay, or sat, in the darkened oak parlour with his eyes bandaged, a prey to wrath, pain, despair. The vitriol from the broken vial had got into his eyes, and there was reason to fear had blinded them.

He was obliged to have the burning balls kept from the light, but he raged under the obligation. He wanted to see, he could not be patient under restraint. He could ill understand that in all things he might not have his way, even in such a matter as this. He chafed also at having been conquered by Glory. That she should have defied and beaten him, and beaten him in such a crushing manner, cut his pride to the quick.

None knew how the accident had occurred save himself and Mehalah. To the doctor he had merely said that in getting the vitriol bottle from the shelf, it had fallen and broken on his forehead.

Mrs. Sharland remained in as complete ignorance of the truth as the rest, and her lamentations and commiserations, poured on Elijah and her daughter, angered him and humiliated her. Mehalah had suffered in mind agonies equal in acuteness to those endured in body by Elijah.

Horror and hatred of herself predominated. She had destroyed, by one outburst of passion, the eyesight of a man, and wrecked his life. What henceforth for thirty or forty years could life be to Rebow?—to one who could not endure existence without activity? She had rendered him in a moment helpless as a babe, and dependent on herself for everything. She must attend to his every want, and manage the farm and his business for him. By a stroke, their relative positions were reversed. The wedding night had produced a revolution in their places of which she could not have dreamed. She felt at once the burden of the responsibilities that came upon her. She was called upon by those on the farm to order and provide for everything connected with it. She had to think for the farm, and think for the master into whose position she had forced her way.

She hated herself for her rash act. She hated the man whom she had mutilated, but more herself. If by what she had done she had in one sense made herself master, in another she had cast herself into bondage. By the terrible injury she had inflicted on

Rebow she had morally bound herself to him for life to repair that injury by self-devotion. Had it been possible for her to love him, even to like him, this would have been light to her, with her feminine instinct, but as it was not possible, the slavery would be inexpressibly painful.

Love will hallow and lighten the most repulsive labours, the most extreme self-sacrifice, but when there is no love, only abhorrence, labour and self-sacrifice crush mentally and morally. She must bear the most fierce and insulting reproaches without an attempt to escape them, she had in part deserved them. These she could and would endure, but his caresses!—no! however deeply she might have sinned against him, however overflowing her pity for his helpless condition might be, she could not tolerate affection from the man who by his own confession merited her profound loathing. He had taken an unoffending man, and had imprisoned him and blinded his reason by cruelty; it seemed to her as if Providence had used her hand to exact a just retribution on Rebow by condemning him to an equally miserable condition. The recompense was justly meted, but would that it had been dealt by another hand!

In one particular she was blameless, and able to excuse herself. She had acted without intent to do bodily harm, and in ignorance of the weapon she had used. She had been carried away by the instinct of self-preservation, and had taken up what was readiest at hand, without a wish to do more than emancipate herself from the grasp of the man she detested. He had brought the consequences on his own eyes by his own act.

But though she quite recognised that he had done this, and that he richly deserved the consequences, yet she could not relieve her conscience from the gnawings of self-reproach, from the scalding blush of shame at having executed a savage, unwomanly vengeance on the man who had wronged her. Had her victim been a woman and a rival, she would perhaps have gloried in her act; but the female mind is perverse in its twists and complexion, and it will tingle with pain for having hurt a man, however little that man may be loved, when it would plume itself for having done the same to a woman who has been a friend. A woman must think and act rightly towards a man, but can do neither towards one of her own sex.

Mehalah's bosom was a prey to conflicting emotions. She pitied Elijah, and she pitied George. Her deep pity for George forced her to hate his torturer, and grudge him no suffering to expiate his offence. When she thought of what George de Witt must have endured in the vault, of his privations there, of the gradual darkening and disturbance of his faculties, and then of how Elijah had stepped between him and her, and spoiled their mutual dream of happiness, and ruined both their lives, the hot blood boiled in her heart, and she felt that she could deal Rebow the stroke again, deliberately, knowing what the result must be, as a retributive act. But when she heard him, as now, pacing the oak parlour, and in his blindness striking against the walls, her pity for him mounted and overlapped her wrath. Moreover, she was perplexed about the story of George's imprisonment. There was something in it she could not reconcile with what she knew. Elijah had confessed that on the night of George's disappearance he had enticed the young man to Red Hall, made him drunk or drugged him, and then chained him in the vault, in the place of his own brother who had died. It was Rebow and not De Witt who, that same night, had appeared at her window, driven in the glass and flung the medal at her feet. But was this possible? She knew at what hour George had left the Mussets' shop, and she knew about the time when the medal had been cast on the floor before her. It was almost incredible that so much had taken place in the interval. It was no easy row between Red Hall and the Ray, to be accomplished in half an hour.

Surely, also, had George De Witt been imprisoned below, he could have found some means to make himself heard, to communicate with the men about the farm, in the absence of Rebow. Would a few months in that dark damp cell derange the faculties of a sane man?

Mehalah lifted the trap and went down. The vault was a cellar not below the soil, but with floor level with the marsh outside, or only slightly beneath. It had a door fastened from within by a bolt, but also provided with a lock; and there was the circular window already described. The shutter had not been replaced, and the sunlight entered, and made the den less gloomy and horrible than Mehalah had conceived it to be. She found the staple to which the chain had been attached, away from the door and the window. It was obvious how the maniac had got loose. The chain had been attached to the staple by a padlock. Elijah sometimes unlocked this, when he was cleaning the straw from the cell and supplying fresh litter. He had carelessly turned the key in the lock, and left it unfastened. The madman had found this out after Rebow was gone, and had taken advantage of the circumstance to break out at the window. The chain and padlock, with the key in it, were now hung over the fireplace in the hall, mocking the inscription below, 'When I take hold, I hold fast.'

Mehalah seated herself in the window of the hall, and took up some needlework. Elijah was still pacing the parlour and beating against the opposite walls, muttering curses when he struck the oak panels. Presently she heard him groping along the walls for the door, and stumbling over chairs. He turned the handle and entered the hall.

He stood before her in the doorway of the darkened chamber, with extended quivering hands, his head bowed, his eyes covered with a thick bandage. He wore his red plush waistcoat and long brown coat. His dark hair was ruffled and stood up like rushes over a choked drain. He turned his head aside and listened. Mehalah held her breath.

'You are there,' he said. 'Although you try to hide from me, I know you are there and watching me. I am in the dark but I can see. I can see you always and everywhere, with your eyes—great angry brown eyes—on me, and your hand lifted to strike me into endless night.'

Mehalah did not speak. Why should she? She could say nothing that could do either any good.

'Have you put the hot fire to your tongue and scorched it out as you have put it to my eyes?' he asked. 'Can't you speak? Must I sit alone in darkness, or tramp alone up and down in black hell, feeling the flames dance in my eye-sockets, but not seeing them, and have no one to speak to, no one to touch, no one to kick, and beat, and curse? Go out and fetch me a dog that I may torture it to death and laugh over the sport. I must do something. I cannot tramp, tramp, and strike my head and shoulders against the walls till I am bruised and cut, with no one to speak to, or speak to me. By heaven! it is bad enough in Grimshoe with two in the shiphold mangling each other, but there is excitement and sport in that. It is worse in that wooden hold yonder, for there I am all alone.'

He stopped speaking, and began to feel round the room. He came to the chimney and put his fingers into the letters of the inscription. 'Ha!' he muttered, 'When I lay hold, I hold fast. I laid hold of you, Mehalah, but I have not let go yet, though I have burned my fingers.'

This was the first time he had called her by her Christian name. She was surprised.

'Mehalah!' he repeated, 'Mehalah!' and then laughed bitterly to himself. 'You are no more my Glory. There is no Glory here for me; unless, in pity for what a ruin you have made, you take me to your heart and love me. If you will do that I will pardon all, I will not give a thought to my eyes. I can still see you standing in the midst of the fire, unhurt like a daughter of God. I do not care. I shall always see you there, and when the fire goes out and only black ashes remain, I shall see you there shining like a lamp in the night, always the same. I do not care how many years may pass, how old you may wax, whether you may become bent and broken with infirmities, I shall always see my Glory with her rich black shining hair, her large brown eyes, and form as elastic and straight as a pine-tree. I shall see the blue jersey and the red cap and scarlet skirt.' He raised his hands and wrung them in the air above his head: 'What do I care for other sights? These long flat marshes have nothing beautiful in them. The sea is not here what it is on other coasts, foaming, colour-shifting like a peacock's neck; here it is of one tone and grey, and never tosses in waves, but creeps in like a thief over the shallow mud-flat, and babbles like a dotard over the mean shells and clots of weed on our strand. There is nothing worth seeing here. I do not heed being blinded, so long as I can see you, and that not you nor all your vitriol can extinguish. Heat skewers white hot in the fire, and drive them in at the eye-sockets through all obstruction into the brain, and then, perhaps, you will blind me to that vision. Nothing less can do it. Pity me and love me, and I forgive all.'

He crept past the chimney-piece and was close to the window. He touched Mehalah with one hand, and in a moment had her fast with both.

'I cannot love you,' she said, 'but I pity you from the depth of my soul, and I shall never forgive myself for what I have done.'

'Look here!' he snatched his bandages away and cast them down. 'This is what you have done. I have hold of you, but I cannot see you with my eyes. I am looking into a bed of wadding, of white fleeces with red ochre smears in them, rank dirty old fleeces unsecured—that is all I see. I suppose it is the window and the sunshine. I feel the heat of the rays; I cannot see them save as streaks of wool.'

'Elijah!' exclaimed the girl, 'let me bandage your eyes again. You were ordered to keep all light excluded.'

'Bah! I know well enough that my eyesight is gone. I know what you have done for me. Do you think that a few days in darkness can mend them? I know better. Vitriol will eat away iron, and the eyes are softer than iron. You knew that when you poured it on them.'

'I never intended to do you the harm,' said Mehalah passionately, and burst into tears. He listened to her sobbing with pleasure.

'You are sorry for me?'

'I am more than sorry. I am crushed with shame and grief for what I have done.'

'You will love me now, Mehalah.'

She shook her head and one of her tears fell on his hand; he raised his hand and put it to his eyes; then sighed. 'I thought one such drop would have restored them whole as before. It would, had there been sweetness in it, but it was all bitter. There was only anger with self and no love for me. I must bide on in blackness.' He put his hands on each side of her head, twisted his thumbs resting on her cheek-bones, and her unrestrained tears ran over them.

He stood quite still.

'This is the best medicine I could get,' he said; 'better nor all doctor's messes. To listen to your heart flowing over, to feel your warm tears trickle, does me good. In spite of everything, Glory! I must love you, and yet, Mehalah! I have every cause to hate you. I have made you, who were nothing, my wife, mistress of my house and estate, with a property and position above everyone else in Salcott and Virley, equal to any of the proud yeomen's wives on Mersea Isle. I have made a home for your mother, and in return you have plunged me in eternal night, and deny me your love.'

'Let us not recriminate,' said Mehalah through her tears, 'or I should have enough to charge you with. I never sought to be your wife. You drove me into the position in spite of my aversion to it; in spite of all my efforts to escape. You have wounded me in a cruel and cowardly manner past forgiveness. You have ruined my life and all my prospects of happiness. George——'

He shook her furiously.

'I will not listen to that name,' he said through his teeth.

'You could bear to hold him in chains there below,' she answered.

'You said, Let us not recriminate, and you pour a torrent of recriminations over me,' he gasped. 'If I have wronged you, you have redressed all with one vial of vitriol in the eyes, where man is most sensitive. With that firejuice you purged away all the past wrongs, I expiated in that liquid flame all the evil I had done you. You don't know what I have suffered. You have had no such experience of pain as to imagine the tortures I have undergone. If the anguish were all, it would be enough atonement; but it is not all. There is the future before me, a future of night. I shall have to trust to someone to do everything for me, to be eyes, and hands, and feet to me. Whom can I trust? How do I know that I shall not be deserted, and left to die in my darkness, a prey to ravenous men? If you loved me, then I could lean on you and be at peace. But you do not love me, and you will leave me when it suits your pleasure.'

'No, Elijah,' said Mehalah sadly; 'that I never will do. I have robbed you of your sight. I did it unwittingly, in self-defence, perhaps also in anger at knowing how cruelly, wickedly, cowardly you had behaved to me and to another whom I loved.'

'Whom you love still!' with a cry of rage.

'One whom I loved,' repeated Mehalah, sadly; 'and I must atone for my mad act as far as lies in my power. I will stay by you. I will never forsake you.'

'Listen to me, Mehalah,' said Elijah, with concentrated vehemence; 'you know what was said—that the person you loved went out in a boat and was lost. The body was never found. Should the man turn up again.'

'That is impossible.'

'I don't care for impossibilities. I live now in a dream-world where there is no line drawn between the possible and the impossible. Should he reappear, what then?'

'Still I would remain at my post of duty,' said the girl, humouring his fancy.

'The post of duty, not of love,' he muttered.

'I said duty,' she replied; 'I will never leave that.'

His thumbs twitched on her cheek-bones and worked their way to the corners of her eyes; she sharply withdrew her head.

He laughed. 'You thought I was going to gouge your eyes out with my thumbnails,' he said, 'that I was going to repay you in kind. No, I was not; but should the dead return to life and reclaim you, I may do it. You cannot, you shall not escape me. You and I, and I and you, must sink or swim together. Say again, Mehalah, that you will stand by me.'

'I promise it you, Elijah, I promise it you here solemnly, before God.' She sank on her knees. 'I have brought you unwittingly into darkness, and in that darkness I will hold to you and will cherish you.'

'Ha!' he shouted. 'At the altar you refused to swear that. To love, cherish, and obey is what the parson tried to make you say; but all you swore to was to obey, you denied the other, and now you take oath to cherish. The wheel of fate is turning, and you will come in time to love where you began to obey and went on to cherish.'

CHAPTER XXVI.
THE FORGING OF THE RING.

Mrs. Sharland was failing. The excitement of the marriage had roused her to activity, but when that was over she relapsed, her energy evaporated, and she took to her bed with the avowed intention of not leaving it again, except for a christening in the family, till carried to her grave. She did not understand Mehalah, she fretted because the arrangements after the eventful day remained the same as before; her daughter shared her room and kept as much away from Elijah as was possible, showed him none of the love of a wife to her husband, and was distressed when spoken to by her new name.

'You are either Mistress Rebow or you are not,' said the old woman peevishly to her daughter one night, in their room, 'and if you are not, then I don't understand what the ceremony in the church was for. You treat Elijah Rebow as coldly and indifferently as if he were naught to you but master, and you to him were still hired servant. I don't understand your goings on.'

'He and I understand each other, that is enough,' answered Mehalah. 'I have married him for his name and for nothing else. In no other light will I regard him than as a master: I told him when I agreed to go to church with him that I would be his no further than the promise to obey went; I take his name to save mine—that is all. He is not my husband, and never shall be, in any other way. I will serve him and serve him devotedly, but not give him my love. That I cannot give. I gave my heart away once for all, and it has not been restored to me.'

'That is all nonsense,' said Mrs. Sharland. 'Didn't I love Charles Pettican, and weren't we nigh coming to a declaration, only a fit of the ague shivers cut it short? I married your father, and loved him truly as a good wife and not as a hired servant, for all that.'

'Elijah and I understand each other,' answered Mehalah. 'I suppose there is something of truth in what he says over and over again, that he and I are different from others, and that there's none can understand us but our two selves.'

'Then you are made for one another.'

'So he says, but I will not believe it. No. That cannot be. Some have peace and happiness drop into their lap, others have to fight their way to it, and that is our fate. But that we shall find it in each other, that I never will admit. In George——' she covered her eyes, and left her sentence unfinished.

The charge of Mrs. Sharland was, to some extent, unjust. Mehalah did attend to Elijah with as much care and as assiduously as she was able, considering the amount of work which had devolved upon her. Her mother was ill and in bed, Elijah helpless. She had to see after and direct everything about the farm and house, beside ministering to the two invalids. Consequently she was unable to devote much time to Elijah, but whenever she had a few moments of relief from work she devoted them to him. She took her needlework either to him in the oak parlour, or brought him into the hall. She had now somewhat lightened her labours by engaging a charwoman, and was therefore more able than before to be with Rebow and her mother. Each complained if left long alone, and she had much difficulty in portioning her time between them. She tried, but tried in vain, to induce her mother to make an effort and come downstairs, so that she might sit with both at once; this would save her from distraction between two exacting and conflicting claims, and some restraint would be placed on the intercourse between Rebow and herself by the presence in the room of a third party.

Elijah was not entirely blinded, he was plunged not in darkness but in mist. He could see objects hazily, when near; he could distinguish figures, but not faces, when within a few yards of him, but nothing distant. The wall and a black cloud on the horizon were equally remote to his vision.

He wandered about, with a stick, and visited his cattle sheds and workmen; or sat under the south wall of his house in the sun. The pump was there, and to it Mehalah sometimes came. He listened for her step. He could distinguish her tread from that of the charwoman. He took no notice of this woman, though she came up to him occasionally and said a few commiserating words.

The men thought that he was gentler in his affliction than he had been before. He did not curse them, as had been his wont. He asked about the cattle, and the farm, and went his way. Mehalah also noticed that he was less fierce; she was able also to attribute this softening to its right cause, to her own influence. He was, to some extent, happy, because she was often with him, sought him instead of shunning him, spoke to him kindly, instead of rebuffing him when he addressed her, and let him know and feel that she thought of him, and was endeavouring to make him comfortable in his great deprivation.

As he sat in the sun and looked up at the bright orb, which he saw only as a nebulous mass of light, she was ever present before his inward eye, she in her pride and beauty. He did not think; he sat hour by hour, simply looking at her—at the image ever before him, and listening for her step or voice. An expression of almost content stole across his strongly marked features, but was occasionally blurred and broken by an uneasy, eager, enquiring look, as if he were peering and hearkening for something which he dreaded. In fact, he was not satisfied that George De Witt would never reappear. Had he been set at rest on this point, he could have been happy.

Mehalah was touched by his patience, his forgiveness of the irreparable wrong she had done him. He had said that if she loved him he would pardon all. He was ready to do this at a less price; though he craved for her love, he was contented, at least for the present, with her solicitude. He had been accustomed to open hostility and undisguised antipathy. Now that he met with consideration and tenderness from her, he became docile, and a transformation began to be operated in his nature. Love him, she could not, but she felt that but for what he had done to George, she could regard him without repugnance. Pity might ripen into friendship. Into a deeper and more rich feeling it never could, for he had barred the way to this possibility by his dealing with De Witt.

She ventured occasionally to approach the subject, but it always produced such agitation in the manner of Rebow that she was obliged to desist from seeking explanation of the particulars which perplexed her. The slightest allusion to George De Witt troubled the master of Red Hall, made his face darken, and brought on an access of his old violence, from which he did not recover for a day or two.

Mrs. De Witt came to see him.

'Lawk a day!' she said; 'what a job to find you in this predicament!'

He turned his whitened eyes on her, with a nervous twitch in the muscles and a tremour of the lips. 'Well! What news?'

'News!' echoed the lady; 'dear sackalive! who'd expect to find news in Mersea? you might as well drag for oysters in a horsepond.'

He was satisfied, and let her talk on without attending to her.

A few days later, he called the charwoman to him as she was going to the pump.

'What is your name?'

'Susan Underwood. I'm a married woman, with three small children, and another on its way.'

He fumbled in his pocket, and took out a crown.

'Any news?—from Mersea, I mean.'

'I don't come from Mersea. Thank your honour all the same.'

'But if there were news there it would get to Virley or Salcott, or wherever you live.'

'It would be sure. I did hear,' she said, 'that Farmer Pooley has been a-wisiting a little more nor he ought at widow Siggars' cottage, her as has a handsome daughter, and so, they do say, has Farmer Pudney; and the other day they met there, and was so mad each to find the other, that the one up with his hunting whip and the other with his bible and knocked each other down, and each had to be carried home on a shutter.'

'Go and tell those tales to the old woman upstairs. I have no patience to listen to them. That's the sort of garbage women feed on, as maggots on rotten meat.'

'But it is true.'

'Who cares whether true or not? It is all the same to me. Has anyone arrived at Mersea?'

'Not yet, sir, but they do say that the parson's wife has expectations.'

'Go back to the kitchen,' growled Elijah, and relapsed into his dream.

A few minutes after, Mehalah came out, and seated herself on the bench beside him. She was knitting. He put out his hand and felt her, and smiled. He raised his hand to her head.

'Glory! when you wear the red cap in the sun I know it, I see a scarlet light like a poppy, and it pleases me. Let me hold the ball, then I can feel every stitch you take with your fingers.'

She put the wool gently into his palm; and began to talk to Mm concerning the farm. He listened, and spoke in a tone and with a manner different from his habit formerly.

Presently his hand stole up the thread, and he caught her fingers and drew her hand down on her lap. Her first impulse was to snatch it away, but she conquered it, and let him feel over her hand without a movement of dislike.

'You have not yet a ring,' he said; 'you have no gold wedding circle like other married women.'

'Our union is unlike all others,' she said.

'That is true; but you must wear my ring. I shall not be happy till you do. I shall think you will cast me off unless I can feel the ring that has no ending round your finger. Where is the link with which I married you?'

'I have it here,' she said; 'I have not cast it off, and I shall not cast you off. I have fastened it by a string and carry it in my bosom.'

He seemed pleased. 'You wear it for my sake.'

'I wear it,' she replied, truthfully, 'because I took a solemn oath on that day, and I will not go from it. What I undertook that I will fulfil, neither more nor less. What I did not promise I will not do, what I did undertake that I will execute.'

'And you bear the ring in your bosom——'

'As a reminder to me of my promise. I will not be false to myself or to you. Do not press me further. You know what to expect and what not to expect. If I could love you I would; but I cannot. I did not promise that then and I will not promise it now, for I know the performance is out of my power.'

'You must wear the wedding ring on your finger.'

'I cannot wear this link, it is too large.'

'I will get you a gold ring, such as other women wear.'

'No. I cannot wear a lie; the gold ring belongs to the perfect marriage, to the union of hearts. It befits not ours.'

'You are right,' he said, and sighed. He still held her hand; she made a slight effort to withdraw it, but he clasped the hand the tighter.

156

'Let me touch and hold you, Glory,' he said. 'Remember I can no more see you, except mistily. You must allow me some compensation. I know what you are now, sitting here in the sun, with your hair full of rich coppery gleams, and your eyes full of light and darkness at once, and your cheek like a ripe apricot. I know what you are, splendid, noble, as no other girl in the whole world; but you have shut my eyes, that I may not see you, so allow me, at least, to feel you.' He paused. Then he went on: 'You are right, our union is unlike any other, as you and I are different from all others in the world. The married life of some is smooth and shining and rustless like the gold, but ours is quite contrary, it is rough and dark and full of blisters and canker. It may be different some day——' he turned his dim eyes enquiringly at her, 'but not now, not now. Nevertheless as the ring is without an end so is our union. Give me the link of iron, Glory, and come with me to the forge. I will beat out a bit of the metal into a ring, one small enough and light enough for you to wear.'

He got up, and holding her hand, bade her lead him to the forge.

Near the bakehouse was a small smithy, fitted up with all necessary appliances. Rebow was a skilful workman at the anvil, and shod his own horses, and made all that was needed in iron for the house and farm.

Mehalah conducted him to the shop, and brought fire from the kitchen for the forge, she worked the bellows and blew the fire into size and strength, whilst Elijah raked the coals together.

'Where is the link, Glory?' he asked, and went up to her. He put his hand to her neck, before she did, and drew out of her bosom something.

'That is not the link, Elijah,' she said; 'it is my medal—the medal that——'

He uttered a fierce cry, and wrenching it off, dashed it on the ground. He would have stamped on it had he been able to see it.

Mehalah's cheek flushed, but she said nothing. She saw where the coin had rolled. She stooped, picked it up, impressed a kiss upon it, and hid it once more in her bosom.

'Here is the iron link,' she said; he took it from her sullenly.

The flame gleamed up blue above the wetted coal, and glared out white through the crevices in the clot, as the bellows panted, and Rebow drew the coals together or broke into the glaring mass with an iron rod.

'I heard a preacher once take as his text,' said he, 'Our God is a consuming fire; and he told all in the chapel that this was writ in Scripture and therefore must be true to the letter, for God wrote it Himself, and He knew what He was better than any man. He said that fire warms and illumines at a distance, but if you come too close it dazzles and burns up. And he told us it was so with God. You can't keep too far off of Him to be comfortable and safe; the nearer you get, the worse it is for you; and to my thinking that is Hell, when you get sucked into the very core of the fire in the heart of God. You must be consumed because you are not divine, fire alone can live in fire; most folks are clay and water, and they are good enough, they get light and warmth, but when they die they burn up like this dock of coke. But there are other folk, like you and me, Glory! who are made of fire and clay; it takes but a word or a thought to make us roar and blaze and glow like this furnace. There is passion in us—and that is a spark of the divine. I do not care what the passion be, love or hate, or jealousy or anger, if it be hot and red and consuming so that it melts and burns all that opposes it, that fiery passion is of God and will live, live on for ever, in the central heart and furnace, which is God. When you and I die, Glory! and are sucked into the great fiery whirlpool, we shall not be burnt up altogether, but intensified. If I love you with fiery passion here I shall love you with fiery passion ten thousand times hotter hereafter; my passion will turn to glaring white heat, and never go out for all everlasting, for it will be burning, blazing in God who is eternal. If you hate me, you will be whirled in, and your fury fanned and raked into a fiery phrenzy which will rage on for ages on ages, and cannot go out, for it will be burning in the everlasting furnace of God. If I love, and you hate with infinite intensity for an infinity of time—that is Hell. But if you love and I love, our love grows hotter and blazes and roars and spurts into one tongue, cloven like the tongues at Pentecost, twain yet one, and that is Heaven. My love eating into yours and encircling it, and yours into mine, and neither containing nor consuming the other, but going on in growing intensity of fiery fury of love from everlasting to everlasting, that is Heaven of Heavens.'

He was heating the link, held between the teeth of long shanked pincers, and then withdrawing it, and forging it on the anvil as he spoke.

'Glory!' he said; 'tell me, you do not hate me?'

She hesitated.

'Glory!' he repeated, and laid hammer and pincer on the anvil, and leaned his head towards her, as she shrank into the dark corner by the bellows, 'Glory! tell me, you do not hate me.'

'Elijah,' she said, 'I must be candid with you. When I think of what, by your own confession, you have done to him whom I loved more than all the world——'

He raised his hammer and brought it down on the link, cutting it in half, and sending one fiery half across the smithy.

'When I think of what you have done to him, I feel that I do hate you, and that I have every cause and right to hate you. I could forgive everything else. I have turned over in my mind all that you have done to me, the cruel way in which you worked till you had brought me within your power, the heartless way in which you got my good name to be evil spoken of, and drove me out of self-defence to take your hand before the altar of God, I have thought of all this, and I feel that my act—unintentional though it was—yet my act, which has blinded you, has expiated all those offences. You have wronged me, and I have wronged you. I have ruined your life, but you have also ruined mine. We are quits so far. You have my frank forgiveness. I blot out all the past, as far as it concerns me, from my memory. It shall no more rankle in my heart. You have shown me a generous forgiveness of my misdeed, and I would imitate you. But what you did to George is not to be expiated. You sinned against him more terribly, more wickedly than against me, and he alone can pardon you. That I cannot forgive; and for that crime I must still hate you.'

He stood trembling—a strange weakness came over him—he was not angry, savage, morose; he seemed a prey to fear and uncertainty.

'Tell me, tell me truly, Glory! Does that alone prevent you from loving me? Had I never done what I said I had done, could you love me?'

'I do not say that,' she replied. 'As I have told you before, I gave my heart once for all to George De Witt. I never could love you with my fresh full heart, as a woman should love her husband, but I feel that I could like you as a friend. I do pity you. God knows how bitterly I have suffered from remorse for what I did unwittingly, and how sincere I am in my repentance and desire to deal tenderly and truly by you, Elijah. I feel sometimes as if I could like you; I do acknowledge that you and I stand apart from others, and alone can understand each other; but then that great crime of your life against George rises up before me and drives back my rising compassion.'

Rebow worked again at the link, beating out the fragment into a wire, and cutting it again. He was thinking whilst he wrought.

'Sooner or later,' he muttered at last, 'all will out.'

He worked with difficulty, and slowly, as he could not see, and was obliged to feel the iron, and cool it repeatedly to ascertain whether it was as he desired it.

'Look here, Glory!' he said, 'when iron is taken from the smelting furnace it is crystalline and brittle; there is no thread and texture in it, but we burn it and beat it, and as we work we beat our stubborn purpose into the metal, and it is the will of the smith which goes through his arm and hammer into the iron and converts it to steel; he drives his will into the metal, and that becomes the fibre in it. You don't find it so in nature. The human soul must part with something and transfuse it into the inanimate iron, and there it will lie and last, for the will of man is divine and eternal. It is much the same with all with which we have to do. I have spent time and labour over you, and thought and purpose have been consumed in making you my wife; they are none of them lost, they are all in you, they have become fibres in your soul. You may not be aware of it, but there they all are. The more one thinks and labours for the other the more he ingrafts himself in the nature of the other. I have heard of sound men having their healthy blood drawn off and injected into the veins of the sick, and restoring them thus to activity and health. We are always doing this with our wills, injecting their fire into the hearts of others, and so by degrees transfusing their natures. You are pouring yourself into me, and I into you, whether we know it or not, till in time we are alike in colour and tone and temperature.'

He had worked the piece of steel into a rude ring, not very cumbrous, and he bade Mehalah try it on her finger. It was too small. He easily enlarged it, and then got a file to smooth off the roughnesses.

'I had rather you wore this than a ring of gold,' he said, 'for there is part of my soul in this iron. I have made it in spite of my blindness, because I had the will to do so. The whole metal is full of my purpose, which tinctures it as wine stains water; and with it goes my resolve that you shall be mine altogether in heart and soul, in love as well as in pity, for now and for all eternity. You will wear that on your finger, the finger that has a nerve leading from the heart. Stretch out your hand, Glory, and let me put it on. Stretch out your hand over the hearth, above the fire, our God is a consuming fire, and this is His proper altar.'

He stood on one side of the furnace, she on the other; the angry red coals glowed below, and a hot smoke rose from them.

She extended her hand to him, and he grasped it with the left above the fire, and held the steel ring in his right.

'Glory!' he said in a tremulous voice. 'At the altar in the church you swore to obey me. In the hall you knelt and swore to cherish me; here, over the fire, the figure of our God, as I put the iron ring on, swear to me also to love me.'

She did not answer. She stood as though frozen to ice; with her eyes on the door of the smithy, where stood a figure—the figure of a man.

Suddenly she uttered a piercing cry. 'George! my George! my George!' and withdrew her hand from the grasp of Elijah. The iron ring fell from his fingers into the red fire below and was lost.

CHAPTER XXVII.

THE RETURN OF THE LOST.

Mehalah was clasped in the arms of George De Witt.

'Who is there? Where is he?' shouted Elijah, staggering forward with his great pincers raised ready to strike.

George drew the girl out of the way, and let the angry man burst out of the door and pass, beating the air with his iron tool. He put his arm round her, and led her from the house. She could not speak, she could only look up at him as at one risen from the dead. He led her towards the sea-wall, looking behind him at the figure of the blind man, rushing about, and smiting recklessly in his jealousy and fury, and hitting bushes, rails, walls, anything in hopes of smiting down the man whose name he had heard, and who he knew had come back to break in on and ruin his hopes.

George De Witt walked lamely, he had a somewhat stiff leg; otherwise he seemed well.

'How manly you have grown!' exclaimed Mehalah, holding him at arms' length, and contemplating him with pride.

'And you, Glory, have become more womanly; but in all else are the same.'

'Where have you been, George?'

'At sea, Glory, and smelt powder. I have been a sailor in His Majesty's Royal Navy, in the Duke of Clarence, and I am pensioned off, because of my leg.'

'Have you been wounded?'

'Not exactly. A cannon-ball, as we were loading, struck me on the shin and bruised the bone, so that I have been invalided with swellings and ulcerations. I ain't fit for active service, but I'm not exactly a cripple.'

'But George! when did this take place? I do not understand. After your escape?'

'Escape, Glory? I have had no escape.'

'From confinement in Red Hall,' she added.

'I never was confined there. I do not know what you are talking about.'

Mehalah passed her hand over her face.

'George! I thought that Elijah had made you drunk and then put you in his cellar, chained there till you went mad.'

'There is not a word of truth in this,' said De Witt. 'Who told you such a tale?'

'Elijah himself.'

'Elijah is a rascal. I have enough cause against him without that.'

'Then tell me about yourself. I am bewildered. How came you to disappear?'

'Let us walk together to the spit by the windmill, and I will tell you all.'

They turned the way he said, and he did not speak again till they had reached the spot.

'We will sit down, Glory; I suffer still somewhat from my leg, so that I am always glad to rest. Now I will tell you the whole story. You remember the evening when we quarrelled. You had behaved rather roughly to Phoebe Musset.'

'I remember it only too well, George.'

'After you had left, I went to the Mussets' house to inquire after Phoebe, who had been well soused in the sea by you; and on my return I fell in with Elijah Rebow. He took me to task for not having gone after you and patched up our little difference. He said that a quarrel should never be allowed to cool, but mended while hot. He persuaded me to let him row me in his boat to the Ray. He said he was going there after ducks or something of that sort, I do not remember exactly. I agreed, and got into his punt with him, and we made for the Rhyn. We had scarcely entered the channel when a lugger full of men ran across our bows and had us fast in a jiffy. I was overpowered before I knew where I was, and taken by the men in their boat.'

'Who were they, George?' asked Mehalah, breathlessly.

'They were some of the crew of the Salamander, a war schooner then lying in the offing, come to press me into the service with Captain Macpherson, who had been on the coast-guard, but was appointed to the command. I was carried off as many another man has been, without my consent, and made to serve His Majesty on compulsion.'

'But, George! how about your medal that I gave you? That was returned to me the same night.'

'I suppose it was,' he replied coolly. 'As I was taken, Elijah said to me, "Have you no token to send back to Glory?" I bade him tell you how I was impressed, and how I would return to you whenever the war was over and I was paid off; but he asked for some token, that you might believe him. Well, Glory! I had nothing by me save your medal, and I handed it to him and told him to give it to you with my love.'

Mehalah wrung her hands and moaned.

'I have a notion,' continued George, 'that Rebow was somehow privy to my being pressed; for he went out that afternoon to the Salamander in his cutter, and had a private talk with Captain Macpherson, who was short of men. Now I fancy, though I can't prove it, that he schemed with the captain how he should catch me, and that Elijah with set purpose took me into the trap set for me. He is deep enough to do such a dirty trick.'

Mehalah's head sank on her knees, and she sobbed aloud.

'And now, Glory, dearest!' he went on, 'the rascal has got you to marry him, I am told. How could you take him? Why did you not wait for me? You were promised to me, and we looked on one another as soon to be husband and wife. You must have soon forgotten your promise.'

'I thought you were dead,' she gasped.

'So did my mother. I do not understand. Elijah knew better.'

'But he told no one. He allowed us all to suppose you were drowned in one of the fleets.'

'It is very hard,' said George, 'for a fellow to return from the wars to reclaim his girl, and to find her no longer his. It is a great blow to me, Glory! I did so love and admire you.'

She could only sway to and fro in her distress.

'It is very disappointing to a chap,' said George, putting a quid in his cheek. 'When he has calculated on getting a nice girl as his wife, and in battle and storm has had the thoughts of her to cheer and encourage him; when he has some prize-money in his pocket, and hopes to spend it on her—well, it is hard.'

'George,' said she between her sobs, 'why did you return the medal? I gave it you, and you swore never to part with it. You should not have sent it to me.'

'Did I really swear that, Glory?' he answered; 'if so, I had forgotten. You see I was so set upon and flustered that night, I did not rightly consider things as they should have been considered.' He stopped.

'Well?' asked Mehalah, eagerly.

'Don't catch me up, Glory. I only stopped to turn the quid. As I was about to say, I did not remember what I had promised. I had nothing else to send you that would serve as a token. The medal was an article about which there could be no mistake. I knew when you saw that you would make sure Elijah's story was true, and my promise would be sacred—I have kept it, I have returned to you, Glory, and if you were not married I should make you my wife. I love you still, as I always did love you. I've seen a sight of fine girls since I left Mersea. There's more fish in the sea than come out of it; but I'm darned if I have seen a finer anywhere, or more to my liking than you, Glory. You were my first love, and the sight of you brings back pleasant memories. The more I look at you now, the more I feel inclined to wring that old prophet's neck. You are too good for such a chap as he; you should have waited for me. You had promised, and might have had patience. But, Lord bless me! how the girls do run after the men! Glory! I have seen the world since I left Mersea, and I know more of it than I did. I suppose you thought that as I was gone to Davy Jones's locker you must catch whom you could.'

'George!' exclaimed Mehalah, 'do not speak to me thus. I cannot bear it. I know you are only talking in this way to try me, and because you resent my marriage. I promised once to be true to you, I gave you my heart, and I have remained, and I will remain, true to you; my heart is yours, and I can never recover it and give it to another.'

'This is very fine and sentimental, Glory,' said George; 'I've smelt powder and I know the colour of blood. I've seen the world, and know what sentiment is worth; it is blank cartridge firing; it breaks no bones, but it makes a noise and a flash. I don't see how you can call it keeping true to me when you marry another man for his money.'

'You are determined to drive me mad,' exclaimed Mehalah. 'Have mercy on me, my own George, my only George! I have loved and suffered for you. God can see into my heart, and knows how deeply it has been cut, and how profusely it has bled for you. You must spare me. I have thought of you. I have lived only in a dream of you. The world without you has been dead and blank. I have not had a moment of real joy since your disappearance; it seems to me as though a century of torment had drawn its slow course since then. No, George! I have married for nothing but to save my self-respect. I was forced by that man, whom I will not name now, so hateful and horrible to me is the thought of him—I was forced by him from my home on the Ray to lodge under his roof. He smoked my mother and me out of our house as if we were foxes. When he had me secure he drew a magician's circle round me, and I could not break through it. My character, my name were tarnished, there was nothing for it but for me to marry him. I did so, but I did so under stipulations. I took his name, but I am not, and never shall be, more to him than his wife in the register of the parish. I have never loved him—I never undertook to love him.'

'This is a queer state of things,' said George. 'Dashed if, in all my experience of life and of girls, I came across anything similar, and I have seen something. I have not spent all my days in Mersea. I've been to the West Indies. I've seen white girls, and yellow girls, and brown girls, and copper-coloured girls, and black ones—black as rotted seaweed. I have—they are all much of a muchness, but this beats my experience. You are not like others.'

'So he says; he and I are alone in the world, and alone can understand one another. Do you understand me, George?'

'I'm blessed if I do.'

She was silent. She was very unhappy. She did not like his tone: there was an insincerity, a priggishness about it which jarred with her reality and depth of feeling. But she could not analyse what offended her. She thought he was angry with her, and had assumed a taunting air to cover his mortification.

She drew the medal from her bosom.

'George! dear, dear George!' she said vehemently, 'take the pledge again. I give it you with my whole heart once more. I believe it saved you once, it may save you again. At all events, it is a token to you that my heart is the same, that I care for and love none but you in the whole wide world.'

He took it and suspended it round his neck.

'I will keep it for your sake,' he said; 'you may be sure it will be treasured by me.'

'Keep it better than you did before.'

'Certainly I will. I shall value it inexpressibly.'

'George!' she went on, trembling in all her limbs, and rising to her feet. 'George! my first and only love! as I give it you back now, I make you the same promise that I made you before. I will love—love—love you and you only, eternally. I swore then to be true to you, and I have been true. Swear again to me the same.'

'Certainly. I shall always love you, Glory! I'm damned if it is possible for a fellow not to, you are so handsome with those flashing eyes and glowing cheeks. A fellow must be made of ice not to love you.'

'Be true to me, as I to you.'

'To be sure I will, Glory!' and added in an undertone, 'rum sort of truth hers, to go and marry another chap.'

'What is that you say, George?'

'Take care, Glory!' exclaimed the sailor; 'here comes the old prophet with a pair of tongs over his shoulder, staggering along the wall towards us. I had better sheer off. He don't look amiable. Good-bye, Glory!'

'Oh, George! I must see you again.'

'I will come again. You will see me often enough. Sailors can no more keep away from handsome girls than bees from clover.'

'George, George!'

Elijah came up, his face black with passion.

'Mehalah!' he roared, as he swung his iron pincers.

She caught his wrist and disarmed him.

'I could bite you, and tear your flesh with my teeth,' he raged. 'All was so peaceful and beautiful, and then he came from the dead and broke it into shivers. Where are you?' He put out his hands to grasp her.

'Do not touch me!' she cried, loathing in her voice. 'With my whole soul I abhor you, you base coward. You lied to me about George, a hateful lie that made me mad, and yet the reality is almost as bad—it is worse. He is alive and free, and I am bound, bound hand and foot, to you.'

CHAPTER XXVIII.
TIMOTHY'S TIDINGS.

'Mehalah!' roared the wretched man, smiting at her with both his clenched fists, and nearly precipitating himself into the mud, by missing his object, 'Mehalah! where are you? Come near, and let me beat and kill you.'

'Why are you angry, Elijah?' asked the girl. 'The man you betrayed to the pressgang has returned, are you vexed at that?'

'Come near me,' he shouted.

'You have gained your end, and may well be content that he is alive. You have separated us for ever; what more could you desire? His hopes and mine are alike shattered by your act. You lied to me about his madness, but though that wickedness was not wrought to which you pretended, you have done that which passes forgiveness.'

'Where is he?'

'He is gone. He would not meet you. He could not deal the punishment you deserve on a blinded man.'

'You have been discussing me—the blinded man,' raved Elijah. 'Yes, you first blind me that I may not see, and then you meet and intrigue with your old lover, in security, knowing I cannot watch, and pursue, and punish you.'

'Go back to the house, Elijah. You are in no fit temper to speak to on this subject.'

'Oh yes! go back and sit in the hall alone, whilst you are with him—your George! No, Mehalah! I tell you this. I will not be deceived. Though I be blind, I can and will see and follow you. I will sell my soul to the devil for twenty-four hours' vision, that I may track and catch and crush your two heads together, and trample the life out of you with my big iron-heeled boots. You shall not see him, you shall never see him again. Give me back my pincers, and I will make an end of it all.'

'Elijah, you must trust me. I married you in self-respect, and I shall never forget the respect I owe to myself.'

'I cannot trust you,' he answered, 'because you are just one of those whose movements no one can calculate. I tell you what, Mehalah. God made most folks of clockwork and stuck them on their little plots of soil to spin round and run their courses, like the figures on an Italian barrel-organ. You look at Mersea island, that is the board of such a contrivance, and on it are so many dolls; they twist about, and you know that if God turns the handle for ten minutes or for ten years, or for ten times ten years, they will do exactly the same things in exactly the same ways, just as He made them and set them to spin. But as He was making the dolls that were to twirl and pirouette His breath got into some, and they are different from the rest. They don't go according to the clockwork, and don't follow the circles of the machine, as set agoing by the organ-handle. God himself can't count on them, for they have free wills, and His breath is genius and independence in their hearts. They go where they list, and do what they will, they follow the impulse of the breath of God within, and not the wires that fasten them to the social mechanism. I do not know what I may do. I do not know what you may do. We have the breath of God in us. I am sure that you have, and I am sure that I have; but I know that there is none in your mother, none in such as George De Witt. The laws of the land and of religion are the slits in the board on which the dolls dance, and they only move along these slits; but you and I, and such as have free souls, go anywhere, and do anything. We have no law. The wind bloweth where it listeth, and thou canst not tell whence it cometh and whither it goeth; so is everyone that is born of the Spirit. I heard a preacher once explain that text, and he said that the wind was the Spirit of God and it went where it willed, and so all who were born of the Spirit followed their wills, and there was neither right nor wrong to them, for they were blown about, across and up and down, where others not so born dare not step, and they never forfeited their sonships whatever they did, for it was not they, but the divine will in them that drove them. Mehalah! you are one with a free, headlong will, and how can I count on what you will do? There is no cut track along which you must run. The puppets dance their rounds, but you rush in and out and upset those that are in your way. I am the same. You have seen and learned my way. Who could reckon on me? I never mapped out my course, but went on as I was impelled; and so will you. But be sure of this, Mehalah! I shall not endure your desertion of me. Beware how you meet and speak to George De Witt again.'

'Elijah,' said the girl; 'I give you only what I promised you, my obedience, never expect more. Your crooked courses are not such as can gain respect, much less regard. You say that you act on impulse, and have not mapped your course. I do not believe you. You have worked with a set purpose before you to get rid of George, and obtain hold over me. Your purpose was deliberate, your plans laid in cold blood. You have got as much as you can get. You have obtained some sort of control over me, but my soul is free, my heart is free, and these you shall never bring into slavery.'

'I was ready half an hour ago to forgive you for having blinded me. I cannot forgive you now. You have done me a wicked wrong. You acted on impulse, without purpose, you say. I do not believe it. There was set design and cold scheming in it all. You knew that George De Witt was not dead—or you thought he might be yet alive and might return, so you dashed the firejuice into my eyes to blind them to what would take place on his reappearance.'

'This is false!' exclaimed Mehalah indignantly.

'So is it false that I schemed and worked,' he said. 'Do you not understand, Mehalah, that what we do, we do for an end which we do not see? We act on the spur of passion, and the acts link together, and make a complete chain in the end. I did at the moment what I thought must be done, and so it was brought about that you became my wife. You acted as anger and love inspired, and now I am made helpless, whilst you sport with your lover. But I tell you, Mehalah, I will not endure this. I don't care if you die and I die, but parted we shall not be. You and I must find our heaven in each other and nowhere else. You are going after wandering lights if you expect a port away from my heart. Wrecking lights attached to asses' heads.' He stamped and caught at her.

'My heart was given to George before I knew you,' said Glory sadly; 'I have long known him, and we had long been promised to each other. We had hoped to be married this spring and then we should have been happy, unspeakably happy. He has been true to me and I will be true to him. We cannot now marry. You have prevented that; but we can still love one another and be true to each other, and live in the thought and confidence of the other. He trusts me and I trust him. He is now bitterly distressed to find that you have separated us, but in time he will be reconciled, and then it will be as of old, when I was on the Ray. We shall see one another, and we shall be true, loving friends, but nothing more; nothing more is possible. You have barred that.'

'Is this your resolve?' he asked, turning livid with anger; even his lips a dead leaden tint.

'It is not a resolve, it is what must be. I must love him, I cannot help it. We must see each other. We can never be man and wife, that you have succeeded in preventing, and for that I shall never forgive you. But I will not be false to my oath. I will still serve you, and I will cherish you in your wretchedness and blindness.'

'This will not do,' he cried. 'My whole nature, my entire soul, cries out and hungers for you, for your nature, for your soul. I must have your whole being as mine, I will not be master of a divided Glory! allegiance here, love there, cold obedience to me and gushing devotion to him. The thought is unendurable. O God!' he burst forth in an agony, 'why did I not take you in my arms when the Ray house was burning, and spring with you into the flames and hold you there in the yellow wavering tongue of fire, till we melted into one lump? Then we should both have been at peace now, both in one, and happy in our unity.' He strode up and down, with his head down.

'Mehalah! have you seen water poured on lime? What a fume and boiling takes place, the two fight together which shall obtain the mastery, but neither gets it all its own way in the end, but one enters into and penetrates every pore of the other, and the heat and the steam only continue till every part of one is impregnated with the other. You and I are mixing like water and lime, and we rage and smoke, but there is peace at the end, in view, when we are infused the one into the other, when it is neither I nor you, but one being. The mixture must be complete some day, in this life or the next; and then we shall clot into one hard rock, imperishable and indivisible.'

'Elijah! try to take interest in something else; think of something beside me. I can be nothing more to you than what I am, so rest contented with what you have got, and turn your thoughts to your farm, or anything else.'

'I cannot do it, Mehalah. I put a little plant once in a pot and filled the vessel with rich mould, and the plant grew and at last broke the pot into a hundred pieces, and I found within a dense mat of fibres; the root had eaten up and displaced all the soil and swelled till it rent the vessel. It has been so with my love of you. It got planted, how I know not, in my heart, and it has thrown its roots through the whole chamber, and devoured all the substance, and woven a net of fibres in and out and up and down, and has swelled and is thrusting against the walls, till there is scarce love there any more but horrible, biting, wearing pain. I cannot kill the plant and pluck it out, or it will leave a great void. I must let it grow till it has broken up the vessel. It grows and makes root, but will not flower. There has been scarce leaf, certainly no blossom, to my love. It is all downward, inward, clogging, bursting tangle of fibre. Can you say it is so with you? You cannot. Your care for that fool George is but a slip struck in that may root or not, that must be nursed or it will wither. Tear it up and cast it away. It is not worthy of you. George is a simple fool. I know him. A clown without a soul. Why, Glory! there are none hereabouts with souls but you and me. Your mother has none, Mrs. De Witt has none, Abraham has none. They can't understand the ways and workings of those that have souls. They are bodies, ruled by bodily wants, and look at all things out of bodily eyes, and interpret by bodily instincts all things done by those spiritually above them. But you understand me, and I understand you. Soul speaks to soul. I've heard a preacher say that once on a time the sons of God went in unto the daughters of men, and what they begat of them were cursed of heaven. That means that men with souls married vulgar women with only instincts and appetites, and such unions are unnatural. The sons of God must marry the daughters of God, and leave the animal men and women to pig together and breed listless, dull-eyed, muddle-headed, dough-hearted, scandal-mongering generations. The curse of God would have rested upon you if you had married George De Witt. I have saved you from that. You have mated with your equal.'

'What happiness, what blessing has attended our union?' she asked bitterly.

'None,' he replied, 'because you oppose your will to the inevitable. We must be united entirely, and blended into one, but you resist, and so misery ensues. I am blinded and wretched, and you, you———'

'I am wretched also,' she said; 'but stay! here comes someone to speak to us.'

'Who is it?'

'I do not know exactly. A young man who came here one day with Phoebe Musset.'

'What does he want with us? I will have no young men coming here.'

The person who approached was Timothy Spark, 'cousin' to Admonition Pettican. He was dressed in a new suit of mourning. He lounged along the sea-wall with his hands in his pockets.

'Your servant, master,' he said to Elijah as he came up. 'Your most devoted servant,' he added with a bow to Mehalah, and a simper. 'Charmed to see my dear and beautiful cousin so well.'

'Cousin!' exclaimed Rebow, stepping back and frowning.

'Certainly, certainly,' said Timothy. 'I am cousin to Admonition, wife, or rather let me say widow of the late lamented Charles Pettican, and he was first cousin to Mrs. Sharland, so my pretty cousin Mehalah will not, I am sure, deny the relationship. Let me offer you an arm,' he wedged his way between Rebow and Glory.

'First cousin once and a half removed,' he said. 'Drop the fractions and say cousin, broadly. Certainly, certainly so. Is it not so, my dear?' In an undertone and aside to Mehalah. 'Let us drop the old fellow behind. I have a word to say in your ear, cousin Mehalah! By the way, how do you shorten that long name? It is such a mouthful. But I forget, where is my memory going? Glory is the name you go by among relatives and friends. Come along, Glory! Lean on my arm. The blind gentleman is a little unsteady on his pins and can't keep up with us. He will be more comfortable taking his airing slowly by himself; we shall distract him with our frolicsome talk. He is in a serious mood, perhaps pious.'

'Say what you have to say at once,' said Elijah surlily. 'I must hear it. What did you say about late Charles Pettican?'

'The poor gentleman is deceased,' said Timothy; 'and his disconsolate widow is drinking down her grief in hot toddy.'

'Mr. Charles Pettican dead!' exclaimed Mehalah with grief.

'Dead as Nebuchadnezzar,' replied Timothy; 'rather rapid at the last, the paralysis attacked his vitals, and then it was all over with him in a snap. Fortunately, he had made his will. You haven't taken my arm yet, my pretty cousin. You won't? well then, I will continue. I flatter myself that my influence prevailed, and he made a will not in favour of Admonition, who had really become too exacting towards myself, and inconsiderate towards him, for us to endure it much longer. He threw himself on my honour, and I told him I relied on his gratitude. We put our heads together. Admonition has had a fall. She gets only a hundred pounds. My friend Charles, in token of my friendship, has kindly, I may say handsomely, remembered me,—and all the bulk of his property he has bequeathed to my good cousin here, Glory. I need hardly say that this has proved as great a surprise to Admonition as it must be to you. Admonition brought it on herself. She should not have attempted to displace me; I am not a person so unimportant as to be dispensed with at pleasure. Admonition cannot recover from the shock and mortification, and I left her at Wyvenhoe, venting it in language not flattering to the late lamented. She led me a dance, and him she treated like a galley-slave, so that she has got her deserts. I saw that she was carrying it on a little too far for the endurance of Charles, so I had a talk with him on the matter, and offered to help him in the management of his affairs for a trifling salary, and he was good enough to see how advantageous it would be to him to have me as a friend and adviser; so we put our heads together, and then Admonition tried to bundle me out of the house, and much to her surprise learned that I was as securely installed therein as herself. I was private secretary and accountant to Charles, and cousin Admonition had to knuckle under then. Curiously enough, she had picked up another cousin about that time, one I had never heard of before in my life, and she wanted to bring him into the house in my place; I did not allow that game to be played. I kept my berth, and Admonition was in a pretty temper about it, you may be sure. How Charles chuckled! He enjoyed it. Upon my word I believe he chuckles in his grave to think how he has done Admonition in the end; and he smirks doubtless to consider also how he has served me.'

'What has he left Mehalah?' asked Rebow surlily.

'I cannot tell you exactly, but I suspect about two hundred and fifty to three hundred pounds a year; a nice little fortune, and dropping in very unexpectedly, I presume. I am executor, and shall have the choicest pleasure in explaining all to my sweet cousin. Is it not near about your dinner-time?'

'Yes.'

'Then I don't mind picking a bone and drinking a glass with you. The drive is long from Wyvenhoe. You happen perhaps to have a spare room in the house?'

No answer was given to this question.

'Because I have brought over my little traps. I thought it best. We can talk over matters, and I will show you what the amount of property is that Charles has left. I have the will with me, it is not proved yet. I shall do that shortly.'

'There's an inn at Salcott. The "Rising Sun." You can go there. We do not take in strangers.'

'Certainly, certainly! only you see,' touching Elijah knowingly in the ribs, 'I'm not a stranger, but a friend and relative of the family, a cousin; you understand, a cousin, and ready to make myself agreeable to one,' with a bow to Mehalah, 'and useful to the other,' with a tap on Rebow's arm.

'You can settle all you have to say on business in an hour if you stick to it, and then you can be gone,' said Elijah in ill-temper, withdrawing his arm from the familiar touch.

'Certainly, certainly,' said Timothy. 'But then, I must call again, and yet again, always I am sure, with increasing pleasure, but still at some inconvenience to myself. I thought I might just settle in here, you might give me a shake-down in any nook, and I would make myself a most invaluable member of the family. You, old gentleman, with your affliction, want an overlooker to the farm, and who could serve your purpose better than myself, a friend and a relation, a cousin, almost first cousin, with just a remove or so between, not worth particularising. I could devote my time to your affairs——'

'I don't want you. I will not have you!' exclaimed Rebow angrily. 'Why have you come here, you meddling puppy? Did I ask you to come? Did Mehalah want you? I know you and your ways. You got into Pettican's house hanging on to the skirts of his wife, and then made mischief between man and wife; and now you come here to play the same game; you come because I am blind and helpless, and sneaking behind my Glory; you want to steal in to play the fool with her and set us one against the other. We want none of you here. We are not so tender together that we desire another element of discord to enter into the jangled clash of bells. Be off with you. As for the matter of Mehalah's inheritance, the lawyers shall communicate with us, and between you and her. I will not have you set your foot inside my house.'

'Stay,' said Glory; 'I must know if this be really true. Am I really inheritor of such a fortune?'

'I have the will in my pocket.'

'Show it me.'

Timothy produced the document and read it to Elijah and Mehalah. Both drew near.

'Let me see it!' said Rebow vehemently, and grasped at the paper with nervous hand.

'My good friend,' remarked Timothy patronisingly; 'the state of your eyes, if I mistake not, will prevent your being able to read it.'

'I must feel it then.'

He grasped it fiercely and in a moment tore it with his hands, and then, biting the fragments, rent it further and further.

'For heaven's sake!' exclaimed the young man in dismay.

'Ha! Glory! Did you suppose you were to be made independent of me? Did you think I would let you get a fortune of your own, to emancipate you from me? That you might go off with it, and enjoy it along with your George De Witt?'

He dashed the tatters about him.

'You mad fool!' exclaimed Timothy Spark. 'Do you suppose that by such a scurvy trick as this you will despoil my pretty cousin of her money, and perhaps of her liberty?'

'I have done it,' shouted Rebow wrathfully. 'You cannot make the will whole, I have chewed and swallowed portions, and others the winds have taken into the sea.'

'Indeed!' said Timothy. 'Do you suppose that this is the original? Of course not. It is an authenticated copy. The original will is left with Morrell the lawyer, and this is but a transcript.'

Rebow gnashed his teeth.

'It seems to me,' said Timothy, 'that after all I shall be called upon to step in between husband and wife, and to protect my pretty dark-eyed, rosy-lipped cousin. I am sure you have a spare room where I can have a shake-down.'

CHAPTER XXIX.

## TEMPTATION.

Elijah Rebow sank into a sullen fierce silence. He scarcely stirred from the house except to the forge, where he groped among the dead ashes for the iron ring, which however he never found. He sat in his hall, smoking, his elbows on the arms of his chair, his head sunk on his breast, with his dull eyes on the floor. He seemed brooding over something, which occupied all his thoughts, and he rarely spoke.

There had been little difficulty in getting rid of Timothy. He lingered a day or two about Salcott and Red Hall, but as he met with angry repulse from Rebow, and no encouragement from Mehalah, he abandoned the ground as unproductive. He was an idle, good-for-nothing young man, hating work, and when he was obliged to leave comfortable quarters at Wyvenhoe, hoped to settle himself into a similar position at Salcott. He was conceited, and fancied himself able to make conquests when he liked, and never for a moment doubted that his looks and address would have ingratiated him with Mehalah, and won him a lodgment in the house. He had been hovering about Phoebe Musset for some time, as she was thought to have money. Her parents had no other child, and the farm and shop would have suited him. When he met with a rebuff at Red Hall he betook himself to Mersea, and was much surprised to be received there with coldness where he had expected warmth. The reason was that George De Witt had returned, a sailor in the Royal Navy, covered with glory according to his own account, and Phoebe was more disposed to set her cap at him than flirt with the shore-loafer, Timothy Spark.

As Mehalah was crossing the farmyard one day, old Abraham Dowsing stopped her.

'I want to speak along of you,' he said in his uncouth, abrupt manner. 'What does the master mean by his goings on? I saw him to-day after his dinner sitting with the great knife in his hand. The door was open and I was at the bottom of the steps, and I looked up, and there he was making stabs with it into the air. Then he got up, and holding the knife behind him, he crept over towards your mother's leather-backed chair. I seed him feel at it, and when he did touch it, then there came a wild look over his face, and he out with the carving knife, quick as thought, and he clutched the back of the chair with his left, and dug the blade right into the leather, and it came through at the back. You look next time you go into the hall. I guess he's going as his brother did.'

'Going out of his mind, Abraham?'

'Yes, I reckon. What else does it all mean? It is either that, or there is something that deadly angers him.'

He looked with a cunning covert glance at her.

'It is not that these matters concern me, over much, but I don't want to change places in my old age. I'm comfortable enough here. I gets my wittles regular, and my swipes of ale. Take care of yourself, Mistress. I've heard as how the master got somebody pressed when he was in the way,—there's a tale about it abroad. He won't stand that party about here much, and I wouldn't adwise the encouragement of him.'

'George De Witt is my friend. He may come when he likes,' said Mehalah gravely. 'He and I have known one another since we were children, and my marriage need not destroy an old friendship.'

'I mentioned no names,' said the old man. 'You can't say I did. One thing I be sure of. Whenever somebody comes here, the master knows it; he knows it by a sort of instinct, I fancy. I see him at the head of the steps looking out as though he could see, and biting at the air, just as a mad dog snaps at everything and nothing.'

'There is George!' suddenly exclaimed Mehalah, as she saw the young sailor's figure rise on the sea-wall.

'And there is the master,' muttered Abraham, pointing to Elijah, who appeared at his door, peering about, and holding his hand to his ear.

Mehalah hesitated a moment, and then went up the steps to him.

'Do you want to come down?' she asked; 'shall I lead you?'

'Yes, help me.' He clutched her hand by the wrist and came out and stood on the stair. Then he grasped her shoulder with the other hand, and he began to shake and twist her.

She could see into his heart as into clear water, to the ugly snags and creeping things at the bottom. She saw that the temptation had come on him to fling her down: but she saw also that it was immediately overcome. He knew she read his thoughts. 'The height is not much,' he muttered; 'you might sprain an ankle but not break your neck. I will not hurt you, do not fear. Hurt you! Good God! I would not hurt you, not give you one moment's pain, I would bear hours of agony rather than make you suffer for one second. But what must be, must be! There is no way out of the marsh but over the dyke. There is no peace which is not won by a fight and wounds. Let me go back.' He drew her in at the door, a ferocious expression flickered over his face, like phosphorescent illumination over dead fish.

'I cannot endure this longer. Mehalah! you are killing me. This is worse than the fire-juice in my eyes, you are drenching my heart and brain in vitriol, I feel it gnawing and stinging and blackening as it consumes a way to the inner core, leaving charred matter behind.'

'What am I doing, to make you suffer?' she asked.

'You are doing all you can. I cannot, I will not endure that agony. Have you seen the coal heap in the forge, how the fire rages and glows within before the blast? Water is thrown on without quenching the fire, it only intensifies its heat. At last the black mass cracks on all sides and the white fury shoots out in spits and knives of flame. It is so with me. The fire is here.' He smote his breast and then his brain. 'It is raging, panting, whitening, intensifying, and at last it will break out on all sides. Who is blowing the fire into vehemence? It is you—you—you!'

He gathered himself up, like a crouching beast, as though to spring on her and strangle or tear her; but she stepped back beyond his spring.

'I give you no occasion for this,' she said; 'you speak and act like a madman.'

'It is you who drive me to act and speak like one,' he cried. 'You are now mistress of yourself, you have money—as much as you want; now you will shake me off. Now you will desert the man who stood between you and your fool. You will go off with him and forget me. It shall not be.' He clutched his hands into his sides. 'It never shall be.'

'I will not listen to this. I will not endure such words,' she exclaimed. 'Remain here and cool.' Then she left the room, and, walking across the pasture to the landing-place, extended her hand with a smile to George. It was a relief to her to be away for a while from the gloom and savagery of the man to whom she was bound for life. In her simplicity and guilelessness she would not believe that there was any wrong in meeting the friend of her childhood, her almost brother. She needed some light on her sad life, and the light shone from him.

'My dear Glory,' he said,' I am delighted to see you. What a colour there is in your cheeks. Has the prophet been in his frenzies again? I fear so. You must not allow it. You should not endure it.'

'How can I help it, George? it is the man's nature to rave; he has it in his blood. I almost fear he will go mad like his poor brother.'

'The sooner the better.'

'Do not say that. You do not know how dreadful was the condition of that miserable wretch.'

'I do say it, Glory, dearest! I say it, because the sooner you are freed from this tyranny and torture, the better for both of us.'

'How so?'

'Glory, dear! is it true that you have been left a small fortune?'

'Yes, it is true. It seems that there is money in various securities, the savings of Charles Pettican's life, and they bring in something like three hundred pounds a year. Sometimes it may be less, sometimes perhaps more.'

'And is this money absolutely your own?'

'Entirely.'

'You may do with it what you like?'

'Yes, altogether; even Elijah cannot touch it. I will give you all if you like, or as much as you like.'

'I would not touch it without you, Glory.'

She sighed.

'Oh, George, George! to think how happy we might have been!'

'We may be, Glory.'

'I do not see how that is possible. I have no more any hopes, but it is a great pleasure to me to see you and to hear you talk. I think of old days and old dreams of happiness.'

'Why, Glory! with three hundred a year we might have lived as gentlefolks, doing nothing. We might have bought a little house and garden just anywhere, at the other end of England, in Scotland, or where you liked, away from all ugly sights and memories.'

'I had no ugly memories in the old days,' she said sorrowfully.

'I suppose not. But you have now. My Glory! how delightful it would be to cast all the horrible past away like a bad dream; all the past from when I was pressed into the service, to now—to drop it all out of memory as though it never had been, and to take up the story of life from that interruption.'

'Oh, George!' She trembled and gave one great sob, that shook her.

'How we should live to one another, live in one another, and love one another. Why, Glory! we should not care for any others to come and disturb us, we should be so happy——'

She covered her face.

'On three hundred a year,' he went on. 'That is a beautiful sum. I suppose you need not live here on it: you might live where you liked on the money. It is not laid out on land in Wyvenhoe?'

'No, no.'

'You might take, let us suppose, a cottage by Plymouth Harbour. I have been there; it is a lovely spot, where you would see ships of all sorts sailing by; and just draw your money and live at ease.'

'I suppose so.'

'And nobody there would know you, whence you came, and what your history. They would not care to ask. That would be a new life, and in it all the past would be forgotten.'

'Why do you talk like this to me, George? I cannot bear it. You raise pictures before me which never can exist. All I want is to live on here in my sorrow and difficulties, and just now and then to see you and talk to you, and thus to get refreshed and go back to my duties again with a lighter heart, and strengthened to bear my burden.'

'I do not understand what you mean by duties,' he said. 'You have told me more than once that you have only formally taken Elijah Rebow as a husband, but that he is nothing to you in reality, you do not love him, and have no tie to bind you to him save the farce you went through with him in church.'

'There is another,' said Mehalah in a faint tone.

'What other? What other can there be? You do not look on him as your husband, do you?'

'No I do not, and I never will.'

'You do not even wear a wedding ring.'

'No.'

'He understood that he was to be regarded by you in no other light than as one who gave his name to you in consideration for some service.'

'That was all.'

'Then I cannot see that you are not free. You promised to be my wife, quite as solemnly as you have promised anything to Elijah, and you made your agreement with him on the supposition that I was dead. He knew he was deceiving you, and that I was alive to claim the fulfilment of your oath to me. He got your promise from you under false representations, and it cannot stand. You did not know how matters stood, or you would never have taken it.'

'Never, never!'

'Through all, you say, you have held true to me.'

'Indeed I have, George.'

'Then Glory, my dearest, our course is quite clear. You are not bound to this man, but you are bound to me. Your tie to him is worthless and is snapped; your tie to me is strong and holds. I insist on the fulfilment, I have a right to do so. I must have you as my own. Come away with me. Come to any part of England, where you will, where we are not known, where our names have never been heard, and we will be properly married in a church, and live together happily the rest of our lives. As for your mother, she is failing fast. I will wait till her death, or we can take her away at once with us.'

'Oh, George, George!' Mehalah's tones were those of one in acute pain. She flung herself on the ground at his feet, and clasped her hands on her brow.

He looked at her with some surprise: 'This will be a change for the better. You will escape out of darkness into sunshine, and leave all your miseries in this hateful marsh behind your back.'

'George! George!' she moaned.

'Elijah deserves not a thought,' he went on. 'He has behaved like a villain from beginning to end, and if he is served out now, no one will pity him.'

'It is impossible, George!' exclaimed Mehalah, lifting herself on her knees and holding her knitted fingers against her heart. 'It cannot be, George. It never can be. There is another tie that I cannot break.'

'What tie?'

'I must own it, though it steep me in shame. It was I, George, who blinded him, I in mad fear and anger mingled, not knowing what I did, poured the vitriol over his eyes.'

George De Witt drew back from her.

'Glory! how dreadful!'

'It is dreadful, but it was done without premeditation. He had me in his arms and told me what he had done to you—' she corrected herself—'what he pretended he had done to you, and then he tried to kiss me, and in a moment of loathing and effort to escape I did the deed. I did not know what was in the bottle. I did not know what I laid hold of.'

'You are a dangerous person to deal with, Glory. I should be sorry to provoke you. I do not understand you.'

'I suppose you do not,' she said, with a sob; 'but you must see this, George. I have blinded him and made him a helpless creature dependent on me. I did it, and I must atone for it. I brought him into this condition, and I must expiate what I did by helping him to bear the affliction.'

'He exasperated you.'

'Yes, but think what he is now, a wreck. I must tow the wreck into port. There is no help for it; I cannot leave him, I have brought this on myself, and I must bear it.'

'Glory! what nonsense! You do not love me or you would at once come away with me, and leave him to his fate. He has richly deserved it.'

'I not love you!' she cried. 'Oh, George! how can you doubt that I do? I have suffered for you, dreamed of you, lived for you. My world without you is a world without a sun.'

'Then come with me.'

'I cannot do it. I have done that which binds me to Elijah. I must not leave him.'

'You will not. Hark!' A burst of merry bells from West Mersea church tower swept over the water. 'There is a wedding to-day yonder, and the bells are being pealed in honour of it. Did the bells peal when you were married?'

'No.'

'They shall when you become mine. Not those Mersea bells, but some others where we are not known.'

'It cannot, it cannot be. George! do not tempt and torture me. I must not leave Elijah. I have linked my fate to his by my own mad act, and that cannot be undone. Oh, George! if it had not been for that, I might have listened to you and followed you; for I am not, and never will be his; but now I cannot desert him in his darkness and despair. I could not be happy with you if I were to leave him.'

'This is too bad of you,' said the young man angrily. 'You are to me an incomprehensible girl.'

'Can we not live on as we are at present, true to each other yet separated?'

'No, we cannot. It is not in nature. I will tell you what, Glory! If you do not come away with me and marry me, I will marry someone else. There are more fish in the sea than come out of it.'

She rose to her feet and stood back, and looked at him with wide open eyes. 'George, this is a cruel jest. It should not be uttered.'

'It is no jest, but sober earnest,' he answered sullenly. 'Glory! I don't see why I should not marry as well as you.'

'Oh, George! George! do not speak to me in this way. I have been true to you, and you have promised to be true to me.'

'Conditionally,' he interjected.

'You could not do it. You could not take another woman to your heart. George! you talk of impossibilities.'

'Indeed! Do you think that another girl would not have me? If so, you are mistaken.'

'You could not do it,' she persisted. 'If you were to, it would not be the George I knew and loved and lost, but another. The George I knew and loved and lost was true to me as I to him; he could no more take another to his heart than can I.'

'But you have, Glory.'

'I have not. Elijah sits nowhere near my heart.'

'I do not believe it. If he did not, you would shake him off without another thought and follow me.'

'Do you not see,' she cried passionately, holding out both her palms, and trembling with her vehemence, 'that I cannot. I by my own act have made him helpless, and would you have me desert him in his helplessness? I cannot do it. There is something in here, in my bosom, I know not what it is, but it will not let me. If I were to go against that I should never be at ease.'

'You are not at ease now.'

'That would be different. I have my sorrow now, but my distress then would be of another sort and utterly unendurable. I cannot explain myself. George! you ought to understand me. If I were to say these words to Elijah he would see through my heart at once, and all the thoughts in it would be visible to him as painted figures in a church window. To you they seem all broken and jumbled and meaningless.'

'I tell you again, Glory, I do not understand you. Perhaps it is as well that we should live apart. I hate to have a knot in my hands I can't untie. If Elijah understands you, keep to him. I shall look for a mate elsewhere.'

'George!' she said plaintively, 'You are angry and offended. I am sorry for it. I will do anything for you. True to you I must and will remain, but I will not leave Elijah and follow you. I could not do it.'

'Very well then, I shall look for a wife elsewhere.'

'You cannot do it,' she said.

'Can I not?' echoed George De Witt with a laugh; 'I rather believe there is a nice girl at Mersea who only wants to be asked to jump into my arms. It seems to me that I owe her reparation for your treatment of her once on my boat.'

'What!'

'Now, Glory! let us understand one another. If you will run off with me—and I see nothing but some silly sentiment to hinder you—then we will be married and live happily together on your little fortune and my pension and what I can pick up.'

She shook her head.

'If you will not, why then, I shall go straight from here to Phoebe Musset, and ask her to be my wife; and you may take my word for it that in three weeks the bells that are now pealing from Mersea tower will be pealing again for us.'

'You could not do it.'

'Indeed I will. I shall go direct to her. My mother wishes it and I know that Phoebe is ready with her yes.'

'You can take her, her, to your heart?'

'Delighted to do so.'

'Then, George! I never knew you, I never understood you.'

'I dare say not, no more than I can understand you. Once again, will you come with me?'

'No, never.'

'You never loved me. I shall go to Phoebe and have done with Glory.'

She lifted her hands to heaven, pressed them to her heart, and then ran with extended arms back to Red Hall, stumbling and recovering herself, and fluttering on, still with arms outstretched, like a wounded bird trying to rise but unable, seeking a covert where it may hide its head and die.

CHAPTER XXX.

TO WEDDING BELLS.

She ran on. Red Hall was before her. The sun had set, and scarlet, amber, and amethyst were the tints of the sky, blotted by the great bulk of the old house standing up alone against the horizon.

She ran on, and the wedding bells of Mersea steeple chanted joyously in the summer evening air, and the notes flew over the flats like melodious wildfowl.

She ran up the steps, in at the door of the hall, where sat Elijah with his finger feeling the inscription on the chimney-piece, with the red light glaring through the western window on his forehead, staining it crimson.

She cast herself at his feet; she placed her elbows on his knees, and laid her head upon them. Dimly he saw the scarlet cap like a broken poppy droop and fall before him, he put out his hand and it rested upon it.

She had come to him, to the only heart that was constant, that was not to be shaken and moved from its anchorage; to the only soul that answered to her own, to the only mind that read her thoughts. The George of her fancy, the ideal of truth and steadfastness, was dissolved, and had disappeared leaving a mean vulgar object behind from which she shrank. To him whom she had hated, with whom she had fought and against whom she had stiffened her back, she now flew as her only support, her only anchorage.

She could not speak, her thoughts chased through her head in wild disorder like the clouds when there are cross currents in the sky.

Now and then a spasmodic sob broke from her and shook her.

'What is the matter, Mehalah? Where have you been?'

She did not answer. She could not. She was choking. Perhaps she did not hear him, or hearing did not understand the import of his words.

She saw only the falling to pieces into dust of an idol. Better had George died, and she had lived on looking upon him as her ideal of manhood, noble, straightforward, truthful, constant. She would have been content to drudge on in her weary life at Red Hall and would have borne Elijah's humours and her mother's fretfulness, without a hope herself, if only she might still have maintained intact her image of all that was honourable and steadfast. She could not bear the revulsion of feeling. She was like a religionist who, on lifting the purple veil of the sanctuary, has found his God, before whom he had offered libations and prayers, to be some grovelling beast.

'Where have you been?' again asked Elijah placing his hands on her shoulders.

She raised her head, and gasped for breath, she essayed to speak but could not.

'Why do you not answer me?' he asked, not with fierceness in his tone, but with iron resolve.

'Mehalah!' he said firmly, solemnly. 'There have passed many days since George De Witt returned, and since Charles Pettican's bequest has rendered you independent of me. I have waited, and wanted to hold you, as I hold you now, firmly, fast in my strong hands. You feel them on your shoulders. They shall never let go. Now that I hold I shall hold fast. Mehalah! we have old scores to wipe out. Days and weeks of blind agony in me, hours, days of horrible internal torture whilst George De Witt has been here. I hold you now and all must now be made square between us.'

She tried to raise her hands, but he held her shoulders so tightly she could not move them.

'Elijah!' she said, 'do with me what you will. It is all one to me.'

'Where have you been? with whom have you been?'

'I have been with him.'

'I knew it. You shall never be with him again.'

She sighed. She knew that he spoke truly. Never could she see him again, in the old light; she never could meet him again on the old footing.

'Mehalah!' he went on, and his hands shook, and shook her; 'I have loved you; but now I hate and love you at the same time. You have caused me to suffer tortures, the like of which I could not suppose it possible any man could have endured, and have lived. You little knew and less cared what I endured in my eyes when they were burnt out. You little know and less care what I have endured in my soul since George De Witt has been back.'

'Elijah,' she said raising her heavy head, 'let me speak. George———'

'No never,' he interrupted, 'never shall you utter his name again.' He covered her mouth with his hand.

'No, I could not bear it,' he went on. 'Mehalah! your heart has never been mine, and I will not endure to be longer without it. Could you come to my breast and let my arms lap round you and our hearts beat against each other's bosom, and glue your lips to mine? No, no,' he answered himself. 'Not now, I cannot expect it. He has stood in my path, he has risen out of the waters to part us. Whilst we are on the earth we cannot be united, because he intercepts the current which runs from my heart to yours, and from yours to mine. Although he might be far away, a thousand miles distant, yet the tide of your affection would set to him. The moon they tell us is some hundreds of thousands of miles from the ocean, and yet the water throbs and rises, and falls and retreats responsive to the impulse of the moon, because moon and earth are both in one sphere. As long as you and he are together in one orb, there is no peace for me, your love will never flow to me and dance and sparkle about me. I must look elsewhere for peace, elsewhere for union, without which there is no peace. Lift up your head, Mehalah! Why is it resting thus heavily on my knee? I do not know what has come over you. Yes—' he said suddenly, in a louder tone, 'Yes I do know what it is. It is the shadow of the cloud, the scent before the rain. You have crept to me, you have cast yourself at my feet, you have leaned your head on my knee, you lift your arms to my heart, for the consummation is at hand. Mehalah! Do you understand me?'

'Yes.'

'Yes. We two understand each other, and none others can. Now, Mehalah! Glory! you shall not escape me. Glory! will you kiss me?'

He put his hand to her head, and felt it shaken in the negative.

'No. I did not suppose you would. You would kiss George, but not me; but you never shall belong to another but me. Hold up your face, Glory!'

He lifted it with one hand, and peered at it through the haze that ever attended him.

'Glory!' he said. 'Will you swear to me, if I let you go one minute, that you will place yourself here, at my feet, in my hands, as you lie now?'

'Yes.'

'It is dark, is it not? I can see nothing, not your flaming cap. I will let you go. I can trust your lightest word. Go and kindle me a candle.' He relaxed his grasp, and she staggered to her feet, and dully, in a dream obeyed. There was a candle on the chimney-piece, she took it to the hearth in the kitchen and lighted it there. The charwoman was gone.

'Go upstairs,' he said. 'There has been no sound in the house this hour. Go and kiss your mother and come back.'

She obeyed again, and crept lifelessly up the stairs; in another moment he heard a low long muffled wail.

He listened. She did not return.

'Mehalah!' he called.

He waited a minute and then called again.

She came down bearing the light. He did not see, but the candle glittered in tears rolling down her cheeks.

'Come to your place,' he ordered. 'Remember you swore.'

She threw herself at his feet.

'My mother! my mother!'

'She is dead,' said Elijah. 'I knew it. I heard her feebly cry for you, an hour ago, and I crept upstairs, and I listened by her bed, and held my hand to her heart till it ceased.'

Mehalah did not speak, her frame shook with emotion.

He took the candle, raised her face with his hand under the chin and held the light close to it.

'I cannot see much,' he said; 'I can see scarce anything of the dear face, of the great brown eyes I loved so well, I can see only something flame there. That is the cap.' He took it off and passed his hand through her rich hair. 'I can see, I think I can see, the flicker of the candle flame in the eyes. I can see the mouth, that mouth I have never touched, but I see it only as a red evening cloud across the sky.'

'Let me go!' she wailed. 'My mother! my mother!'

'We will go together to her,' he answered; 'stay one moment.'

He put down the candle, and once more laid his hand on her head, and now he pressed it back with his left hand. Did she see in the dull eyes a gathering moisture, the rising of a tide? A tear ran down each of his rugged cheeks. Then he suddenly rose, and he struck her full in the forehead with his iron fist, heavy as a sledge hammer. She dropped in a heap on the floor.

'Glory! my own, own Glory!' he cried, and listened.

There was no answer.

'Glory! my love! my pride! my second self! my double!'

He caught her up, and she hung across his knee. He held his ear to her mouth and hearkened.

'Oh Glory! my own! my own!'

He stretched his hand above the mantelpiece and plucked down the chain and padlock; he secured the key. Then he cast the chain over his arm and drew the inanimate girl to him and held her in his firm grasp, and lifted her over his shoulder, and felt his way out at the door and down the steps.

No one was in the yard. No one on the pasture.

The sun had set some time, but there was blood and fire on the horizon, clouds seamed with flame, and streaks of burning crimson.

He cautiously descended the stairs, and crossing the yard, made his way over the pasture to the landing place. He knew the path well. He could have trod it in the darkest night without error. He came to the sea-wall, and there he laid Mehalah, whilst he groped for his boat, and unloosed the rope that attached it to the shore.

He returned, and took up the still unconscious girl.

He felt her feeble breath on his cheek as he carried her, but he did not see the spot of returning colour in her face. He was eager, and hasty. He knew no delay, but pressed on. He carried her into the boat and took his oars and began to row, with her lying in the bottom.

The tide was running out. His instinct guided him.

The bells of Mersea tower were dancing a merry peal.

The windows of the 'Leather Bottle' were lighted up, and the topers were drinking prosperity to the married pair.

George De Witt was making his way to the Mussets, little conscious that Mehalah was lying in a boat, stunned, and being carried out seaward.

Presently Elijah felt sure by the fresher breeze and increased motion that he was out of the fleet in deep water. Then he quietly shipped his oars.

He lifted Mehalah, and drew her into his arms and laid her against his heart.

'My Glory! my own dearest! my only one!' he moaned. 'I could not help it. You would have left me had I not done this. There was no other way out of the tangle, there was no other path into the light. Glory! we were created for each other, but a perverse fortune has separated your heart from mine here. We shall meet and unite in another world. We must do so, we were born for each other. Glory! Glory!'

She stirred and opened her eyes, and drew a long breath.

'Are you waking, Glory?' he asked. 'Hark, hark! the marriage bells are ringing, ringing, ringing, for you and me. Now Glory! now only is our marriage! now only, locked together, shall we find rest.'

He took the iron chain, and wound it round her and him, tying them together tight, and then he fastened the padlock and flung the key into the sea.

'Once I turned the key in the lock carelessly, and he who was bound by this chain escaped. I have fastened it firmly now, it will not fall apart for all eternity. Now Glory! Now we are bound together for everlasting.'

She sighed.

'Do you hear me?' he asked. 'It is well. Glory! one kiss?'

He put down his hand into the bottom of the boat, and drew out the plug, and tossed it overboard. At once the cold sea-water rushed in and overflowed his feet.

'Glory!' he cried, and he folded her to his heart, and fastened his lips fiercely, ravenously to hers.

He felt her heart throb, faintly indeed, but really.

Merrily pealed the musical bells. Cans of ale had been supplied the ringers, and they dashed the ropes about in a fever of intoxication and sympathy. Joy to the wedded pair! Long life and close union and happiness without end! The topers at the 'Leather Bottle' brimmed their pewter mugs and drank the toast with three cheers.

The water boiled up, through the plughole, and the boat sank deeper. Life was beginning to return to Mehalah, but she neither saw nor knew aught. Her eyes were open and turned seaward, to the far away horizon, and Elijah relaxed his hold one instant.

'Elijah!' she suddenly exclaimed, 'How cold!'

'Glory! Glory! It is fire! We are one!' The bells pealed over the rolling sea—no boat was on it, only a sea-mew skimming and crying.

THE END.

Printed in Great Britain
by Amazon

# pulse & cocktails

## Exclusive Offer

# £14 Discount

When you spend £14 or more on sex toys or lingerie at Pulse & Cocktails.

*conditions apply

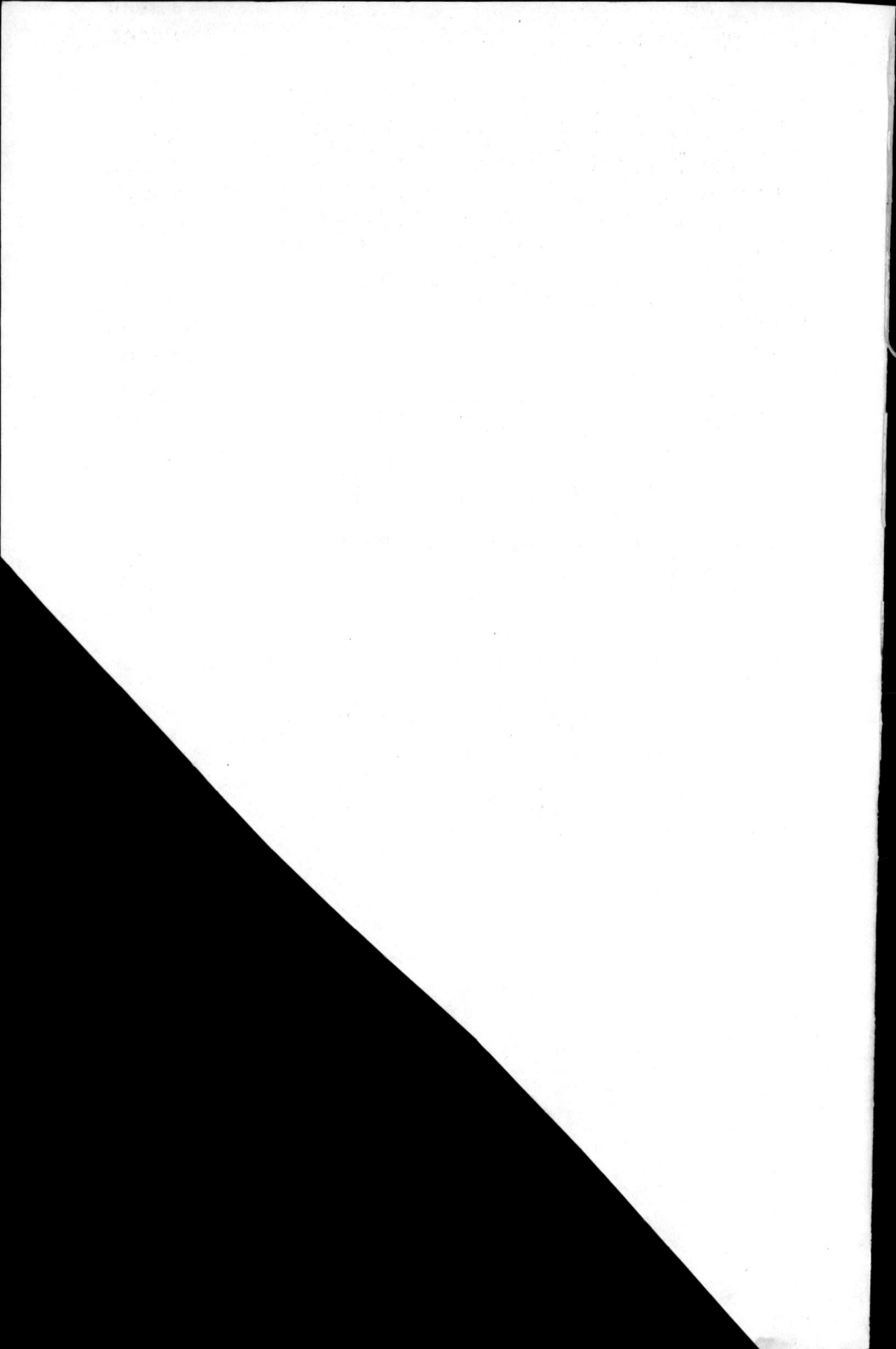